No Ordinary Thunder

Mark A. Keith

No Ordinary Thunder

No Ordinary Thunder

To my mother, Mary,

who lost her way

No Ordinary Thunder

Chapter 1

October, 1869

Tennessee, in the fall of the year, could not have been more beautiful. The trees represented every color imaginable. Some, Harley Macon couldn't even describe. The creeks and rivers flowed cold and clean, the sky a brilliant blue. Every bend in the road produced a scene more inspiring than the last. But the scene Harley longed for most turned out to be a horror.

He stepped off his tired horse and surveyed the charred rubble where his love, Abigail Mendenhall, used to live. Grass and weeds grew up through the ruins. The house had been destroyed long ago. December would mark seven years since he'd been here. The time he'd spent in this gracious home, accounted for some of the happiest days of his life.

Only a corner of the house remained. The room where he'd helped her with the Christmas decorations—the room where they'd talked and danced. Everything else was gone. The barns, the slave quarters, the orchard, all burnt to ash. What happened? Where was everyone? Where was Abigail?

Harley loosened his cinch and hobbled his horse, allowing him to graze on the grass beside the road. They'd ridden for nearly three weeks from Fort Belknap, a lonesome outpost in West Texas. The horse deserved a good, long rest. So did Harley, but he could see he wasn't going to get it. He searched through the blackened remains, looking for what, he didn't know. Just something, anything to relieve the pressure in his throat. The pressure only intensified when he heard the hammers of a shotgun click.

"What you doin' here, mistuh?"

No Ordinary Thunder

Harley raised his hands, but didn't turn around.

"I come to visit a friend. Looks like I'm too late."

"You three years too late. You touch that pistol, I'll cut you in half."

Harley turned, his hands still in the air, and looked critically at the double-barrel eight-gauge. "I believe you, but there's no need. I'm friendly."

The old black man holding the shotgun only stood about five-foot six, but his trigger finger looked just as big. His weather-beaten face and arthritic hands showed years of brutal work. He could well be a man with nothing to lose. Harley had no doubt the old man would shoot him.

"Name's Harley Macon. I rode in from Texas. I met the Mendenhalls during the war in '62. They took me and my outfit in for a while. What's your name?"

"Otis George. The Mendenhalls is dead. Buried 'em back there in the woods myself."

"All of 'em? What about Abigail? Is she dead, too?"

"No, suh. She ain't dead, but I wish she was. She in the asylum, over 'round Cooksville." Otis lowered the shotgun and let the hammers down slowly.

"Oh, God. What happened to her?"

"Confederate home guard. The Mendenhalls was feedin' too many freedmen."

Otis took a seat on a piece of the porch, stoked his pipe and took a long drag. He laid the shotgun across his lap, but kept it pointed in Harley's general direction.

"Only they feet was free," he said. "They stomach was still a slave. Well, the guard didn't want no nigras gettin' fat, so they took all the Mendenhalls had. And when they didn't have no more, they killed 'em and burned 'em out. Do I have to tell you what they did to Miss Abigail?"

Harley went weak at the knees. He steadied himself, leaning on the porch post, staring far off into the

No Ordinary Thunder

woods. The asylum. Good God. How could he have been so foolish? Why hadn't he come back to her? The war, that's why. The damn war. And Texas.

Reconstruction was hell throughout the South, and Texas was no exception. Crime was rampant all over the state, but wasn't the woman he loved more important? Couldn't he have taken her to Texas with him? And what good did it do to go back, anyway? Only months before, half his Ranger troop had been massacred. He wasn't able to save them. Maybe he couldn't save anyone. The war was lost. His men were lost. And now, Abigail.

"How far to Cooksville?"

" 'Bout sixty mile north. You ain't goin' up there, are you? Best not. It won't do you no good. Miss Abigail past helpin' now."

"I've come all this way. I expect I'll see for myself. Much obliged."

The men shook hands and Harley rode north, sickened at the thought of what he might find.

#

Harley tied his horse at the rail, outside the foreboding stone walls of the Tennessee State Asylum. He leaned on his saddle, studying their structure long and hard before resigning himself to venture inside. Every step he took toward the large double doors required a tremendous effort. He was not prepared for what awaited him.

At recreation hour, the dismal halls teemed with lost souls trying to find their way. The rancid stench of vomit and waste seemed to bother no one but Harley. The lye used to clean the place only made it worse.

Mr. Batton, the hard looking man leading Harley through the crowd, avoided eye contact with anyone. He just weaved his way through them as if in a room full of

No Ordinary Thunder

furniture, never speaking, maybe not hearing. But Harley could hear them.

They screamed and cried, laughed and cursed, all without notice by Mr. Batton. Harley had seen the same behavior in the war. Men went about their daily duties as if it wasn't happening to them, but to someone else. The blood, the bodies, none of it seemed real after a while. Only the memories were real.

"Are you sure you want to do this, Mr. Macon? You're not going to like it."

"I've come this far. Where is she?"

"That's her there, in the corner."

Harley turned to glue inside. He couldn't move, nor speak, nor even think. There sat Abigail, the most beautiful woman he'd ever seen—the woman he loved—sucking on her fingers, asking someone invisible not to hurt her. Repeatedly, she'd pull her smock up around her waist, and again ask not to be hurt. She'd pulled handfuls of her golden hair out, showing scabbed-over sores where she'd scratched herself down to the blood. Her fingernails were broken off, her toenails far too long. The sight turned Harley's stomach. He whirled on Mr. Batton in a rage.

"Is this the best you sons o' bitches can do for her?"

"We have to sedate her to do anything with her. If we even try to touch her, she goes into fits. We can't keep her under all the time. I wish we could medicate them all. Most would probably benefit, if we could. I'm sorry, Mr. Macon. I know it's hard. Most visitors stop coming in a short while. It's just more than they can stand."

"Can I talk to her?"

Mr. Batton hesitated to answer. "I doubt she will know you, but you can try. I warn you though, she often becomes violent when approached. We don't want her agitated."

Harley stepped over a young man with no legs, lying on the floor. The young man didn't even notice. His

No Ordinary Thunder

tattered Confederate uniform sent a shiver down Harley's spine.

"Abigail? It's me, Harley. Do you remember me?"

"Harley?"

"Yes, honey, it's me, Harley. Do you remember when the soldiers came to see you? Hanging the Christmas decorations? Do you remember when we danced, while your mama played the spinet?"

"Oh, yes. I remember now. Mama's dead."

"I know. I'm sorry. But you ain't, honey. You're alive, and you're gonna get well."

"I'll be all right when Daddy gets home. Mama cooked a roast. What's your name?"

"Why it's me, honey. Harley Macon. Remember?"

Abigail looked at him, trying to recall, then screamed at the top of her lungs.

"Don't hurt me! Please don't hurt me again!"

Harley swallowed hard and took a few steps back. Abigail put her fingers in her mouth and pulled her smock up over her face.

An old man with one arm and a long gray beard, slid his hand down his pants at the sight of Abigail's stained undergarments. The young man with no legs continued his silent stare.

Mr. Batton had seen enough. "I'm sorry, Mr. Macon. I think we should leave her alone now. You can't help her. She's far passed that."

Harley wanted to go, but couldn't. He was as mesmerized by her agony as he had been by her grace and beauty. He'd known women like this before, in Texas, after being held captive by Indians. Abigail would never find her way back.

Why had he come? It was folly to think she'd be waiting for him all these years. A woman as beautiful as Abigail would have suitors calling day and night. He'd

No Ordinary Thunder

been hoping against hope, but it didn't matter now. His love was gone forever.

The old man with one arm approached Abigail, and dropped his pants to the floor. He offered himself to her and was quickly subdued by a stout young orderly, who helped the man with his pants. The orderly led him away by the hand, promising candy if he'd behave.

Harley wanted to run. God, how he wished he could remember her as she was. Young, beautiful, perfect. Now his lasting memory would be of a pitiful, wounded creature, so lost she probably didn't know her own name. He could do nothing to save her.

He backed away a few steps, then turned and made for the door. Pushing through the crowded hallway, he saw a woman lift her smock and relieve herself on the floor. A scurvy looking boy about twenty years of age, made advances on a woman old enough to be his grandmother. The woman giggled like a schoolgirl showing a big smile with no teeth.

Harley quickened his pace. He nearly jumped out of his skin when the loud bell rang to sound the end of recreation. The inmates cried and cursed at the thought of going back to their wards. Harley hit the outer door so hard he broke the glass, and bolted for his horse.

Mr. Batton, observing through the broken glass, appeared to whisper something into a smiling girl's ear, as Harley mounted and spurred his horse to the gallop.

#

San Antonio, Texas

May, 1874

"Wake up, Harley," the jailer said. "You've got a visitor."

No Ordinary Thunder

Harley rolled over and turned his back to the door. He wasn't ready to receive visitors just yet. He was still too drunk for that.

"Tell 'em to come back after I've had my breakfast."

"No breakfast this mornin'. This man's paid your fine."

"I don't think so," Harley said. Without looking at the man, he stuck his head under the pillow to shut out the light. "Get out. I need some more sleep."

Tubb, the jailer, turned the key in the lock and opened the squeaky door, then slammed it hard to get his prisoner's attention. Harley jumped off his bunk, instinctively reaching for a gun he didn't have.

"Damn you, Tubb. Leave me alone!"

Through the eye that hadn't been swollen shut in Teeters' Saloon the night before, Harley took notice of the runty little man standing beside the jailer. He chewed vigorously on an unlit cigar. His bearded face carried a revolted expression. In his broadcloth coat, white shirt and string tie, he looked like a preacher on a mission to save someone's soul.

"What the hell do you want?" Harley asked.

"I'm looking for Harley Macon of the Texas Rangers. Have I found him?"

"No."

The man took a seat on a stool in the hallway. Harley thought he looked fair tuckered out. He was sure the man's feeble appearance belied his age.

"That's him, Captain. That's Harley Macon," Tubb said.

Harley gave the jailer a stern, threatening stare.

"I'm Captain Leander McNelly. Cole Ellsworth told me I might find you here. Looks like you need something else to do. How would you like to go to work for me?"

No Ordinary Thunder

"No thanks. You got any whiskey?"

"I don't use it. You've probably got enough in your system to last awhile."

Harley shook his swirling head. "How's Cole? I ain't seen him in a year or so."

"He's doing well. Raising some fine horses. He and Rebecca have a new baby, a boy."

"Well, I swear. They had a girl about three years ago. I guess they've got a full house now. Tubb, you got any coffee?"

"Yeah. You want some, Captain?"

"Thank you, but I'm in a hurry."

Tubb left the cell block to fetch the coffee. When they were alone, McNelly confronted Harley on a more serious note.

"Are you planning to wear a path between here and the saloon for the rest of your life? Or are you ready to get back on the horse? Texas needs you."

"What for?" Harley squeezed his temples with his shaky fingertips.

"I'm putting together a special troop of Rangers to clean out the Nueces Strip. I need a man who knows the country on both sides of the border. Governor Coke says you're the one."

"Yeah? What makes him think so?"

McNelly abruptly came to his feet. His cordial manner quickly disappeared.

"I didn't ride all the way to San Antonio to dance with you, Macon. I understand you've been a drunk for five years. Your reasons are your own, but that should be long enough for anyone. If you want to die lying in your own piss, that's your choice. But if you want to go with me, and ride like hell again, I'm staying at the hotel until tomorrow."

McNelly turned and walked out the door, thanking Tubb for his trouble as he went.

No Ordinary Thunder

"How about that coffee?" Harley shouted.

"Yeah, yeah." Tubb handed him a cup too hot to hold and sat down on the three-legged stool.

"So that's McNelly. I heard he was with the State Police."

"He was," Harley said. "Quit when he found out how crooked they were. Coke said he'd reinstate the Rangers if he got elected governor, but I didn't believe it. McNelly raised hell with the Yankees in the war. I expect he'll do the same with the Mexicans. Ain't we gonna have breakfast? This is a helluva way to treat your regulars."

"I'll get you some breakfast, but you oughta take McNelly's offer. You've spent enough time in this jail. I'm gettin' sick o' lookin' at you."

Harley's eyes flashed cold blue fire. Tubb shut the cell door and locked it.

"You've sure got a sweet disposition," he said. "By the way, you owe Pap Teeters twenty dollars for the damage on his saloon."

"I'll be owin' damages on this jail if you don't shut up and go get me my breakfast."

Tubb put on his hat, and slammed the door on his way out.

Captain Leander McNelly. Now Harley knew he looked older than he was. Everyone in Texas had heard about his guerilla scouts in the war, mostly operating behind enemy lines.

You could say the man was famous. He'd tricked eight hundred Union troops into surrendering at Brashear City, Louisiana, by marching around them all night, convincing them of superior power. McNelly had only forty men. There was even a rumor that he'd once carried out a spy mission on his own, dressed as a woman.

Countless tales circulated of his boundless courage and absolute conviction that there were only two kinds of people in the world—the lawless and the law abiding. Not

No Ordinary Thunder

many law abiding citizens occupied the Strip, and those that did paid the price. Rustlers, killers, and rapist ran rough-shod over the population. McNelly would have his hands full if he thought he'd clean up that mess.

It was a mess fifteen years in the making. General Juan Cortina led a highly organized band of rustlers, stealing thousands of Texas cattle to fill large beef contracts with Cuba. The rustlers were so brazen that often the cattle were loaded on ships just off the coast at Brownsville. The Texas ranchers had little chance to stand against their numbers. And it had only gotten worse since the Rangers were disbanded, after Davis's gubernatorial victory in '69. His answer to crime in Texas was the hated State Police, an institution every bit as corrupt as Cortina's band of thieves.

But now it seemed Governor Coke would keep his campaign promise and reinstate the Rangers—with McNelly in charge.

Harley lay back on his bunk, to rest his pounding head on what passed for a pillow. His coffee had gone cold, but he didn't want it anyway. He wanted a drink to settle his shaky nerves.

He'd tried his hand at many jobs since the Rangers were disbanded, but his drinking always got in the way. Maybe the jobs were just too tame for him. He was a man of action. A man of war. Nothing would ever change that.

After he'd had his breakfast and slept awhile longer, he'd go see McNelly. He didn't want to spend his life in jail. And after seeing what happened to Abigail, maybe dead wasn't so bad after all.

#

Captain McNelly sat in the dining room of the Menger Hotel, finishing his lunch when Harley came in.

No Ordinary Thunder

He ordered coffee, which Harley refused—his hands were shaking badly. McNelly's conversation was short and to the point.

"I don't allow drunks in my troop, Macon. You'll sober up or I'll leave you flat. We're going to shut these border gangs down, and I need men I can count on. Can I count on you?"

Harley hadn't been confronted so directly in quite some time. Of course, bartenders, whores, and jailers were supposed to keep their mouths shut. They were about the only people he saw anymore.

"What're you countin' on me for, Cap?"

McNelly's mouth tightened considerably. "You can call me Captain, or Captain McNelly. Not Cap. Is that understood?"

Harley wasn't sure he was going to like this man.

"Yes sir, Captain. What are you countin' on me for?"

"I want you to spy for me. Make yourself known to the rustlers. Keep me informed."

Harley felt a little insulted. After all, he was a known man, too.

"Beggin' your pardon, Captain, but nearly everybody in Texas knows me, and knows I was a Ranger. I doubt the bandits are gonna let me in among 'em."

"They know you *were* a Ranger. Now they know you're a drunk *ex*-Ranger. That might be just the cover you need."

Now, Harley was sure he didn't like him.

"Besides, you won't be working alone. I want you to go to Laredo. You'll be met there by a Mexican—Jesus Sandoval. You'll be working closely with him. I've got some work to do in DeWitt County. Might be a good while before I get down there. Just learn what you can, and make yourself known. You want the job?"

Harley wished he had a drink. His head felt kind of

No Ordinary Thunder

empty.

"Yes, sir. I reckon I do. But I ain't got a horse, nor outfit, nor nothin' but my pistol."

"There's a horse, a blue roan, waiting for you at the livery, along with an outfit and a new Winchester. Cole Ellsworth sent them down for you. He said you could pay him when you get rich."

McNelly dropped forty dollars on the table. "That's your first month's pay. I'd advise buying some decent clothes. I want you on the road in two hours."

"Two hours? Now wait a . . ."

"Two hours!" McNelly barked. The effort seemed to take a great deal of energy. He left the table and walked to the lobby, coughing violently into his handkerchief, as he made his way up the stairs.

#

Delgado, along with two other bandits, pushed one-hundred and forty-three head of steers through the dusty chaparral of South Texas. They planned to cross the Rio Grande at La Bolsa, only a few miles further.

The afternoon was warm and dry. The bandits looked forward to the crossing. They'd been pushing the steers for about ten miles, at a fairly rapid pace. Men and cattle alike could all use a good drink. Maybe the men could get a bath if everything went well.

They'd left one dead at the site of the theft, a boy no more than sixteen. He'd been foolish enough to think the bandits only wanted to water their horses. Rojas roped the boy around the neck, and dragged him through the cactus until he died.

Rojas had his nose cut off when he refused to pay a hot tempered whore. As a result, he could be very cruel. Besides, ammunition was expensive and someone might

No Ordinary Thunder

have heard a gunshot.

Stealing cattle was easy, to Delgado's way of thinking. Even easier than trading guns with the Comanche. But those days were gone for good. A few Comanches still raided in the north, but the gun trade all but stopped when Macon and Ellsworth killed Zendejaz.

He had barely escaped with his own life, when the Rangers charged into the stronghold on the caprock. As far as he knew, every bandit there had been killed including Lean Wolf, whose murder of the five Rangers on the llano had inflamed Ellsworth's dogged determination—a mistake the outlaws didn't live to regret.

But there were no Texas Rangers now. The very reason it was so easy to steal cattle and drive them to Mexico.

Large ranchers like Richard King and Shanghai Pierce did their best to mount small armies. But Cortina had a big army. And not many men were willing to die for another man's cattle. The smaller outfits were helpless.

So lucrative was the trade that Delgado expected to live out his days lying in a hammock with two pretty *señoritas*. But the bullet that tore off Castro's face, reminded him that he wasn't there yet.

In a moment, they were in a hail of gunfire. The bullets buzzed around them like hornets. Castro lurched forward, his gunbelt hanging on the saddle horn, as the bandits stampeded the cattle. The horse leaped. Castro rolled off to the side, the gunbelt holding him to the saddle.

Castro flopped like a flag in the breeze, his arms and legs slapping the horse with every stride. Soon the horse lost his balance and fell, crushing the already dead bandit. A bucket of blood erupted from his mouth, when the weight of the horse fell on him.

Delgado and Rojas pushed hard for the river. Losing Castro didn't slow them down. The fallen horse struggled to regain his feet, but couldn't get up with the

No Ordinary Thunder

body hanging to his side. He kicked and screamed in wild terror, cutting his own legs with flailing hooves.

The river shined like a ribbon in the bright Texas sun. The bandits drove the cattle across, taking time for neither drink nor bath. Once safely in Mexico, they turned to see their pursuers.

There were four of them, all still firing, but now well out of range. They'd given up the chase, and stopped to free the downed horse of his burden. While three of them worked to get the horse up, another threw a loop around Castro's neck and dragged him through the brush.

The dragging would serve no purpose. The man couldn't be any deader. But Delgado and Rojas watched intently, happy that it wasn't them being dragged. They heard a single shot, probably to put the horse down, then turned east toward Matamoros, the bawling cattle leaving a trail of dust rising to the sky.

No Ordinary Thunder

Chapter 2

Harley rode south at a leisurely trot. The blue roan had plenty of bottom, and could undoubtedly make better time, but Harley was in no hurry. He hadn't been in the saddle for a while. He felt like he might break in two.

He had taken McNelly's advice and bought some new clothes, but compared to his worn out rags, the clothes were hot and uncomfortable. His shirt was already soaked with sweat—the effect of a steady diet of whiskey.

Before leaving town, he'd gone into Pap Teeters' saloon to pay him half of the damages he owed. Teeters, bristling, demanded full restitution, but opted for half when Harley laid his pistol on the bar and ordered a drink.

Harley didn't mind paying what he owed, but damn, twenty dollars for that broken down joint? The place didn't look much different after the fight, than it did on any given evening. But Teeters had settled for half which, after paying the barber, buying the clothes, a few supplies, and the drink, left Harley with a total of eight dollars. He thought that if he lived long enough, he'd get the rest to Pap as soon as he could.

Afternoon passed into evening, the ride an uneventful bore. Harley hadn't seen a soul since clearing the outskirts of San Antonio. He supposed he'd made nearly twenty miles, when he saw the campfire off to the east. Being close to dusk, he decided to ride over and see about spending the night. A little conversation was usually welcomed around the fire. Maybe the camper had a nip of whiskey. Harley was feeling nervous and sick. He wished he'd brought a bottle with him.

Three men stood around the fire. One of them, the man with darker skin, looked more than a little worried. The other two, both white men, held their pistols on him. They didn't act like they wanted company.

"Hello the camp," Harley shouted.

No Ordinary Thunder

The men turned quickly, their guns pointed at Harley, then one turned back to cover the prisoner. The gunman facing Harley was no more than a boy, but he held his pistol rock steady.

"You better keep movin', mister," the boy said. "This ain't none o' your lookout."

"Got you a greaser?" The prisoner showed no offense at the remark. Harley thought the man looked a little more Indian, though his vision was pretty blurry.

"We don't know what he is, but he ain't got any business around here."

The smell of the rabbit roasting on the spit, made Harley's dry mouth water.

"Mind if I step down? I could use a cup o' coffee, and a taste o' that rabbit."

The gun arm of the man covering the prisoner seemed to be sagging somewhat.

"I told you to keep ridin', mister!"

The boy's nerves were getting frazzled. Harley could hear it in his voice. No doubt he'd been a lot steadier when they had only one man to watch.

Harley took a chance and slid out of the saddle, keeping the roan between himself and the boy's gun. The prisoner's guard shifted his gaze for a moment. The prisoner saw his opportunity, and knocked him cold with one punch. The boy turned away from Harley to face the dark-skinned man. He tried to keep both men covered, unsure of what to do next. Harley drew his pistol with a shaky hand, and leveled it at the boy.

"That's enough, son. Put your gun down. I don't wanna shoot you."

The boy froze in his tracks, embarrassed and afraid. He dropped his gun, and with Harley's permission, knelt down to check on his brother. The prisoner kicked his guard's gun out of reach, but made no attempt to pick it up.

"Thanks, mister." His mouth turned up in an easy

No Ordinary Thunder

grin. "Guess I'll know better'n to extend my hospitality so free next time. These boys were gettin' restless."

"What they holdin' you for?" Harley asked. "You steal from 'em?"

"Nope. Didn't steal. Just built a fire and killed a rabbit. That against the law in Texas?"

"Not if you share it." Harley turned his attention back to the boy. The other one was just coming around.

"All right, son. What's your story?"

"Ain't got one."

"Were you plannin' to rob this fella?"

The boy answered the question when he looked at the ground.

"That's what I thought. Drop your gun belts and start walkin'. Come back in the mornin' and get your horses after we're gone. Get your friend up and get goin'."

"He's my brother. Hell, mister, we . . ."

"Outlaw leads a tough life, son. Move out."

The men surrendered their weapons and walked away seething, the brother still reeling from the effects of the punch. When they'd gone a fair distance, Harley took a closer look at the man with the easy grin.

Five foot nine, maybe a hundred and fifty pounds. Of mixed race, definitely Indian, maybe mulatto. Late twenties, long black hair, with a wispy mustache and goatee. Square shoulders, deep chest, and straight, powerful limbs. He grinned the grin at Harley's inspection.

"You lookin' me over to sell me, or you wanna wrestle?"

"I ain't in the mood to wrestle. Besides, I've got the gun."

"That you do. Least I can do is share that rabbit with you. Them fellas got the drop on me good."

Harley was reluctant to holster his weapon. His host had a pile of guns.

"I expect you'd need a pack horse to haul all that

No Ordinary Thunder

iron. You don't look like a drummer."

"I ain't. But if you'll quit pointin' that pistol at me, I give you my word I won't touch a one."

Harley nodded his agreement.

"Fair enough. What's your name?"

"What's yours?"

Harley waited. Maybe this man worked for Cortina. But hell, someone would identify him sooner or later. No point in complicating things.

"Name's Harley Macon."

"Harley Macon? Of the 8th Texas Cavalry?"

The man's response was not what Harley expected. He fished his cup out of the saddlebag and blew the dust from it. "Yeah. And you?"

"Call me Dixon. You know, like the Mason-Dixon."

"I've heard of it, as I recall."

The conversation dwindled as the rabbit disappeared. The food helped Harley's queasy stomach, but his nerves were going to keep him awake. Dixon sensed his visitor's condition, and reached for his possibles bag. Harley drew and cocked his pistol. Dixon carefully produced a bottle of whiskey.

"This'll help you settle down. I'm afraid you might wake up and shoot me."

Dixon filled Harley's cup, took a drink and put the bottle away. He groped under his saddle and came up with a fiddle, wrapped in a fine sheepskin. The fiddle piqued Harley's curiosity. It was hardly something the average horseback traveler carried.

"Fiddler, huh? You any good, or you just tote it around?"

"Oh, I can play a little. My pa taught me. Taught me how to shoot, too."

"Handy things to know. Let me hear somethin' sweet."

Dixon played a haunting tune that Harley didn't

No Ordinary Thunder

recognize. Something about the dark-skinned man had him puzzled. He didn't seem the kind to be found wandering on the prairie.

Harley stretched out and sipped his whiskey. He thought of the task that awaited him, of the years he'd been out of action—of Abigail in that pitiful place. He tossed off his drink, and fell asleep to the sweet refrain of "Barbara Allen".

#

Dixon woke to the repulsive sound of Harley throwing up his supper. Thankfully, he'd made it a few steps from the camp, before falling to his hands and knees.

Dixon stirred the coffee pot, and walked in the opposite direction to check the horses. When he did, he saw the four riders. Two were the men who wanted to rob him. It looked like they'd found some more guns. The other two were a little older, a little rougher.

Dixon strapped on a wide leather belt, and shoved three pistols in it. He checked his rifle, a Henry repeater. Full load, sixteen rounds.

"Get up, Harley. We got company comin'."

Harley made it to his feet. Dixon could see he was pretty shaky, but he went through the motions of checking his guns, though he'd checked them before going to sleep.

"Damn!" Dixon said. "I'd hoped we'd be gone before they came back. Brought some help with 'em this time. I don't think they came just for the horses."

"Yeah. Looks like they mean it. The coffee hot? I could use a cup, and maybe a shot o' whiskey. I feel kinda jumpy."

"You look worse than that. You think we can take 'em?"

"I guess we'll know in a few minutes."

No Ordinary Thunder

Harley shook the cobwebs from his head. He sipped his coffee with both hands on the cup and tried to keep from shaking. By the time the riders reached the camp, both men were ready to greet them.

"Mornin'," Harley said. "You boys are out early. Can we offer you some coffee?"

"We come to get them horses you stole from my boys."

The speaker was an older man of maybe sixty, with tobacco juice dripping off his chin. He spoke directly to Harley, while giving Dixon only a contemptuous glance.

"You got it wrong, mister. Your boys were up to mischief with my friend here. We thought maybe a long walk would do 'em good. We didn't harm 'em, but we could've."

"Been worse for you, if you had. As it is, we're gonna take them horses, and yours. Maybe a long walk'll do *you* good. If you'da harmed my boys, I'da killed you."

Harley grew tired of the conversation. He felt like he might throw up again.

"I've grown pretty fond of that roan. I don't think I'll let him go cheap. You boys take your horses and ride outta here, now. We don't want any trouble."

The old man smiled. So did the boy who talked to Harley the night before. If there was movement, it was so subtle Harley didn't see it. But evidently, Dixon did. He pulled two pistols and emptied two saddles, before Harley had his gun out. The old man drew, a curse on his lips. Harley shot him in the throat, then leveled his pistol at the boy.

"Get off that horse, you little bastard!"

The boy swung down, but not fast enough. Harley grabbed him, took his gun, and slammed him to the ground. Holding him by the shirt, Harley punched his face to a bloody pulp.

No Ordinary Thunder

"Three dead men, you son of a bitch. Your daddy's dead because o' you. Your brother's dead. Damn you little bastard!"

Harley kept on punching the boy, while Dixon busied himself stripping gun belts and checking pockets.

Harley soon wore out. He wasn't in as good a shape as he used to be, but the boy was unconscious anyway. He had a bad cut above his left eye, and there was a piece of one tooth cradled in his ear. Harley rolled off and lay beside him, trying to catch his breath. When he finally did, he rolled over again and started heaving, but nothing came up.

"No wonder they're thieves," Dixon said. "They ain't got two dollars between 'em."

Harley sat up, his face gray and sweating. "Give it to this boy when he wakes up. Maybe he's got a ma somewhere."

"I got a ma, Harley. Least I did when I left home."

"Yeah? Where's home?"

Dixon took his time answering.

"Somewheres else," he said.

The boy was starting to come around. Harley snatched him off the ground to help him along. "You load these bodies on their horses, and get the hell outta here. That's twice now I've let you go. You can keep your gun, but if I ever see you again, you'd better be ready to use it. Get busy."

Harley and Dixon drank their coffee and waited for bacon to fry, while they watched the boy struggle with the bodies. When he had them loaded, Harley repeated his speech and sent him on his way. Dixon was perturbed at having to give up the money, but Harley wouldn't have it any other way.

"Y'know, we coulda ate on that money for two or three days," Dixon said.

"We?"

No Ordinary Thunder

"Well...yeah. I thought we might stick together for a while. Kinda look out for each other. Ain't none o' my business, but where you headed?"

"Down Laredo way. I've got some things to see to down there."

"I ain't ever been to Laredo. You want some company?"

"You may not want any part of this. It ain't gonna be no holiday."

"Maybe not. But I owe you, Harley. You saved my hide. That's enough for me."

"Well, you're handy with a gun, I'll give you that. You don't owe me nothin', but I guess I don't mind if you care to ride along."

"You're pretty handy yourself, what with that throat shot and all."

Harley shook his head. "My hand was shakin'. I aimed for his chest. If it ain't any trouble, I could sure use a touch o' that whiskey."

#

Laredo, Texas, was like Hell with the hide off. Harley and Dixon rode in after sundown to the sounds of music and laughter, cursing, yelling, and occasional gunfire. Cowboys roamed from saloon to cantina, ducking into alleys with friendly women. Harley couldn't remember what day it was. He'd long since quit keeping track. They'd been on the road for several days, but it didn't feel like Saturday.

It had been a long ride from San Antonio, and Dixon was sparing with the whiskey. Harley felt a little better, not as sick, but still a bit shaky. He knew the best place to get information was the saloon, but he hadn't been sober very long. Maybe he wouldn't stay that way if he

No Ordinary Thunder

went inside. Why had he agreed to this? How could he play the drunk ex-Ranger and stay sober at the same time?

"I'm hungry," Dixon said. "Let's find a place to eat."

"Carlita's, just down the street. I ain't been here in a while, but I expect it's still there."

It was, and so was Carlita. She looked just like Harley remembered. A beautiful, buxom woman of rare talent, both in and out of the kitchen, Carlita had gone through many men. Mostly because she'd never felt the urge to quash her desire for the next cowboy to come through the door. She loved them all, at least for a while. Carlita lived life free and easy, the devil take the leavings. Her black eyes sparkled when Harley stepped inside.

"Ahh, Harley, my love!" She ran to him and threw herself in his arms, covering his face with kisses. The customers took little notice. Harley was not the first old flame they'd seen Carlita greet in such a manner.

"How you been, darlin'?" Harley asked. "You been true to me?"

"Hell, no. You stay away too long. The nights can be cold on the river."

"Well, we'll see what we can do about that. This is my friend, Dixon."

Carlita looked him over critically, like she was buying a horse built for stamina.

"He is not very tall, but he is handsome." She grabbed Dixon firmly by the buttocks. "Ah, he is strong where it counts."

Harley snickered. Dixon looked stunned. "I just want somethin' to eat, ma'am. I'm a married man, but thank you just the same."

"We're hungry, that's a fact," Harley said, "but it looks like you're full up."

Carlita clapped her hands. A young man with a big knife in his belt stepped out of the backroom, ready for

No Ordinary Thunder

anything. She pointed to a drunk, face down in his tamales. The young man quickly threw the drunk into the street.

"Sit down," she said. "I'll bring you some food."

She walked away laughing, tossing her hair and swinging her hips.

The men sat down at the drunk's table. Harley finished the drink he'd left and pushed the tamales to the side, while the young man with the knife cleared the dishes.

"So, you're married, huh?" Harley said to Dixon.

"Yeah," was the answer he got.

"Kids?"

"Three."

"Where'd you say you were from, again?"

"Somewheres else."

Carlita returned with plates overflowing, hot coffee, and a raft of tortillas. She pulled her blouse a little further off her shoulders, and sat down to join the conversation.

"I heard you and Ellsworth killed Zendejaz," she said. "Then no more Rangers, *que no?*"

"Nope. No more Rangers, honey. Ain't been one for years." Harley thought he saw Dixon stiffen a little at the mention of the Rangers.

"Did you come to Laredo to see me?" She put her hand under the table, and massaged Harley's quivering thigh. "I always like to see you."

"I like to see you, too. I guess you get prettier with time. But mostly I'm lookin' to make a livin'. I don't know nothin' but ridin' and shootin'. Ain't much call for that anymore."

Carlita eyed Harley suspiciously.

"The famous Ranger cannot be a sheriff somewhere?"

"Sheriff? Collar drunks and wife beaters? No thanks. Besides, you gotta be sober to be a sheriff. I ain't had much luck at that lately."

"You could be the sheriff in Laredo. He is a good

No Ordinary Thunder

man, but just as drunk as everyone else. If you are the sheriff, then I can see you more, *eh?*"

"I've had enough law and order. It don't work. Look at this town. Swarmin' with drunk cowboys, and not a lawman in sight."

"It is not like this all the time. The cowboys drove a herd across the river. They have lots of money to spend. In a day or two, they will all be poor again."

"Then what?"

Before she could answer, the cantina doors burst open with a bang. Harley and Dixon laid hand to their guns. The eyes of the customers grew wide with fear, when the three *vaqueros* sauntered in.

"*El Chacal*," Carlita whispered.

She pulled her blouse back up on her shoulders, and ushered the men to a table near the kitchen. Several customers decided they were no longer hungry. They eased their way to the door, leaving coins on the tables as they left.

Dixon looked the *vaqueros* over with a keen, curious eye. "*El Chacal?*"

"The Jackal," Harley said, returning to his meal.

"My, oh my. He sure looks like a scary fella."

"I suppose he don't scare you, though."

"Why should I be afraid? I got more guns than him. Besides, I'm with a famous Ranger."

"Ex-Ranger."

"And a Captain of the 8th Texas Cavalry."

"Long time ago. How do you know about the 8th?"

"I ain't deaf. You boys sure gave them Yankees fits through Kentucky and Tennessee."

"Yeah. Well, they kicked our ass anyway." Harley tried to change the subject. He didn't want to talk about Tennessee. Thoughts of Tennessee always turned to Abigail, and she was the last thing he wanted to think about. "Where were you goin' when I run into you?"

No Ordinary Thunder

"No place particular. Just out seein' the world."

"Lotta you boys from back in that country comin' west."

"And what country would that be?"

"I'd say likely Carolina, by the way you talk."

"Let's just say I'm from somewheres else."

"Like Robeson County?"

Dixon cleaned his plate with the last tortilla, and popped it into his mouth.

"Is one of us gonna die here, Harley?"

"If so, it'll be you. I've got a pistol leveled at your guts under this table. But there's no need, Mr. Lowery. You are Henry Lowery, ain't you?"

"How'd you know?"

"I ain't deaf, neither. I heard about you. Fiddle playin' mulatto Injun, with enough guns to arm a squad? I can't recall the last time I saw one. I says to myself, Harley, you're in the company of the notorious Henry Berry Lowery, guerilla raider and enemy of the Ku Klux Klan."

"What now? Turn me in for the reward?"

"How much is it?"

"Was twenty thousand, but me and the boys stole the money before I lit out."

"Stole your own reward money?"

"Yeah. Even Jesse James never did that."

Harley broke up laughing. "No, I ain't gonna turn you in. Anybody who fought the home guard is all right by me. Let's get outta here."

The drunk the young man had thrown into the street earlier, still lay where he landed. He'd fouled himself, but didn't know it. Only the dogs would come near to investigate. Dixon took pity on the wretched soul, and dragged him onto the boardwalk.

"Well, what now?" he asked Harley.

"Find us a fleabag hotel, I reckon—unless you've

No Ordinary Thunder

still got some o' that reward money."

"Oh, I might have a dollar or two. I think we can do better'n a fleabag."

"If you've got money, why'd you try to rob that kid back yonder?"

"Force o' habit. Let's have a look around."

Carlita took a seat on Chacal's lap the second Harley left the room. The swelling she felt beneath her confirmed that he wasn't there just for her cooking. Chacal smiled a wicked smile, exposing perfect white teeth and a devilish eye. He slid his hand up under her skirt, while she fed him the best enchiladas in Laredo.

"You are bad for business, *Amante*. The people leave when you come in. How am I to make a living?"

Chacal fumbled through his vest pocket and came out with five dollars gold. He tossed the coin into the air. It landed on the table with a ring that startled the few remaining customers. "Who is the *gringo?*"

Carlita neither spoke nor moved to pick up the coin. Chacal returned to the pocket and produced another two dollars.

"Harley Macon," she said, dropping the coins into her blouse. "He used to be a Texas Ranger. Ellsworth's partner."

"Ah, yes. The famous Ellsworth and Macon. Do you know him well?" Chacal touched her where many others had, to accentuate the question.

"I know him. Very well."

"Why is he in Laredo?"

"He said he is looking for work. He didn't say what kind."

"And the other one?"

"I don't know him," Carlita sighed. "But I hope I see him again."

No Ordinary Thunder

Chacal pinched her on the thigh. She slapped his face without hesitation, sending the *vaqueros* into fits of laughter.

"Do you think he is working with the law? Or did he come to Carlita to taste the honey?"

"He told me he is through with the law. That the law is no good for him now."

"Do you believe him?"

"Maybe he is lying. All men do."

"If I told you I want to take you on this table, would you believe me?"

"Oh, I would believe you, *Amante*. But I would not do you on the table. At least, not until we are closed."

Chacal drew his pistol and stroked her cheek with the shiny barrel.

"You keep an eye on Macon. Tell me if he is doing anything suspicious. I will see that you make plenty of money."

Carlita wrapped her long fingers around the barrel of the gun, and slowly massaged its length.

"I am sorry," she said to the patrons. "We are closing early tonight."

No Ordinary Thunder

Chapter 3

Sweat dripped from Jesus Sandoval's beard, as he hacked out a grave in the rocky ground. The wife and two daughters of the murdered rancher stood near the body, the woman begging God for vengeance. The youngest of the girls, three or four years old, seemed to be crying mostly because her mother and sister were. Her *papa'* lay on the ground, rolled up in a blanket. Why he wouldn't come out, she didn't know.

Jesus himself had once owned a small *rancho* north of the Rio Grande. It was a quiet place where he and his family could be happy. But the southern bandits raided one day while he was gone to help a neighbor. When he returned, his wife and daughter lay dead in the yard, his few head of cattle driven off. Jesus never spent another night in his home. Since the raid, he'd been living in the brush like a wolf. His only reason for living was to kill the bandits. And kill them, he did. He was sure he'd eliminated all those who murdered his family, but exacting his revenge had become a habit. A habit that Jesus took great pleasure in.

"Why don't you take the girls for a walk *Señora?* I will finish here and come to the house."

"No," she said. "We will stay and see it finished."

The rancher was heavy. Jesus felt awkward trying to drag the body to the grave in front of his family. All three of them gasped when he was rolled into the hole.

"*Por favor*, *Señora*. Please, go to the house."

The widow cursed Juan Cortina, and led her children away.

Every stolen cow on the Nueces Strip was attributed to Cortina. And he was responsible for thousands of them. But some, especially the smaller bunches, were often driven to remote villages and butchered on the spot. The village would therefore have plenty of food, and Cortina

No Ordinary Thunder

would get the blame.

The rancher had been shot only this morning, along with the one horse he owned. The widow said they had only a dozen head of cattle. They sold a few each year and kept the rest for food.

Now they would have no food, no way to survive, unless Jesus could find the cattle and bring them back. He had no intention of bringing the rustlers back. They would only cause him trouble.

Jesus didn't understand the *gringos'* law, so he made up whatever he could live with. His conscience didn't bother him much. He could think of no fate bad enough for men who killed women and children. He crossed himself when the chore was finished, and walked back to the house.

The heartbroken girls sat on the bed, held each other and cried. The widow hustled around the little kitchen, preparing some food for Jesus to take with him. He had to insist that she keep the food for herself and her girls.

"You will need the food more than me," he said. "I will try to find your cattle and bring them back, but you may want to move closer to a town. It's not good for you to be here without your man. What was his name?"

"Reynaldo Gutierrez. He was a good husband, and father to our children. The girls are Rosa and Theresa. My name is Elena. We thank you for what you did."

"*De nada.* I am Jes. . ."

"I know you. Everyone knows you."

Jesus felt uncomfortable. He needed to leave, but didn't want to say goodbye. Seeing their sadness brought about memories of his own murdered family. He asked the widow for a brief description of the two men who killed her husband, tipped his sombrero and made for the door.

"If I'm not back in a few days with the cattle, you'd better go. *Adios.*"

No Ordinary Thunder

#

Confident there would be no pursuit, the rustlers hadn't traveled far from the Gutierrez place. The lookout, a Mexican, kept an eye on the countryside, while the other, a *gringo*, napped under a mesquite tree.

The rustlers lazed around a little creek, letting the cattle drink their fill. The water was cool and inviting, and they were in no hurry. The lookout entertained thoughts of a bath, of the women he'd known and would know. There was little else to think about on the trail.

He was just nodding off when he felt the loop drop over his head. He grabbed at the rope, but too late. It was already tight around his throat. He was being dragged through the brush, the rope burning his neck, strangling him. He tried to reach his knife, but he carried it in his boot. Each time he thought he had it, in panic he would reach for the rope again.

The dust boiled up around him. He tried to scream at his partner, but couldn't get the words to come out. Suddenly the ground fell out from under him, as his assailant pulled him over the edge of a rocky arroyo. He hit the ground hard, and was dragged up the other side to an open flat.

The rider began to lope circles, making each one smaller than the last. Every few strides, he shortened the dally on his rope. As the circles grew smaller, the lookout rolled over and over, dragging ever closer to the horse's hooves.

The horse kicked and missed—kicked again and struck the man in the top of the head. He felt the blows coming more often now, but didn't feel the pain. The horse kicked him full in the face, but all he could think of was the big tree at his mother's house. The tree he'd climbed a thousand times. Of his grandfather, who taught him to

No Ordinary Thunder

smoke cigarettes. And of his sister, Carlita.

Jesus removed his *reata* from the lookout's neck, and quickly searched through his pockets. Like most rustlers, he didn't have much. Nine dollars, a small crucifix, two pictures, one of a naked blonde on a burro, and one of Carlita Ramirez, who owned the cantina in Laredo. He'd lost his weapons, but Jesus would find them and give them to the widow, along with his fine silver spurs.

He swung to the saddle and galloped back to the creek. The cattle were still there, but the *gringo* was gone. Jesus could see him making dust in the distance. No matter. He had a good description of the man.

He gathered the lookout's horse and started the cattle back north. The widow and the girls could use a good horse, or could sell him if they moved to a town. The man's belongings would never make up for the loss of her husband, but it would help. She would be glad to know one of the killers was dead.

Jesus would keep the pictures, especially the one of the blonde. Maybe the picture of Carlita could lead him to the lookout's identity. Not that it made any difference. Jesus would not be surprised to find a picture of Carlita in the pockets of many men. The *gringo* would not be hard to find. He was headed straight for Laredo.

#

Sheriff Eli Plummer lay across the bed in his broken-down jail, hovering between drunk and unconscious. A young Mexican girl named Felicia rubbed his dirty feet.

Felicia was one of several wayward girls in Laredo,

No Ordinary Thunder

who dropped by to procure favors from the sheriff. He supplied their whiskey, never failed to offer them a little money for their services, and always allowed them to sleep it off in his bed if they were too drunk to go anywhere else.

But Eli didn't care about the girls—he cared only about Carlita Ramirez. Her beauty was astonishing, not to mention her sultry demeanor. She'd invited him to her bed a few times, only strengthening his need for her. But it took many men to keep Carlita happy. She would never be satisfied with a drunken sheriff.

Eli had been holed up in the office for several days, as was his habit when the cowboys came to town. The less he saw of them, the less chance he would have to attempt any sheriffing.

Twice a day he'd send a girl out for whiskey and food, and get his exercise going to the privy. He thought he remembered Felicia saying there were two strangers in town, neither of them cowboys. One was white, she didn't know about the other, but he carried three pistols in his belt. He sounded like a man Eli hoped would leave soon.

The heavy pounding on the door startled him so, that he kicked Felicia in the chest and knocked her to the floor. Eli drew his pistol from the holster hanging on the bedpost.

"Who is it?" he shouted.

"Sheriff. It's me. Bell."

"Let him in," Eli said to the girl.

Felicia raised herself from the floor, favoring an elbow she'd banged in the fall. She walked over, cursing, and unlocked the door, leaving a trail of bare footprints in the dust. The man entered the room looking haggard and drawn. Eli knew he'd been riding hard.

"How many'd you bring in?"

"None," Bell said. "Some *vaquero* roped Ramirez. He's dead."

Bell walked to the barrel that passed for a table, and

No Ordinary Thunder

poured himself a glass of whiskey. He didn't elaborate on the man's gruesome end. Death by dragging was not uncommon in South Texas.

"One *vaquero*?"

"I think it was Sandoval," was all Bell said, or had to.

Jesus Sandoval was known all over the border country. Often parents would use his name to make their children behave. "Be good, or Jesus Sandoval will get you," was usually enough to quiet the children down. But it was not the children who needed to fear him. It was the bandits—like Ramirez and Bell.

"Where'd it happen?"

"Ten miles south of Carrizo Springs. We had to kill the rancher. He only had a dozen head."

"You killed him for a dozen cows? Are you out of your mind?"

"A man's gotta eat. Beef is money, and money's what I want. Money's what we both want, right? Sheriff?"

The way Bell emphasized his final word made Eli feel hollow inside. He'd once been a respected Ranger, having served under Captain Cole Ellsworth. He was there when the Rangers took down Zendejaz and his band of comanchero gun-runners. Now, everything was different. Now he was just a drunk, a pawn, paid to look the other way.

There were plenty of places to cross cattle on the river, but not many towns where a man could spend his money. That made Laredo a popular hangout for thieves of every description. Wanted men could feel safe there, knowing a few dollars and a drink would buy the sheriff's silence.

Eli's cut of the cattle profits usually didn't amount to much. And often he was so drunk the rustlers cheated him out of the little he had coming. He supposed the only reason they let him live was the thought of Laredo getting

No Ordinary Thunder

an honest lawman.

"You told Carlita?"

"Nope. Just got to town." Bell took a long look at the black-eyed girl sitting quietly in the corner.

"Why don't you go tell her, and leave me and the girl alone for a while?"

Felicia giggled at Bell's suggestion. Eli rolled onto his side and fumbled under the bed, trying to find his socks. He reached too far and fell out, bloodying his nose on the floor.

"It's plain you can't do her no good," Bell said. "She looks kinda lonesome to me."

Felicia giggled again. Eli made it to his feet, wobbling noticeably, his stinking socks in his hand. They were hard and crusty. A mouse had chewed a hole in one. Eli threw them in the corner and searched for another pair. He soon gave up and sat down on the bed, to pull his boots onto bare feet.

"I'll tell her. I'm due for some fresh air anyway. Might be good for you to stay outta sight if Sandoval's lookin' for you."

"I don't think he got a good look at me." Bell flopped down hard in the chair, and lifted his leg for Felicia to pull his boot off.

"Well, she'll keep you busy for a while. I'll see what I can find out." Eli walked out and headed for Carlita's, his boot quickly rubbing a blister on his heel.

#

Harley dozed in the shade, while the farrier nailed the last shoe on the roan. Things were quiet. Most of the cowboys had left town, probably gone to steal more cattle. Henry Berry Lowery, or "Dixon" as Harley agreed to call him, spent most of his time cleaning his many weapons.

He and his brothers had taken to the swamps of Robeson County, North Carolina, when Henry was only

No Ordinary Thunder

fourteen, to avoid conscription into the Confederate labor forces. Indians and blacks alike were taken to Wilmington in chains, to build the yellow fever-infested coastal forts the Confederacy needed. They died by the hundreds, faster than they could be replaced. Henry Berry, his brothers, and a growing number of rag-tag boys, preferred life on the run.

They soon became heroes to the Lumbee Indians, the blacks, and all the oppressed of Robeson County. But they were not heroes to the Confederate home guard.

On March 3, 1865, the home guard murdered Henry Berry's father and brother, for harboring escaped Yankee prisoners. The Civil War, at that time, was coming to a long-awaited end. But the war in Robeson County had just begun.

After Lee's surrender, the home guard re-emerged as the Ku Klux Klan, continuing to spew their hatred for any law other than their own. The outrages against the blacks and the Indians became more frequent and violent. So did the retaliations of the Lowery gang, turning Robeson County and the surrounding area into a bloody battleground.

Finally, in 1872, after stealing their own reward money, the gang disbanded, and Henry Berry Lowery, the outlaw chief, was never seen in Robeson County again. Lowery, like so many others of his stripe, had faded into legend.

"You're gonna rub a hole in that gun if you don't quit," Harley said.

"I like a clean weapon. Never know when you'll need it. Especially travelin' with an ex-Ranger. Likely lots o' folks wanna shoot you."

"Can't argue with that. But I'm gonna eat before they do. It's a worrisome thing to carry a bullet when you're hungry. I'm feelin' kinda puny."

Harley paid the farrier and led his horse back to the livery. Dixon walked alongside, his eyes catching every

No Ordinary Thunder

movement on the street. The scream that came from the cantina startled them both.

Carlita burst through the doors, sobbing into her hands. She reeled and wailed until she fell to the ground, the dust turning to mud on her wet face. Harley ran to her and held her in his arms.

"Carlita! What is it? What happened?"

"My brother. He is dead."

"What happened to him?"

Carlita didn't answer the question. Dixon thought she was holding something back.

"Harley?"

The voice rang so familiar, Harley smiled before he turned.

"Eli Plummer. What the hell are you doin' in Laredo?"

"I'm the sheriff," he said, without much pride.

"What're you doin' here?"

"Well, right now I'm tryin' to comfort this woman. You know what happened to her brother?"

"Uh, somebody killed him. We ain't exactly sure. Is the Cap'n with you?"

"Nope. Cole's got a real life now. I ain't a lawman anymore. I'm down here lookin' for work."

Carlita had settled down a little, but the tears still flowed in torrents.

"You be still now, honey," Harley said. "Eli, this here's Dixon. You know, like Mason-Dixon?"

"Howdy." Eli offered his hand. Dixon took it, but said nothing.

"Let's get outta the street," Harley said. "Come on, honey. We'll get you inside."

Carlita stumbled back to the cantina with the help of Eli and Harley. Dixon kept a wary eye on the street. He heard her curse Jesus Sandoval every step of the way. Wasn't he the man Harley was supposed to meet? Was he

No Ordinary Thunder

her brother's killer? And where was he now?

#

Jesus slipped into Laredo a little past midnight, his paint horse tired and hungry. His friend, Banda, who owned the livery, put his horse in a back stall out of sight.

"Macon?" Jesus asked, when he saw the blue roan.

"*Sí, and another one.*" Banda poured the paint a good ration of oats, and started forking him hay.

"Another? Who is he?"

"I don't know. But he is almost as spooky as you. I have heard something bad has happened to Carlita's brother. She thinks you did it, *amigo*."

"Her brother? *Aiee*, I thought he was a lover. I found her picture in his pocket."

"Her young brother. She loved him very much. Maybe you rest awhile and leave town, *eh*?"

"I have to talk to Macon first. Do you know where to find him?"

"*Sí*. He is at the sheriff's office. They have been drinking a lot. The sheriff and Macon were Rangers together."

Jesus had little tolerance for drunks. McNelly told him to be careful of Macon, until he was sure the man could do his job. But if he and the sheriff were old friends, it might be the way for Macon to get in with the bandits, and report to McNelly. Or, he might find the money irresistible and cross over to the other side. If he was drunk, he would be useless. As useless as his drunken friend, the sheriff.

"I'm hungry, Banda. If you would please get me some food, then go tell Macon his horse is sick."

"I'll have my son bring the food around back. If Macon is too drunk?"

No Ordinary Thunder

"Bring him. He's cavalry. He won't be too drunk to care for his horse."

#

Though Eli had given him a description of the man, the face Harley saw when he stepped into the livery did not fail to shock him. A light-skinned, blue-eyed Mexican with red hair and beard. He carried the look of a madman.

"You Sandoval?"

"*Sí*. Harley Macon?"

"Yeah." The men shook hands, while Harley looked into the scariest eyes he'd ever seen. Eli, between drinks, had spoken freely about Sandoval and his vengeance on the southern bandits. He'd wreaked havoc on some of the northern bandits, too. Apparently, Jesus Sandoval had only one purpose in life.

Harley left Eli asleep in his chair, but Dixon didn't feel comfortable waiting around the jail, so he came along to see if he could help with the horse. He'd plainly become suspicious when Harley told him to wait outside and watch the door.

"What do you hear from McNelly?" Harley asked.

"The feud in DeWitt County does not go well. It may be a long time before the Rangers come south."

"What are we supposed to do, twiddle our thumbs?"

"Many cattle cross here. It's a long way to the ocean, nearly two hundred miles. I don't think they drive little bunches all the way. I think they hold them somewhere across the river, then drive them down when they have a big bunch."

"Any idea where they're bein' held?"

"Large herds of cattle are not hard to find, *Señor*."

"And when we find 'em, then what?"

"I think they will drive them to Las Cuevas, or

No Ordinary Thunder

maybe all the way to Matamoros. There must be bed grounds, or maybe holding pens, along the way for such a long trip. If we find them, maybe *Capitán* will know where to strike, *eh*?"

"Sounds like they know what they're doin'. They'll likely post outriders to the rear. I doubt we could follow 'em without gettin' killed. Too much open country."

"No. We can only follow from a long distance, unless they travel at night. Maybe you can go with them."

"Go with 'em? How the hell can I do that?"

"Your friend...the sheriff. He is one of them."

No Ordinary Thunder

Chapter 4

"Eli? Are you sure?"

"I'm sure, *Señor*. He has been the sheriff almost two years," Jesus said. "I did not know he was your friend."

The news cut Harley like a knife. He felt angry and sad, both at the same time. Eli Plummer was the last man he thought would go bad. He plainly had his head in the bottle. Harley could see that from their visit at the jail. But he had to admit, the whiskey went down easy and he'd wanted more himself. It was difficult keeping control. If Banda hadn't come with the ruse of the sick horse, he might be passed out next to Eli, right now.

"Damn!" Harley's nerves got the better of him. He wished he had another drink. Staggering a bit, he sat down on an empty keg, removed his hat, and mopped his brow.

"Why you suppose he went to hell like that?"

"Money. It's always the money, *Señor*."

"Hell. Eli never worried about money before."

"All men worry about money. It is the curse of the living. Maybe your friend can work both sides for us."

"Too dangerous. Now the word's out that we're old partners, they'll be watchin' him close. Better just play it like it lays. I don't want any harm to come to him, if we can help it."

"Stealing cattle is a harmful profession. Cortina has some very bad men."

"Yeah. I won't say anything to Eli yet. Let's meet here tomorrow night about ten o'clock. We'll slip across the river and see if we can find the holding ground. If they've only got a few head, it might buy us some time. But if they've got a bunch, we'll have to move fast. You all right with that?"

Jesus answered with a big stretch and a smile. "*Sí*. I will eat my fill and sleep all day. Banda's wife is a very

No Ordinary Thunder

good cook. The horses will be ready when you get here. What about your other friend outside?"

"I don't know. I'll tell you later."

Harley stepped out into the night to find Dixon sitting on the ground, his back to the wall, holding a sick kitten in his lap. The kitten's eyes were matted shut, and discharge ran from its nose. It didn't look long for this world.

"Who's your sidekick?" Harley asked.

"He didn't say his name. I'm callin' him Sick Kitty. My little girl, Sally Ann, had one the same color."

The mention of his daughter caused Dixon to look away, toward the hills of Carolina, where he'd lived and loved his family. And the swamps, where he'd hidden for so many years.

"Think you'll ever get to go back there?"

"No. I can never go home, now. Sure wish I could. My wife, Rhoda, is the prettiest gal in Robeson County. Everybody says so, not just me. And she can shoot straighter and faster than most men. Everybody says that, too."

"Well, maybe you can bring your family to Texas. We can always use another pretty gal, especially one that can shoot. What about your kids?"

"Sally Ann, Henry Delaney, and Neelyann. Sally Ann and Henry are good shots, too. Neelyann will be when she gets older. Her ma'll see to that."

Harley thought he might as well spit it out. "I'm ridin' to Mexico tomorrow night. Gotta look over some things. Don't know when, or if I'll get back, so I guess this is good-bye. It's been good knowin' you. You don't have to wonder. Your secret's safe with me."

Harley stuck out his hand, but Dixon paid no attention. Without rising, he started digging a hole with his knife. Sick Kitty had breathed his last breath.

"I think I'll ride along, if you don't mind. Your

No Ordinary Thunder

friends in the livery talk loud, *Seenyor*. I guess you're a Texas Ranger, after all."

"Yeah. Nothin' you have to worry about. Am I gonna have to shoot you?"

"Nope. I can keep a secret, too. I'm an outlaw, remember? Besides, you saved my life."

"I told you before. You don't owe me anything. This bunch down south is a bad outfit to fool with."

"Worse than the Ku Klux? I doubt it. Sons o' bitches killin' and terrorizin' innocent folks. I enjoyed killin' 'em, I don't mind tellin' you. Maybe this bunch needs killin', too."

Dixon covered the kitten, stood to his feet, and tamped the dirt down flat with his boot heel. By daylight the grave would be unnoticeable, like the many graves he'd left behind in the Carolina swamps.

"You've got a family, Dixon. I don't want you to go. You could damn sure get killed if you come with me."

"If I do, I'll die game. That's how I always planned to go."

#

Chacal made a pass around the holding area before he rode in, just to be on the safe side. Everything looked about like he'd left it, but one couldn't be too careful.

The noonday sun baked down on the stolen cattle. They lay in the sparse grass, panting in the heat, puffs of dust billowing up around their noses. A little creek provided all the water they needed, but for the most part, they seemed content not to move. Some of the cowboys napped in the shade, while others dozed in the saddle, instinctually aware of what happened around them. Bell approached Chacal on a keen little buckskin, the horse's neck and flanks dark with sweat.

No Ordinary Thunder

"I count two hundred forty-one," he said.

Chacal didn't hide his disappointment. He needed to push the cattle to Las Cuevas. Salinas was waiting for the three hundred head Chacal had promised him. He was not the kind of man who liked to be kept waiting.

Las Cuevas was the headquarters of General Juan Flores Salinas, considered to be the chief of all cattle thieves on the border, and the *alcalde* of Camargo. Three miles south of the Rio Grande, in the brushy country of Tamaulipas, the *rancho* lay surrounded by a vast expanse of cattle pens, the biggest bandit camp on the river, with the exception of Cortina's main camp at Matamoros. Most of the cattle stolen upriver were crossed and driven down to Las Cuevas, or Cachuttas, a line camp between Las Cuevas and the river. They were held there until Cortina secured passage to Cuba.

Chacal's men had been holding the herd south of *Nuevo Laredo* and adding to it for nearly two weeks. They would have to move them to new grass soon, two or three days at the most. He'd lost a good man in Ramirez, but was mostly disgruntled because he and Bell had attempted to drive back only a dozen head—a long way from the sixty needed to swell the herd. Salinas would expect what was promised. The loss of a good *vaquero* would not change that.

But now he had only seven riders. Eight would have been barely enough to push a herd this size in the dark. Many rustlers who brought in small bunches disappeared after they'd been paid, not to be seen again until Chacal started building another herd. Well, time was against him. He'd just have to do with what he had.

"We need to fill out this herd," he told Bell.

"I think maybe some of us will cross over and sweep the area to Rio Grande City. The rest will start pushing this bunch downriver."

"We're shorthanded as it is. How you gonna do it?"

No Ordinary Thunder

"We will need a few more men. There must be someone around who needs a few dollars. I will go see Carlita tonight."

#

There were no customers in the cantina when Chacal walked in, only Carlita and a few of the girls who worked the streets. With no cowboys in town, and little money to be made, they chose to join Carlita in her grief. They took turns crying with her, assuring her that her brother was in Heaven now, and that she would see him again when she got there. Chacal didn't believe in Heaven or Hell, or any of that nonsense. When you died, you were dead. That's all. The girls got up and made their way into the street, when he joined Carlita at the table.

"I'm sorry about your brother," he said, taking a seat facing the door. "He was one of the best *vaqueros* on the Strip. It will be a hard thing to replace a man like him, but replace him I must. We have to move the cattle soon. Are there any cowboys in town?"

Most men would have wilted at the fire in Carlita's eyes, but Chacal just waited patiently for her answer.

"Replace him? You bastard. He lays on the prairie for the coyotes to eat. No one even buries him. That son of a bitch, Sandoval. If you were a man, you would go kill him."

Chacal slapped her hard, and knocked her out of the chair. The young man, Ramon, burst from the kitchen, a big knife in his hand, a fierce look on his face.

Chacal laid his pistol on the table. His glare made it plain he was in no mood to fool with interruptions.

"Go wash the dishes, *chico*, and you will live another day. Stay here, and I will kill you."

Ramon stood defiantly.

No Ordinary Thunder

"Has he hurt you, *Señorita*?"

"No. I'm not hurt. Go back to the kitchen. Quickly! Go now!"

Ramon backed out of the room, but stayed close to the kitchen door to keep an eye on things. Carlita used the chair to help herself up. Her lip was split and bleeding, but she showed Chacal no fear, only contempt.

"Can we talk business now?" he asked her.

"There is no business to talk. There are no cowboys in town. Only Macon and his friend."

"Have you been watching him?"

"*Sí*, but he does nothing. He only says he is looking for work. If you want him watched, you watch him. I have other things to do. *Vayate*! We close now."

Chacal slapped her again, but this time not so rough. "I am not ready to leave, Carlita. I think I am ready to take you upstairs."

"You will not take me tonight, you bastard! I am in mourning for my brother."

He drew her close, kissed her hard on the lips, and headed for the door. Carlita spit on the floor in anger—then, in a moment, thought of calling him back.

Chacal stepped out onto the boardwalk. The cantina door slammed behind him. Why hadn't he thought of it before? Maybe the best way to watch Macon was to keep him and his friend close by. Besides, what could the two of them do against so many? It would be a simple matter to outnumber them until he had all the facts.

He would do it. He would hire them to drive the cattle downriver. If he saw or heard anything suspicious, he would have them killed and be on his way.

Chacal mounted his horse and rode through the maze of ramshackle buildings, until he reached the sheriff's office. He looked through the window and saw Eli there, leaning on the desk, his pants around his ankles, with Felicia on her knees in front of him. Both looked like they

No Ordinary Thunder

were enjoying themselves. He waited until they'd finished before he banged on the door.

"Sheriff," he shouted. "It is Chacal. Save some for me, *eh*."

Eli jumped at the sudden disturbance, while Felicia, drunk, only laughed. He buttoned his pants, unlocked the door and let Chacal in. The bandit's excitement showed plainly through his trousers.

"Wait here, *chiquita*," he said. "The sheriff and I will talk outside."

Felicia giggled, wiped her chin, and took another drink. Eli strapped on his pistol and the men stepped out. Chacal got right to the point.

"Where is your friend, Macon?"

"Don't know. I ain't seen him this evenin'. If I know Harley, he's likely doin' the same thing I was doin'. I ain't seen Dixon neither. What you want with him?"

"I want him to drive the herd to Las Cuevas with us. Do you think he can be trusted?"

Not much blood had returned to Eli's brain—it was mostly swimming in whiskey. He had a hard time choosing his words, but finally was able to speak.

"Harley says he's through lawin'. I've known him a long time. He's kinda crazy, but he ain't a liar. I expect he means what he says."

"Good. We'll take him along and keep an eye on him. From what I've heard, he is a good man to have on your side."

"And a damn bad one to have against you. Harley's all right, but I don't know Dixon. He looks pretty cagey."

"Cagier than *El Chacal, amigo?*"

Chacal turned and stepped into the office. Eli heard him lock the door. He watched through the window for a while, saw Chacal drop his pants and Felicia take her position. Forcing himself to turn away, he relieved himself in the alley, and walked down the street to get a drink.

No Ordinary Thunder

#

Harley and his men rode north of Laredo, circled west and crossed the river in an isolated spot. They wound their way through the chaparral, unsure of their destination. Only a few miles into Mexico, they began to hear the lowing of the cattle.

Jesus was right. The herd was easy enough to find. Being held on the same patch of ground for so long, the whole area reeked of manure. The cattle were on their feet, moving about in the cool night air. A few cowboys rode their circles, singing softly about everything from gunfights to lost loves, the latter fouling both Harley and Dixon's mood.

"Damn, there's a bunch of 'em," Harley said. "How long you reckon they can hold 'em here?"

"Not much longer," Jesus said. "By the smell, they have been here a while. There can't be much grass left. They will have to move them soon."

"I count three riders," Dixon said, "but that can't be all, can it? I never drove a cow in my life, but I'll bet it takes more'n three men to move this bunch."

"*Sí.* The others must be sleeping, or in town maybe."

"About ten days to Las Cuevas," Harley said. "Ten more to Matamoros. Hot as it's been, they'll need plenty o' water. I expect they'll stay pretty close to the river."

"If they travel at night, they will make better time," Jesus said. "Maybe eight days to Las Cuevas, if they rest through the heat."

"Well, I guess now all we gotta do is figure a way to get in with 'em."

The sound of hoofbeats at a lazy walk alerted the nighthawk closest to the intruders.

"*Quien es?*" he said softly. The rider drew near

No Ordinary Thunder

enough that Harley could see he held a rifle across his saddle.

"Chacal," came the reply. "Any trouble?"

"No. The cattle move easy. There is coffee on the fire."

"Good. Let's ride in. I want to talk to everyone. Swing around and tell the other riders."

Chacal rode to the camp, while the nighthawk gathered the men. Soon they all stood at the fire, drinking coffee, listening to Chacal's plan.

"Wish I knew what he was sayin' to 'em," Harley said. "Must be somethin' important, to wake 'em all up."

"Maybe they plan to move tonight," Jesus said.

"Yeah, maybe."

Harley suddenly looked left and right. "Damn it all! Where's Dixon?"

#

The camp looked about like Dixon expected. A pile of coffee grounds dumped at the edge of the fire, sardine and food tins scattered about, cigarette butts, liquor bottles, and a stack of old papers with a rock on top, to be used on the men's trips to the bushes. He had once lived much the same way, himself—an outlaw on the run.

Dixon moved through the brush like a ghost—the cows swishing their tails made more noise. It was quiet, eerie, the kind of night that made his heart pound. The kind that made him crave action. He came within twenty feet of the firelight, as Chacal told the men of his scheme.

"There are no cowboys in town. I want to take Macon, the ex-Ranger, with us. I don't trust him. We can keep an eye on him if we take him along, and kill him if he gets out of line. Maybe after we deliver the herd, we will kill him just for the fun of it."

No Ordinary Thunder

"You'll have to move fast if Delgado finds out he's with us," Bell said. "I doubt he'll give Macon much of a chance."

"Ah, that is a good idea. I have a feeling Delgado would love to see Macon again."

"What about his friend? You gonna take him?"

"We can use the help. If he wants to come, we'll take him. Maybe we can have some fun with him, too"

"They don't look much like the kind to have fun with. I'd like it a whole lot better if there was just one of 'em."

"We will think about that later. For now, we rest and prepare for the trip. We leave tomorrow at sundown, with or without them. Riders, get back to the cattle."

Dixon looked the men over closely. All wore their pistols low and tied down, a sight fairly common in Texas. They were men who would go down hard if it came to that, and Dixon was sure it would. A herd this size must be worth a lot of money, something most men did not give up easily. He didn't know exactly what Harley's intentions were, but the man had saved his life, and that was reason enough to stick with him, at least until he learned the play.

Dixon made his way back to Harley's location. The men were not where he'd left them. Fearful of speaking out, he slipped through the rocks as quietly as possible, taking care with every step. Just then he saw a shadow. He gasped at the burn of a garrote around his throat. Harley put a knife to his breast, but chuckled when he recognized him.

"Dixon," he said, "you take a lotta chances. You could've been killed goin' down there…or comin' back here, for that matter. Let him go, Jesus."

Jesus released the garrote, but it took a great effort. Dixon noticed a frightening glaze over the man's scary blue eyes. He seemed to have gone to another place—a place hard to come back from.

"What'd you hear?" Harley asked

No Ordinary Thunder

"Well, you ain't gotta figure a way in. Chacal wants to take you with him, to keep an eye on you. Me too, if I wanna go."

"By God, I like doin' things the easy way. They say when they're gonna leave?"

"Tomorrow at sundown. I guess they'll come find us."

"Good. You've still got a chance to get outta this, Dixon. Once we sign on, they won't let us leave."

"Oh, I wouldn't worry about that. They don't plan on us leavin'. Sounds like they plan to kill us when we get wherever we're goin'."

"Well, they'll have it to do. Anything else?"

"Yeah. They said there's a fella lookin' forward to seein' you again. A fella named Delgado."

No Ordinary Thunder

Chapter 5

Rio Grande City came alive with the news. Governor Richard Coke had reinstated the Texas Rangers. Rojas heard little else as he made his way around town.

The soldiers from Ringgold Barracks drank too much and talked too loud. What did they need the Rangers for? The army was in Texas, now. They needed no help from a bunch of wild Texans, who were half outlaw themselves. Anything that needed handling in Texas, the army could more than handle it.

Rojas scoffed at the bragging soldiers. The way he saw it, the army was doing a damn poor job of handling anything. The Indians, though their numbers had depleted, still did pretty much as they pleased in the west, and the bandits completely controlled the border. He could not remember one time when the army captured or killed any rustlers. With all their pomp and ceremony, it took them too long to move. The dust from their columns could be seen for miles. An experienced bandit could cross his bunch and be soaking in a bathtub across the river, before the army could locate his trail.

The citizens, on the other hand, were glad to hear of the Rangers' reinstatement. But there had been Rangers on the border before. They were no match for the *Cortinistas,* as they were always grossly outnumbered. It was said that Cortina could muster fifteen hundred to two thousand men in just a few days. What were a few Rangers going to do? Since Cortina started shipping cattle to Cuba, it seemed there was not enough beef in Texas to satisfy the need. But it was the raping and killing that concerned the citizens the most. One could maybe get more cattle, but life was a one-time affair. To have it taken or destroyed, was forever.

Rojas stepped up to the bar, and ordered a tall tequila. Several of the men hanging around the cantina made their living as small time bandits. Rojas could see

No Ordinary Thunder

they had a lot on their minds. It was funny how the U.S. Army worried them not at all, but just the mention of the Texas Rangers had them thinking of finding new jobs. The army had far more men, but few could fight or ride like a Ranger.

Half of the army's scouts probably sided with Cortina. There was no telling how many merry chases the soldiers had been led on. But it wouldn't be like that with the Rangers. They had learned to track and fight, warring with the Comanche and the Kiowa. Rojas had no doubt they could find whoever they were after. The Rangers were more interested in justice than looking good or filling out reports.

He called for one more tequila, tossed it down and went for his horse. The bay had been standing tied a long time. He was more than ready to ride.

Rojas mounted and headed for the river. The bay pranced through the town's dusty streets, snorting, his head held high. Rojas slacked the reins and they were off like a shot, splashing across the Rio Grande, shining by the light of the moon.

#

Delgado cursed, and slammed his fist down on the pit-rail. He had five dollars bet on the brindle bitch and she was clearly losing the fight. The red bitch held her firmly by the cheek, gradually working down to the brindle's throat. The brindle was helpless in such a hold, and would soon be killed when the red reached her goal.

Of course, the owner could always concede the fight. Delgado hoped he would. After all, the brindle had shown no bad signs of turning, and scratched hard every time, even after the red had damaged her stifle. She was game, just overmatched. The superiority of a good head

No Ordinary Thunder

dog could not be denied. The red was plainly in control. No need to lose a brave dog over it.

Rojas pushed his way through the crowd, making a path to where Delgado stood. His attempts to get the man's attention were rudely brushed aside, Delgado being only interested in the dog fight.

Rojas lit a cigarette and waited, the smoke, in great puffs, exiting the hole where his nose used to be. Finally, at one hour and four minutes, the brindle's owner forfeited and Delgado paid his five dollars. The crowd cheered for the winner and the loser, both being great, brave fighters.

"What is it?" Delgado snapped.

"I've been across the river," Rojas said. "I heard the governor has re-formed the Texas Rangers."

"What? Who told you?"

"It is all the talk in the saloons. A Major Jones is in charge of the Frontier Battalion. They have gone west to fight the Indians. A captain, McNelly I think, is in charge of Special Forces to stop feuds and outlaws. Do you think the Rangers will come back to the Strip?"

"No. They could do nothing before, and we are stronger now than ever. Even the army cannot stop us. If the Rangers are foolish enough to come back to the Strip, we will kill them all. It is only a matter of time before we run the *gringos* out, and take the Strip back for Mexico!"

Rojas had heard it all before. Mexico would never get the Strip back. If Sam Houston had fulfilled his dream, all of Mexico would belong to the United States. Maybe they should feel lucky they had anything left. The *Norte Americanos* usually got what they wanted.

"Maybe we should go tell Salinas, *eh?*"

"Not yet," Delgado said. "There is someone I want to see first."

"A woman?"

"*Sí,* a woman. Don't say any more about this to

No Ordinary Thunder

anyone until I get back. We will ride to Las Cuevas at sunrise."

Delgado left the building at the first scratch of the next fight, males fifty-one pounds. The yellow dog raced across the pit so fast that the opponent's handler was unable to release his dog, thus bearing the brunt of a vicious attack.

Rojas looked across the pit to see a homely young woman, laughing at the smoke coming out his nose hole. He smiled at her, showing her a mouthful of gold teeth. She smiled back and the two disappeared in the crowd.

#

Delgado tied his horse to a post, outside the one-room adobe a half mile west of town. Hanging from the walls were skulls, and bones, and hides of all types. Snake skins littered the ground.

A large black pot sat in the darkened, dying embers of a fire, emitting the aroma of some kind of meat. Delgado didn't care to know what it was.

He saw a shadow move across the dimly lit window, just as the heavy door creaked open. A sliver of light revealed the old woman. Sophia, the witch of Camargo.

Sophia came from somewhere far to the south, and when angered spoke a language no one understood. She was tall and black-skinned, and frightening to look at. Delgado had heard the stories about her, but wasn't prepared for the chills that ran up his spine. She swung the door open and he followed her in, reluctant to close the door behind him.

The room was hot and stank of cats, of which he counted seven. All sat about staring, their tails curling patiently, as if waiting for something to die. Sophia

No Ordinary Thunder

pointed to a chair at the table covered with candle wax, sat down opposite her guest and waited. Delgado caught his breath at the sight of her sitting so close.

Her eyes were large and yellow colored. They seemed to have no pupil. Her skin was black as ten feet under, her few teeth only a slightly lighter shade. She wore a cap fashioned from a spotted hide and a necklace strung with the skulls of rats. The lobes of her ears stretched near to her shoulders, under the weight of her heavy earrings. Delgado thought they could be made of solid gold, but would make no attempt to take them. He didn't have the courage to kill a witch, and if he let her live, she might put a curse on him.

Sophia stared vacantly around the room.

"One dollar," she said.

Her voice snapped Delgado out of his trance. He took a dollar from his vest pocket and laid it on the table, trying not to look at the gnarly hand that picked it up.

"What troubles you, boy?"

Delgado couldn't look into her eyes. He bowed his head and tried to focus on the floor. "I've heard news of the Texas Rangers. That they may be coming back to the Strip."

"Ah." Sophia pressed her hands into the candle wax on the table. When she removed them, the imprint didn't look like hands, but more like the wings of a bird. She studied the imprint carefully, humming an ugly, guttural chorus, until her yellow eyes rolled back in her head.

"There is a chicken hawk flying to Mexico," she said. "His talons are long and sharp. When he flies low and puts his talons in the water, the Rio Grande will turn to blood. The hawk will devour everything in his path, he has no mercy on his prey. His wings are wide, and far reaching, like the dragon."

Sophia pushed herself up from the table. All the cats

No Ordinary Thunder

moved as one and met her at the door, crying to be let outside. The cool air rushed into the hot little room, drawing Delgado from his motionless state. Sophia stood silhouetted in the doorway, and waited to usher him into the night. He caught the smell of something dead as he brushed past her and untied his horse.

"I do not understand your prophecy, woman. Are the Rangers coming to the Strip or not?"

Sophia dipped some meat from the old black pot and threw it to the cats. Whatever is was, it was quickly devoured, the cats squalling and screaming for more. She rattled the necklace of skulls at Delgado, muttered a few unintelligible words to the sky, shrugged her shoulders and went back inside.

Delgado shook his head, mounted his horse and rode back to town. The crazy bitch. He hadn't come to talk about birds, or see her stinking cats. If she couldn't tell a Texas Ranger from a chicken hawk with wings like a dragon, he guessed she wasn't much of a witch. As he drew near to town, the festive atmosphere of Camargo made him wish he could get his dollar back.

#

The manpower shortage forced Chacal to keep the men together, and drive the herd downriver. Somewhere along the way, they would bed the herd, cross over to Texas and steal the cattle they needed to fill the contract with Salinas. It would also give him a chance to see which side Macon and his friend were really on.

Macon seemed at ease among the bandits, telling stories of the old days in the war, women he had known, and Indians. Dixon, though, said little. He mostly cleaned his guns and played his fiddle. The bandits knew few of the tunes he played, but the music settled cattle and men

No Ordinary Thunder

alike, so it was always welcomed around the fire.

In the red dawn of the fourth day, Chacal let the cattle drift out on good grass, and ordered the men to get some sleep. "We're going to Texas tonight. We will be there until we have sixty head or more. Three men will stay with the herd. The rest will go with me. Let the cattle drift today. They are tired. They won't go far."

"Might be a good idea to gather some fresh horses, if we can," Bell said. "Some o' these were wore out when we started. If we're gonna chouse around Texas, we're gonna need 'em."

"We will if we get a chance, but we don't have time to look for them. Salinas is waiting and I want to be paid."

"We all wanna get paid, but we can't run beef on wore out horses. I say we get the horses first, then the cattle."

"Shut your mouth," Chacal said. "I decide what we do. Tend to your horses. We'll rest until sundown."

The men unsaddled, set up camp and found shade wherever they could. It was going to be another hot, miserable day, and the tension was growing among them. The all night rides, coupled with trying to sleep in the heat, were wearing them down. Soon they would be at each other's throats.

"That's a fine horse you're riding, Macon," Chacal said. "Where'd you get him?"

"Oh, he come from up north a ways."

"How far north? Everything is north of Mexico."

"Too far to go on this trip, unless you wanna add a few weeks to it."

"Maybe not this trip, but horses like him would be worth a long ride. Someday, I might want to go get them."

"Well, I don't think I'll show my face around there for a while. It ain't like I got a bill o' sale with him."

"We'll wait a while before we go. I wouldn't want you to get in any trouble."

No Ordinary Thunder

Chacal took a bottle of tequila from his saddlebag and offered it to Harley, who refused.

"I don't care much for tequila," he lied. "Think I'll just get some sleep. But you go right ahead. I won't take it as you bein' rude."

Harley lay back on his saddle and pulled his hat down over his eyes. Chacal snorted, took a drink, and picked a spot to rest under a big oak tree.

Dixon played the men to sleep with "The Girl I Left Behind Me," then threw his blanket under a mesquite bush. Before he closed his eyes, he made a mental note of where every man slept, in case he had to come up in a hurry.

Jesus Sandoval, watching from a distance, prepared to cross the river, where he would meet his friends to form a welcoming party for the bandits.

#

Harley rested through most of the day, but didn't get much sleep. He peered from beneath the brim of his hat, keeping a close eye on the men. They were a bad bunch. Not the kind you'd turn your back on. And they had solely one thing in mind—money. Harley had no doubt they'd kill each other, if that was the only way to get it.

The men had their fill of coffee and tortillas before crossing the Rio Grande. Seven riders, Harley and Dixon among them, splashed through the warm water, unsure of their destination or their fate. The three who stayed behind to watch the cattle, stretched and scratched and had a few drinks to celebrate their good fortune.

Once across, Chacal picked up the trot and maintained it for four or five miles. He seemed to know exactly where he was going, though no one had voiced any plan. They held a north-easterly direction toward the village of Randado and the old Garcia place. Harley had to

No Ordinary Thunder

wonder if there was anyone still living there. At its peak, only about fifteen people inhabited the village. Maybe they would travel on to the King Ranch, but that was a good hundred miles. A long way to go for sixty head. No matter. Sandoval's friends were to be expecting them, if everything went as agreed. They may well have them in sight right now, just waiting for the opportune time. The time came within ten miles of the river.

Sandoval's vigilantes emerged from the arroyo, firing their rifles high and wide. In the dusk, the confusion became general, each man retreating at speed. There was no cover anywhere near. Harley and Dixon stayed close together, hoping to take down a bandit or two if they could.

The vigilantes whipped their horses into pursuit, being careful to keep their distance, and extra careful not to hit Harley and Dixon. The bandits returned fire with their pistols as they ran, but the interval was too great. There was no hope of hitting the men who chased them.

One of the bandits' horses was shot in the neck, by a fellow outlaw riding closer to the front of the bunch. The horse went down hard right in front of Harley, whose own mount had to jump the beast to avoid being part of the wreck.

The man was none the worse for the fall. He shouted for Harley to come and pick him up. Firing behind him at the rifle flashes, he chased after the escaping bandits on foot.

Harley hauled the roan around and raced back to meet him. When the bandit reached for the saddle horn, Harley shot him in the chest. The man hung on for two or three strides, a confused, frightened look on his face, then fell and died alone on the dark Texas prairie.

The whole thing had taken no more than a minute. Harley passed the body of another dead bandit, as he whipped to catch up with the riders. The man had been shot in the back of the head. It was probably Dixon that killed

No Ordinary Thunder

him.

Now there would be no slowing down. Chacal headed for the river at breakneck speed. Harley hoped they'd given Jesus enough time.

#

Jesus and four riders kept a close eye on the camp. All were experienced *vaqueros* and moved through the cattle with minimal disturbance. The three men seated around the fire would hardly have known otherwise. They'd broken Chacal's cardinal rule, and had too much to drink.

The conversation was typical—women, money, horses, and women. Of course, they felt terrible about Carlita's brother. He was a good hand with a horse and friendly enough, but sometimes he tried to stand in the way of his sister's happiness. Who was he to say who could approach her? If Carlita wanted a man, that was her business. It was not for her brother to choose who was good enough for her. The three of them together could show her a good time. Maybe they would do just that, when they returned to Laredo.

One of the men had drifted off to sleep, when Jesus stepped into the firelight. He held two pistols, cocked and ready. The bandits were taken completely by surprise.

"Don't get up," Jesus said. "Throw your guns over here."

The men cautiously did as they were told. The sleeping bandit woke abruptly, and mistakenly reached for his weapon. Jesus shot him in the face, just as two ropes dropped around the necks of the others. They were jerked out of the camp and disappeared, dragged away behind galloping horses. Jesus called to his remaining men. They rode into the camp, dismounted, and finished the whiskey.

No Ordinary Thunder

"Saddle their horses," he said. "The others will be back soon."

#

The big oak tree, where Chacal had spread his blanket only that morning, was now decorated with three hanging corpses. One of them had his face blown off, drops of blood spattering the ground beneath him.

The others hadn't been shot. Their eyes bulged in disbelief. They appeared to be staring into the abyss, and not liking what they saw. Their horses and the cattle were gone. The tracks showed they'd been driven upriver a short distance, then crossed over into Texas.

"Let's get after 'em," Bell said.

"Our horses are washed out!" Chacal snapped. "We've already lost five men tonight. How do you know they're not out there waiting for us?"

No one could get a grip on what happened. The bandits ranted their anger. Long days of hard riding had all come to naught. Five men dead, the cattle gone, and Salinas was still waiting.

Nothing like this had ever happened before, and of a sudden Harley Macon was the center of attention. He thumbed the thong from his pistol, took a wide stance and prepared to go down shooting.

"If you think I had anything to do with this, spit it out," he said. "We could've been killed back there as easy as any of you. But if you think you've got a case, have at it."

Dixon came alongside him, and laid hand to pistol. Together they faced the vengeful bandits.

The horses shuffling and munching grass was the only sound for a while. A warm breeze set the limb to creaking under the weight of the three dead men. Not far away a night owl screeched, as he made a dive for his

No Ordinary Thunder

dinner.

"Pull 'em or back off!" Harley said.

They didn't want to back off, but they did. Chacal didn't like losing face. Harley knew there would be another time.

Dixon walked to the tree and cut the three ropes. The bodies dropped heavily, side by side.

"Let's get them buried," Chacal said. "Tomorrow we ride to Las Cuevas, to tell General Salinas what happened."

No Ordinary Thunder

Chapter 6

The ride to Las Cuevas took longer than expected. Harley could see that Chacal was in no hurry to face Salinas. Besides, the tension among the men made it hard to cover much ground. No one wanted to expose their back, but Harley and Dixon had to stick with the bandits if they were to get the information McNelly needed.

Every stop along the way was somber and suspicious. Few words were spoken, or needed to be. Harley knew they didn't trust him, and he damn sure didn't trust them. Dixon kept his eye on Harley, always ready to get into action.

Mid-morning of the third day brought them in sight of the *rancho*. Harley had expected the place to be a fine *hacienda*. Instead, he saw a few small houses of poor construction, several thatch-roofed *jacales* made of sticks and mud, and more cattle pens than he knew existed.

Harley figured there must be nearly a thousand head of cattle, all of them bawling from the heat. He'd been seeing the dust for a mile or two, and smelling the manure even farther. This looked like the same situation as Laredo. The herd couldn't be held much longer. They would have to move them soon.

"Quaint little *rancho*," Harley said. "I was expectin' somethin' a little more elaborate for a general."

Chacal was in no mood for small talk. "General Salinas was an officer of the *Rurales,* not the Mexican Army."

Harley could smell the fear on Chacal. Salinas would no doubt take it hard that they'd lost the cattle. The loss of the men, he assumed, would be of little consequence. There looked to be plenty of hands milling around, though many of them were in chains. Mostly Apaches, Harley thought, and maybe some Yaquis, too.

To the south stood a large post corral, filled near to

No Ordinary Thunder

bursting with some mighty fine horseflesh. Harley was anxious to check the brands. He was sure the horses had come from Texas.

The inhabitants of the ranch looked disappointed to see Chacal ride in with no cattle. They'd planned a welcoming celebration, just as they always did, but this time it appeared there would be none.

A pretty, barefoot girl, plainly anxious to greet the *vaqueros*, ran to the main house and came out with a rough, dangerous looking man. He carried two pistols in a bright yellow sash, and had a wicked looking knife strapped to his right leg. His broad, gray mustache covered his whole mouth, but somehow Harley knew he was scowling. The man was General Juan Flores Salinas.

"Chacal, my friend. You do not have my cattle. Where are they?"

"I am sorry, General. We lost them. We went to Texas to fill out the herd, and when we came back the cattle were gone. I lost five men, too. Three hanged, and two shot."

The broad mustache drooped a little further. Harley eased the thong off his pistol. He'd heard stories about Salinas. It would be no surprise if the old man started shooting.

"Who took my cattle from you? Was it Indians? Or ranchers? . . . Or *Texas Rangers?*"

Harley felt a catch in his throat. Dixon scanned the area with a critical eye, but otherwise appeared indifferent.

"Rangers?" Chacal said. "What do you mean, *Señor?*"

"I mean," Salinas said, "the Governor of Texas has re-commissioned the Rangers."

"I've not heard of any Rangers on the border, General." Chacal turned in his saddle, and calmly addressed the rider to his left. "Maybe this man can tell us about them."

No Ordinary Thunder

All eyes turned to Harley, who did what he always did when things became too tense. He laughed, and spit on the ground.

"Howdy, General. Name's Harley Macon. I expect you've heard o' me."

"*Sí.* I know you, Macon. I know you were once a Ranger."

"Yeah, but not for five years, now. I don't know anything about this reinstatement. I'm just lookin' to make a livin'."

"A living stealing Texas cows?"

"I fought four years for the Confederacy, General. Wounded three times. It didn't do any damn good, at all. Nine years with the Rangers, wounded twice, and all I got was fired for my trouble. I don't owe Texas anything."

"Maybe not. But maybe you want my cattle, *eh*?"

"I don't give a damn about your cattle. I came down here to make some fast money, and your man here let the deal slip away. If I was you, General, I'd keep an eye on this fella."

Dixon grinned the easy grin, and shifted in his saddle.

"And this one?" Salinas said. "Who is he?"

Harley started to speak, but was abruptly cut off. Dixon stepped his horse forward, and looked into the black eyes of General Salinas.

"Name's Dixon, General. You know, like the Mason-Dixon?"

Apparently, some of the men in the crowd didn't appreciate Dixon's cavalier humor. They slowly began to drift closer to his horse. Dixon saw no reason to let them. He pulled two of the three pistols from his wide leather belt, so fast Harley barely saw it. Every man reached for their guns. Women screamed—children ran—Harley pulled his weapon and covered the general.

"I'll kill him!" he shouted. "Back off. This ain't the

No Ordinary Thunder

way we want it, General. But if your boys wanna open the ball, you'll be the first man dead. Now, tell 'em to get back, or make your play."

Salinas was stunned. He could hardly imagine such a bold move, yet here he stood, in his own front yard, staring down the muzzle of a .44 Colt. He'd never seen anyone faster than Dixon, and there was little doubt Macon would kill him at such close range. The only thing he could think to do was what Macon had done before. He laughed and raised a hand to stop his men.

"Well, Macon, you have the nerve of a Ranger, I'll say that for you. Holster your weapon and step down."

Harley followed the general's instructions, but Dixon kept his seat, weapons in hand.

"Put your guns away, Dixon," Harley said. "We accept your hospitality, General."

Dixon did as he was told, but never removed his hand from the gun butt.

"You know my men will be watching you," Salinas said, "but from here they have orders to leave you alone. Is that clear, *amigos*?"

The crowd mumbled their agreement and randomly dispersed, many of them offering hard glances as they went. They would be watching—make no mistake.

"Bell will show you to the stable, and where you will sleep. Chacal, I will speak with you inside."

The men dismounted, numb from the riding. They shook their legs and stomped their feet, to get some feeling in them, then made their way down the dusty road that led to the stable. Harley spoke to Dixon in a whisper.

"Damn, you did that kinda sudden, didn't you? What if they'd started shootin'?"

"There was only eleven of 'em. Between us we have twice that many bullets."

No Ordinary Thunder

"Only eleven? Are you crazy? I admire your sand, but next time give me a little warnin', will you?"
"Why, Harley. You weren't scared, were you?"
"Course not. But damn it, I could sure use a drink."

#

Eli could hardly keep up with the thoughts racing through his head, as he watched Sandoval and his vigilantes drive the stock through the streets of Laredo. Having no knowledge of Harley's connection with Sandoval, he wondered if his old partner was dead. He knew Sandoval for a brutal killer. His stomach went queasy at the thought of Harley suffering such a death.

He wanted answers, but could not reveal what he knew about the cattle, Harley, Chacal, or any of it. The only thing he felt sure of was that, with Sandoval involved, some, or all of the men were dead. He swallowed hard when the wild-eyed Mexican rode up to speak with him.

"I am Jesus Sandoval. Maybe you have heard of me, *eh*?"

"I've heard of you."

"Good. I know most of the brands on these cattle, Sheriff. I have sent riders through the country telling the owners they can reclaim them north of town. My men will hold them there until the owners arrive."

"Where'd you get 'em?"

"Downriver. Some bad men had them. Some of those men will not go home. But then, life can be short. *Adios*."

Just as Jesus turned to ride off, a bullet smashed the sheriff's office sign, hanging over the door of the jail. Eli dropped to his belly on the boardwalk. Jesus crouched off the side of his horse, as three more shots rang out.

"Carlita, no!" Eli shouted.

No Ordinary Thunder

Carlita Ramirez stood in the middle of the street, her skinny arms trying to steady the big pistol.

Jesus wheeled his horse and galloped toward her, as she fired her last two rounds. Her pistol empty, she threw it at him, the gun sailing five feet over his head. Jesus kicked her to the ground as he rode past.

He jumped from his horse and put his knife to her throat. Eli drew his pistol to defend her, but Sandoval's men already had him covered. He had no choice but to holster his gun and wait to see what happened next.

"*Cabron!*" Carlita screamed.

"You killed my brother!"

Jesus pressed the knife to her throat. A drop of blood fell into the dust beneath her. "Your brother was a murdering thief, *Señorita*. He killed a man with a wife and two little girls, for only a dozen cows. *Sí*. I killed him. And I will kill a hundred more like him, if God lets me live long enough." Jesus held her by the throat, and pressed the blade lightly to her cheek. "If you are wise, you'll get out of this before you end up getting hurt very bad."

"I will kill you if I get the chance," she said. "I will kill you and feed you to the pigs!"

"Get away from these men. Soon they will all be dead or gone. Don't die for them, Carlita. They will not die for you."

Jesus sheathed his knife and swung into the saddle. He was nearly out of town before Carlita regained her feet. Eli reached her just as she was about to faint.

"Lean on me, girl. I'll get you inside."

The dark, cool cantina helped to bring her around, along with a tall glass of beer. Eli chose whiskey to settle himself. He tossed it down with a shaking hand.

"What you reckon happened?" he asked her.

"What do you think happened? That son of a bitch ambushed them and killed them all."

"He told me some of 'em wouldn't go home.

No Ordinary Thunder

Maybe they ain't all dead. Maybe some of 'em got away."

"Oh, yes. And maybe my burro will fly to Mexico City."

Eli called for another whiskey. The more he thought about Harley, the more nervous he became. Harley Macon was a hero of the Civil War, and one of the most respected Rangers there had ever been. To be killed by a Mexican madman, while driving stolen cattle, would not go down easy with the citizens of Texas. On the other hand, he himself could be implicated in the whole stinking mess by anyone left alive. Maybe it was time for a new job, in a new place.

But Harley was his friend. They'd ridden together for thousands of miles, tracking Indians, bandits, killers, rapists, and every kind of vermin the world offered up. He couldn't just leave without knowing what happened. But how could he find out? The idea of dangling from Sandoval's rope made his stomach start turning again.

"What you think we should do?"

"You are the sheriff. Maybe you should go and arrest the bastard. Or maybe you are a coward."

Eli was not a coward. His record of service with the Rangers proved as much. But he wasn't about to go after Sandoval alone. That business could wait until another time. Maybe he could sneak out to the holding area north of town and learn what happened. Then he would decide what to do. Until then, he would just lay low and be ready to run.

He walked out of the cantina without a word, and made his way back to his office. It was no more than a shack with a desk and a bed, and one cell the lock didn't work on. He had to keep a chain and padlock handy, in the event he had a prisoner.

But Eli couldn't remember the last prisoner he had. He hadn't been made sheriff to enforce law and order, but to keep up appearances and stay out of the way. Chacal

No Ordinary Thunder

and the bandits ran Laredo. Further downriver it was Salinas and Cortina, and the pack of wolves that followed them.

The weight of the predicament fell heavily on his shoulders. He collapsed on the bed and tried to think it through, but all he could ponder was Harley hanging in a tree, or something worse. Some of Sandoval's victims had been found with their heads missing. Some were found hanging upside down over a burned out fire. If Sandoval wanted information, he knew how to get it, and had no problem doing it.

Eli felt his stomach churning again. He rolled onto the floor just in time to keep from vomiting in his bed. He found a dirty shirt lying in the corner, and used it to clean up the mess.

A drink, that's what he needed. A drink to settle his nerves. He pulled a half-empty bottle from beneath his pillow, drank nearly all of it and lay down to sleep. Tonight he would locate the holding ground, and see what he could learn about Harley.

#

Carlita spent the rest of the day in her room, her heart broken over the death of her brother, and the circumstances of the life he'd chosen. His greed, and the greed of those he rode with, had turned him into a killer. To murder a man—a man with a family—for only a dozen cows? How could he have gone so far? Why didn't he get out? Now the woman and her children had no one to care for them. No one to tuck the children into their beds at night. No one to make love to their mother.

Bell had escaped without injury. Had he left her dear brother to that murdering bastard, Sandoval? Had he run to save his own skin? Was he actually the killer? How

No Ordinary Thunder

would she ever know who fired the shot that killed the rancher? All but a few of the men she'd met, were cowards in Carlita's estimation. Men willing to do or say anything, to keep themselves from harm.

Maybe she was no better. Bandits came and went from her cantina, boasting of their wicked deeds, throwing their money around. Often they persuaded her to sell them what they wanted most, capitalizing on her own greed. As long as the money came in, she was willing to keep her mouth shut. But she had never committed murder, nor would she. At least, not for money.

For love she might do anything, but love was a hard thing to find. She'd loved Harley Macon once, and happily would have again. But Harley was dead. She could not love a dead man.

Chacal was a passionate lover, but she didn't love him, and he certainly didn't love her. He'd spent many nights in her bed, only to leave in the morning. She never knew when she'd see him again.

In that regard, Chacal and Harley were no different. Each man came and went as he pleased, without anything as frivolous as love to hinder him. Anyway, he was dead, too.

And how many others? All that went downriver with the herd? How many more were to die? Carlita threw herself on the bed and sobbed into her pillow, hoping, at least, that Jesus Sandoval would be among them.

#

Harley could learn nothing of the plan to move the cattle by talking to the men. He doubted they would tell him, even if they knew. The plans were clearly known only to Salinas and Chacal.

He and Dixon were pretty much ostracized, only

No Ordinary Thunder

speaking to others at meals and around the fire. He'd neither met, nor heard mention of Delgado. Evidently, he was not at the *rancho*. Harley looked forward to meeting him. When he got the chance, he would kill the only man to escape the stronghold of Zendejaz. Harley didn't like to leave things undone.

Dixon sat in the shade, playing a mournful rendition of "Home, Sweet Home." His dark, handsome features had captured the attention of several *señoritas*—another reason for the men to distrust him.

Harley trusted the man's courage and skill, but the altercation the other day still had him a little rattled. Never had he seen guns come out so quickly. If the shooting had started, they would've surely been killed. The idea that they would've taken a few bandits with them didn't make it go down any easier. Dixon was one of those fearless types. The kind you had to keep a close eye on.

Harley was right about the pen of horses. Nearly every one he checked had a Texas brand. Most of them wore Richard King's running W. King was known all over Texas for his outstanding horseflesh. At this rate, he'd soon be known all over Mexico, as well.

The horses were to be the remuda for the drive. With such a big herd, the men would need a lot of extra mounts. It was a good hundred miles to Matamoros, and a thousand head would be a chore to handle.

A few *vaqueros* had ridden in since they'd arrived, all of them pushing additional stock. These were directed to the pens at Cachuttas, a line camp closer to the river. Harley wondered if the cattle had a different destination.

The pace around the ranch was rapid. Horses being shod, the cook wagon being prepared, young bronc riders topping off the remuda horses. Tomorrow they'd be leaving, and Harley was ready. He was anxious to get to Cortina's camp. To meet the man who, it was said, had stolen over a million cattle out of Texas in the last fifteen

No Ordinary Thunder

years. To meet the man to whom murder and rustling were such a common thing.

What would happen when they met, he could only guess. He hadn't figured the word about the Rangers' reinstatement would be released so soon. He and Dixon were in the lions' den, and hadn't yet heard a thing about McNelly. It had been said that General Lee made his plans, then fought his battles. And that McNelly made his when he'd located his enemy, while swooping down for the kill like a chicken hawk. Whatever the case, Harley knew they were in deep, and a long way from help.

He thought he'd try to cross the river into Brownsville, after they delivered the herd. He'd learn all he could about Cortina's set-up, then try to get word to the Captain. What the hell could be taking so long in DeWitt County? Now that the news was out about the Rangers, McNelly better show up soon, or he'd be missing a spy. Harley didn't think Salinas believed a word of his story.

One thing was certain. They'd be watching him every minute, now. Getting across the river would be easier said than done.

Dixon finished the song and began cleaning his weapons again. He was a solemn man, quiet and mysterious. He never seemed to have much to say, yet he was always in a cordial mood. He had impeccable manners for a man who'd spent half his life hiding in the swamp. Harley knew he pined for his family, as he, himself, pined for Abigail. He hoped, someday, Dixon would see them again.

But he was in a damn poor position. Harley would've been glad to call it square, when Dixon shot the men out on the prairie. He could've never taken all the men alone, in his drunken, hung-over condition. But Dixon needed to be somewhere. Harley let the man make up his own mind.

The sky in the west was turning gold, putting a

No Ordinary Thunder

shine on everything, as only a western sunset could do. Soon there would be guitars and dancing, the last celebration before the journey to come.

#

Eli had no idea how to get close to Sandoval's camp. His men were not paying much attention to the herd. The cattle were not bunched, but scattered throughout the brush. Any attempt to get past them might set them off.

The mesquite glowed in the light of the fire, but Eli couldn't see anyone, nor could he hear any voices. Cowboys liked to sing to the cattle, but these men made not a sound. It was eerie, hearing only the cattle drifting through the brush. Then Eli had a sobering thought. If the men weren't at the fire, and he could not hear them riding, where were they? His question was answered by the voice behind him. He froze in position when he heard it.

"Macon told me you would come, Sheriff. He says you're not a bad man, but I'm not sure yet. If you try to shoot me, I will kill you. Turn around."

Jesus pointed his rifle at Eli's nose. "Drop your gun belt. Then we'll talk, *eh*?"

Eli did as he was told. He wished he'd taken one more drink before leaving town. His nerves had the best of him. His hands were shaking badly.

"What do you mean, Harley told you?"

"He told me you wouldn't run. That you'd come to see about him. He must know you well."

"We rode a lotta miles together. Is he all right?"

"*Sí*. He is at Las Cuevas, by now. Have you heard of the Rangers' reinstatement?"

"What?"

"The Texas Rangers have been reinstated. Have you heard?"

No Ordinary Thunder

"Why, no. Where'd you hear that?"

"From Captain McNelly. Macon and I are working for him. Macon is back with the Rangers."

"Leander McNelly? He's in charge of the Rangers, now?"

"Some of them. Some are in the west, fighting Indians. McNelly is in DeWitt County, trying to stop a feud. He will come to the border when it's settled."

"Well, I'll be damned. Harley could be in bad trouble if Salinas knows about this."

"*Sí*, but the news is bound to get out. Macon knows the chance he is taking. He is hoping to get information on Cortina's outfit, when they take the cattle to Matamoros."

Eli fell silent. He plainly had something serious on his mind.

"What is it?" Jesus asked.

"The cattle don't go to Matamoros from Las Cuevas. They go to Monterrey, a hundred miles into Mexico."

No Ordinary Thunder

Chapter 7

Harley pulled his saddle cinch tight, just before the sun came up. The roan took it well, not being cinchy, but others were not so lucky. A few of the horses bucked across the lot, dumping their riders in an effort to get the kinks out.

Sunrise at Las Cuevas was not a thing of beauty, but of dust, bawling cattle, and hung-over *vaqueros*. Harley no longer felt such a grave need for the whiskey, though he'd never been one to turn it down. He had a few drinks to maintain his cover, but Dixon, as was his habit, had only one.

Though the evening celebration was relatively quiet, there had been one fatality. A knife fight between two of the women left one dead and one badly wounded. The women had been fighting over a handsome *vaquero*, who apparently knew them both intimately. Dixon liked to be fully aware when such things took place.

While the women kissed their men good-bye and all made ready to leave, Salinas and Chacal secretly huddled to themselves.

"Give us a few days before you begin," Salinas said. "We will let the Texans know they cannot take cattle from us. Steal and burn everything you can. Kill them if they stand in your way. Delgado should meet with Cortina tomorrow, to tell him about the Rangers. I have sent another rider to tell him of the cattle. This will not happen again. We'll wreak vengeance on the Texans like they've never seen before."

"*Sí*, General. Just as you say."

"Find Sandoval and kill him. He must be in this, some way. Take another look at Macon's friend, the sheriff. If you even suspect him, kill him. *Entiendes*?"

"*Sí*. We will handle it, General."

"*Bueno*. I should be back in two weeks with the

No Ordinary Thunder

gold. Then, *amigo*, we will take war to the Texans. The Rangers will never stop us."

The bandits shook hands and mounted their horses. Salinas drew his pistol and fired a single shot—a signal to start the cattle moving. The cows pawed and bawled, and some tried to get back to the holding pens. But a few minutes of hard pushing saw them headed south.

Harley was impressed with the *vaqueros*. They handled cattle and horses like they were born to it. In the time he'd been with them, he'd witnessed some of the best roping he'd ever seen. They went at their work with a joy, like a calling, he hadn't seen in the Texas cowboys.

Harley figured Salinas had his reasons for not following the Rio Grande. But after two hours on the trail, he began to wonder why they weren't swinging east. He noticed signs throughout the broken brush, that large herds of cattle had come this way before. They were beginning to drift to the west. Dixon's expression told him that he was wondering the same thing.

"Is this the way to Matamoros, Harley?"

"No. We should've cut east a long ways back. I don't know what's goin' on, but I don't like it."

"Me neither. My scalp's crawlin'."

"Why, Dixon. You ain't scared, are you?"

"Course not. I just can't help wonderin' if I oughta be."

"I hate to ask too many questions. I've got a feelin' they're just waitin' for us to make a bad move. We'll just drift along for a while. Maybe we'll hear somethin' when we stop."

"What if they're plannin' to kill us when we stop? If that's the case, I'd rather keep goin'."

"Just relax. We'll find out soon enough. Try not to shoot anybody, if you can help it," Harley teased. "I'd like to make it back to Texas alive."

They pushed the cattle through the heat of the day,

No Ordinary Thunder

and made camp beside a small creek. The herd spread out for nearly half a mile, so that all could get a good drink.

The men looked like ghosts, they were so covered with dust. They took turns washing in the little creek until finally they looked human again.

A quick meal of *frijoles* and *tortillas* was laid out for the men. Most accepted it eagerly, as there had been no meal at noon. But Harley was dissatisfied with the fare. He thought he might as well say so.

"When I was told I'd be travelin' with a general, I expected a little more style. I hope we get fed better'n this in Matamoros."

"Come now, *Señor* Macon," Salinas laughed. "You can see we are not going to Matamoros. This herd is going to Monterrey, to feed the army of Mexico. They live very well on Texas beef."

Harley did his best to hide the disappointment.

"Damn. That's a shame. I know a pretty gal in Matamoros, that really knows what for. I was lookin' forward to seein' her again."

"Ah, not this trip. I'm sorry you will miss her, but there are women in Monterrey, also. Maybe one of them really knows 'what for'."

All who spoke English burst into laughter, while the rest followed suit, so as not to be left out of the joke.

"Bell," Salinas said. "You and Macon make the first swing. Dixon and Valejo the second. I'll work the rest out later."

"If you don't mind, General, I'd rather stick with my partner," Harley said.

"You will make new partners on this trip. Maybe Dixon is tired of your company."

Dixon shrugged and pulled out his fiddle. He tuned the strings for a minute or two, and played "Tenting Tonight on the Old Campground." He was as cool as Harley had ever seen him, which meant he was ready for

No Ordinary Thunder

anything.

Harley took up his saddle and headed for the remuda. The wrangler roped him a tough little sorrel with a blaze on his face, and four hard, black feet. He was one of Richard King's.

Bell stood waiting, rolling a cigarette, while the wrangler chose his horse. Later, after the horses had been tried, the men would know which were the better night mounts. Until then, they would just have to take their chances.

Harley rode out to the herd without waiting for Bell. He hadn't handled cattle that much, but he knew this bunch was tired, and unlikely to run in the heat. He needed time to think.

Maybe the next herd would go to Matamoros. The change had thrown him for a loop, but McNelly would want to know the play, no matter where the cattle ended up. If it was Monterrey this time, then so be it. He'd learn all he could and take the information back to Texas, if he didn't get killed in the process.

Sundown came slowly to the dusty brush country. The temperature dropped a little bit, but the horses continued to sweat. Bell sang to the cattle as they lay down to rest from the long days journey. Harley listened as Dixon played "Black, Black, Black", and then the camp fell silent.

#

Juan Nepomuceno Cortina had led an interesting life along the Rio Grande. He'd gone to war with the Texans in '59 over depredations upon the Mexican people. After retreating to Matamoros, he declared himself Governor of Tamaulipas, and was later awarded the rank of general in the Mexican Army, by Benito Juarez himself. He'd sided with the Union forces against the Confederacy

No Ordinary Thunder

in the Civil War, and saw no reason to stop taking "grandmother's cattle" back from the Texans.

He was a charming, handsome man of medium height, fair complexion, brown hair and a full, reddish beard. His green-gray eyes betrayed his cunning, fearless manner.

Cortina had done battle with the Texas Rangers before, and knew them as fierce, bloody fighters. But he had never had more men at his disposal. The United States Army was no match for his forces, and besides, the Rangers were not likely to come back to the Strip anyway.

If anything, the governor would probably request more soldiers, which was fine with him, as the soldiers could be easily persuaded with whiskey and women. Still, any mention of the Rangers deserved serious consideration. He'd heard about the reinstatement before Delgado arrived.

"I'm not worried about the Rangers," he said. "The government never gives them enough money to stay active very long. The Texans are losing their hold on the Strip. I doubt they will have it much longer."

"I agree, General." Delgado sipped a glass of fine brandy, while standing more or less at attention. Cortina wore his army uniform, even on the hottest days. He cut a dashing figure that commanded respect. "I hear most of the Rangers are fighting Indians in the west. General Salinas just wanted you to know."

"You will thank him for me when you return to Las Cuevas. Tell him we will continue operations without interruption. If the Rangers return to the Strip, it will just be their bad luck, *eh*?"

"It will be their *very* bad luck, General." Delgado polished off the brandy and wiped his mouth with his shirt sleeve—an action Cortina obviously found distasteful.

"Go now," Cortina said. "Have a bath and eat. Enjoy yourself. In two days, the men are going to Texas. You will go with them. We need another five hundred

No Ordinary Thunder

head for the next steamer to Cuba. Then you will return to Las Cuevas."

Delgado nodded and walked out of the cool, comfortable home, into the blazing hot Mexican sun. The afternoon heat left little to do but find shade and comfort wherever it was available. A bath and a bottle sounded just fine to him—a good meal, clean clothes—and a woman.

Delgado crossed the plaza to the public baths, his big roweled spurs dragging through the flour-like dust. He purchased a bottle of whiskey from the old man at the bar, took the hand of a pretty, bored *señorita,* and vanished behind the curtain.

# #

Eli tied his horse to the hitch rail in front of Carlita's place. His meeting with Sandoval left him rattled and scared. He'd begun to wish Harley had never come to Laredo. There was no telling what kind of mess his old friend was in. Or if he was still alive. Salinas wasn't a man to take spies lightly. He'd been a success at the rustling game because he was smart. Too smart to let an ex-Ranger go unnoticed.

Eli stepped into the cantina and tossed his badge on the table. It made a hollow sound as it spun and wobbled its way into Carlita's lap.

"I'm gettin' out," he told her. "If you're smart, you will, too. Come with me. I'll take you someplace safe."

"Safe? Hah! I knew you were a coward. A drunken, foolish coward. How could Harley Macon ever ride with a man like you?"

"That was then, this is now. Don't stay here, Carlita. Come with me, now. You can leave that badge for

No Ordinary Thunder

the next fool to take this job."

"Do you think they will let you walk away? You know too much. They will find you and kill you. If I go with you, they will kill me, too."

"Maybe. Don't forget, a bunch of 'em are already dead. Besides, we'll be long gone before nightfall."

"I'm not going with you. Go ahead. Run, you rabbit."

Eli saw it was hopeless. Just because he wanted her, didn't mean she wanted him. "That's damn good advice. I believe I'll take it. Good-bye. I…"

"Get out!" she screamed.

Eli backed away from the table, keeping an eye on Carlita until he slipped out the door. Her cold stare followed him, threatening revenge. He heard a glass break against the wall.

"They will find you," she shouted, as he mounted his horse. "They will find you and kill you. You bastard!"

Eli rode out of town at the gallop, following the river to the west. His horse had been idle for most of two years. Within a half mile, the animal began to sweat and blow. Eli soon had to break him down to a walk. His sides heaved as he tried to take in the air. Eli dismounted and loosened his cinch. He had to lead the panting horse upriver on foot.

Shame and anger overcame him as he made his way west. He'd lived much of his life by the horse and the gun. Now he lived by the bottle, on scraps and handouts the bandits gave him.

If Captain Cole Ellsworth saw his horse's condition, he would be sorely disappointed. "I can order you into trouble," the Captain would say, "but it's your horse that will get you out." Funny how, after seeing Harley again, he remembered so many things the Captain said.

The sun was hot. Eli, being soaked with whiskey, drank up his water quickly. He refilled his canteen, hung

No Ordinary Thunder

his gunbelt on the saddlehorn and jumped into the river. The water felt so inviting, he wished he could stay there until dark. But maybe Carlita was right. No telling how soon someone might be after him.

He let the horse drink his fill, then stepped out of the river and started walking. By the time he'd made a couple of miles, his clothes were bone dry, and he'd finished nearly half of his water.

The whiskey made him stink with sweat. His tongue felt like a stick in his mouth. The water did little to satisfy his thirst. His hands shook as he tried to drink.

Eli stopped to lean on his saddle. God, how he needed a drink. Just one to take the edge off. Just one to keep from throwing up.

He took a bottle of whiskey from his saddlebag, pulled the cork and started to drink, but instead, changed his mind and threw it in the river. He drew his pistol, took aim at the bottle, and fired every round. He never came close to hitting it.

Then a single shot rang out, and the floating bottle disintegrated. Eli jumped at the sound of the gun. He turned with an empty weapon.

Jesus dismounted to let his horse drink and reloaded the spent chamber. He spun the cylinder, twirled the gun twice, and replaced it in its holster.

"You could not persuade Carlita to leave with you, *eh*?"

"No. She didn't want any part of it. She called me a rabbit."

"Well, are you ready to go to work, *Señor*?"

"I'd like to think I am, but I'm in awful shape. Maybe we oughta lay low a day or two, until I dry out."

"You don't look so good, *amigo*. You may be right. There is a run-off no more than two miles from here. We can hide there a few days. When you feel better, we'll go see about Macon."

No Ordinary Thunder

"I wonder how long they'll be at Las Cuevas?"

"Who knows? They may be on the trail to Monterrey already."

"I hope you're wrong. That's a damn long way into Mexico. I've got a bad feelin', and it ain't from the whiskey."

"We'll see, when we see. Let's ride. I'm hungry. I'll go hunting after we've set up the camp."

The men mounted and continued to ride upriver. Eli was a shaking, sweating mess. Twice he vomited off the side of his horse. The rocking made him queasy, so he chose to dismount and walk. Jesus stayed with him, though Eli encouraged him to ride on ahead.

"I have to look out for you," Jesus said. "Macon told me you would come around, but I didn't think so. I thought you would run."

"Well, I ain't runnin'! Right now, I ain't even walkin' good."

The run-off was a good place to hole up. Access to plenty of water, a little mesquite hanging over for shade. Jesus got a fire started and put the coffee on.

Eli unsaddled and hobbled his horse. There was a little graze in the run-off. The horse couldn't get out the other end, so Eli turned him loose to make his own way for a while. He pitched his blanket under the sparse shade, and tried to settle down.

"I'll go and find us something to eat," Jesus said.

"Drink the coffee. It will make you sick and get the whiskey out. *Adios*."

Eli had never felt so alone. His guts were churning. He needed a drink. Why had he thrown his bottle away? He thought to go back and try to find it, but remembered Sandoval shot it with his pistol.

He couldn't hold his legs still. He kept scratching and digging in the dirt with his heels. He had sweated through every dry thread he had on. He stripped his clothes

No Ordinary Thunder

in an effort to cool off, until he lay naked in the shade of the mesquite.

He poured coffee and drank it down, only to throw it up again. He thought of Carlita, of Harley, of death. His guts were on fire, and he couldn't stop sweating.

He stumbled to the river, cutting his feet on the rocks, but it was worth it when he fell in the water. Though the water was warm, it felt cool to him. As cool as the water that flowed off the mountains in the spring.

#

The news of the stolen cattle put Cortina in a rage. The upcoming trip to Texas, now would have a second purpose. To show the Texans they could not win. To show them they had better abandon the Strip and let well enough alone, or suffer more vengeance than they could bear.

The Texans were fighters, no question about that. But once their cattle and horses were across the river in Mexico, it was generally accepted that they were lost for good. Now the Texans were so bold as to cross the river, kill five men and take the stock back. And all at the time the Rangers had been re-commissioned. Cortina didn't believe in such a coincidence. There would be hell to pay when his men crossed the Rio Grande.

"You will go tomorrow night," he told Delgado.

"Two hundred men will ride with you. Go as far north as the King Ranch. Travel only at night. Hide in the thickets through the day. Do no damage on the ride north. When you get there, break your men into four groups. Have them swing as far west as Laredo. Steal and burn your way back to the river. If the Texans try to fight you, kill them. This has gone on long enough. We will take the Strip, if we have to kill them all."

"*Sí*, General. And maybe bring back some women,

No Ordinary Thunder

eh?"

"Do what you want with the women, but don't bring them back. Leave them so the Texans can see them every day. So they can watch their bellies grow fat with the children of *Cortinistas!*"

Cortina cleared the room with the wave of his hand. Delgado and the messenger were about to step out, when the young man remembered something he'd forgotten to tell, in the midst of the general's outburst.

"Forgive me, General. I have more to tell you. There are two men with General Salinas. *Norte Americanos.* One man was a Ranger once. His name is Macon."

Cortina recognized the name, but it went through Delgado like a bullet.

"Harley Macon? Harley Macon is with the General?"

"*Si.* He has a man with him that nobody knows. Macon is friends with the sheriff of Laredo. That's where he met *El Chacal.*"

"Well," Cortina said, "now that is interesting. The sheriff of Laredo is a friend of the Ranger, Macon. He is your old enemy, *eh,* Delgado?"

Delgado went numb. He took his time answering.

"That is old business. I never thought to hear of him again. The last I knew, he was a worthless drunk."

"The world has never known such coincidence," Cortina said. "What does the general think of this?"

"He has his men watching Macon all the time," the messenger said. "His friend, too. Macon's friend carries many guns, and he is as fast as the lightning."

"He'd better be," Delgado said. "When they show up, we will shoot them to rags, and drag them naked across the river."

Cortina laughed a villainous laugh that set the young messenger shaking.

No Ordinary Thunder

"Delgado," he said, "when the time comes to finish Macon, you can have the pleasure. Unless of course, General Salinas doesn't let him live that long."

No Ordinary Thunder

Chapter 8

Carlita lay alone in her bed, the pitch black night a perfect reflection of her troubled, aching heart. The world was crashing in on her. She'd lost her dear brother at the hands of that bastard, Sandoval. Now she mourned that Harley and Chacal had probably suffered the same fate. She'd never heard of Sandoval leaving anyone alive to tell the tale. The man was a vicious killer, known and feared throughout the border country.

But Carlita had not heard of him doing something like this before. Did Sandoval think he could take on the southern bandits with just a few gun hands? Sneaking around killing one here and one there, kept the bandits aware of his presence, but this time he had gone too far. General Salinas would have his revenge.

How wonderful it had been to see Harley after all this time. Years before, when the Rangers spent much of their time chasing Comanche horse thieves, they'd met when Harley's troop camped near her father's place on the western frontier. The frontier was a dangerous place to live in the time of the Comanche, but live there they did. And for the six days the Rangers camped, she learned to love there, too.

So taken was she with the handsome Ranger, that she gave herself to him at the first opportunity. Every night, she would sneak from her bed to meet him down by the creek. Harley would be waiting with a sip of whiskey he'd stolen from the medicinal supply. He taught her things not many sixteen year old girls would know. And then he left. The following year, she heard he'd gone to the east to fight the Yankees.

News of the 8th Texas Cavalry and their daring exploits never failed to reach her. Night after night she dreamed of her lover, dashing through the Yankee lines, riding through thunderous cannon fire, not only to save the

No Ordinary Thunder

Confederacy, but to save her. Ahh, but they were only the dreams of a young girl in love—dreams of a brave soldier willing to die for her.

They'd enjoyed each other a few times since his return from the war, but Harley was never the same after that. Somehow he'd maintained his devilish humor, but often he seemed to be somewhere else. As if something were calling him back to the east. This time he seemed even farther away. Not once had he found his way to her bed.

Since her romance with Harley, Carlita had never given much thought to having just one man. Her experience taught her that they sometimes became grouchy and mean when confined, so she gladly let them go on their way, and she would do the same.

But as the years rolled by, she'd come to realize that she wouldn't be pretty forever. Someday her looks would be gone and the parade of handsome *vaqueros* would stop. Then she would be alone. Not alone for a night or two, like she was now. But alone forever. The thought broke her heart and she burst into tears.

Her feeling was more than just a desire. It was a need that she had. A need for a man to hold her in his arms. To make passionate love to her, if only for a night. A need to quench the fire in her body, and reduce her lover to a limp, quivering mass. It was the only power she had over men and she knew it. They could come and go, and maybe get themselves killed, but while she had them, they were hers to do with as she pleased. Most never even knew they were submitting.

But Chacal was different than the others. Chacal never submitted. Rather, he would force *her* to submit to the raw, raucous things he enjoyed. The thought that she would never see him again put an aching in her she found hard to control.

If that damn sheriff had any courage, he would find

No Ordinary Thunder

Sandoval and avenge his partner's death! Sadly, Carlita knew she was being too harsh in her judgment. Eli had ridden with the Texas Rangers. And with Captain Ellsworth, at that. She knew there were no cowards in Ellsworth's troop. In the two years he'd been in Laredo, she had no idea he was a friend of Harley's. Nothing had been said about his days with the Rangers.

Though he wasn't handsome, she occasionally used him, until his drinking got too bad. One night he was so drunk he fouled her bed. After that, she never invited him back. He'd walked a little taller when he first came to town, but it didn't take long for the bandits to get their hooks into him. Anyone could become a drunk, if that's all they had to do. If only he were to knock on her door tonight, she would forget all that. She would remember that he was once a good man, a man that tried to do right. She would ask him in, draw him to her, and use him until they were both worn out.

Carlita tossed and turned until the wee hours of the morning. The night was hot, her bed damp with sweat. She walked to the window and looked into the darkness. The air was heavy and stifling.

She thought to go down to the river to swim, but it was dangerous to walk the streets at night. Too dangerous even for a woman with so many bandit friends. She wondered how many of them would be friendly, when they heard that Chacal was gone. More than likely, they would turn into animals.

She jumped and caught her breath, when she heard a loud banging on the cantina door. Who could it be at this hour? There was just a sliver of gray in the east. No one would be out for breakfast so early. Maybe it was someone who had heard of Chacal's fate. Someone who thought they would be welcomed in his absence. Or maybe one of the street girls needed help. Maybe someone had hurt her.

Carlita took the shotgun from beneath her bed,

No Ordinary Thunder

checked the loads and started downstairs. When she reached the bottom step, the banging started again. Carlita cocked both hammers.

"*Quien es?*" she shouted. "Who is it?"

"It is me, *Chiquita*. Open the door."

Carlita breathed a sigh of passion and relief. "Chacal, my love. My darling."

Chacal told Carlita of the incident with the cattle over a man-sized breakfast of eggs and coffee. He saw a great relief in her eyes when he told her that Macon was alive.

When she told him that Sandoval had driven the cattle through town, he immediately wanted to talk to the sheriff.

"He is gone," she said. "He ran like a coward when Sandoval came through."

Carlita walked to the cupboard and retrieved something from a drawer. She returned and placed Eli's badge in the bandit's hand.

"He told me to give this to your next fool."

Chacal picked his teeth with an ivory handled pen knife, then threw it down and stuck the blade in the table.

"How long ago did he leave?"

"Two days. I think he planned to go far and fast. He could be anywhere, by now."

"Sandoval," he said, and stuck the knife in the table again. "I knew it had to be him. Salinas thought so, too. Well, Texas will pay for their foolishness. Delgado has gone to Matamoros to inform Cortina. He will likely send an army across the river. Have you seen any *vaqueros* in town?"

"A few come and go. I think they wonder if you will come back."

"Then they are through waiting. We will put out

No Ordinary Thunder

the word that I need men. Men who are willing to make war with the Texans. They will take no more cattle from us. We will make sure of that." Chacal folded the knife and put it back in his vest pocket. "I think I am ready for sleep, *Chiquita*. I will think about the sheriff when I wake up."

Carlita slipped off her shoe and placed her foot between Chacal's legs. She stroked him vigorously to a quick reaction, and giggled at the devil in his eyes.

"I know something that will help you sleep, *Amante*, if you don't think you are too tired."

Chacal held her foot, applying more pressure until he was fully aroused. Carlita pulled her nightgown off her shoulders, and exposed her dark-nippled breasts.

"On the table?" he asked her.

"No. Ramon will be here soon. It is almost time to open."

Chacal took her by the hair and kissed her hard. He lifted her from the chair like a sleeping child, kissed and fondled her naked breasts, and carried her up thestairs to her room.

#

Within twenty-four hours, the word circulated through the countryside that Chacal was looking for hands. Jesus and his men started driving the cattle further north, as soon as Banda got the news to him. Some of the stock had been retrieved by the owners, but Chacal wasn't coming just for cattle this time. He was coming to teach the Texans a lesson. A lesson they would not soon forget.

Jesus thought they'd done the right thing by taking the cattle back. Harley did, too. But now he saw it as a terrible mistake. No one had ever done such a thing. He had no idea the reaction it would generate.

No Ordinary Thunder

Eli plodded along like a sick calf, when he wasn't unconscious or having visions. Sometimes he'd see spiders crawling on his legs, or a snake swimming in the stew. Sometimes he'd sleep like a dead man. Sometimes in his sleep, he'd talk to his mother.

Jesus didn't know if she was dead or alive, but Eli often apologized for the turn his life had taken. Evidently his Christian mother didn't hold with the human vices, of which Eli was subject to many.

Jesus thought Eli would work his way through it, but drunks were unpredictable. He'd once known a man who'd been sober for years, then one day he got drunk, stuck a shotgun in his mouth, and painted the ceiling with his brains. Who knew how life would end?

"Where we takin' 'em?" Eli asked. He woke to find that Jesus had tied him to his saddle.

"A big thicket with a little water, north of here. I've already sent riders to find the owners of the cattle. If they can't find them, the men will drive the cattle home. We must tell the people to prepare for war. If Chacal is looking for warriors, it is because Salinas ordered it. If he did, Cortina probably will too. I'm afraid we've made a bad mistake, *amigo*."

Eli only heard about half of it. His head buzzed like he had a bee in his ear. He felt like he had to piss again, but the last two times he dismounted, nothing happened. It was just a holdover symptom from so much drinking. Like the constant feeling he was about to throw up. At the moment, there was nothing he wouldn't do for a drink, but Jesus wouldn't allow whiskey in the camp. The way he felt, it was a damn good thing.

"We better get where we're goin' pretty soon," Eli said, "or you're gonna have to leave me here. I ain't gonna make it much farther without a rest."

No Ordinary Thunder

"It's not far, a few miles maybe. You'll make it. I hope your friend Macon is doing better than you. You both drink too much. McNelly doesn't like drunkards."

"Yeah? Well, maybe drunks don't like McNelly, neither! I wouldn't worry about Harley. He's a better man drunk, than most are sober. He'll get his end of it, you can bet on that."

"I'm glad you have so much confidence in him. He's been drunk for five years over a woman. He was in jail when McNelly found him."

"A woman? I never knew Harley to care that much about one woman. Who was she?"

"A woman in Tennessee, that's all I know. Maybe I shouldn't have told you."

Eli searched the corners of his muddled, hazy mind. He remembered Harley talking about a woman, back when they Rangered together, but he couldn't remember her name. Annabelle, he thought. No, something else. Well, no matter. He couldn't think about it now.

His head was swimming, and he was glad to be tied to the saddle. Damn, it was hot. If sundown didn't come soon, he thought his brains might cook. No more than he'd used them lately, he figured he deserved it.

Eli nodded off again, but was rudely awakened when the cattle pushed into the thicket. Thorns tore at his clothes and scratched his face. A mesquite branch hung in his off stirrup, causing his horse to jump sideways and nearly unseat him.

"Damn, boys!" he shouted. "Couldn't you give a man a little warning?"

Sandoval's men paid him no attention. Eli didn't expect them to. Moving cattle in the thickets was a part of daily life for them. They were *vaqueros* and proud to be so. Men of the horse, who could think of no higher calling. After all, they would say, "What else is there, but riding fine horses?"

No Ordinary Thunder

Their traditions ran deep and were closely guarded. The talents that made a man a good *vaquero*, unfortunately, also made him a good rustler. One could not tell the difference just by looking.

"Let them spread out," Jesus shouted. "They will find the seep when they get thirsty. Rest your horses. The cattle won't go far."

A grinning *vaquero* rode up beside Eli, and cut him loose from his saddle. Eli tried to thank the man, but blacked out and fell off his horse.

#

Delgado had many things on his mind, as he crossed the Rio Grande well to the west of Brownsville. One of those things was Harley Macon.

While he'd made good his escape from the stronghold on the caprock, he knew it was luck and nothing more. Harley Macon. That son of a bitch. Well, he could only be thankful Ellsworth wasn't with him.

Two hundred men rode behind him, all good men with a gun and a rope. Cortina had been plundering Texas for years, but this was war—all out war—in an attempt to finally drive the Texans out of the Nueces Strip.

Never had Delgado led so many men. Far more men than even Zendejaz had commanded. He hoped he was up to the task. One had to get respect among such a mob, or they would soon disregard any order given. They were not the kind of men one ordered much, anyway. Cortina had given the orders before the men left, and they were not hard to follow. Ride north peaceably, ride back south, steal and burn everything in your path. Simple.

It was just over a hundred miles to Richard King's ranch. Three nights riding should see them there without wearing out the horses. They would have even better

No Ordinary Thunder

mounts on the way back. King Ranch horses, bred for toughness, stamina, and incredible bursts of speed. Many of the men were probably riding one now. King's horses were highly prized in Mexico.

    The night was warm. The moon gave no light. The men spoke little, traveling only with the sounds they were accustomed to—creaking saddle leather, jingling spurs, a horse snorting dust from his nose. The gentle, monotonous rocking of a horse could easily lull men to sleep. They kept a sharp eye, relying on each other to stay awake on the long, boring ride.

    They were a mixed bunch, all trying to scratch out a living where it was hard to do so. Mexicans who felt their land had been stolen, Indians who seized every opportunity to get back at the whites. Black outlaws, white outlaws, expatriated Americans who had lost everything in the war. They rode north with one thing in mind. To get something they didn't have. Money, cattle, horses—revenge.

    The place Delgado planned to stop was only a few miles farther. The slight chill in the air told him of the approaching dawn. Soon the men could stretch out and rest, only to repeat the ride at sundown. Delgado thought little about the upcoming mayhem, but he couldn't help but think about the women. His lust for them had always been his only weakness. To have a woman give herself to him was a thrill he enjoyed immensely. But to take her against her will, fighting and screaming, begging him not to. Well, that was a thrill beyond compare.

#

    Dixon had never known temperatures like he felt in Mexico. He thought it must be well over a hundred degrees, and dry as a Quaker's preaching. Salinas must have his reasons for traveling by day, but Dixon couldn't

No Ordinary Thunder

imagine what they were. He thought it better to travel at night, if for no other reason than they wouldn't have to look at such a desolate wasteland. The cattle raised a dust one could hardly navigate through, the oppressive heat acting as a lid to keep it from rising above them.

The stinking cattle bawled for water. Every time they came within a mile of a creek or waterhole, they would cut and run until they reached it, stirring up even more dust. At such times, the *vaqueros* would just let them go. There was no point trying to stop them. Someone would probably just be killed in the stampede. Why anyone would want to be a cowboy, Dixon didn't know.

Salinas seemed to be going out of his way to keep him and Harley separated. In the past few days, he'd only seen his partner when they stopped for the night. Salinas didn't believe in noon meals. The separation only confirmed Dixon's theory that Salinas didn't believe a word of Harley's story. He wouldn't believe it either, if it had been told to him. The story was too convenient.

The previous evening, Salinas told them they were half-way to their destination. When the cattle were sold, there would be a big fiesta before they returned to Las Cuevas. Maybe Dixon could entertain the soldiers with his fiddle. There would be wine and women, dancing and more women. They'd go home with their pockets filled with gold.

The gold sounded good, but his wife, Rhoda Lowery, was the only woman he cared about. He wanted to hold her in his arms again, to love her while their children slept in the other room. To eat her cooking, and sleep with his head in her lap.

He'd had to leave Robeson County. There was no other way. Sooner or later, the Ku Klux would have come after his family. He wanted to stay and fight, to wipe them off the face of the earth, but his followers were being whittled down. He couldn't do it alone. The swamp was

No Ordinary Thunder

not where he wanted to live, and though Rhoda's every move was observed, the money he'd left her would last a lifetime, if she spent it inconspicuously. The children would have what they needed, if not all they desired. Everything they needed, but a father.

What the hell was he doing here? He'd been given every chance to get out, yet here he was, tied in with some of the most dangerous men he'd ever known, in a land no more than a scorching desert, driving stolen cattle to God knows where. He trusted nothing about Salinas or his cohorts. The further into Mexico they traveled, the less chance anyone had of determining what happened to them.

Maybe he was worried about nothing. Half the men riding with this bunch probably weren't what they claimed to be. He knew from his own experience that the best of men could turn outlaw, if the conditions called for it.

He himself had studied to be a preacher, an ambition his mother was so proud of. But then the home guard killed his pa and brother. There was no sermon to right that wrong. He chose to send as many of them to Hell as he could, so they'd have a good long while to think about it.

The cattle were slowing, milling into a bunch, creating a dust cloud that nearly hid them from view. There had been no mad dash for water. Something else must have brought them to a stop, but what? Harley pushed his way through the herd, a bandana over his face to filter the dust. He looked like he'd fallen into a barrel of flour.

"What's the holdup?" he shouted.

"Hell, how would I know?" Dixon said. "I can't see ten feet in front o' me."

"I don't like it. Let's ease on to the point and have a look."

The cattle began to drift through the brush. The *vaqueros* had abandoned them to see why the herd had

No Ordinary Thunder

been stopped. Through the haze, Harley could see a conversation taking place, but could not tell who was involved. The army, maybe? Possibly someone expecting a toll? He and Dixon made their way closer, then Harley pulled up and ducked into the brush.

"Come on," he said. "Follow me."

Safely behind cover, Harley looked to his guns and told Dixon to do the same.

"What is it, Harley?"

"Apaches. Looks like a bunch of 'em. I expect they wanna cut the herd."

"Apaches?" Dixon said, a touch of excitement in his voice. "Is one of 'em Geronimo?"

"Geronimo? Why, hell no! Geronimo's in the Arizona territory."

Dixon went glum. "Well, he's the only Apache I ever heard of. Rhoda's got a picture of him."

Harley surveyed the brush, but to no real purpose.

"There could be fifty Apaches out there and we'd never see 'em. Masters of camouflage. An Apache ain't seen until he wants to be."

"They've been talkin' a long time. Maybe they're makin' a deal."

"I doubt it. Salinas don't strike me as the type to give in to herd cutters."

The voices grew louder. *Vaqueros* and Indians alike began to jockey for position. The confrontation was getting tense. It plainly wouldn't last much longer.

"These cows must be gettin' thirsty standin' around in the heat," Harley said. "Let's see if we can't drift 'em towards water."

Dixon didn't immediately understand, but caught on when Harley started shooting to stampede the herd. They rode out from their cover, screaming and shooting, the cattle instantly stirring up a thick cloud of dust.

They heard general gunfire from the point of the

No Ordinary Thunder

herd, but couldn't see anything. In another moment, the cattle charged at a dead run, racing through the sandy fog, taking down everything in their path.

Harley and Dixon passed a few dead Apaches, but saw none left alive. If any of them survived, they must be caught up in the stampede. None of the *vaqueros* were spotted. They'd probably all made for the flanks and let the herd run by.

"How you plannin' to explain this?" Dixon shouted through the haze.

"I'll worry about that later. Right now I wanna get the hell outta here. I've seen what a band of Apaches can do. Shoot 'em down, and let's ride!"

No Ordinary Thunder

Chapter 9

Harley didn't know how many Apaches were killed in the fray. He'd counted seven bodies lying in the dust, but there might have been more strung out along the trail. One of the *vaqueros* was lost. His horse went down in the midst of the stampede. Both horse and rider were trampled to death.

The cattle ran for nearly three miles before the men could turn them. A few were trampled, a few gave up and died in the heat, but for the most part, everyone seemed happy with the outcome. They all knew the chances men took when they chose to make their living stealing cattle. Swollen rivers, lightning storms, stampedes—not to mention getting shot or hung. Rustling was a rough game for rough men, and Salinas had a bunch of the roughest. When informed of the death of their fellow bandit, they all formed a circle and fired a shot into the ground, one of them citing a proverb in Spanish that translated, "Life is but a vapor." Harley thought Dixon, who said almost nothing, could've come up with something better than that.

Three more days would see them in Monterrey, though Harley couldn't imagine any specific information he could glean there. The cattle were going to feed the Mexican army. What else was there to tell? When Salinas returned to Las Cuevas, he would start replenishing the pens. Harley assumed it was the same with Cortina. Deliver the cattle and go get some more. It hardly seemed like espionage.

The vastness of the country made the Texans particularly vulnerable. A lone, isolated rancher didn't have a prayer against a pack of coyotes like this bunch. And if Salinas could muster such a force, there was no telling how many men Cortina had rustling for him. The only thing a man needed to know was when and where they were going to strike. So far, Harley hadn't been privy to

No Ordinary Thunder

such intelligence. On the trip into Texas with Chacal, he never learned the destination. Sandoval would have his hands full, if he had to keep an eye on the whole Rio Grande.

Harley and Dixon had been under close scrutiny since joining with the bandits, and though suspicions had subsided somewhat, Harley doubted Salinas would confide much information. The man didn't get where he was by being careless.

Harley didn't think the *vaqueros* knew much more than he did. Probably only a chosen few were permitted to hear the details. Without them, McNelly was beating a dead horse. If the army couldn't patrol the border and keep things under control, it was unlikely the Rangers could.

One Ranger equaled three soldiers to Harley's way of thinking, but how many would the governor send? If the past was any measuring stick, it wouldn't be near enough. The Rangers were accustomed to being outnumbered. It was just a fact of life.

The *vaqueros* would be hard to keep track of. They were expert at their occupation, knew what the cattle would do before they did it, and could get more miles out of a good horse than Harley believed possible.

They had all of Mexico to hide in. The empty prairie would just swallow them up. The Rangers were not allowed to pursue them across the river anymore. It was a short ride to freedom from Texas. Harley wondered if McNelly knew what he was in for.

The bawling and the heat were never ending. Harley guessed the dust could be seen for ten miles, though at times, he could barely see the cattle at all. He gave a start when the *vaquero* rode up beside him.

The man's name was Bedoya and he was known for two things. The one black tooth he had left in his mouth and the largest endowment in camp. He pulled the bandana down, exposing his face and the single black toothed grin.

No Ordinary Thunder

"*Amigo*," he said, "do you know Monterrey?"

"Nope," Harley said. "Never been there."

"Ah, there are many beautiful women there."

Bedoya held the pommel of his saddle and rocked his hips back and forth. "It makes me hard to think of them. When we get there, I will take you to Ayala's. He has the most beautiful whores in the city."

"Well now, I look forward to meetin' 'em. You reckon he's got a redhead, say about five-seven, maybe in a dark green dress?"

Bedoya let out a scream Harley feared would spook the cattle. "If he does, I may have to fight you for her."

"No need for that. Hell, I expect she's woman enough for both of us."

The *vaquero* laughed, spurred his horse, and disappeared into the wall of dirt.

Ayala's—the most beautiful whores in the city. That would be the *vaqueros*' first stop. If they stayed in town very long, they would begin to seek out the cheaper, less refined women. Women more likely to talk. But all women would talk, refined or not, if given enough to drink.

A whorehouse was always a good place to get information. Harley had tracked down plenty of men that way. But there was also room for caution. A man couldn't spend his money if he was dead or in jail. What Salinas said about men going home with pockets filled with gold was folly. Most of these men would be flat broke before they left Monterrey. The girls wouldn't want to hinder their cash flow.

Other than how often the herds were delivered, Harley didn't know what the girls could tell him. But that was something. He guessed he'd just call it a pony ride, and get to Texas with what he could.

#

No Ordinary Thunder

Delgado sat his fine black horse and rolled a cigarette, while the three herd guards kicked and strangled, the rawhide *reatas* stretching their necks. The youngest of them, a boy of seventeen or eighteen, took the longest to die. He was light, not much more than a hundred pounds. The *reata* didn't break his neck when he came off his horse. He choked and kicked and fouled himself for longer than Delgado cared to wait. He ordered one of his men to rope the boy's legs, take a turn around the saddle horn and jerk. The boy's neck snapped and grew three inches in length. His blue eyes closed to the world. The bandits looked on, relaxing in the saddle, complaining of needing sleep.

"That is a fine bunch of horses," Delgado said.

"Maybe we will take them, and let the others worry about the cattle."

The horses belonged to Richard King, whose home was nearly six miles to the east. It was said that King had five thousand horses, but this bunch numbered about four hundred. Horses were easier to handle than cattle and they traveled a lot faster. Besides, a good horse was always worth more than a dozen cows.

"We'll wait until dark. Spread out. Keep an eye open for more guards. If you see them, kill them, and we'll go."

The bandits made a wide circle around the horses and settled down to relax. They had a three hour wait until sundown. The rest would do them all good.

Delgado saw no future in attacking the King Ranch. He knew the place to be heavily fortified. The men there would give their lives for Richard King, and would gladly take as many lives as necessary to defend his holdings. No need to get into all that. There were plenty of others to rape and kill on the way south.

He'd broken the men into four groups like Cortina said, and sent them to various locations to the west. Soon

No Ordinary Thunder

the Strip would be burnt and bloody. Delgado almost felt bad for the Texans. They would suffer terribly for taking the cattle back. Many of them were his own people, but if they chose to side with the Texans, they would get what they deserved.

And what about the Rangers? And Harley Macon? Delgado was sure he'd heard the last of both, but now they were again in his thoughts, in his dreams.

Macon was only one man, but a man not like many others. He was known all over Texas as a man quick to kill. A man unyielding in his pursuit of justice. If they met again, one of them would surely die. And what of the man riding with him? The man who carried so many guns? Did he know Macon was a Ranger? Or *was* Macon a Ranger? If he was, Salinas had probably killed him already. Maybe there was nothing to worry about.

But Delgado worried anyway. Harley Macon was not a man to be taken lightly. Goddamn him! Why couldn't he stay drunk?

A soft breeze carried the smell of salt water, though they were at least thirty miles from the Gulf of Mexico. Delgado liked the smell of the ocean, and as a boy had fantasized of going to sea to be a pirate. He dreamed of sailing to faraway ports, of boarding rich vessels and stealing all they held. Of kidnapping beautiful women and taking them to his island paradise.

He'd been to the gulf and seen the great ships, their billowing white sails like clouds against the blue sky. He'd even thought of making the trip to Cuba on one of the steamers transporting the stolen cattle. Well, maybe someday. Maybe someday soon. But for now, he would get a little sleep. He would dream about the Cuban women, and try to forget about Macon and the Texas Rangers.

The bandits started south about an hour after

No Ordinary Thunder

sundown. The horses moved gracefully under the dim light of the rustlers moon—just a fingernail of silver hanging in the starry night sky.

Delgado had his first target already in mind. A small *rancho* only a few miles away, with maybe just a hundred cows, a few horses and a lot of goats. Cortina needed the cattle to fill his contracts, but the stock was not really as important as the message. The message that Cortina didn't give a damn about the Rangers. As far as he was concerned, the Nueces Strip belonged to Mexico, and that meant everything in it.

Delgado had given the men their orders. Drive the horses through the property, sweeping all the livestock with them. Burn the buildings, be careful of the children if there were any. Do what you want with the women if you get the chance. Kill the men.

He doubted there would be much of a fight at such a small place. No more than a few people could live there. But one never knew how a man would react to his woman being raped. Most men would not take it well, but it did no one any good to get killed over it. There were plenty of women in the world.

There was no light burning in the little *jacale*. Evidently the family had already gone to bed. Delgado fired the first shot to start the horses running. Within seconds the herd was out of control. The bandits rode hard. They tried furiously to turn them, but to no avail. The horses ran blindly through the *rancho,* breaking down the makeshift fences and trampling the *jacale* just as the light came on. The screams Delgado heard coming from inside the ruins told him there was a child in the hut.

In less than a minute, the screaming stopped. The horses were only a dust cloud in the distance. There were two little sheds that hadn't been touched. Delgado stayed behind and set them on fire. The home was just a pile of rubble. In another moment, the thatched roofing burst into

No Ordinary Thunder

flame. Then Delgado heard the child begin to scream again.

The screams sounded like a wounded animal—shrill and blood curdling. Delgado leaped from his horse and ran to the fire. He had to try to save the child, but the intensity of the flames held him back. There were no other voices. Everyone else must be dead. He froze for a second, listening in terror to the horrible din, then quickly drew a pistol and emptied it in the area the screams came from. There was no sound, but the crackling of the fire. The silence told him the child's suffering was over. But still it left him cold and afraid. Afraid of how far this might go.

He stayed a few moments, in case he heard any more screams. But the sweet smell of burning flesh always made him sick, so he mounted and rode after the others. He felt awful about the child dying. Children should have their chance at life, or at least a chance to fight for it. The world had plenty of ways to kill you, and there was always another opportunity to die. But this child would not get that chance.

Delgado looked behind him one last time, then spurred his horse to the gallop. The herd had gained a lot of ground and showed no signs of letting up. King's men would be right behind them, as soon as they found the horses were missing. There would be no slowing down now. Maybe, if they followed the smoke, King's men would bury the bodies.

#

The plateau city of Monterrey guarded the high passes through the Sierra Madre, which would lead one south to the *Ciudad de Mexico*. After ten days on the trail, constantly watching his back, Harley was glad to be there.

A fashionable municipality of twelve to fifteen thousand people, Monterrey lay surrounded by mountains within the crooked elbow bend of the Santa Catrina River.

No Ordinary Thunder

As the capitol of *Nuevo Leon*, Monterrey maintained a heavily armed garrison, complete with walled fortress and cannon to protect the Governor's Palace.

The people, rich and poor, ran to the streets in droves to see the cattle driven through the gateway. There was always something to do in Monterrey, but when the cattle came from Texas, the town erupted into *fiesta*.

"By God, they make a party out of it, don't they?" Harley said.

Bell popped his rope against his leg, encouraging the cattle to keep moving.

"Yeah. And tonight…when that sun goes down…well, the women wake up and the real party starts."

"That sounds good to me, but my friend, Dixon, don't take notice o' such things. I expect he'll find somethin' else to do."

"No. I think we'll stick together. General Salinas wants it that way."

"I see. Does that mean you're gonna watch me take a bath?"

"You've gotta admit, Macon, showin' up when you did draws a lot of attention."

"Ain't you heard? Why, I'm a famous war hero. I draw attention everywhere I go."

"Salinas don't give a damn what you did in the war. Nor what you did as a Ranger, neither. He just wants to make sure you don't get more famous at his expense."

"You boys sure have a suspicious nature. Didn't we save your ass back there with them Apaches? Y'know we could've just let 'em kill you and rode away."

"I reckon that's true, but then you wouldn't get paid. As I recall, you said you came down here for the money."

"You're right, I did. But back once when I was Rangerin', I found a man tied to a cedar post. He was a short time dead, and every inch of his skin had been peeled

No Ordinary Thunder

off. Apaches done it. There ain't enough money in the world to buy a new hide."

"Damn! How'd you know it was Apaches?"

"We followed 'em to their camp that night. Two of 'em."

"And?"

"Well…let's just say they died a hard death."

A platoon of soldiers met the cattle at the holding pens. They opened and closed gates, separating the herd, like they'd done it a thousand times. The whole thing was orchestrated like a ball room dance, the *vaqueros* moving the cattle with a grace and ease Harley found most impressive. Dixon, on the other hand, couldn't have cared less. His thoughts were plainly somewhere else.

When the last cow was penned, Harley approached his sullen companion. He seemed so preoccupied that Harley had to speak abruptly just to get his attention.

"Hey! Where the hell are you?"

"None o' your damn business. I'm ready to get outta here. My skin's crawlin' again."

"Well, I don't think Salinas is gonna let us ride off, just yet. Hell, he ain't even been paid for the cattle. Besides, why not enjoy some of the amenities? I've had enough dust in my diet for a while."

"So have I, but Texas sounds real good right now. This place gives me the willies."

"You'll feel better after you've slept in a bed and filled up on good food. 'Course me, I've got other things on my mind."

"Like?"

"Like findin' out all I can about these deliveries. I didn't come down here to see the sights, remember?"

"What you got in mind?"

Harley shook his head and laughed. "I swear, Dixon. You've lived in the damn swamp too long. I've got a trip to the whorehouse in mind. That's where we'll find

No Ordinary Thunder

out."

The *vaqueros,* along with Harley and Dixon, rode proudly through the mass of onlookers, waving and smiling as if it were a grand parade. The young girls in the crowd blew kisses and winked, no doubt dreaming of romancing the valiant horsemen. The young boys dreamed of being one—of riding a fine horse through the streets of the city, waving and smiling at all the girls who dreamed of romancing *them*. A young boy could hardly think of a better life.

To Harley's surprise, a company of soldiers had marched onto the parade ground, led by the garrison commander on an exquisite chestnut stallion. The horse had too much fire to stand at attention. His hindquarters motionless, he pranced on the fore as if in time to a drum beat. The horse, and the gold-braided colonel that sat him so proudly, truly were a sight to behold.

"Damn," Harley said. "I expect that's the prettiest soldier I've ever seen."

"I think maybe you'd better get on to the whorehouse," Dixon said, his dark eyes staring a hole through the colonel. "I'm ready to get the hell outta here."

Harley didn't like it. Dixon wasn't the nervous type, and up to now had been cool as can be. Something was eating at him. Something more than just the usual caution.

Salinas halted his men and rode up to meet the colonel. They spoke quietly, even had a few laughs, then the colonel spoke sharply to his lieutenant, who handed Salinas a large, heavy bag of gold coins. The *vaqueros* cheered when Salinas held the bag aloft.

"Well, it looks like payday," Harley said.

"An overdue payday," Bell complained, "since we lost that herd upriver. There's a barracks behind the garrison for us. That's where we'll get paid."

Salinas dismissed his men, with the exception of Harley and Dixon. He called them over to introduce them,

No Ordinary Thunder

so they would be known when seen around town. Both men had their senses on full alert.

"*Señor* Macon, *Señor* Dixon, may I present *Coronel* Garralaga, garrison commander at Monterrey."

"Howdy, Colonel," Harley said. Dixon offered only a suspicious nod.

"General Salinas has told me of your effort to save the cattle from the Apaches. On behalf of my men, I thank you."

"No trouble, Colonel. We're lookin' forward to the hospitality of your city. As soon as I can get un-stuck from this saddle, I'm gonna take four baths, eat ten meals, and sleep 'til I feel like doin' somethin' else."

"Ah, that is a fine plan," Garralaga said. "But I am afraid you cannot do that, *Señor*. You and your friend are under arrest."

No Ordinary Thunder

Chapter 10

Dixon woke to the sensation of a rat scurrying up his pant leg. He took a swipe at the rat and jumped to his feet, only to fall on his face, having forgotten for the moment that his legs were shackled. He heard voices snicker, though he couldn't see a thing.

The cell was dark and smelled of human waste, the dirt floor soaked with urine. One chamber pot in the corner served the number of men occupying the cell on a given day. Dixon thought it must have been a good, long while since the pot was last emptied.

Four other men occupied the cell, not counting Harley. They were thrown inside well after sundown. The men's faces were nearly impossible to make out. They introduced themselves, but had little to say, other than Harley and Dixon were soon to learn the fundamentals of making adobe bricks. Within moments the men fell asleep, exhausted, oblivious to their new cellmates.

Dixon doubted there would be much light in the cell, even in the daytime. The stuffy little room had no window—the door only a shuttered opening big enough to pass a plate through. Choking down a meal in such a filthy place would be hard to do.

A sudden gasp meant the rat had found another leg to crawl on. But this time it was not quick enough to escape. The voice was young and sounded a little crazy. Dixon couldn't recall the boy's name. He crushed the rat in his bare hands, cursing and crying all the while. When the boy felt satisfied the rodent was dead, he threw it hard up against the wall. It fell into the chamber pot with a plop that only served to stir up the smell.

"You all right, son?"

"Who is it?" the boy asked.

"It's me, Dixon. Me and my friend came in last night, remember?"

No Ordinary Thunder

"Yeah. I remember. Y'all drove the cattle in."

"Right. Did you get bit?"

"No, but I've been bit before. My leg swelled up somethin' awful that time. You won't get much doctorin' in here."

"What's your name again?"

"Name's Fallon. Bobby Fallon."

"Well, that sounds like a fine name, Bobby. You been in here long?"

"Almost a year, I think. What month is it?"

"August."

Bobby wept at Dixon's reply. "I guess it's been more than a year. I had a birthday last month."

Dixon thought to leave the boy alone and let him cry it out. But Bobby was scared. He plainly wanted to talk.

"How old are you, son?"

"I'm seventeen, now." Bobby wiped his eyes on a dirty shirt sleeve. "I expect my ma's quit lookin' for me."

"Where is your ma?" Harley asked from the darkness.

The cell went silent until Dixon cleared the air. "It's all right, Bobby. You can tell him. He's my friend."

"My ma's in Mississippi. That's where I'm from."

"How'd you end up in here?"

"I came to Texas lookin' for trouble and I found it. Ended up broke. Robbed a hardware store in Brownsville and cut for Mexico. Fell in with a bad bunch and here I am."

"How much you get?"

"Thirty-eight dollars. Sure wish I could do it over. Didn't even get to spend the money."

"Well," Harley said, "maybe we'll get you back home, yet. I ain't plannin' on takin' root."

"You ain't goin' anywhere," an old, gravelly voice chimed in. Dixon remembered it belonged to a man called Salyard.

No Ordinary Thunder

"Who says?" Harley shot back.

"Garralaga says! And what he says is the law around here. You even think about runnin', and they'll bury you out there with the others. After they beat the hide off you."

"How many others?"

"A lot," Bobby said. "There must be fifty, sixty graves back in the grove. They take at least one back there, almost every week."

"They kill 'em?"

"No need to. The work kills 'em."

"Damn!" Harley said. "How long you been in here, Salyard?"

There was a lengthy pause as the old man calculated his stay. "Since '70, I reckon. I come down here with General Shelby, after Lee surrendered in '65. Had a good life too, until Maximilian was executed in '67. Then the government told us we had to leave the country. Me and some o' the other boys decided to stay on and try to steal ourselves a livin'. Didn't work out so good. Some of 'em escaped capture. But most of 'em are buried out in the back."

"You were with Shelby's Iron Brigade?"

"Yeah. Maximilian gave us some land for a colony down around Vera Cruz. By God, it was all in front of us then."

"Rank?"

"First Sergeant. What damn difference does it make, now?"

"It makes a lotta difference. First Sergeant Salyard, I'm Captain Harley Macon of the 8th Texas Cavalry. And as you well know, it's our duty to attempt an escape."

Harley's statement set the cell buzzing. These men had obviously given up any hope of escape, and now, with nothing more to go on than a few words from a Civil War legend, they were ready to storm the palace.

No Ordinary Thunder

"When will we try, Captain?" Bobby asked. The boy's voice fairly trembled with excitement. Salyard, though, was not as enthusiastic.

"Didn't you boys hear what I said? We ain't goin' anywhere. I've heard about you, *Captain Macon.* But this ain't Kentucky or Tennessee. Your hero days are over. Nobody's ever escaped from this place, and ain't nobody ever goin' to."

The room fell silent—ominously so—then Bobby began to cry again.

"Now hold on there," Harley said. "Maybe nobody's escaped because they gave up too soon. We ain't gonna do that. We're gonna get outta here, no matter what. Do you understand me?"

Harley made a forceful effort, but the moment was gone. The men had slipped back into their complacency. He became more keenly aware of the stench inside the cell.

"Well, Dixon, looks like it's just you and me. I should've known this bunch didn't have the sand for it. First Sergeant Salyard, you're a damn disgrace."

"To hell with you, *Captain!* The war's over. You ain't got the authority to tell me anything. You might be a big auger in Texas, but in here, you're nothin', just like the rest of us. I'm tellin' you, if we try this you'll get us all killed."

"And if we don't try, we'll all end up buried out back, anyway."

"Just a minute," Dixon said. "Somebody's comin'."

"It's time to make bricks," Salyard said. "Now you'll see what I'm talkin' about, Macon. After one day in this hell hole, you'll see that tryin' to escape is insane."

Insane was a word Harley had come to detest. Whenever he heard it, he thought of Abigail, alone in that asylum, with all those crazy bastards pawing at her. If she could, she'd escape—and that's what he planned to do.

"Well, that might be," Harley said, "but I intend to

No Ordinary Thunder

die tryin' to live. How about the rest o' you boys?"

The door swung open with the same loud screech they'd heard the night before. Harley and Dixon shaded their eyes, but there was no need. The sun wasn't even up yet.

"What's for breakfast?" Harley said, to the guard outside the cell.

"You'll get breakfast when they think you've done enough work," Salyard said. "There's been plenty o' times we didn't get any at all."

"*Vayate!*" the guard commanded.

The prisoners were marched to a six-foot adobe wall, being built to surround the cathedral plaza. Harley saw several other prisoners being marched in another direction. They looked no different than the men he was with—beaten and defeated.

"Where they takin' those men?" he asked Salyard.

"Down in the pits to dig the clay. They bring it back in wagon loads, along with barrels o' water. We'll work up here a few days, then we'll go down there. This is better. It's a hot son of a bitch in the pit."

"*Callate!*" the guard shouted.

"What the hell's that mean?" Dixon asked.

"It means shut up," Harley said. "I expect this jasper ain't much for mornin' chit-chat."

"I hope they give me time to learn the language before they shoot me."

"Oh, you'll learn the language, all right," Salyard said. "Shut up, sit down, stand up, get to work. And it'll be taught with a lash across your back, if you don't catch on pretty damn quick."

Even the early morning hours were stifling. Not a breeze moved through the cathedral plaza. The air was heavy and warm. The work load, along with the abhorrent conditions, had taken a brutal toll on the men. Harley could see why so many gave up the fight.

No Ordinary Thunder

Bobby Fallon appeared thin as a rail and plainly scared to death. His blond hair hung below his shoulders, no doubt a point of harassment the guards and other prisoners took advantage of. The boy's face showed not a glint of hardness, his features almost feminine. Harley doubted the boy could put up much of a defense.

Salyard looked just like he sounded—ugly, hard and mean. A man of large frame, he was also down to skin and bone, as were the other two cellmates.

One, a Yaqui Indian named Emilio, looked about thirty, though his condition made it hard to tell. He carried the scars of numerous battles, and a patch of hair had been removed from the back of his head. Evidence that he'd once been scalped. Trying to age Paulo, the old Mexican, was a waste of time. His eyes were covered by a milky film that made him difficult to look at.

Salyard, if not really in charge, appeared to have his bluff in, though Harley had no doubt the Yaqui could hold his own in a fix. He might well play an integral part when the time came to escape.

Dixon and Harley manned the shovels, while Salyard explained the process of turning clay and straw into bricks. Under the watchful eyes of many armed guards, the day's work began.

By mid-morning, the men, already depleted, had still seen no sign of breakfast. Just as Harley was about to complain, a handsome young priest Salyard identified as Father Molino, stepped out of the cathedral carrying a platter of tortillas and a large vessel of water. He approached the prisoners without hesitation, paying no attention whatever to the guards. The men went at the tortillas like there was no tomorrow. The guards, though they carefully observed, didn't make a move to stop them. Harley thought this priest might be a man to know.

"*Padre*," he said, "I sure wanna thank you. This bunch was gettin' a little peaked. Name's Harley Macon.

No Ordinary Thunder

This here's my friend, Dixon."

"It is nothing, my son. Only flour and water."

"Well, just the same, we thank you."

Salyard sat by himself, wolfing down the tortillas, casually studying the man called Dixon. But he knew Dixon wasn't his real name. His name was Lowery—Henry Berry Lowery—the guerilla fighter from North Carolina.

Salyard had seen a few sketches of the man circulating throughout the South, and heard all about his war with the Confederate home guard, and later the Ku Klux Klan. He supposed there must be a damn big reward on him. Hell, if there wasn't, he could sell him to the Klan. This made things look a little different. Maybe, just maybe, if they could escape, he might become a wealthy man.

#

Jesus waited impatiently for a messenger from across the river at Camargo. The word circulated through Rio Grande City that Salinas was back in Las Cuevas. But he'd not yet heard any news of Harley Macon.

Eli couldn't sit still. His nerves had the best of him. Jesus did his best to encourage the man, though he too was deeply concerned about Macon's safety. Had he any idea of the reaction taking the cattle would incite, they might have done something less drastic. But they'd made a terrible mistake, and now they'd have to live with it.

"Dammit! If we don't hear somethin' soon, I'm goin' over there," Eli said.

"No. We'll wait. If we start snooping around, they *will* kill them. We have to be patient, *amigo.*"

"I've been patient long enough. Damn, I could sure use a drink."

No Ordinary Thunder

"Maybe you should get some food, instead. The whiskey will not help you."

"No. But just a sip wouldn't do me no harm, neither."

"We should hear something soon. If not, I will send someone else over. Someone less conspicuous than a tall *gringo* with the shakes."

Eli thought he'd had enough of being ridiculed by Mexicans. He'd taken Chacal's abuse for nearly two years, and all he got for his effort was more abuse. Carlita treated him like a puppy unless she needed him for something. She'd invite him to her bed if she wanted a man—the next day she wouldn't know him. Now it was Sandoval. How could he begrudge a man a drink, when he plainly needed it so bad?

When he served as a Texas Ranger, he felt like a man of importance. But then Davis disbanded the Rangers and he quickly became a nobody, drifting from one town to the next. His old partner, Asa Moody, joined the hated State Police, only to be hanged by an unruly mob who couldn't accept a black man having authority over them. Eli didn't know how much more Mexican authority he could take.

"Ah, he is coming," Jesus said.

The old peddler crossed the river, walking in water up to his waist. His stout little burro followed behind. The burro's legs were barely long enough to keep the peddler's pack goods out of the water, but the old man seemed unconcerned about his property. In fact, he didn't seem concerned about anything. He stopped mid-stream, fumbled with his pants, then stood with a relieved expression on his face. In a minute, he fumbled with the pants again, and finished his trek across the river.

"Who is he?" Eli asked.

No Ordinary Thunder

"His name is Eduardo. He walks all over the border country, selling and trading. He knows everything that happens on the river. He will know about Macon and his friend."

"He looks old enough to have lived two lifetimes."

"He is not as old as he looks. He has seen so much bad in the world, that he is happy just to be alive and breathing the clean air. Now he goes through life with a song on his lips, though he can't sing very well. But there is nothing wrong with his hearing.

"Eduardo listens to the talk in the cantinas. He listens to the conversation of those he trades with, the political news, which wives are cheating on their husbands. Precious little escapes him, and for a price, he will gladly relay the information."

Eduardo made his way up the narrow road and stopped beside a tiny grove to check his burro's foot. His slow progress went unnoticed by everyone, with the exception of the two men waiting in the trees.

"Eduardo! You are moving slower these days," Jesus said. "What news do you have to tell me?"

"Your friend Macon did not return from Monterrey, *amigo*." Eduardo worked his way around the burro, inspecting each foot carefully. "The people say he was killed in a fight with the Apaches."

"Oh, God!" Eli said. "Are they sure?"

"That is the news I hear. Many Apaches were killed, but so was Macon and the other one. I am sorry for your loss, Jesus. You will pay me now, *eh*? My burro is hungry. I would like to buy her some oats."

Eduardo stroked the burro's long ears, goading her into the annoying bray that Eli hated so much.

Jesus tossed a coin in the air. Eduardo deftly removed his sombrero, caught the coin and replaced the sombrero in one fluid motion. He spoke softly to the burro and walked away without another word to the men, though

No Ordinary Thunder

his voice could be heard singing a bright, festive tune all the way into town.

Eli slid down the trunk of a tree and took a seat on the warm, hard ground. His face had gone pale. He shook worse than ever. If he'd needed a drink before, he certainly needed one now. Harley Macon dead—that was hard to believe. And what about Dixon? He didn't look like the kind to go down easy, and Harley definitely wasn't. To have survived the war, and all those years as a Ranger, only to be killed by a bunch of murdering Apaches with a taste for Texas beef. Well, there was no telling how a man might lose his life. At least he didn't die in jail.

"Are you ready to travel, *Señor?*"

"Where we headed?"

"North."

"North? What for?"

"To take the news to McNelly. Don't you think he should know?"

"Hell, let's go find out for ourselves, first! That old man could be wrong. I thought Harley was dead once before, remember?"

"I remember, but then you thought the whole bunch had been killed. Eduardo doesn't carry tales, *amigo*. If Macon's death is the talk of the town, then it is probably true."

Eli couldn't get his mind to accept such bad news, but Sandoval was right. Every man had to meet his maker. Eli got to his feet with some little effort and pulled his saddle cinch tight. He mounted the horse and rode north toward town, not waiting for Sandoval. It was a long ride to DeWitt County. They might as well get started.

#

Forty miles north of Rio Grande City, Eli and

No Ordinary Thunder

Sandoval came across a burned-out ranch—a bloody sight not uncommon on the Nueces Strip, but becoming more prevalent since the bandits started retaliating with a vengeance. An elderly couple lay dead in the yard, along with several ranch hands. A multitude of spent shells littered the ground. A bloated horse lay on his back, with all four feet in the air.

"Must've been one hell of a fight," Eli said. "Looks like over a hundred rounds were fired. Just a couple days ago, I'd say. I can still smell the fire."

Jesus dismounted, crossed himself, and made a closer examination of the bodies. Eli rode a wide circle, trying to determine the number of the gang. There were so many tracks, he had no way of telling. But there were a lot of them, no question about that.

On his return, Eli found Jesus digging a grave. He'd located a shovel that had somehow made it through the fire, and saw no point in wasting any time. Eli searched for blankets or a tarp, anything to wrap the bodies in. But there was nothing. Not a single thing from the house could be salvaged.

The men spent a long, grim day digging the graves of the fallen. They found the only survivor, a wounded dog, lying in the brush as they left. The dog probably hadn't had a drink since before the battle—and a drink wouldn't do him any good, now. He'd been shot in the belly with a small caliber weapon. There was no way to save him.

Jesus stepped off his horse and approached the dog, who growled at first, then whimpered and let him come close. Jesus stroked the wounded animal, tugged his ears, spoke softly to him, at the same time drawing his knife. He quickly, deliberately, cut the dog's throat, remounted, and rode away.

"Damn," Eli said. "Why didn't you just shoot him?"

"Because we may need that bullet before we get where we're going."

No Ordinary Thunder

"Yeah, I guess you're right. But it seems like a hell of a way to kill a dog."

The trip to DeWitt County took much longer than expected. Every day they found more rubble, more bodies. Every day they dug more graves. The stark realization of what they'd done haunted Jesus. He guessed it would haunt him the rest of his life.

No Ordinary Thunder

Chapter 11

Eli knew Leander McNelly only by reputation. He'd heard the Captain was by nature a quiet man—solemn, congenial, prone to self discipline. And as hard on himself as he was on his men. He had no use for man or horse that couldn't go thirty-six hours without rations. When in hot pursuit, there was no stopping for anything other than bodily functions. And even in that, he expected the utmost efficiency. He told his men what to do and demanded they do it, or face the consequences. At the moment, he paced back and forth in front of his tent. He'd chewed his cigar down to a nub, and considered the repercussions of the terrible mistake that had been made.

"You're sure he's dead?" McNelly asked Sandoval.

"There is little doubt, *Capitán.* The whole town speaks of it."

"Damn! I didn't tell him to interfere, just to get me information."

"We agreed. It was not his decision alone."

"I wondered why the activity picked up so much. It's like a damn war. But I've been ordered by the governor to stay here and take care of this mess. I don't know when I'll get down there."

McNelly tossed his soggy cigar and took out another. He didn't smoke them. He just chewed them up and threw them away. The more upset he was, the more aggressively he chewed. The Rangers, huddled around the camp, commented that this one wouldn't last long.

"You say your name's Plummer?" McNelly asked.

"Yessir, Captain. Eli Plummer. I rode with Captain Ellsworth and Harley Macon a pretty good while. I was with 'em when they got Zendejaz."

"If you were with them, then you got him, too."

"Well, yessir, I guess so."

McNelly's statement shocked Eli back into that

125

No Ordinary Thunder

feeling of importance. He glanced at the Rangers, all of whom were taking note of him. He felt the old camaraderie he used to know. The feeling that he was a part of something special.

"Let's take a walk," McNelly said. "Jesus tells me you were the sheriff in Laredo?"

"Yessir. Almost two years."

"Why'd you quit?"

Eli wasn't sure what to say. He was ashamed of his behavior and wasn't anxious to talk about it. But McNelly would find out sooner or later.

"I quit because things were gettin' too hot around there."

"So you know something of the border gangs?"

"Yessir. I know some of the people involved."

"Good. What do you plan to do, now?"

"Can't really say I've thought about it much. But if you can use another man, I'd be proud to ride with you, sir."

McNelly looked him up and down. Eli didn't know why. There wasn't much to see—just a tall, gaunt, unshaven man, who had been a long time in the saddle.

"You a drinking man, Plummer?"

"I have been in the past, Captain. But I ain't been for a while. Jesus can vouch for that."

"I didn't ask Jesus. I asked you. You told me the truth, didn't you?"

"Yessir. I just thought you might want another's say so."

"I don't need that. I need to trust *you*. Can I trust you, Plummer?"

"Yessir, Captain. You can trust me."

"All right then. Take your horse to the picket line and fall in with these men. In a few hours, you'll partner up and sweep the county. You'd better get some rest. Jesus, I need to talk to you."

No Ordinary Thunder

McNelly walked away with Jesus to discuss something privately. And Eli Plummer, the former drunken sheriff of Laredo, marched to the picket line with a fresh bounce to his step. The deaths of Harley and Dixon still weighed heavy on his mind, but every man got a turn to die. There was nothing he could do to bring them back. He would try to get word of Harley's death to Captain Ellsworth as soon as he could. He knew the Captain would take it hard. But he, himself, was a Texas Ranger again, and that made him feel like a man of some importance.

#

Delgado and his band of thieves rode boldly into Matamoros, driving nearly a thousand head of cattle and more than six hundred horses. No one bothered to count the goats. When they arrived, they found there was no place to put so much stock. The pens were full. The grazing land south of town couldn't feed any more. Cortina's men were bringing them in so fast, the town was overflowing.

Vaqueros roamed the streets with money to burn, and the girls were glad to help them spend it. In such a festive atmosphere, one could hardly be unhappy. Wine, women, dancing in the streets—what more could a man ask for?

There was nothing to be done but to drive the herd south, and let them mix with the other stock. He couldn't leave them in the middle of town, though he'd heard it was sometimes done in Dodge City.

According to the stories, there were more sporting women in Dodge City, Kansas, than any other cow town in the West. Delgado would love to see those women. He could appreciate the talents of his own people. Their dark-eyed beauty, their eagerness to satisfy. But he truly loved the *gringas,* with their soft, white skin, their golden hair.

No Ordinary Thunder

He even remembered one in Dallas with hair like fire. Her temper, as he recalled, was much like fire as well. Her eyes were as green as mountain grass. Well, before he got too carried away, he'd better get the herd settled, then he could do what he wanted.

"Rojas," Delgado said to his partner, "when we get paid, I am going to find a woman—no, *two women,* who need money, very bad."

"I don't know, *amigo.* There are so many. These women may already have all the money in town."

"They don't have mine yet. But I would be happy to give it to them."

"Ah, but you look very tired, *no?* Maybe you cannot keep up with two women."

"*Quien sabe?* If they are too much for me, I will call on my old friend, Rojas, to help me. Together, maybe we will have four women, *eh?* Maybe we will have all the women in this town."

"Delgado, with a handsome friend like you, I can get beautiful women. On my own, I only get the ugly ones. Some of them are too ugly, even for me."

"There will be no ugly women for us tonight, *amigo.* Tonight, we will have the most beautiful women in Matamoros."

With the stock in place, Delgado and his cronies raced through the streets, to the home of General Juan Cortina. His aide met them at the door, carrying a bag of gold coins as big as his head.

None but Delgado were allowed inside, as the general liked to keep his home clean and free from the smell of manure and trail dust. The aide carefully doled out each man's pay, after Delgado reported the head count. One by one, they swung into their saddles and galloped away like the devil was on their trail.

"A good trip?" Cortina asked. He offered Delgado a glass of brandy, which was accepted and downed

No Ordinary Thunder

immediately.

"*Sí*, General. The Strip is a bloody battlefield—with many fewer cows than before. We brought back over six hundred horses. Four hundred of them came from the King Ranch. They are fine horses, indeed."

"*Bueno*! The battle has just begun, my friend. By the time we are through, the Texans will beg us to take back the Strip. Go now. Collect your pay. You have earned it. Take a few days rest. Enjoy yourself. Then we'll decide what to do next."

After receiving his money, Delgado left the spacious home, paid a young boy to lead his horse to the stables, and made his way through the crowded streets of Matamoros. He'd walked no distance at all when he heard several shots ring out.

The shots came from the bath house across the plaza, resulting in a number of naked people running into the street. It was not hard to imagine what happened. Someone probably touched something they shouldn't have, or said something to the wrong person. With so much drinking, and so many naked bodies, it would be easy to get the wrong impression. But Delgado had to admit, it was a hilarious sight, watching all the body parts bouncing and swinging in the moonlight.

The gunman appeared from the bath house momentarily, roaring drunk, wearing a bright red dress belonging to one of the girls, and holding a pistol in each hand. He raised the guns to fire and was immediately shot to pieces by a half-dozen men.

A large-breasted woman standing near Delgado, attempted to cover herself with only her hands. She wept openly, but not for the life of the gunman. Apparently it was her red dress.

Delgado placed his arm around her, promising to buy her a new dress, any color she wanted, if she would accompany him into the alley. It was an offer he was sure

No Ordinary Thunder

she would agree to. After all, she was already naked and had plainly had enough to drink.

The woman smiled a pretty smile, if more than a bit woozy. A trip to the alley seemed to be exactly what she wanted. She took Delgado by the front of his shirt and led him into the darkness, where she quickly unbuckled his gun belt and fumbled with the buttons on his pants. Soon, everyone passing the alley could hear Delgado's groans. A group of young boys giggled into their hands, trying quietly to get a better look.

#

The prisoners were allowed to stop digging clay, only long enough to load the corpse into a wagon already filled. Harley didn't know the man's name. He'd been arrested just a few days before in connection with a small time robbery. Far too old to be digging in the pit, the blazing Mexican sun killed him quickly.

The guards saw no reason to make a special trip to remove the body from the sweltering pit. They let the man lie bloating in the heat until the wagon was full, then ordered him thrown on top of the pile. The wagons had carried nine men out of the pit in the short time Harley had been a prisoner. He'd seen several others carried out of their cells. He didn't plan to add to that number.

Each time a prisoner was loaded into the wagon, the guards removed his shackles and put them under the wagon seat. As they were not always the same guards, Harley assumed that each man carried a key. The shackles were the old screw locking type, so the key was universal. It was something to keep an eye out for.

Certainly there was no way to escape from the clay pit. Any attempt would have to be made from the building projects above. But so far, Salyard's prediction was correct.

No Ordinary Thunder

No one had even tried to escape. Those who had been there the longest had just given up. Dixon, though, had not. His spooky eyes never stopped searching for a clue, a weapon, anything he could use when the time came.

Salyard kept a very close eye on Dixon. In his mind, he'd spent the reward money a hundred different ways. He knew such rewards increased when collected outside the state where they were issued. The payoff for an outlaw like Henry Berry Lowery might well be enough to live out his days in comfort and with style. Of course, Lowery left plenty of dead men behind him. Salyard had to be careful his payoff wasn't a stylish funeral.

"Hey, Salyard!" Harley shouted. "If you're through makin' eyes at my partner, maybe you could shovel some o' this clay. Then maybe the guards won't shoot us."

"Don't get in an uproar, Macon. You ain't runnin' this outfit, remember?"

"Yeah, I remember. I remember a dead man bein' hauled outta here not ten minutes ago, too."

"Well, don't you worry about it, hero. I'm sure you've got a plan to save us all, don't you?"

Dixon's face grew dark and terrible. He whirled on Salyard with a chilling stare—a look that frightened even Harley.

"Shut your mouth, you son of a bitch. If anybody's gonna get us outta here, it'll be Harley. One more word and I'll kill you right here."

"Dixon. Keep it down," Harley said. "Everybody get back to work."

Bobby was scared. Scared of dying, and scared of living the rest of his life as a slave. He'd helped throw the old man into the wagon, wondering if he was better off

No Ordinary Thunder

dead than alive. Wondering if there really was a Heaven, or if Hell was a Mexican prison. He felt relatively safe with Harley and Dixon, but some of the guards watched him too closely, made comments about his hair, followed him to the latrine. When he asked to have his hair cut, the guards told him they liked it the way it was.

Bobby didn't think he could take it much longer. If Harley had a plan, the sooner he enacted it, the better. But it was only wishful thinking. Salyard was right. No one had ever escaped and no one was going to. Bobby's mother would just give up on finding him. She'd just figure her boy for dead, and he likely soon would be. He would die in this miserable place. Or worse yet, he might live a long life building walls in Monterrey, eating *frijoles* whenever he could get them, trying to avoid the curious guards.

The workday dragged on endlessly, with only occasional breaks for water. Not so much as the slightest breeze descended into the pit. The temperature soared well over a hundred degrees, forcing men to pause, or fall. Some of them cried, some of them threatened, but the merciless guards pushed all the harder. Mexico was crawling with bandits who could lift a shovel. There was no need to pity the labor force.

"This is the kind o' thing I took to the swamp to avoid," Dixon told Harley. "The Confederates killed men as fast as they could find 'em, buildin' those damn forts. If we don't figure a way outta here, these Mexicans are gonna kill us, too."

"We're gonna figure a way out. But I sure ain't figured it, yet."

"*Callate!*" a guard shouted.

The men went back to shoveling clay. They were exhausted. Their bodies ached from the back-breaking work. The sun finally dropped below the rim of the pit, lending encouragement that the work day would end within the hour.

No Ordinary Thunder

Harley took stock of his fellow prisoners, and didn't like what he saw. Most of them could never attempt an escape. They were beaten, worn, defeated men, destined to die hopeless, digging clay for Colonel Garralaga.

Well over a month had passed since he and Dixon left Las Cuevas with General Salinas. Surely Sandoval would be looking into their disappearance, by now. Maybe he just assumed them dead. Hell, maybe Sandoval was dead himself. There was no way of knowing. And what about McNelly? Was he on the border? Had Eli joined with Sandoval? Did he run, or had Sandoval killed him?

Harley didn't feel like a very successful spy. So far, he had no answers, only questions. What would become of him in this prison, he could only guess. There had to be a way out, but how? The guards never slacked up for a minute. He hadn't been close to a saddle horse since the roan was taken from him. Garralaga didn't care how many men he killed beautifying his city. Most of them looked like they'd rather be dead, anyway. Well, a chance would come. It always did. But for now, he'd keep his head down, his mouth shut, and wait.

#

Jesus slowly, carefully, made his way back to Laredo. He traveled mostly at night, stopping often to conceal himself from passing herds, reckless bandits and vigilance committees bent on hanging every Mexican they found.

The Nueces Strip was under siege. Innocent Mexicans were hanged with no more evidence than being caught horseback with a rope tied on their saddle. Homes were burned, ranchers killed, women raped in retaliation.

No Ordinary Thunder

Hundreds of stolen cattle crossed the Rio Grande almost daily. Texans had turned on one another, not knowing who to trust. The Strip would soon be a barren wasteland if something wasn't done.

With Macon dead, McNelly needed another spy. Someone who could report the inner workings of the rustler gangs. There was no more time to waste.

But if Macon couldn't succeed in infiltrating the gang, Jesus certainly couldn't. He'd be hanged on the spot without a second thought. No man was more reviled by the southern bandits.

Maybe Banda would know what was going on. Laredo was not a big town. People heard things, told things. As far as Jesus knew, no one was aware of his friendship with Banda. He'd slipped in and out of Laredo many times, with no one being the wiser. And if Banda had no information, Jesus knew someone who would—Carlita Ramirez.

No Ordinary Thunder

Chapter 12

Carlita loved the steady stream of cash that flowed through Laredo. The cowboys were wild and reckless with their money. The saloons, cantinas, the cafes all turned a tidy profit. And the girls had never done better. Some had taken to traveling all the way to San Antonio, to purchase new dresses and sundries that appealed to ladies and gentlemen alike.

But Carlita didn't like so much violence on the Strip. Too many innocent people were being killed, too many women degraded. She'd just recently heard of a group of honest cowboys who were killed when mistaken for rustlers. The cowboys, under the orders of their employer, were simply moving horses from one grazing point to another, when they were ambushed and shot to death. When the dust settled and the dead were identified, it turned out that some of the killers knew some of the victims—had worked with them, drank with them. Other victims had been found hanging in the trees, their bodies decomposed from the heat. Rustling in South Texas had taken a wicked turn.

The Strip was becoming too bloody, too vicious. Chacal had set himself up as the sheriff, so that now there was not even the pretense of law.

The rustler gangs would hit Laredo like a whirlwind, still reeking from their ugly, heinous deeds. Some carried scalps on their belts, offering to trade the scalps for goods or services. Others sat and drank with a vacant stare, a look Carlita had grown accustomed to.

She liked to think that she knew about men, what they needed, why they did the things they did. But lately she was seeing things that were hard to explain. Things she'd never dreamed she would see. If not for the money, she could easily be persuaded to leave Laredo. But the money was just too good.

No Ordinary Thunder

By the time things settled down, she would have enough money to do as she pleased, to go wherever she felt like going. How long it would take, she couldn't say.

One thing she'd learned in her life among men was that you could only push a Texan just so far. The army would send more soldiers. The Texas Rangers would come to the border, and they would come waging war. Only a fool would think otherwise. The Rangers would come to avenge Harley Macon. No matter what end he'd come to, Harley would be remembered as a hero.

Carlita had been so happy to hear that Harley was not killed on the way to Las Cuevas, only to have that happiness dashed when she heard he'd been murdered by Apaches en route to Monterrey. Oh, the Rangers would come, all right. They would come riding with the devil himself—and then, only Hell would be satisfied.

Jesus patiently sat his horse along the bank of the river. Laredo howled. The cowboys raced their horses in the streets. The music drowned out all but the gunfire.

Banda's place was not far from the river, but Jesus chose to wait. There would be plenty of time to get to his friend's house. At the moment, he wanted to rest both himself and his horse.

The trip from DeWitt County had been sobering. He'd come across so many corpses, so many burned out homes, that, for a while, he thought of simply riding west, never to return. Living with the idea that he and Macon had set this thing off would be hard. And now, Macon was dead. His scary friend, too. The mission had gotten off to a bad start. Jesus, like Plummer, found it hard to believe that Macon was dead. He'd done so much in the war and as a Ranger. Well, every man had to face his own death.

No Ordinary Thunder

Maybe Plummer could take up the slack. He claimed he'd ridden with Macon for years. Surely he'd learned some of the man's tactics.

But learning tactics was one thing, executing them quite another. Harley Macon was a brilliant soldier, that could not be disputed. His legend kept even the most hardened criminals awake night after night—but no longer. Macon was dead and that was that.

McNelly keenly felt the loss. He had counted heavily on Macon's expertise. Now that was a thing of the past. Well, the Rangers would have to press on without him. For now, Jesus decided it was time to eat some of *Señora* Banda's good cooking.

The food and hospitality in the Banda home were a welcome distraction from the chaos outside the window. The moon slowly drifted far across the sky and still the racket persisted. Banda's son and baby daughter slept soundly on their pallets, oblivious to what had become an accepted part of their lives. The noise would cease when everyone was too drunk to make it anymore. Sometimes it lasted for days.

"I'm afraid I do not have good news to tell you," Banda said. "We have no way of knowing when more cattle will arrive, or when they will stop arriving. They are coming through now, almost every day. We hear the terrible stories from the north, but the bandits are not concerned with the bloodshed. They only want more money."

"What about Carlita? Will she have information?"

"I don't think so, *amigo*. There is nothing to tell. Before, there was a plan. Steal the cattle, bring them south. When you run out of money, go get some more. Now, the cattle hardly stop coming. They cross the river day and night."

No Ordinary Thunder

Jesus dropped his head and stared at the floor. In trying to help, he had only made things worse. Looking back, taking the cattle was a crazy idea. He should have known Cortina wouldn't stand for it. Now hundreds of people were dying. Not all of them innocent, but plenty of them were. He feared he'd started a war that no one could win.

"If you stay very long, Chacal will find out you're here," Banda said. "Maybe you'd better go, *eh*?"

"I've learned nothing for my long ride. I need to tell McNelly something."

"Tell him you are still alive, *amigo*. Tell him there is nothing to tell. If you keep hunting, you will only be another dead man. The *banditos* will not be kind to you."

Jesus thanked his friends for the hospitality and pushed himself up from the table. He was tired, bone tired. He knew his horse would relish a few days rest, but he could not linger. McNelly wanted information, and it was his job to get it. Though how and where he would get it, he couldn't say.

Knowing Chacal, the rustlers themselves probably had little, if any, knowledge of the proceedings. Jesus saw no point in questioning them. A man couldn't tell what he didn't know, regardless of how forcefully you asked him. Maybe, if he couldn't gather the intelligence he needed from the rustlers, he could slow down the mayhem by taking matters into his own hands.

He would bypass Carlita. Approaching her may only serve to warn the townspeople of his presence. Besides, if what Banda said was true, she may not know anything.

But Chacal would know. Yes, Chacal would know everything. The times, the places, all of it. Of course, he would first have to capture the man.

#

No Ordinary Thunder

Chacal's horse stood tied at the hitch rail outside the sheriff's office. Jesus saw no sign of life there, but with the horse left standing at the ready, he chose to investigate anyway. His time was not wasted. Chacal slept hard in a drunken stupor. He didn't move a muscle when Jesus quietly came through the door.

The room was dark, with only a faint beam of lantern light shining through the filthy window. Jesus waited for his eyes to acclimate, crouching low in the darkest corner. Chacal wore his gunbelt, though shirtless and barefoot. The room smelled of *tequila*, dirty socks and women.

In time, Jesus eased across the floor, pulled Chacal's pistol from its holster, and quickly covered the man's face with the pillow. Chacal struggled to get free, cursing and threatening his unknown assailant. Jesus pressed the muzzle of the gun into the pillow.

"Be still, *bandito*, and I will let you live. If you give me trouble, I will beat you to death. *Entiendes*?"

He struck the pillow with the grip of the pistol, just to be sure the struggling figure was no longer a threat.

"Get dressed," he said, "and don't try anything foolish. I already want to kill you."

Jesus stepped back to let the man rise and put on his clothes. The shirt and hat were fairly easy, the boots a bit of a chore. Though Chacal was nearly blind drunk, he recognized Jesus immediately.

"So, it is you, *Cabron*. I'm surprised someone hasn't killed you yet."

"Oh, they have tried. But it will take a man to kill me—not a worm like you. Where do you keep the money?"

"What money?"

Jesus rapped him on the head with the pistol.

"The money you get for buying and selling the cattle. *Where is it*?"

"You know, I could split the money with you. All

No Ordinary Thunder

men love money. You could ride away as if you were never here."

Jesus cocked the pistol and put it to Chacal's head. "I will not ask you again."

Chacal hesitated, but saw it was pointless. Sandoval would kill him. There was no doubt about that.

"In my bedroll."

Jesus retrieved the money—a generous sum a man could live easy on for a while. He rolled it in the blankets again, and tucked them under his arm.

"*Vamonos, El Chacal.*"

"Where are you taking me?"

"Shut your mouth!"

Jesus gagged Chacal with two stinking socks, secured his hands behind his back with the man's own belt, and dragged him into the street.

"I am taking you to meet the Texas Rangers. The bandit killers."

He pushed Chacal into the saddle, and mounted his own horse. The two galloped out of Laredo, Jesus leading the bandit's mount.

#

Jesus rarely traveled the same trail twice, at least not in succession. If he had, maybe they would have found fewer bodies. He'd spent much of his trip to Laredo burying people.

But now he had someone else to do the burying. The old woman and the two young boys had been in the sun a long time. Remarkably, no animals had molested them. They had probably run from a nearby home, only to be shot down like dogs on the prairie. There was not much left to bury, but Jesus thought the experience might do his prisoner some good. They would search for other bodies

No Ordinary Thunder

when the burying was done.

He turned a fat armadillo over the fire, and watched as Chacal toiled at the digging. The man looked like he'd fallen in a creek, so soaked he couldn't wipe his face fast enough to keep the sweat out of his eyes. Jesus sat back in the shade of a mesquite and cleaned his pistol, holding Chacal's at the ready in his lap.

"Do you think the lives of these people are worth no more than the money you get for the cattle?"

Chacal grunted as he pushed the old woman into the grave. "These lives mean nothing to me. They are people with nothing to live for. They try to make a living, in a place better suited for death. Would you not rather be dead than poor?"

"I have been poor all my life. I, too, lost everything to bandits like you, remember? But I still have something to live for. Now I live to kill those bandits—to kill all the bandits who murder and steal. I will take great pleasure in killing you."

"You may not find me so easy to kill."

Chacal drug the two boys to the common grave, holding them by the hair. He tossed them in the hole with little effort. The bodies had decayed beyond being heavy.

"Many have tried to kill me, Sandoval, just like many have tried to kill you. We are both still alive, and I intend to stay that way."

"No one lives forever. When I deliver you to McNelly, he will decide your fate."

Chacal, on his knees, scooped armfuls of dirt into the hole. The grave was shallow. There was not much dirt to move. "Now they will be happy together, *eh*?"

Jesus tore a leg off the armadillo and pitched it to Chacal. "Put something in your mouth. I'm tired of hearing you talk."

"Ah, that's good, because I am tired of talking. I think I would like to sit in the shade, and rest from my hard

No Ordinary Thunder

work."

"You sit in the sun. It will help to dry your sweat. You stink like a pig. I don't want you in my shade."

"You are a hard man. But I am a hard man, too. You will never get me to McNelly. Sometime you will sleep, or look away, and when you do, I will tear your guts out. It's a long way to DeWitt County. Do you think I don't know where the Rangers are?"

Jesus hadn't figured on Chacal knowing where they were headed, but it didn't matter. By now, probably everyone knew the Rangers were back in business, where they were, what they were doing. Besides, McNelly didn't know he was bringing Chacal back. If the man became too much of a problem—well, it *was* a long way to DeWitt County.

#

Jesus rode into the camp with his prisoner, and found Eli in the last few minutes of his watch. He swallowed hard when he saw Chacal.

The man had absorbed some serious punishment. His hands were swollen, tied to the saddle horn. All in all, he looked about done in. His nose appeared to be broken and he had a bad gash over his right eye. But he hadn't given up. His face became even more menacing when he saw Eli standing beside his horse.

"Jesus," Eli said. "Had a rough trip?"

"Not rough for me, *amigo*, but a little rough for this one. He tried to escape and fell off his horse."

"Uh-huh. The Captain's in that wagon over yonder. He ain't feelin' too good."

Jesus and his captive approached the wagon, the Rangers eyeing them both suspiciously. He tossed Chacal's reins to one of the Rangers, cut the lash on his hands and

No Ordinary Thunder

pushed him out of the saddle. Chacal hit the ground hard, knocking the wind out of him. He responded with only a seething glare.

Jesus dismounted and stuck his head through the canvas flap.

"*Capitán*, I have brought you a bandit to talk to. I think he is anxious to meet you."

McNelly lay covered with a blanket in the wagon, trying to sweat out a fever. His chest ached and rattled with the agony of consumption. He tossed off the blanket and pulled on his boots. Though it was the last thing he wanted to do, he put on a stern face, wiggled his way out of the wagon, and did his best to intimidate Chacal.

"I'm Captain Leander McNelly. What's your name?"

Chacal didn't answer.

"He is *El Chacal, Capitán*...from Laredo," Jesus said.

"Hard case, huh? Well, I'm going to give you some good advice, mister. You cooperate with me and my men, and it'll go a lot easier on you. You tell me what I want to know, and I'll see you get a fair shake."

The intimidation didn't work. Chacal smiled, cleared his nasal passage, and spit on McNelly's boot. Instantly, a Ranger took hold of his arms, and another had him by the neck.

"Wait!" McNelly said. "Take him out of camp. Over there in those trees. Jesus, you come with us."

Chacal began to fight. The Rangers had to work hard to control him. He kicked and threatened to kill the Rangers, until one of them struck him a wicked blow to the chin. Chacal didn't lose consciousness, but the punch slowed him down long enough to get a handle on him.

Jesus led his weary horse into the timber. On McNelly's orders, the Rangers tied Chacal's hands behind his back. He continued to kick, and fight, and curse. Jesus

No Ordinary Thunder

placed his loop around the man's neck, pitched the rope over a tree limb, and the Rangers put him up on the horse. Jesus tied the rope fast to the tree trunk, and walked forward to take the bridle.

"Now," McNelly said. "I want to know everything *you* know about the rustling going on along the Strip."

Chacal refused to answer. Jesus led the horse two steps ahead.

"How many men does Salinas have?"

Chacal only grinned.

"Jesus."

Jesus led the horse another step, the rope around Chacal's neck getting visibly tighter.

"What do you know about Cortina's operation?"

Chacal tried to spit again, but he couldn't summon any moisture.

"All right. You men come back to camp with me," McNelly said. "Jesus, you handle this."

The men returned to camp, mumbling among themselves, unsure of what they'd just witnessed. Was this how the Captain planned to clean out the Strip? Was he planning to use torture to get his information? Jesus Sandoval was just plain scary to be around. His reputation as a killer preceded him. From the looks of his prisoner, the man had obviously gotten on Sandoval's bad side. What would he do to get the information McNelly wanted?

"Ah, so now it is just you and me, *eh, Cabron?*"

"How many men ride for Salinas?"

"General Salinas has many men, but it only takes a few to steal cattle in Texas."

Jesus led the horse forward, the strain on the rope lifting Chacal from the saddle.

"Wait!" he gasped. "I will tell you everything."

Jesus backed the horse two steps. Chacal settled back into the saddle and laughed.

"It was only a few who raped and killed your

No Ordinary Thunder

family, Sandoval. Your woman screamed like a hog. I remember your daughter. Ahh, so young. She cried a lot, but she was very sweet."

Jesus, furious, slapped his horse on the hip. The paint leaped forward, unseating Chacal. The bandit's neck snapped with a horrid crack—and El Chacal was dead.

In a moment, Jesus realized he'd reacted too soon. McNelly didn't want a dead man, he wanted answers. The Rangers needed as much information as they could get, if they were to defeat a foe like Cortina. But the thought of Chacal with his daughter was more than he could stand.

Jesus knew about McNelly's tuberculosis, but he also knew that he was trying to keep it quiet. If word got out that the Captain was failing, the bandits would know it was just a matter of outlasting him. Jesus was aware that McNelly's time was short. He had to get his work done quickly. Hanging Chacal had only slowed things down.

Jesus walked into camp leading his horse, with Chacal draped over the saddle. The man's neck was longer than before. His head flopped side to side with the movement of the horse.

"Well?" McNelly asked.

"*El Chacal* had nothing to say."

No Ordinary Thunder

Chapter 13

Days turned to weeks in the dank Mexican prison, and weeks slowly turned into months. The seasons changed with monotonous regularity, and still Harley saw no opportunity of escape. The diligent guards kept a watchful eye, rarely taking time for even the shortest break. The shackles the prisoners wore around their ankles were removed only after the prisoner was dead. So far, everyone Harley had seen leave the prison, did so in the back of a wagon.

A chilly wind blew off the mountains surrounding Monterrey, carrying a soft dusting of snow with it. The snow danced across the cathedral plaza reminiscent of little cyclones. The dark, heavy cloud cover made the day seem that much colder.

Harley and Dixon had lost considerable flesh—a condition far easier to take in the warmer months. But they, along with all the others, suffered terribly through the cold.

Paulo, the old Mexican they'd shared the cell with, had given up his life and taken a ride in the wagon. However, the Yaqui, Emilio, held on with a vengeance, having fully committed to Harley's escape proposal. Salyard had embraced the idea as well, a far cry from his original dismissal. Bobby Fallon had been taken from their ranks a month earlier, to live out his time in the guard house. Bobby didn't have to make bricks anymore. He was forced to pay his debt in other ways.

The wall encompassing the cathedral was nearly finished. What the next project would be, Harley had no idea. Maybe the change would bring about an occasion, however slim, to make some kind of play. Whatever transpired, they couldn't leave Bobby to the wolves. They had to get him out of the guard house—but how? How could Harley convince the rest of the men to risk their lives to free the boy, when all they wanted was a chance to run?

No Ordinary Thunder

Bobby meant nothing to them. Why would they care what happened to him? In an awful place like this, why would anybody care about anything?

Father Molino kept Harley informed as to Bobby's condition. He saw the boy nearly every day, offered him guidance, prayed for him. According to the good Father, Bobby had taken about all he could. The guards were many and unrelenting.

Father Molino was sympathetic to all the prisoners, but especially to the horror that Bobby lived with. Harley had given the youngster hope of escape. Now his plight was even worse than before. When the time came, he'd get Bobby out, or die in the guard house with him.

The water used to mix the clay floated just a skiff of ice. The men's hands were freezing, their feet numb from the cold. While the others complained, Harley took notice of the effect the weather had on the guards. Cold temperatures made men sleepy, sluggish. He'd seen it many times during the war. The cold, if endured long enough, would eventually put the men to sleep, often resulting in the loss of toes and fingers due to frostbite. It was unlikely the temperatures would drop that low, but even if they didn't, the guards' attention span would begin to decrease. Their thoughts would start to wander.

Harley shifted his attention to the wagon coming out of the pit. It carried two dead men along with a load of clay, and was driven by a soldier half-awake at best. Disarming and disabling the man could be done in an instant, but that was as far as the attempt would take them. They'd be shot to rags and thrown in the wagon, to be buried out back with the others. Waiting around was not Harley's strong suit, but it was better than being shot to death on a cold March day in Mexico.

"Hey, *amigo*," he said to the driver, "looks like you've got some work to do. You gonna bury those men all by yourself?"

No Ordinary Thunder

"*Sí. Coronel* Garralaga allows only one man to dig the graves. He says the dead are not much trouble. Unload the wagon."

Harley and Dixon climbed aboard and shoveled the wagon clean. They'd seen the victims a few times before. Both had been reasonably healthy men not long ago. The grim reality of the prisoners' situation became even more apparent. They would escape or die trying, or they would end up like these two—starved and worked to death.

"You'll have hell diggin' in this cold ground," Harley said, as he stepped down off the wagon.

"I will manage. Get back to work!"

Harley watched the wagon roll away, the origin of a plan formulating in his head.

"One grave digger," he whispered to Dixon. "If a man was to die just long enough to get to that graveyard, he could take out that soldier and get away. Go for help and come back."

Dixon looked at Harley like he was crazy. "And which one of us is gonna take that chance? Somethin' goes wrong and tips our hand, them guards'll kill us all. Looks like this job's about finished. Maybe they're gettin' tired o' feedin' us."

"Yeah, and maybe we'll stay here until they bury us for good! We've gotta do somethin'. If anybody was comin' to help us, they'd be here by now. We're on our own, Dixon. We've gotta get the hell outta here. Before long, we'll be like the rest of 'em…too weak to even try."

"Quiet! Here comes the Father."

Father Molino carried a pot of coffee and his customary platter of *tortillas*, both of which had gone cold the minute he stepped out the door. He carried no cups. The men would have to share and drink from the pot.

Harley marveled at the freedom allowed the handsome young priest. He came and went without the slightest interference from the guards, mingling and

No Ordinary Thunder

chatting with the prisoners as if they were part of his congregation. In light of what he preached, Harley guessed maybe they were.

"Mornin', *Padre*," Harley said. "A man don't have to worry about gettin' too hot, today. I expect that coffee tastes mighty fine."

"I'm sorry. The coffee isn't hot either, my sons. I wish I could take you all inside to get warm."

The men anxiously passed the coffee pot, and gulped the cold *tortillas* like fine cuisine. Harley, as always, waited until each man had some before he took his share.

"How's Bobby?"

"He is not good," the Father said. "The soldiers have broken his spirit. He sits in the corner crying, fearing their return. Bobby will die soon. I think he wants to die."

The image of Abigail Mendenhall, crouched in the corner, sucking her fingers, begging not to be hurt, tore at Harley's very soul. Now Bobby suffered the same way. Harley couldn't help but feel responsible, both for Abigail *and* for Bobby. He'd gone off and left the woman he loved to an awful, horrendous fate. He'd preached escape, given Bobby hope. Now that hope was gone. Now the boy only wanted to die.

"Is there anything you can do for him, *Padre*?"

"How I wish I could. I am searched before the guards allow me in the cell. If I were to get something through, he would only use it to kill himself. I cannot in good conscience do that. He has been moved to the third floor. Only a miracle will free him."

"Well, miracles are right up your alley, ain't they?"

"I cannot do the miracle, my son. I only know how to pray for one. Besides, you will soon need a miracle yourself. When the wall is finished, you and these men are to be taken to Tampico. There you will be put on a ship and sent to Cuba."

No Ordinary Thunder

"Cuba? What for?"

"Cuba needs soldiers. You are known as a great soldier of the American Civil War. *Coronel* Garralaga has highly recommended you."

Harley choked down the last bite of his cold *tortilla*. Cuba—a damn long way to go, just to get killed for somebody else.

"I don't think I wanna go to Cuba. I think I'd rather go back to Texas. Which side o' the guard house is Bobby's cell on?"

"You can see his window from here. It is the last cell to the west, on the third floor. You do not think you can save him, do you?"

"A man never knows what he can do 'til he tries. But I know *one* thing. When I leave this place, that boy's goin' with me, or we'll die right here, together. But we *ain't* goin' to Cuba. Is there a guard on his cell?"

"No guard on the third floor. Bobby is the only prisoner up there. There is always a guard to escort me when I go to see him. He lets me into the cell. There is another guard on the second floor. He has the key. We have to pass him in the stairway when we go up. He gives the key to the escort."

"Just the one?"

"*Sí*, only one."

"Will you see Bobby today?"

"I have already seen him. I will not see him again until tomorrow."

"Well, when you see him, tell him to hang on. This thing ain't over yet."

#

Bobby sat on the floor in the corner of his third tier cell, briskly rubbing his arms and legs, trying to get warm.

No Ordinary Thunder

There was no bunk in his cell, no blankets, no comforts of any kind, though he was thankful for the glass in the window. At least it kept the wind out. He couldn't reach the glass through the iron bars. If he could, he'd break it and cut his own throat.

Father Molino had been to see him just a few minutes earlier, but already he felt he'd been alone forever. As if everyone he'd ever known was a character in a dream. The Father had prayed for him, told him that God knew of his misery. But so far, God had done nothing to alleviate his suffering. Bobby didn't think he believed in God anymore. How could God allow the guards to abuse him so?

Bobby rose to his feet and ran around the cell until he felt a little warmer. He went to the window and saw Father Molino talking to Harley at the wall. The men had stopped working and were passing the coffee pot, eating the Father's *tortillas*. He thought he saw Harley glance at the cell window, then look away before the guards noticed.

Harley talked about escape, but he should have known better. Everyone talked of escape in the beginning. It didn't take long to give up on the notion. Harley and Dixon had probably given up, too.

The sound of a guard coming down the hall brought tears to Bobby's eyes. He turned to face the door when he heard the key in the lock.

For two days and nights, Harley and the other prisoners worked through various escape plans, none of which would be easy—all of which could get them killed. The one they settled on was relatively simple, but it would involve Father Molino, a girl of questionable morals, and probably killing a few guards.

No Ordinary Thunder

Early Sunday morning would be the right time, somewhere around two o'clock. There was a twelve o'clock curfew on Saturday nights within the garrison. Most of the soldiers would be sleeping off *tequila* by then. The guard mount would be cold, tired, and bored, their minds wandering, thinking of women and warm beds.

Two armed guards patrolled the ground floor, where Harley and his cohorts were jailed. Each man walked from the center of the building, past the cell doors to their respective corners, and back again.

Harley had posted enough guards in the war to know they'd be sleepy targets. The shift changed at midnight. They'd be freezing by two. That part of the plan was up to the good Father Molino, and his angel fallen from grace. The rest would require men hardened to violence, men who had no qualm about killing. Harley felt sure he had those men behind him.

Dixon, he trusted explicitly. They'd been through too much together to doubt him. Emilio, the Yaqui, would do whatever it took. He was ready to get back to his people.

But Salyard—well, Salyard was a different story. It was hard to put much faith in the man, though Harley didn't think he'd have a problem with the killing. Something about him rubbed everyone wrong, especially Dixon. It had not been easy to convince him that Bobby was worth saving. He felt it was too much of a risk. But the others disagreed and voted him down. It would pay to keep an eye on him.

Harley would keep Salyard at his side. Their job was to secure the horses. It was up to Dixon and Emilio to free Bobby. Their dark skin would help them pass for Mexican guards in the middle of the night.

The biggest gamble was the girl. Would she show up when she was supposed to? On Saturday night, she might find herself otherwise engaged. The lure of money might make her think the plan unworthy of her time. It

No Ordinary Thunder

would be Father Molino's responsibility to pick a girl they could count on. In their cold, dark cell, they sat and waited on another work day.

"You worried?" Dixon asked Harley.

"I'm always worried when my life's at stake. And the lives of so many others."

"Well...we've made our decision. We can't back out, now."

"I ain't backin' out. I just don't wanna lose anybody."

"Always a chance o' losin' somebody. Even if we do, it's better'n dyin' in this damn place."

"Yeah. Well, let's try to get some sleep. It'll be daylight in a few hours."

They were worn and tired, and needed rest, but sleep refused to come. In forty-eight hours, they would attempt an escape so reckless, so daring, they all wondered if they'd even survive.

#

Bobby didn't know whether to believe Father Molino or not. He hadn't told him any specifics, just to hold on, that things would get better soon. But Bobby didn't see how that could happen. Other than a guard bringing his *frijoles* twice each day, Father Molino was his only visitor—except the guards who brought him the pain and fear.

He often looked out the window, and saw Harley and the others working. He wished he could be with them, making bricks, digging clay, instead of where he was—locked in a cell where every crazy could get at him. The soldiers showed no mercy. He could do what they said, or he could be beaten, and *then* do what they said. It wasn't much of a choice, but it was the only one he had.

No Ordinary Thunder

The faint light at the window told him it would be another cold, cloudy day. Before long the prisoners would be marched out to work. Bobby hoped he'd see Harley and Dixon working on the wall. He always felt a little better when he could see them. Not that it mattered. There had been times when the guards had taken him while looking out that window, watching his friends at work. Times he'd tried to call on them to help him, to kill the guards and save him. But no one ever heard his cries.

And Bobby didn't think anyone ever would. Chances were, he would die right here in this cell, tortured and abused. The guards made it plain enough that they weren't trying to keep him alive indefinitely. There would always be another young prisoner to abuse.

Bobby's legs began to shake when he heard footsteps coming down the hall. It took a moment for him to realize it was only the guard delivering his breakfast. The scratching sound of the key in the lock sent shivers all the way through him. The guard pulled mightily on the massive door. The screeching hinges hurt Bobby's ears.

The guard set the *frijoles* on the cold, damp floor, along with a small jug of water. He replaced the chamber pot at his fellow guards' request. They didn't like the cell to stink so bad. Bobby pressed himself into the corner and waited for the guard to leave.

But the guard stayed a few minutes longer, making suggestions, demonstrations of what they might do before he left.

Bobby had never seen this one before, but that made the man no less dangerous. He pushed himself harder into the corner.

The guard merely laughed and blew a kiss, stepped out and slammed the door behind him. He turned the key in the scratchy lock and walked away, his footsteps seeming to echo forever.

Bobby raced to the cell door and tried to peek into

No Ordinary Thunder

the hall. But there was no one there to see. The guard was gone. Bobby was alone again. More alone than he'd ever dreamed he could be.

He wolfed down the *frijoles* using a rolled up *tortilla* for a spoon, and drank a third of the water. He slid the plate under the door as instructed, sat down against the wall and stared.

The guard would soon come back to get the plate. The jug he'd keep under meticulous care. He'd broken a jug once, in a suicide attempt, but the clay pot was so soft it wouldn't cut his throat. It only skinned his neck. The guards let him go three days without water, to teach him not to break things.

Sounds of activity rose to the window. The prisoners were being marched outside. Bobby leaped to the window to see them, to see anything other than the cracks in the walls, the rats, the roaches, and the heavy door that kept him from freedom. He would watch them all day, entertain himself with their labor. And pray to God the guards didn't come back.

No Ordinary Thunder

Chapter 14

The distant, festive sounds of Monterrey could plainly be heard through the crisp night air. The horses stood braced against the cold in the central corral, great fogs of hot breath billowing rhythmically from their nostrils. Heavy clouds blotted out the moonlight. The garrison lay in near total darkness.

Harley waited, his nerves raw and jangling. For the first time in months, he felt like he really needed a drink. But he knew it wasn't fear that had him so jumpy. It was the anticipation of going back into action. The exhilaration of righting a wrong—of shooting and riding, and taking down your enemy. Well, they still had it to do.

The guard mount had been changed at midnight, as scheduled, but he found it hard to estimate the time. The minutes dragged by, the guards' footsteps seemed endless. Back and forth the guards plodded along, occasionally stopping to pass a few moments in conversation, then returning to their rounds in an effort to keep their feet warm.

The mood in the cell was tense, silent, as if any talking might somehow alert the guards to their plan. The prisoners sat in obscurity, unable to see the faces of the men they'd soon risk their lives with. But Harley knew what the others were thinking of—home, family, freedom—death. Death probably more than anything else. Each man knew their chances of pulling off the escape were slim. So many things could go wrong. They could be shot down in the attempt, or if captured, they would certainly hang. It was a lot to think about.

"Surely it must be two hours, by now," Dixon whispered. "Where the hell is she?"

"It ain't been two hours yet," Harley said.

"How do you know?" Salyard joined in. "Dammit.

No Ordinary Thunder

Maybe she ain't comin'."

"Relax. The *Padre* said she'd be here. We've gotta trust him."

"I trust *him*! But how you gonna trust some damn whore?"

"Look. If she don't show, we ain't any worse off than we were yesterday. We'll just have to try again. Now shut up."

Black silence filled the cell. The men tried to rest, but their nerves wouldn't allow it. What if she didn't show? What if she was laid up with some drunk? What if she turned them in for a reward? What was more enticing to a whore than money? Each sound they heard, each second that passed, only made them all the more anxious.

They waited an eternity. Finally, they heard voices. Harley stepped to the door as if walking on ice. It was the girl. She was talking to the guards—who would be first, who would stand watch.

"Get ready, boys. This is it," Harley said.

Soon there was only one guard's footsteps. As agreed, the girl had taken the other to the far end of the building. Now, they waited for the good Father.

#

Father Antonio Molino had not always been a believer. His conversion came about at the age of sixteen, after killing his mother's rapist. As she lay on her deathbed, beaten and bloody from the crime, she forgave her attacker for the sin he'd committed and begged God to forgive her son for his. She assured Antonio that he would.

Such faith and conviction changed him, made him see things in a different light. But evil was still evil, there was no arguing the point. Colonel Garralaga's men were evil. Father Molino could no longer tolerate the brutal way

No Ordinary Thunder

they treated the prisoners, the horrible things they did to Bobby Fallon. After tonight, God willing, the boy's suffering would end.

Much depended on him. He'd struggled with the idea of getting involved in the escape plan, but felt he had no choice. Something had to be done. If Macon and his cellmates were willing to try, how could he do any less?

He approached the solitary guard wearing a heavy outer robe to shield him from the cold wind—as well as to conceal the knife, two pistols, and small sack of food he had hidden in its folds. He carried a coffeepot, but he had no coffee. The pot was filled to the brim with rocks. He was careful not to shake it. The guard saw the Father coming, and waved a friendly hand.

"Ah, Father, you are just in time to save me from freezing," he said, slapping his hands and stomping his feet.

"I am cold all the way to my bones. Thank you for bringing the coffee."

"It is nothing, my son. The night is cold. You should have what you deserve."

Father Molino brought the pot down hard across the bridge of the sleepy guard's nose. The man went to his knees, but did not lose consciousness. He dropped his rifle with a noisy clatter, tried to retrieve it, but could not make his hands obey. He gaped at the Father, confused and angry. Father Molino bashed his head in, striking him three times to make sure he could not retaliate. He said a quick prayer for the guard, and for himself.

"Get the keys, Father. Hurry up!" Harley said.

Father Molino searched the guard's pockets for keys, found them, and unlocked the door.

Harley and the Father rushed to pull the guard into the cell, where Emilio and Salyard began to strip him of his uniform. Dixon's shackles were the first removed. On his way out, he grabbed the guard's weapon and headed for the far end of the building.

No Ordinary Thunder

"You've done your part, *Padre*," Harley said. "Wait here. When Dixon gets back, him n' Emilio'll go get the boy. Me n' Salyard'll get the horses. What about the girl?"

"She's been told to disappear. I asked her to go with you, but she refused."

"Don't you mean go with *us*?"

"I am not going, my son. The people of Monterrey are my flock. I will not leave them."

Harley didn't like the Father's answer. He took a firm tone with the man.

"If Garralaga finds out you were in on this, there's no tellin' what he'll do to you!"

Father Molino smiled a contrite smile. "You are not planning to leave witnesses, are you?"

"No, *Padre*. I guess we ain't."

Emilio fit into the guard's uniform, with only a little room left over. He was ready. Now all they needed was for Dixon to return.

Every man in the cell jumped when he did. He had already changed clothes with the unfortunate guard, and scared the wits out of everyone when he came through the door dragging the body.

"He give you any trouble?" Harley asked.

"One bayonet thrust through the spine. It was over."

"The girl?"

"Gone before I had him stripped."

"Well...I expect we're ready, then. *Padre*, we can't thank you enough. You take care now, and look out for that girl."

Father Molino accepted handshakes all around, and passed the weapons and the food to Harley.

"*Buena Suerte*, my sons. God watches over you."

The Father quietly closed the door, as he turned and walked away.

"Damn, I thought he'd never leave," Salyard whispered. "This guard he hit's still breathin'."

No Ordinary Thunder

"Cut his throat," Harley said. "We'll wait 'til the Padre's safe outta the way, then we'll go."

#

The lone guard, huddled against the chilly wind, could see nothing out of the ordinary, yet there was no mistaking the remuda's reaction. The horses grew restless. Something was troubling them. Horses were flighty animals, even more so in cold weather. But generally, in such a confined space, they would take comfort in their numbers.

Coyotes were known to occasionally prowl through the town, searching for food of any kind. In the winter months, with nourishment at its scarcest, they would significantly decrease the stray cat population. That's probably all that bothered the horses—a coyote.

From time to time a bear would come down from the mountains, and kill goats, or dogs, or anything he could eat. Bears generally shied away from people, fearful of their strange, noisy ways. But when hungry enough, a bear shied from nothing. The weather hadn't been bad enough to drive the bears out of the mountains, but still a man needed to be careful. The guard pulled his collar up, scanned the area, and hoped it wasn't a bear. In a moment, he saw the man drawing nearer.

The man was taller than the average Mexican, and walked humped over, as if he'd been hurt. He made gurgling noises, held his chest. When he had come within a few feet of the corral, the man fell on his face and let out a gasp.

The guard knew he needed to be cautious, but he couldn't let a man die right before his eyes without at least trying to help. He advanced on the man, speaking to him, asking him questions, but the man gave no response. He

No Ordinary Thunder

crouched beside him, listening intently. The poor soul was still breathing. The guard gently took the man by his ragged clothes, lifted and turned him onto his back—only to have Harley Macon rise up, and stab him in the throat.

The guard was game. He tried to stand up, but couldn't free himself from the knife. Harley twisted the blade in deeper. The guard struggled to get control of his killer's hand. Harley slashed the knife to the side, ripping the guard's throat open. The knife became slippery from the blood running down his arm.

At that moment, Salyard attacked the guard from behind and bashed his skull with a pistol. He knocked the guard a good three feet, not knowing he was already dead.

Each man grabbed an arm and dragged the guard out of the street. They waited just a moment to detect any stir, but there was not a sound.

"Start saddlin' the horses," Harley said. "There's a blue roan in there somewhere, and I want him back."

"We ain't got time for pickin' and choosin'. We've gotta get outta here."

"That's where you're wrong, *First Sergeant* Salyard. We can't afford *not* to be choosy. If we're gonna get outta this, we need the best horses in that pen."

The second-floor guard began to laugh when the door at the bottom of the staircase creaked open. Two uniformed soldiers stepped in from the cold.

"Ay, *amigos*," he said, as they made their way up the stairs. "It is a busy night for the boy. There are two up there with him already. Do you wish to wait? Or would you rather go now and join them?"

Dixon and Emilio thrust their bayonets simultaneously. Emilio's attack was perfectly executed, the

No Ordinary Thunder

long bayonet puncturing the guard's heart, exiting through his spine.

Dixon's rifle struck the barrel of Emilio's weapon, deflecting his thrust into the stunned guard's face. His bayonet pierced the guard's left cheek. The blade emerged at his right temple. The guard's fall jerked Dixon's rifle from his grasp. Both men froze at the racket it made.

Emilio withdrew his bayonet with a firm, steady pull, but try as he might, Dixon could not free his from the guard's skull. He placed his foot on the dead man's neck and pulled with all his strength, but was forced to detach the blade from his rifle, and leave it protruding from the ghastly wound.

They quickly turned out the guard's pockets, relieving him of what little money he had. Grabbing his weapons, they raced up the stairs.

"Damn!" Dixon said. "I didn't count on anybody bein' with him."

"We kill 'em," Emilio said.

The hallway leading to Bobby's cell seemed a half-mile long. Every step the men took, they held their breath, for fear it would be heard. The closer they came to their destination, the more prominent were the moans and groans of the soldiers—the clearer they could hear Bobby cry. The boy was being tortured.

Emilio took a chance, and peeked through the tiny window in the door. He ducked down, nodded, and held up two fingers. He gestured to his clothing and shook his head, *no*. He did the same with his weapons.

Dixon understood. He checked the bayonet on the dead guard's rifle, left his own weapon leaning against the wall, and nodded for Emilio to open the door.

The screeching hinges warned the soldiers, but not soon enough. Dixon drove his bayonet through the broad back of the soldier positioned atop young Bobby. The boy screamed, the soldier tried to, but death came quickly to

No Ordinary Thunder

him. His lifeless body dropped to cover his victim, Bobby crying, straining, to push him off.

Emilio leaped over the bodies. He buried his bayonet into the naked breast of the second assailant. The impact of the blow knocked the soldier backward, crashing into the wall. Emilio pulled the bayonet from him, and drove it in twice more. The soldier's corpse slid down the wall, leaving a bloody trail to the floor.

"Get dressed, Bobby!" Dixon demanded. "Put on a uniform. Harley's gettin' the horses."

"Wait," Emilio said.

Bobby looked almost as dead as the soldiers they'd just killed. His slight build was even slighter than before—his skin pure white, his eyes black and empty. He cried and stared at his rescuers, as if he didn't know who they were.

"We ain't got time to wait. Get him dressed. Let's get the hell outta here."

After checking the soldiers' pockets, Emilio stuffed Bobby into a uniform, while Dixon kept an eye on the hallway. The boy was unable to do for himself. He just stared, trying to recognize the man helping him dress.

"Come on, dammit. Let's go," Dixon shouted.

Emilio handed Bobby a rifle and pushed him out the door. Just as he did, Bobby whirled and ran back into the cell. He stabbed the corpses of the dead, naked soldiers, cursing them, slashing with the bayonet. Emilio grabbed him by the long mane of hair, and slapped him a vicious blow.

"We go. They're dead!"

Dixon hit the staircase running, taking the steps to the second floor three at a time. Emilio and Bobby followed close behind, though they were not able to maintain Dixon's rapid pace. Bobby was weak. He weighed no more than a hundred pounds. Emilio all but had to carry him. He'd wasted away in the lonely cell.

No Ordinary Thunder

Dixon stopped at the first cell he came to, unlocked the door, and handed the key to a Mexican prisoner who spoke no English. He tried to make the man understand what was happening, but couldn't bridge the language barrier. Emilio, in passing, informed the prisoner to free the others, but to keep it quiet. If they made too much noise, they would all be killed.

"One more flight o' stairs, Bobby-boy, and we're bound for Texas," Dixon said.

"Go," Emilio said. "Go, now."

They could hear the cell doors opening and the men running out. How long they could hope for the prisoners' silence, only time would tell. Dixon reached the bottom of the stairs, and carefully peeked out the door. Harley and Salyard were not there.

"Dammit! I don't see 'em," he said.

"I hear 'em," Emilio said. "I hear horses coming."

Harley slid the roan to a powerful stop outside the staircase door. He led one horse, Garralaga's chestnut stallion. Salyard bridled up to a halt behind him, also well mounted, and leading two just as good. The garrison's remuda stampeded through the streets.

"You get him?" Harley asked.

"We got him," Dixon answered.

"Put him on a horse and let's git!"

Emilio tossed Bobby into the saddle of a horse being led by Salyard. He threw a leg over the second horse, while Dixon straddled the Colonel's chestnut, mounting on the run.

There was no need to be quiet now, as the escaping prisoners, still in the jail, were making plenty of noise. Harley whipped the roan to a gallop, his four companions hot on his tail. By the time they'd cleared the limits of Monterrey, they could hear scattered gunfire coming from the garrison.

The men rode in silence, maintaining good speed,

No Ordinary Thunder

again as if conversation would bring the whole thing down around them. They pushed the horses hard for two hours, then dropped them to a walk.

"How's the boy?" Harley asked.

"Not good," Dixon said. "I don't hold out much hope for him."

"That bad?"

"Yeah. He's bad."

"Maybe when we get him to Texas, we can take him to a doctor."

"Hey," Dixon said. "Ain't this Garralaga's horse?"

"Yeah. I thought you'd like him."

Harley couldn't remember being so happy. Freedom made a man feel good. It was a long ride to Texas, but somehow he felt sure they would make it. Whether Bobby would make it was a different matter.

No Ordinary Thunder

Chapter 15

Carlita hastily packed her bag, in preparation to leave Laredo. The town had turned itself inside-out since receiving word of Chacal's demise. Originally it had been believed that he'd absconded with all the money. But when the bandits learned he'd been taken prisoner and hanged by the Texas Rangers, they began preaching even more revenge. The problem was, they had no *Jefe*.

Chacal kept the bandits organized, kept them focused on the task at hand. For months they floundered, fought amongst themselves, unable to successfully perform even the simplest assignment, much less go against the Texas Rangers. Soon they were crossing hardly any cattle at all. Inevitably, they began to drift away. The few who were left spent half their time loafing around town, and the other half shooting each other. Carlita's money well had dried up.

She'd thought of trying Denver, or maybe San Francisco, but Carlita had been born on the frontier. She herself was a Texan, though times being what they were, that didn't count for much if you also happened to be a Mexican.

With activity in Laredo essentially shut down, she decided she'd go to Rio Grande City. General Salinas' operation lay across the river at Las Cuevas. There would be plenty of money flowing back and forth, and plenty of young soldiers to keep a woman occupied. If Salinas would trust her, she could get information from the soldiers and report to him or one of his men. Soldiers, especially young ones, rarely kept their mouth shut in the presence of a woman. A touch here, a kiss there, and soon they would tell her everything they knew. She would get money from the soldiers, money from the bandits, and money from Salinas. Before long, she could do what she wanted, whenever she wanted, and have all the fun she wanted in the meantime.

No Ordinary Thunder

She'd heard that Delgado was often seen in Rio Grande City. He was an old flame, and handsome—even more handsome than Chacal. She hadn't seen him since he rode with Zendejaz, but Carlita was sure he'd remember their good times together. And if he didn't, she had only to remind him.

Delgado might well be the best contact she could have. He was one of Cortina's most trusted men, and probably knew everything about the General's operation. His influence with both Salinas and Cortina carried a lot of weight. To be associated with the two greatest bandits in Mexico could take a woman a long way. Who knew? Maybe General Cortina himself would fall in love with her and move her into his spacious home, where she would live the rest of her days as a queen of sorts. Ahh, to be Cortina's queen and Delgado's lover. Could a woman ask for anything more?

Carlita left the old cantina to the boy, Ramon, and his family. She had little invested, as the building had only been an empty shell when she came to live in Laredo. She swept out the place and moved right in without a word to anyone. Ramon took care of his mother and siblings. The cantina would help them survive.

The noon stage pulled to a bouncy stop on the main street of Laredo at precisely two-thirty, just moments ahead of the huge dust cloud that had been following but finally caught up. The cloud enveloped stage and team alike. The passengers cursed the driver.

Carlita hurried down the stairs, excited at the prospect of new surroundings. The stage always ran late. It would wait only a few minutes, just long enough for the passengers to relieve themselves.

She hugged Ramon and wished him well, then scurried out the door, only to bump into a pair of rough looking men returning from the outhouse. One was broad-shouldered, narrow in the hips, with a perfectly groomed

No Ordinary Thunder

mustache and lightning-blue eyes. The other walked with just a bit of a limp, and had jug-handle ears that folded down under his hat brim. Each man wore two pistols and a knife in his belt.

"Pardon me, ma'am," the mustache said. "Are you takin' the stage?"

"Why yes, *Señor*," Carlita said, looking the handsome man over. "Are you?"

"Yes ma'am. Me and my partner are bound for Corpus Christi. Can we help you with your bag?"

"Yes, you may…and thank you."

The mustache relieved Carlita of her burden and passed the bag to Jug-ears, who placed it on top of the coach. Carlita offered her arm and the mustache helped her inside, taking great pains to see to her comfort. Jug-ears joined them in a moment or two, and the three of them sat waiting for the driver.

Carlita busied herself searching through her handbag, generally ignoring the two spellbound passengers. She did it purely for her own amusement. When the handsome one began to speak, she held up her hand to stop him. She was far too engaged for conversation at the moment. At least, that's what she wanted them to think. When she finally produced the tiny mirror she'd so earnestly been looking for, she took a quick glance at her reflection, smiled, and put it away.

"Now," she cooed, "you were about to say?"

"My name's Ira, ma'am," the mustache said. "Ira Newton. This here's my partner, Lewis Gould."

"Proud to know you, ma'am," Lewis said, tipping his hat. He was uncomfortable in the company of a beautiful woman. Something Carlita was keenly aware of.

"I am glad to meet you, *Señores*. I am Carlita Ramirez," she said, a wicked smile on her lips, as if the men should recognize the name.

"Where you headed, *Señora* Ramirez? Or is it

No Ordinary Thunder

Señorita?"

"It is *Señorita*, but please, call me Carlita."

"Thank you, ma'am," Ira said, a hungry look in his eye.

"I am going to Rio Grande City. I think when I get there, I will open a nice whorehouse. A place where lonely men can come to drink, and dance, and have lots of fun."

Ira returned her wicked smile. Lewis Gould's face turned a pale shade of pink. He removed his hat and placed it over his lap.

The driver rocked the stage when he climbed into his seat. With a quick shout of goodbye, the stage rolled out of Laredo, the powerful six-horse team easily out-running the trailing dust cloud.

"It's chilly, ma'am," Ira said. "Would you like me to lower the blinds?"

"Why, yes. Thank you *Señor*. You are very kind to a lady."

The men got right to the task, unrolling the blinds. In doing so, Lewis dropped his hat on the floor, exposing the excitement in his trousers.

"Well...Carlita," Ira said, "maybe when we finish our business, we'll swing back by your place and have some fun."

"Oh, please do. I would be happy to see you again. What business are you in, *Señor*?"

"We're Texas Rangers, ma'am."

Carlita, well versed in covert conversation, paused at the handsome man's answer.

"Texas Rangers," she said. "Ah, it must be exciting and dangerous."

"Nothin' we can't handle, ma'am," Lewis said, trying hard to impress her. "There's a lotta trouble around Corpus. We're gonna meet some other Rangers there and take care of it."

Ira slipped a bottle from his coat pocket, pulled the

No Ordinary Thunder

cork and offered Carlita a drink. "Just a little somethin' against the chill, ma'am."

Carlita graciously took the bottle and sampled the whiskey. When she finished, she handed the bottle to Lewis and gave him a subtle wink.

"Whiskey always makes me feel warm," she said.

"Yes, ma'am. Me too."

Lewis tipped the bottle back and took a generous swig. He passed it to Ira without taking his eyes off the beautiful woman sitting across from him. Ira took his drink and put the bottle away. His expression told Carlita he was ready.

She raised her heavy skirt above her knees, exposing dark stockings, secured with pink garters, approximately the same color as Lewis Gould's face. The contrast of the garters against the olive skin of her thigh, nearly put the man over the edge.

Ira, on the other hand, unbuckled his gunbelt and confidently worked his way through the buttons on his trousers.

They were not young soldiers, Carlita thought, but by the time the stage reached Rio Grande City, they would tell her everything she wanted to know.

#

Dixon led the way north through a blistering wind, his sharp eye searching for a place to rest. The escapees made poor time on the long, cold trip back to Texas. They spent much of it hiding from Garralaga's soldiers, who showed no signs of letting up. Evidently the Colonel took their flight from Monterrey as a personal affront to his dignity.

They saw search patrols passing every day, sometimes carrying torches, tracking well after dark. The

No Ordinary Thunder

wanted men traveled only at night, riding bent over their horses' necks, clinging to them, trying to stay warm. They could not afford a fire at any time, for fear it would be seen or smelled. They knew Bobby would never make it under these conditions. The boy was dying. There could be no doubt.

Daylight found them taking cover in a deep arroyo. They'd put nearly forty miles behind them, with scant opportunity to graze the horses, or even feed themselves. The little food Father Molino had given them, would have maybe seen them to Texas if they hadn't been forced to travel so slow. As it was, they'd be lucky if it lasted another day. The men picketed their exhausted horses and collapsed—all but Dixon, who took the first watch.

He was accustomed to sleeping in short intervals, as he'd essentially been on the run for ten years. Many times, back in Carolina, he'd napped in the swamps while the Ku Klux and their bounty hunters searched incessantly for him. As long as he could hear them, he knew where they were. The problem at the moment was that he couldn't hear anything. The freezing wind howled across the Mexican prairie blowing dust and sand everywhere. The wind made it difficult to determine if any of the dust was created by riders.

Without question, the soldiers would be looking for them before the day got much longer. If they were cornered in the arroyo, they'd have a fighting chance for a while, but sooner or later the soldiers would block the exits and they'd be trapped. Maybe, if the wind kept up, the soldiers would be unable to track them. Hoof prints disappeared quickly in such a wind. Maybe they could afford to relax for a bit.

But relaxing wasn't something Dixon did well. Especially when he mistrusted one of his own. Salyard was up to no good. He could feel it. He often caught Salyard looking at him, like a man with something on his mind. More than once he'd thought of confronting the man,

No Ordinary Thunder

forcing him into the open. But at the moment, he had other things to worry about. Sooner or later, Salyard would show his hand. When he did, Dixon would take care of it. If Salyard thought he'd catch the outlaw chief off guard, he'd better think again. Many had tried to no avail. Henry Berry Lowery hadn't forgotten himself.

He'd been watching the wind blow across the prairie for two hours, and was just about ready to call for relief when he saw dust rising out of the far end of the arroyo. The dust traveled fast, approaching from the south. Dixon felt the earth vibrate, the dust cloud getting closer. *Horses*! He threw a pebble and hit Harley in the chest.

Harley gained his feet in a second, pistol drawn, ready for whatever came next.

"What is it?"

"Horses. Looks like a bunch of 'em."

"Soldiers?"

"I can't tell yet."

Harley woke the men, and ordered them to gather their horses.

"We'd better get ready to ride," he said. "They're closin' fast."

"We ain't got time, Harley," Dixon snapped. "They'll be here any second!"

Harley could hear the riders' voices, now. They were Mexicans, probably soldiers.

"Emilio," Harley said, "take Bobby and his horse further up the arroyo. If this don't work out, get him back to Texas. Salyard, get your ass up here."

Salyard came forward, checking his rifle as he did.

"Damn Mexicans! Still using these old single-shots. Three rifles and two pistols, against how many? At least the damn pistols hold six. I hope there ain't any more than that."

Emilio led Bobby's horse out of sight, but he didn't go much further. Bobby's faint, ragged voice halted him.

No Ordinary Thunder

"We ain't gonna leave 'em, are we? Harley saved our lives. He freed us from that prison. You ain't plannin' to leave him, are you?"

"No, I ain't gonna leave 'em," Emilio said. "Just thought we might get some better cover."

"Salyard! You take the point, where I can see you," Dixon said.

"What the hell do you mean by that?"

Dixon gave the cylinder of his pistol a spin and pointed it in Salyard's direction.

"I mean, get the hell up there where I can see you! Don't make me tell you again."

Salyard, reluctantly, did as he was told and without a moment to spare. Five riders rounded the bend, all well mounted, all well armed. *Vaqueros* or bandits, who could tell? They were more than surprised to see three men blocking the way, with guns at the ready.

"You men stop right there," Harley said. "Don't touch your weapons. You know what'll happen if you do."

The men looked to one another in question, while the rider at the front of the pack tried to play it cool. He was a tough looking character, apparently fearless, with the unmistakable posture of a leader. His long, hooked nose and narrow, searching eyes, gave him the appearance of an eagle on the hunt.

"*Señores*! Have you become lost in the wind?"

"No, we ain't lost," Harley said. "We're out here lookin' for women. You got any with you?"

The rider laughed. "No, we have no women, *Señor*. We are hunters. We cannot take women along when we are so busy."

"Don't look like you're havin' much luck. I don't see no meat. Damn shame. Me and the boys here been gettin' kinda hungry."

The riders were getting fidgety. Though they had numbers on their side, they were caught unprepared. Dixon

No Ordinary Thunder

could see they wanted to make their move, but nobody wanted to be the first to die. The riders in the back tried to be inconspicuous. They were plainly canvassing the area, looking for two more men. They were hunters all right, bounty hunters, sent by Garralaga to find the escaped prisoners.

"Why don't you have a fire in this cold wind, *Señor*? Are you afr...?"

The leader's chest exploded, drenching his horse's mane with a gusher of blood. He turned a flip off the back of his horse, and then all hell broke loose.

The arroyo came alive with the smell of smoke, deafening gunfire echoing off the walls. The riders tried to fight, tried to shoot, tried to run, but there was no escaping the fusillade of bullets.

The hunted fired until every hunter fell dead, their lifeblood soaking into the cold, dry ground.

"Damn you, Dixon!" Harley said. "I told you to give me a warning before you do anything sudden."

"That was a rifle shot, Harley. I ain't shootin' a rifle."

"Salyard? You fire that shot?"

"Wasn't me, but I got one with the shot I had."

"Emilio!" Harley said.

The men began to search the dead bodies, for money, weapons, anything of value to them. They caught two of the horses, but the others made a dash down the arroyo. Each had a blanket tied to the saddle, something at the moment more precious than money. They stripped the bodies and replaced their stolen uniforms with anything that would fit.

Dixon whirled, pistol in hand, when he heard a horse approaching. It was Emilio. The Yaqui led Bobby's horse, the boy clinging to the saddle horn.

"I swear," Harley said. "I thought I told you to get that boy outta here."

No Ordinary Thunder

"You did," Emilio said, "but I thought you might need me. Looks like you did."

"Well, we'd better get movin'. If anybody heard those shots, they'll likely be here soon. We'll travel in the arroyo as long as we can."

Dixon wrapped Bobby in both of the blankets. The boy was cold as death. They mounted and quietly made their way north, the brutal Mexican wind drowning out any noise they made.

No Ordinary Thunder

Chapter 16

The bandit raid on Nuecestown and the outlying areas of Corpus Christi, had the coastal prairie in an uproar. Delgado took great pride in the way most of it was handled. The bandits worked well together. Raiding in groups of twenty-five to one hundred, they robbed travelers, looted stores, burned ranches, and reportedly killed several citizens. The Texans had been warned.

Outraged vigilante groups took the law into their own hands, deeming the killing of a Mexican, no matter where they were from, an act of justice and therefore no crime at all. In turn, the southern bandits declared the murder of a Texan something a man could be proud of.

Thomas Noakes, who owned a store and ran the post office in Nuecestown, was hit hard in the raid. Though he was able to usher his five children to safety, Mrs. Noakes was quirted and mistreated by the bandits. She also suffered burns when she tried to retrieve her feather bed after the store was set ablaze. Everything in the post office went up in flames.

The bandits pretty much cleaned out the store, including eighteen top-of-the-line Dick Heye saddles—one of which adorned Delgado's recently stolen steeldust gray, tied at the hitch rail outside Carlita's place. In no time at all she'd found suitable digs and furnished them with the best she could afford, which was nothing to sneeze at. Carlita had done well in Laredo.

The soldiers from Ringgold Barracks came through in a steady stream, along with anyone else having a few dollars to spend. Girls flocked to the safety of Carlita's place. Servicing the soldiers in the streets and in the alleys was a dangerous way to live—and a damn easy way to die. The soldiers could come to them now, and there would always be someone to call for help, if a customer got too rough. It looked as if Carlita had found another gold mine.

No Ordinary Thunder

Opening a whorehouse in an army town was no real trick to speak of.

She and Delgado sat at a dark corner table watching the activity, as the girls hustled men from the parlor to the back rooms. He slid his hand up her thigh and touched her in a familiar place. Carlita smiled and kissed his cheek.

"Do you have five dollars?" she asked.

"Five dollars? You would charge me more than you charge the others?"

"Not for that, my love. For information. I must make a living, you understand."

"How do I know you have *good* information? You may tell me something I already know."

"Do you know that Captain McNelly and the Texas Rangers have started moving south?"

The statement brought Delgado up short. He finished the whiskey at the bottom of his glass, and carefully poured another. Digging into his vest pocket, he produced a five dollar gold piece and dropped it into the folds of Carlita's ample bosom.

"How do you know this?"

"I rode on the stage from Laredo with two Rangers. They were foolish, lustful men. It was easy to get them to talk. The raids around Corpus Christi have forced the governor to act. McNelly is riding south, building his troop as he goes."

"How many men does he have?"

"I don't know. The Rangers I traveled with were going to meet him in Corpus. They said he might have as many as the Frontier Battalion. Maybe six companies."

"Six companies? That's four hundred and fifty men. Are you sure that's what they said?"

"*Sí*, I am sure. They said with the Indian trouble so slow in the west, that the governor might send the Frontier Battalion downriver if they are needed."

The idea of going to war with nine hundred Texas

No Ordinary Thunder

Rangers did not appeal to Delgado. Would Governor Coke really do such a thing as send the entire Frontier Battalion to the Rio Grande? If he did, he would only open the west to more Indian depredations. The people on the frontier would be screaming as loud as those on the Nueces Strip. Still, there was little doubt that the governor had to do something. It seemed the day long predicted had finally arrived.

"I'd better go tell General Salinas," Delgado said. "He will want to send a rider to Cortina."

"He can do nothing until tomorrow, *Amante*. Why don't you spend the night with me? We will make warm love, and I will help you forget your troubles."

Carlita refilled Delgado's glass and whispered softly into his ear. She stroked his leg ever higher, until his reaction no longer went unnoticed.

"In all these years you have not changed, Carlita. You have only one thing on your mind."

"Oh, I have many things on my mind, *Amante*. This is just one of them. Another is money. How much will Salinas pay for such important information?"

"General Salinas is a charitable man. I'm sure he would pay you well for information. But first he will need to know if it is true. If he thinks he can trust you, he will take good care of you. If you do all the things I like tonight, I will take good care of you, too."

Delgado took Carlita by the hand and led her to a room in the back. It was Carlita's private room, decorated with comfortable furnishings—the kind an up-and-coming businesswoman might have. Soft rugs on the floor, colorful curtains at the windows. Her bed was large and heavily built, decked with pillows and fine tapestries.

Delgado shucked his boots and stretched out on the bed. He watched, enthralled, as Carlita hurried to undress. In her haste, she jerked a knot in her shoelace, deftly pulling a knife from her garter to rectify the problem. She

No Ordinary Thunder

struggled with her buttons, her hands shaking in anticipation. Moments later, she stood before him naked but for her stockings. Her breasts rising and falling, her breathing coarse and deep.

Delgado smiled at the woman. Carlita, he knew, would never change. But for the next few hours, the last thing on his mind would be McNelly and the Texas Rangers.

#

Sergeant John Armstrong walked through the Ranger camp, barking orders and taking head count. The men occupied their time as they always did—brushing horses, oiling saddles and cleaning their weapons. McNelly had seen better troops, and worse. But it wasn't so much the quality of the men that worried him. It was the number.

"I count forty-one men, Captain," the sergeant reported.

"Not many, is it," McNelly said. "Steele's a competent adjutant general, but he should've known Texas couldn't afford to mount another battalion. With so many people making a profit from the rustling, we'll do well to get any more men."

"You reckon maybe there'll be more waitin' at Corpus? Bound to be. Don't you think?"

"Hard to say. From the destruction and killing we've seen on the trail, there's plenty of men who'd rather go vigilante than Ranger. I expect they'll be as much trouble as the rustlers."

"How we gonna handle it, Captain?"

"First, we'll have to shut down the vigilante groups. That won't be easy. The people down here are damned mad. They've got every right to be. But we can't fight them and the rustlers at the same time. We'll disband them

No Ordinary Thunder

wherever we find them. And if they won't disperse, they'll be treated no different than the outlaws. Any private citizen caught shooting or hanging a man in reprisal will be hanged or shot himself. Texas has tried the court system. It didn't work. The governor sent us down here to put a stop to the rustling and the carnage, Sergeant. We're going to do it, no matter what it takes."

"But, Captain…"

"That'll be all, Sergeant. Have the men ready to move out in fifteen minutes."

"Yes, sir. *Movin' out in fifteen minutes, men! Saddle up!*"

The Rangers quickly secured their gear and saddled their waiting horses. A few complained that neither horse nor man had eaten a bite since breakfast. But such things mattered little to Captain Leander McNelly. They could complain all they wanted, as long as they did it from a saddle. When the time came to move, he moved.

The Rangers rode out of their camp three miles west of Burton, well before sundown on the road to Corpus Christi. Some of them knew McNelly from the war, some from other times past. But most were young, tough adventurers, ready to fall in behind a bona fide war hero, and do their bit for Texas. Eli, though no longer young, felt exactly the same way. McNelly was a man anyone would be proud to serve with. His war record was impressive, as was everything Eli had ever heard about him.

The familiar sounds of horseback travel put Eli in a pensive mood. He didn't know what made men ride headlong into danger. He just knew that, like Captain Ellsworth said, when Texas needs you, you saddle up.

Now Harley was dead and Captain Ellsworth crippled, at least to the point he couldn't Ranger anymore. Harley said he was doing fine raising horses and a family.

Well, the Texas Rangers' job was to protect families, including Captain Ellsworth's. Eli vowed that

No Ordinary Thunder

when the time came, he would do his job and make both Captains, McNelly and Ellsworth, proud they'd signed him on.

An all-night ride found the Rangers skirting the coast shortly before sunrise. With the eastern sky a brilliant pink, its reflection shining on the water, they turned south and headed for Corpus.

The town, though fair-sized, was quiet, almost eerie. Streets were near empty, with only a few men visible. All were heavily armed and disappeared quickly at the sight of the riders. Women and children were not seen at all. Corpus Christi had forted up and drawn the blinds, braced for another attack.

Captain McNelly led his men down Main Street, fully aware of the eyes peeking from behind the shades. He had no doubt that any number of guns covered them. He reined his horse to a stop outside the sheriff's office, and with a shout, he made himself known.

"I'm Captain Leander McNelly—Texas Rangers! I'll speak to the sheriff!"

Sheriff John McClure stepped out the door, a double-barreled shotgun held tightly in his grasp, an expression of complete relief on his face. Pat Whelan and Mike Dunn joined him on the boardwalk, each looking equally thankful. From these men, Captain McNelly got a detailed report.

"Just yesterday, Captain," Pat Whelan said, "me and the remainder of my posse brought in a prisoner. The people took him over to that pecan tree yonder and hung him. We jumped a small bunch o' bandits on the Little Oso River and had quite a scrap. I lost two men and they lost three. I brought the prisoner in to try and get information from him, but soon as the folks saw him, they dragged him over there and hung him."

No Ordinary Thunder

"Was this posse under the command of Sheriff McClure?"

"No, sir. Private militia."

"You're the law," McNelly said, addressing McClure. "Why didn't you stop them?"

"We couldn't stop 'em, Captain. I ain't sure anybody could."

"That's where you're wrong, Sheriff. My men and I *will* stop them. And starting right now, all private militias will immediately disband. If I hear of such a thing happening here again, you will be held personally responsible. Hanging that man was no less than murder in the eyes of the law. If I see such a thing happen, I will hang the perpetrators, myself. Is that understood?"

"Yes, sir, Captain, but…"

"No buts, Sheriff. Anything else?"

"Yes, sir," Mike Dunn chimed in. "The bandits hit Nuecestown. Looted the store and burned it down, along with the post office. They abused the Noakes woman. Her and her husband owned the store. Whipped her with a riding quirt. And stole eighteen silver-conchoed saddles. Dick Heye saddles. The best on the market."

. Sol Lichtenstein had approached the gathering, as Mike Dunn told his story. Sol owned the biggest store in Corpus Christi and thought he'd throw in his two cents.

"I've got some of those saddles ordered, Captain, but they haven't come in yet. I can tell you exactly what they look like, though."

"Good," McNelly said, "but don't sell any until I tell you different. Give Sergeant Armstrong a complete description. Sergeant, make sure every man has a description of those saddles."

"Yes, sir, Captain."

"Prepare the men to move out in one hour."

The order was all the men had to hear. They dismounted, tied up, and headed for the wagon, ready to eat

No Ordinary Thunder

anything old Dad Smith, the cook, had to offer. Since there wasn't time to cook breakfast, they settled for yesterday's leftover biscuits and coffee.

"I need supplies, Mr. Lichtenstein," McNelly said.

"The legislature didn't give me any money, but I need coffee, flour, corn meal and the like. I also need ammunition and weapons if you have them. I'll have to sign a note."

"Hell, I'd rather give them to you, than have the bandits take them. I have everything you need, Captain, including a new shipment of rifles off the last boat from the East—Henrys, Spencers, Winchesters."

"How about Sharps?"

"I've still got a few from the buffalo days, maybe thirty."

"I want them, and plenty of ammunition."

"That's a mighty big gun for shooting men, Captain. And slow to reload if you miss."

"We're not planning on missing, Mr. Lichtenstein. Sergeant Armstrong," McNelly shouted, "have old Dad pull the wagon around to the store."

"I've got a couple boys in my jail, Captain," Sheriff McClure said. "Came to join up with you. Said they're from the Frontier Battalion."

"Rangers?"

"That's what they said."

"What's the charge?"

"Public intoxication."

McNelly shook his head in disgust. "Let's have a look."

Sheriff McClure led Captain McNelly to the cellblock in back of the office. The two men he found there were a terrible mess. Skin ashen, eyes bloodshot—they looked in need of a doctor. Both were unconscious. McNelly rapped on the bars with his pistol to wake them up.

No Ordinary Thunder

"Morning, boys. I'm Captain McNelly. You looking for me?"

The sudden commotion caught the two men off guard. Each grabbed his throbbing head as if it were about to burst. They quickly swung their bare feet to the floor and tried to stand at attention.

"Yes, sir, Captain. I'm Ira Newton and this is..."

"Let him speak for himself, if he can."

"I'm Lewis Gould, Captain."

"You men are from the Frontier Battalion?"

"Yes, sir," Ira said. "Recently discharged."

"Honorably?"

"Yes, sir."

"Why didn't you stay where you were, if you're looking for more Ranger service?"

"Things're gettin' slow in the west, Captain. We thought we'd like to stay a little busier. Sounds like you're gonna open the ball down here."

"We are. Got your discharge papers?"

"Yes, sir."

McNelly looked the papers over and handed them back. "Either of you ever kill a man?"

"We both have, Captain," Ira said.

"Military service?"

"Yes, sir, Captain. We..."

"I don't allow drunks in my troop. Is this a habit with you?"

"No, sir. We just had a little time on our hands, waitin' for you to get here."

Lewis Gould was beginning to wobble. "Mind if I sit down, Captain?" he asked.

"No time for that. Get your boots on. We're leaving."

The small contingent of Rangers came as a surprise

No Ordinary Thunder

to Ira and Lewis. They expected to see the six companies they'd heard Adjutant General Steele had requested. Instead they saw less than one company. Hardly a force to take on Cortina. They wished now that the lie they told Carlita was true. That the Frontier Battalion would come to McNelly's aid.

"I expect we'll meet the rest of your men down south, Captain?" Ira said.

"We might pick up some more, but I wouldn't count on it. This may be the whole of it. You haven't signed on yet. You're free to leave if you like."

Leaving didn't seem like such a bad idea, but Ira and Lewis were fighters. They'd served together with the 18th Kentucky Infantry and had heard that McNelly didn't care if you were Union, just so you did your job.

"I guess we'll stick, Captain."

"Good. Glad to have you. Do you have horses?"

"Yes, sir. We bought some when we got to town. They're over at the stable."

"Go get them. We're ready to move. Sergeant, mount the troop."

"Ain't we gonna eat first, Captain? Me n' Ira ain't had a thing since last night," Lewis said.

"Get a biscuit from Dad and mount up."

The Texas Rangers rode out of Corpus Christi better armed, but barely fed. Apparently, McNelly's plan was to make for Richard King's ranch, where the Rangers could eat their fill and try to requisition more suitable horses. Some of the nags the volunteers rode in on wouldn't last a week chasing bandits.

They were in it now, mounted against an overwhelming force. They needed every advantage they could get. Captain McNelly and Sergeant Armstrong led the column southwest, a band of hard men bound to each other and an unknown fate.

"Sergeant," McNelly said, "sign those two men on

No Ordinary Thunder

when we stop. And relay an order. Any man that sees a Dick Heye saddle, empty it. No questions, no arrests. Shoot the man sitting that saddle, leave him where he lays and bring the saddle into camp. Is that clear?"

"Yes, sir, Captain."

No Ordinary Thunder

Chapter 17

The weather had warmed considerably by the time Harley and his men reached the Rio Grande. The trip had been an awful trial for Bobby Fallon. The running, the hiding, the lack of good food, had nearly done the boy in. The men still debated whether he'd make it.

They waited south of the river, upstream from Camargo, for Emilio to return from his scout. The lights and sounds of Rio Grande City could be distinguished from their hideaway, as well as the activity at Ringgold Barracks. Emilio, dressed in the garb of a Mexican bounty hunter, would easily pass for one and hopefully bring back some useful information. At least, that was the plan.

Bobby coughed and shivered relentlessly, even on such a warm night. Harley thought the fresh air would eventually bring him around, but by now he had his doubts. The boy was still as white as a sheet, and seemed to be losing ground. The men did all they could for him. They gave him the blankets and most of the food, but nothing helped. The consensus was that he may be bleeding inside. Dixon had become Bobby's primary caretaker, rarely leaving the boy for more than a minute.

"He'll be dead by mornin', if we don't get him to a doctor," Dixon whispered.

"Yeah," Harley said.

"That's it? Yeah?"

"What the hell do you want me to do? We can't just ride in there with him. Don't you think Garralaga's men have made it this far? Half the people in that town probably know about the escape. They'll gun us down for the reward in two seconds."

"We've gotta do somethin', Harley. Dammit, we've gotta do somethin'."

"You know what to do," Salyard said. "Why don't you just do it?"

No Ordinary Thunder

"That'll be enough o' that," Harley said. "We ain't gonna kill him, so shut your mouth."

"I'm through takin' orders from you, Macon. The damn Mexican Army's runnin' up our backside, and all you can think about is savin' a sick kid that's gonna die anyway. We need to get across that river."

"We sure do. But when we go, Bobby's goin' with us. Is that understood?"

"No, it ain't understood! We've done all we could for him, and he's slowed us down every step o' the way. We shoulda left him there in the first place."

Salyard never saw the punch coming. He was helpless to get out of the way. Dixon threw the straight right hand, breaking the man's big nose. He followed with a fast left hook to the jaw that rocked Salyard back on his heels. The final blow, a hard kick in the groin, left the old man rolling on the ground. He groaned in agony, his face a bloody mess. Dixon quickly relieved him of his weapon, cocked it, and laid the muzzle between his eyes.

"I've had all I'm gonna take from you, mister. If I hear one more word about that boy, I'm gonna show you some tricks you've never seen before. I can keep you alive a long damn time, so shut your mouth or I'll shut it forever…understand?"

Salyard was a little slow in answering. Dixon whacked him with the barrel of the gun.

"I said, *do you understand me, mister?*"

Salyard spit a tooth in the dirt and mumbled that he did.

The excitement sent Bobby into a coughing fit. This time he brought up some blood. Dixon rushed to his side and wiped the boy's chin, securing the blankets he'd nearly thrown off.

"Easy Bobby-boy. We're gonna get you to a doctor, as soon as Emilio comes back. He'll fix you up just fine."

The coughing continued. The wait seemed

No Ordinary Thunder

interminable. Dixon did all he could to comfort the boy, but nothing relieved his misery.

"I wish them damn Mexicans hadn't taken my fiddle," he said. "Maybe I could ease his passin'. My ma said a little music always helps when they make the journey."

"Well, mothers are usually right about them things," Harley said. "But let's not give up on him, yet."

Three hours before sunrise, Harley heard the splashing of a horse crossing the river—no, two horses. He recognized one of the riders as Emilio. He had no idea who the other man was. In the dim light of the moon, Harley saw that Emilio held the second rider at gunpoint.

"Dixon!" he said. "We've got company."

Dixon came to his feet and cocked his pistol, as the horses stepped into Mexico and shook the Rio Grande from their wet bellies. Salyard moved back out of sight, to cover the approaching riders.

"Who's your friend, Emilio?" Harley asked.

"I'm not his friend," the rider said. "I'm Dr. Warner. And I don't appreciate being dragged from my bed in the middle of the night, with a gun stuck in my back."

"We're sorry about that, Doc. It wasn't the plan, but Emilio likes to do his own thinkin'. We've got a mighty sick boy here."

"What's wrong with him?"

"He's sick," Emilio said. He felt the question rather foolish.

"Hear anything in town, Emilio?" Harley asked.

"Bounty hunters everywhere. Afraid to show my face. Decided just to grab the doc and get out."

"I'll need some light to examine him," the doctor said.

Harley shook his head. "Sorry, Doc. We can't build a fire."

"Uh-huh."

No Ordinary Thunder

Dr. Warner knelt beside Bobby, and opened his ragged shirt. With no more light than he had to work with, he could plainly see the deep bruises covering much of the young boy's body.

"Damn!" Dixon cursed. "I didn't know they beat him like that."

"Who's they?"

No one answered Dr. Warner's question.

"Who did this to you, son?" he asked the boy.

Bobby also refused to answer, but their silence accomplished nothing. It only confirmed what the doctor already suspected.

"So you'd be the escaped prisoners from Monterrey that everybody's talking about. Colonel Garralaga's put a big price on your heads. Two hundred dollars apiece. Like your friend said, you've got plenty of gun hands looking for you. How long since this happened?"

"I expect they started in on him four or five weeks ago," Harley said. "And that ain't near the worst they done to him."

"What's his name?"

"His name's Bobby," Dixon said, his voice taking on an angry, cruel inflection.

"Bobby," Dr. Warner said, "we've got to move you across the river into town. You'll die if you stay out here. I won't lie to you. You may die, anyway. You could be hurt bad inside, son. I won't know how bad until I can get a better look at you. Think you can make the trip?"

The boy turned to Dixon for confirmation. He received it in the form of a nod, and with a faint whisper assured the doctor that he could do it.

"Good man. We'd better get moving then. If Garralaga catches you here—well, a man who'd hang a priest is liable to do anything."

The shock wave hit them all at once.

"Hang a priest?" Harley gasped.

No Ordinary Thunder

"Yes. The bastard hanged him for treason," Dr. Warner said, a great measure of disdain in his tone.

"Something about helping prisoners escape. I heard he hanged a young girl, as well."

The men were stunned. Their mood turned dark and vindictive. Harley's fear had become Father Molino's fate—and the young whore who helped him, as well.

How Garralaga learned of the Father's participation in the escape plan didn't matter. The only thing that mattered was that two more lives had been lost. Two more lives in a long, growing list of corpses left in Harley's wake. He should have forced Father Molino and the girl to come with them, but the *Padre* had his mind made up. The conviction on his face, in his voice, made it plain. He would not leave Monterrey, and that was that.

But the girl—how could even Garralaga do such a thing? Well...maybe there would be another day. A day he'd meet the murdering colonel again.

Bobby's coughing returned the men to their task. Dixon bundled the boy in his blankets, and gently lifted him into the saddle. He weighed hardly anything at all.

"Ride up there with him," Harley said. "I'm afraid he'll fall on his own."

The men mounted their horses and crossed the river. Once on the other side, Dr. Warner made his worries known.

"There are a lot of people in and out of my office. I'm afraid if someone sees the boy, they'll put two and two together and figure out where he came from. With so many people looking for you, and so much going on, we'd better find another place to take him."

"What do you mean, with so much goin' on?" Harley asked.

"About eight months ago, a band of vigilantes stole back a herd of cattle from the southern bandits and drove them upriver. Cortina and Salinas have declared open war

No Ordinary Thunder

on Texas. Now the Rangers are headed south to take up the fight. Last I heard, they were over around Corpus Christi. Captain McNelly hanged the bandit connection from Laredo. *El Chacal* they called him. Since then it's gotten even worse. The violence is almost as bad as the Comanche Wars."

Harley held his breath through the doctor's explanation. The thought that it had all gotten worse than before, proved hard for him to process. McNelly had killed Chacal. What happened to Eli? Where was Sandoval? How many men did McNelly have?

Dr. Warner led the long way around, and entered Rio Grande City from the north. The main thoroughfare had mostly quieted down. It was just over an hour until sunrise.

The drunken soldiers had found their way home, and would soon be rudely awakened by an obnoxious, yelling sergeant. Before long, the merchants would be sweeping the boardwalks, preparing for another days business. The town mutts were already waiting behind the restaurants, for any scraps that might be thrown out.

Dr. Warner made for a nice adobe house, well back from the main street, that still had a few lights burning. The men were cautious, but the doctor persuaded them of their safety.

"I know the woman that lives here…well. On a…professional basis, you might say. She owes me a few favors. She'll take good care of the boy. Her name is Carlita Ramirez."

"Carlita?" Harley said.

"Yes. Do you know her?"

Harley smiled. "That name sounds familiar."

#

No Ordinary Thunder

Dr. Warner went inside first, to be certain it was safe to bring Bobby in. The bed squeaks that came from an upstairs room told him there was at least one customer in the house. He hurried to Carlita's room in the back—an avenue he knew well.

"Who is it?" she asked, when he knocked on the door.

"It's Harold, my sweet."

"At this hour? Has your wife thrown you out?"

"Open the door. Hurry up!"

"Ahh, you are in a hurry?"

Carlita, teasing, opened the door, her mane of black hair seductively tossed, her lacy nightgown most revealing. Dr. Warner pushed past her and closed the door behind him.

"You are anxious, but you don't have to be rude," Carlita said.

"I've got a sick boy outside. I need a place to hide him."

"What is wrong with him? Will he make us all sick?"

"No. He's been badly hurt. There are men looking for him. I don't want them to find him until I have a chance to examine him. Can you help us?"

"Why are they looking for him?"

"I'd rather not say. He's hurt. Does it really matter?"

Carlita already had a pretty good idea, but never being one to miss an opportunity, she made the doctor an offer.

"The next time you come to me, you will bring me something nice from the ladies shop, *eh*?"

"All right." Dr. Warner turned and made for the door. "We'll bring him in the back way."

"Put him in my room, and be quiet."

If the boy was who she *thought* he was, he had a

No Ordinary Thunder

two hundred dollar reward on his head. And so did the others, if they were with him. The report was that five men had escaped. They'd be worth a thousand dollars if they were all still alive.

A thousand dollars could make her somebody important, somebody people listened to. With a thousand dollars, she could move to San Antonio, or maybe even Austin. There she would attract a much higher grade of clientele—politicians, judges, men of power. Carlita loved the cowboys, with their wild, reckless spending and their voracious ways. But they only had money occasionally. Politicians had money all the time.

If McNelly accomplished what he'd set out to do, business along the river would slow down next to nothing. Besides, the violence was becoming too much for her. She hated it. Day after day, more people were murdered on the Nueces Strip. More cattle were stolen, more ranches burned. It had gone far past commerce.

The cattle, and sometimes only the hides, were now being sold in Mexico for a mere pittance. The money hardly seemed to matter anymore. General Cortina wanted the Strip back, and didn't care how many people he had to kill to get it.

Carlita directed the men to her room, when they came in with the sick boy. He looked pale and lifeless, his blond hair half-way to his waist, with a trail of dried blood on his chin. The boy fit the description of one of the escapees perfectly. The men carrying him could easily be two of the others. One gringo, tall and old, and one Yaqui, short and young.

Dr. Warner followed them in, quietly hurrying them along. Carlita had just moved to close the door when Harley stepped inside, wearing the grin she'd fallen in love with, so many years before. She clasped her hand over her mouth to keep from screaming.

Harley grabbed her and swept her off her feet,

No Ordinary Thunder

twirling her until they both became dizzy. Carlita let the tears flow freely. She hugged him, kissed him, and cried like a baby, doing her best to keep it all quiet.

"You been true to me?" Harley asked.

"Hell no," Carlita said with a smile, "you stay away too long."

Harley kissed her, long and deep, Carlita's tears salting his lips.

"My God, Harley, they told me you were dead. We were told the Apaches killed you. What happened? You have been in prison all this time?"

"Yeah. I'll tell you about it later. Let's go have a look at that boy."

"Where is your scary friend, Dixon?"

"He's watchin' the horses."

Dr. Warner had Bobby stripped naked on the bed. His body was bruised from head to toe, some of the worst being on his thighs. His rattling breath made a frightening sound—a sound more clearly identified in the quiet of the comfortable room.

The doctor removed the stethoscope from his ears.

"Pneumonia," he said. "He can't be moved for a good, long while. He needs all the rest and care we can give him. The bruises are bad, but not life threatening. I've ruled out internal bleeding."

"Damn!" Salyard said. "Now we've *gotta* leave him. Sometimes you've gotta leave 'em to the clemency of the enemy. You know that, Macon."

"Now all the sudden you're a soldier again, huh, Salyard?"

"I ain't a soldier anymore, but I ain't gonna swing for this kid."

"Shut your mouth and let me think."

"How damn much thinkin' you need to do?"

"Get out," Harley said. "Go relieve Dixon."

Salyard hesitated, but stormed out the door, angry

No Ordinary Thunder

and fed up with Macon's tone.

"I'm going to give him some laudanum to help ease his pain," Dr. Warner said. "He'll need some other drugs. I don't have them with me. I'll bring them back later. As for the pneumonia, he'll just have to rest and let it run its course. The drugs will help. I wish I could tell you he'll make it because he's young, but I don't know. It's pretty bad. We'll have to wait and see."

Harley obtained instructions as to Bobby's care, and a firm promise from the doctor to keep his mouth shut. Dr. Warner also promised that he would return before sundown to check on the boy.

"Carlita," Harley said, "we'll have to leave him here. Listen, honey, I know you've been involved with the border gangs, and you know about the reward, but I'm askin' an old friend for her help. Will you take care of this boy for me?"

"Old friend? I think we were more than friends, my love. Yes, I will care for him. How could anyone be so cruel?"

"Just comes natural to them guards in Monterrey. Can you gather up some food to take with us?"

Carlita left for the kitchen without a word. She quickly returned carrying a flour sack filled with fruit, snacks, cups, coffee and a pot, all things she made available to her customers.

"We'll hide somewhere in the brush, and come back tonight before we light out," Harley said.

Carlita's heart sank at the thought of Harley leaving so soon.

"Where are you going? Can you not stay a little while?"

"I've got things to do, honey. Important things. But don't you worry. I'll be back after dark. We can't afford to be seen in town."

Harley took her in his arms and kissed her again.

No Ordinary Thunder

"You give me your word you'll take care of him?"

"I will."

With one last look at Bobby Fallon, Harley and Emilio bounded out the door. They found Dixon mounted, holding the horses, with Salyard's body draped over the saddle.

"Dammit!" Harley said. "What the hell happened here?"

Dixon shrugged. "He fell and hit his head. Let's go."

No Ordinary Thunder

Chapter 18

Harley took the risk and built a fire, while Emilio peered through the scrubby brush, watching for anyone approaching from town. They needed coffee and something to eat. The strain of the trip, and Bobby's condition, had their nerves on the ragged edge.

Harley was sure Carlita would keep her mouth shut about the boy, but Dixon hardly knew her, and Emilio not at all. They couldn't help being suspicious. With so many men traipsing through her place, Carlita would certainly know about Garralaga's reward money. She was a woman who liked nice things and would do whatever she had to, to get them. Harley didn't think she'd turn *him* in, but he couldn't be sure what she'd do about the others. And if any of them discovered who Dixon *really* was—well, a reward like that would be hard to turn down.

Now they had another casualty to care for. Salyard lay unconscious under a mesquite bush, a wicked gash on the back of his head. The wound needed stitches, but no one felt inclined to attempt the surgery. It was plain to everyone that Dixon could have killed him. What wasn't plain was why he didn't. Not a man trusted the old Rebel. He obviously had more than escape on his mind, but what it was, nobody knew.

Harley wasn't the kind to throw one of his own to the wolves, but if a man ever tempted him, it was Salyard. He thought of leaving him with the doctor, but couldn't bring himself to do it. They had escaped together. Salyard did his part. Besides, if he let the man out of his sight, he would probably sell them out to save his own skin. Things sure would've been easier if Dixon had killed him.

"What now, Harley?" Dixon asked.

"I expect we'll head east."

"Not me," Emilio said. "I'm going home to my people."

No Ordinary Thunder

Emilio had made it plain that, if the escape was a success, he would return to his homeland. But Harley had grown accustomed to the man and wanted him to stay.

"Sure you wanna do that?" Harley laughed. "Why, we're bound for even greater adventures."

"I don't know what adventure is."

"You just had one," Dixon said. "Bustin' outta that prison was a good'n."

Emilio looked at them like they were crazy. "I'm going to Sonora. All there is to worry about there are Apaches. I should not have gone to Monterrey."

"Why did you?"

Emilio shrugged and went back to his scouting. Evidently his reasons were his own. "I will leave tonight, after we go see the boy."

"That's fair enough," Harley said. "We'll move in just after sundown, before Carlita's business picks up. We'll take another look at Bobby and ride. Should be a long way from here by sunup."

"What about Salyard?" Dixon asked. "He don't look like he'll be ready."

"He would be if you hadn't bashed his head in. Ready or not, we're goin'. Salyard'll have to bow up and ride. We've got a lotta miles to cover."

"I don't think he'll make it."

"Then he won't make it. We're leavin' and that's the end of it."

"Y'know, Harley, for a man with no authority over any of us, you sure take a lot for granted."

"Yeah. Just my nature, I guess. Let me put it this way. Any man who wants to ride with me, be ready to leave by sundown. Any man who wants to take his chances with the bounty hunters, can do as he pleases. How's that?"

"Well, that's a convincin' argument, all right."

"Fine. I'm glad you think so. Now let's have some o' that coffee."

No Ordinary Thunder

The coffee went down good and easy, the snacks and fruit even better. The men ate like they were just learning how, having to force themselves to save some of the food for Salyard. He awoke about the time they were ready to turn in. Emilio had agreed to continue the first watch.

"Heard you bumped your head, Salyard," Harley said. "How you feelin', now?"

"I'll live. Take more than a little headache to do me in."

"Good. We'd hate to lose you. If you're up to it, come and get somethin' to eat. Or would you rather somebody bring it to you?"

"No. I think I can manage. If I need your help, I'll ask for it."

Salyard struggled to his feet, catching himself twice before he made it. The back of his shirt was covered with blood, a knot the size of an apple on his head. His milky eyes drifted side to side, like they were trying to find something to focus on. He walked three steps beyond the fire, before he noticed what he'd done.

"You'd better sit down before you fall down," Harley said. "We've got a lotta ridin' to do tonight. Unless, o' course, you wanna stay here."

"Think I'll just ride along. Wouldn't want you boys to get into any trouble."

"Well, Emilio," Harley said, "you keep an eye on things. Me n' Dixon are gonna get some sleep."

Dixon was already asleep. At least, as asleep as he ever was. He'd crossed his arms over his chest, like a man lying in a coffin. He held a pistol in each hand.

"Sure hope nobody wakes him up too sudden," Harley said. "If I was you, Salyard, I'd stay real quiet."

Salyard worked his way through the coffee and

No Ordinary Thunder

food, all the while wondering if he could take the three of them, now that two were asleep. Emilio would have to be first. A careful shot in the back would finish him. Neither of the other men slept soundly. If he was fast enough, he could take Lowery first, then Harley.

The bounty on Henry Berry Lowery was likely payable dead or alive, though he didn't know that for a fact. Such things usually required only a positive identification. No doubt someone in Texas could provide that. Maybe someone right here in Rio Grande City. Many of the soldiers stationed at Ringgold Barracks probably served in the East during the war. Surely someone there had heard of the outlaw chief.

Still, Salyard's faculties hadn't returned. His vision blurred and his ears rang like chapel bells. He wasn't exactly sure why Lowery hit him, but he knew him as an incredibly dangerous man. Robeson County, North Carolina, could more than attest to that. He was happy the man didn't shoot him.

Countless Klan members never lived to tell of his prowess with a gun—reported to be so stupefying as to defy description. Soldiers, bounty hunters, angry plantation owners, all sought to rid Carolina of Lowery and his followers. That he'd survived in the swamp all the years that he did, said a lot about him.

Salyard had just about worked up the nerve to try his plan, when he glanced across the camp and saw Emilio watching him. He decided to wait. The Yaqui would kill him, and probably enjoy it. He would get his chance at Lowery, now that they were back in Texas. Sooner or later, he would get his chance.

Juan Cortina sat astride his fine palomino, the wind

No Ordinary Thunder

and salt spray pelting his face. He periodically checked the great, gray clouds, and watched the distant steamer make its way to Mexico. It would arrive before much longer.

The captain and crew were always anxious to start loading. But he was short on the head count for this cattle shipment, two or three hundred short. He had to make another trip to Texas.

The Texans fought back and fought back hard, but it made little difference. They could never hope to stand against the terrible onslaught of crime and depredation. He'd heard that McNelly was shutting down the private militias. A good many of the people they killed were not even bandits, but honest Mexicans caught up in the vigilante violence.

The Texans had been given enough chances to return the Nueces Strip to Mexico. There had never been peace in all the years since they stole it, and there never would be. The War of 1846 created more problems than it solved. The time had come to take the Strip back, no matter what the cost.

At last report, McNelly had only forty Rangers. A long way from the four hundred and fifty that Carlita Ramirez spoke of. How could the Texans believe that would ever be enough? On any given day, he could send a regiment of bandits to wipe McNelly off the face of the earth. Even if the governor sent the Frontier Battalion as was rumored, that would account for less than half the men Cortina could engage—though that many Texas Rangers would be a fighting force beyond belief.

The army had proven itself insufficient to handle the problem. Between the soldiers at Fort Brown and those at Ringgold Barracks, there were nowhere near enough troops to take on the bandits. The army was poorly equipped to do battle with such an elusive foe. The people of Texas looked on them as no help at all.

The sound of horse hooves crunching the sand

No Ordinary Thunder

brought Cortina back to the moment. Delgado approached at an easy lope, his handsome steeldust snorting appreciation for the cool ocean breeze.

"I have news for you, *Jefe*," Delgado said. "The news is not good. A rider has come from Las Cuevas. Macon and his friend have escaped *Coronel* Garralaga's prison. The *Coronel* has many men searching, but so far they have not been found."

Cortina shook his head and scowled. "I knew Salinas should have killed them. But what can they tell? They know nothing of our business, but where the cattle go. McNelly will know that, by now. Still, I don't like the idea of doing battle with Macon *and* McNelly. One of them will be bad enough."

Delgado rolled a cigarette, bending over in the saddle to protect it from the wind. He had a hard time lighting it in the damp sea breeze, and finally just threw it away.

"Only a few more hours, and the ship will be here," he said. "When will we go to Texas for the cattle?"

"You and your men will start north tomorrow. We will begin loading while you are gone."

"How many men shall I take with me?"

"Twenty or twenty-five. Don't bring back any more cattle than we need for this shipment. Our pens are in poor condition. We should get them in better shape before we start refilling them. You must hurry. Time is against us."

"*Sí, Jefe*. We will leave by sunrise."

"Arm yourselves fully. Extra weapons and ammunition. Now, with McNelly on the border, we must be ready for anything."

"I will take my best men."

"When you return and the pens are being rebuilt, you and I will go to Tampico. There we will meet many women we don't know. Women who have never known great men like us."

No Ordinary Thunder

"Ah, we will have a good time there, *eh?*"

"*Sí, amigo*, we will have a very good time."

The two men began the ride to Matamoros, the salt spray gradually turning to rain. The blaring steamship whistle echoed in the cloudy distance.

#

Carlita feigned illness to keep the select daylight clientele away from her door. The evening visit by Dr. Warner essentially went unnoticed.

Her heart broke for Bobby. The boy suffered terribly, his beaten, tortured young body all but lifeless, but for the pain. She administered the laudanum and the other drugs, just as Dr. Warner advised. It helped subside the pain for short periods, but Bobby thrashed so violently in his dreams that he soon was moaning again. His recovery would be long and slow.

Carlita still reeled from the sight of Harley walking through her door. For months she had believed he and Dixon were dead, murdered along the trail by Apaches. Now here they were, alive, but in awful shape. All the men were skin and bones. They looked like they hadn't had a good meal in a year. The other two, she didn't know, but if they'd risked their lives with Harley to save this boy, she didn't see how she could turn them in. The main problem would be to make sure nobody else found out about them.

She often dreamed of how life with Harley would have been, had he asked her to marry him. When he walked into the cantina in Laredo, she remembered every detail of their time together. The walks by the creek, the occasional midnight liaisons whenever he was in the area. Her father's threats to shoot him if he ever caught him with her. She thought of the ranch they might have had, of the children and the grandchildren. But it was only a dream. Harley

No Ordinary Thunder

wasn't bred that way. Harley Macon was bred for war.

Bobby began to cough again. A horrible, racking cough that raised him up to a seat. He gripped his ribs against the pain, while Carlita held him in her arms and tried to keep him quiet. A trail of blood ran from the corner of his mouth, the veins bulged in his forehead.

"Shhh. Quiet, Bobby, quiet. Try to be still. You are all right. I will get your medicine."

Bobby collapsed, his head striking the bedpost. Carlita inspected the bump and deemed it nothing to worry about. When she placed the spoonful of laudanum in his mouth, Bobby, for the first time, was able to make out the shapely woman caring for him.

"Who are you?" he asked her.

"I am Carlita Ramirez," she said, throwing her chest out, teasing the boy. "Have you ever had a nurse like me?"

"No, ma'am. I ain't ever had a nurse, at all. Where am I?"

"You are in the best whorehouse in Rio Grande City. When you are well, we will take good care of you."

"You're already doin' that, ain't you?"

"Yes, but you need to build up your strength. My girls are very good at what they do. If one came to you now, they would kill you."

"Wouldn't have far to go. I feel like I'm already dead."

"No, you are not dead. But you would be, if Harley hadn't brought you here."

"Where is he?"

"He will be here soon, after the sun goes down."

"How long have I been here?"

"Since this morning. You've been asleep most of the day."

"I appreciate your help, ma'am. But when Harley gets here, I've gotta be ready to ride."

"Are you crazy? You have pneumonia. You've been

No Ordinary Thunder

beaten half to death. You can't leave. If you try, you'll be dead in ten miles."

"If Harley tells me to, I will."

"Harley won't tell you to. He brought you here for me to take care of. You may be here a long time."

The conversation exhausted Bobby. He slid down into the covers, at that moment realizing he was naked. When he lifted the blankets to look beneath, the sight of his own body repulsed him. Bruises in shades from yellow to black covered him from the knees up. He laid his head on the feather pillow, and stared at the rough-beamed ceiling. A tear rolled down his hollow cheek and settled in his ear.

"You will be all right. I will take good care of you," Carlita said, softly. "Can I do anything for you, now?"

"Yes, ma'am. Would you please cut my hair?"

Carlita did the best she could with Bobby's tangled mane. She'd cut off enough hair to stuff a small pillow, and had just about finished the job when Harley tapped on the bedroom window. It was still early. The girls hadn't occupied the parlor yet, so sneaking the men into the house was easy.

Emilio stayed with the horses. Harley, Dixon, and Salyard went in. The expression on their faces showed their concern.

"How is he, honey?" Harley asked.

"Not good. He hurts bad when he coughs. His head is hot, and he is afraid."

Bobby opened his eyes and saw the men who had saved his life. He did all he could to put confidence in his barely audible voice.

"You boys look almost as bad as I feel. I don't think I've ever seen a more ragged bunch. Dixon, how you like my new haircut?"

"Why, that's just fine, Bobby-boy. Won't be long,

No Ordinary Thunder

we'll have to get you outta here before them girls find you. I expect they'll wear you down to a nub."

"He already looks like a nub to me," Harley said.

"We're gonna have to leave you here, Bobby. Got things to do, but you'll be all right with Carlita. She's taken care o' me plenty o' times. 'Course that was a little different."

"Are you comin' back for me?"

"Sure, we'll be back. But by then, you won't wanna leave all these women."

"Can't stay here," Bobby said. "What about Garralaga?"

"Look, son. You've got a long recovery ahead of you. If we take you with us, you'll die. The doc says that's certain. You're in good hands here. We'll be back as soon as we can."

"Can you, at least, tell me where you're goin'?"

"I'd like to, son, but if you don't know, you can't tell. You understand?"

"Yes, sir."

"Good."

Dixon brushed a lock of hair out of Bobby's face, turned, and walked out of the room. Salyard followed, never having acknowledged the boy. Harley walked Carlita to the door, lowering his voice to a whisper.

"I'm countin' on you, honey. That boy didn't deserve what he got in that prison. He needs somebody to take care of him. I'll pay you the two hundred if you don't turn him in."

Carlita gave Harley a brutal slap, then kissed him long and hard. "I told you I would care for him, and I will. You don't have to pay me!"

Harley touched her cheek, slid his arms around her waist and pulled her close to him. Her sweet breath, her firm breasts, made it hard to do what he must. He kissed her, wiping a tear from her eye.

No Ordinary Thunder

"Don't cry, honey. I'll be back before you know it."

He turned on his heel and rushed out of the room, as if waiting another moment might lead him to change his mind. Carlita quietly closed the door. She heard the girls laughing and teasing, as they made their way down the stairs to the parlor.

Carlita wanted to believe that Harley would come back, but she had no idea where he was going, or how long he'd be gone. Maybe he wouldn't come back at all.

Harley was a dangerous man, and he lived a dangerous life. Anytime he walked out the door, she knew it could be the last time she saw him. Why had the rumor been spread that he had been killed? Why had he been imprisoned in Monterrey? He'd said he would tell her about it, but he hadn't. Even if he did come back, Carlita knew he wouldn't stay. She began to wonder if any man ever stayed.

Emilio shook hands with the men all around, mounted his horse and rode west into the darkness. Harley hated to lose a good man, but held no hard feelings for his leaving. Emilio had been rock steady through everything. If he wanted to go home, that was his business.

Harley didn't know what to do about Salyard. What would his reaction be when they met up with the Rangers? Should he just tell him that he was a Ranger himself and send him on his way? Something told him that would be foolish. He hadn't trusted the man up to now, and saw no reason to start. Well, it was a long way to the coast. Maybe Dixon would solve the problem, himself.

No Ordinary Thunder

Chapter 19

Jesus steadied his field glasses on a rotten post marker and watched the three riders from a distance. They picked their route carefully, checking their back trail often, as though expecting someone to give chase. One of them rode a magnificent chestnut, another a hearty blue roan. They were not close enough for him to make out their faces. The broad sombreros they wore kept them too well hidden. The third rider wobbled and weaved in the saddle, putting forth a great effort to keep his seat.

Jesus scanned the horizon behind them, but saw no sign of pursuit, nor dust clouds made by trailing cattle. The men looked and acted like border bandits, heavily armed, well mounted, and wary. Yet the way two of them sat their saddles made him wonder. Something about them—the horses maybe? Yes! The roan. Harley Macon's roan. The bandit must have stolen him, or maybe he was with Macon on the trail to Monterrey. Maybe he took the horse after Macon was killed. Jesus determined the roan too nice a horse to belong to a murdering bandit.

In a few hours, the sweltering hot day would end. He would follow the riders until they pitched their camp, then in the darkness he would steal Macon's horse away. And the fine chestnut, too.

Jesus had become an accomplished horse thief in the years he'd done battle with the bandits—a crime that would readily get a man hung in Texas. But since he only stole the horses to return them to their rightful owners, and since Macon wasn't around to press charges, he felt he owed it to his *compadre* to get the roan back. Besides, he'd taken a shine to the roan the first time he saw him. The horse exhibited excellent conformation, and proved sound in both wind and limb. Surely Macon would rather he have the horse, than a bandit. Either way, Macon would never know.

No Ordinary Thunder

Jesus maintained a safe interval while following the riders through the maze of mesquite and chaparral. They weren't looking for an easy trail, but one that kept them well under cover. Surprisingly, they stopped sooner than expected and made camp in a little draw.

Though accustomed to living in the brush like a wolf, often waiting on his quarry until his bones ached, Jesus dearly wanted a cup of the bandits' coffee. There was still too much daylight to walk into camp, but he was sorely tempted. The smell of the coffee reminded him just how long it had been since he'd had some.

Sundown was painfully slow in coming. Sitting in the shade of his old paint horse, his shirt and britches soaked with sweat, Jesus sipped water from his canteen. The banks of the draw were sheltered in heavy brush. Even in daylight he couldn't see into it. Exactly where the horses were, Jesus couldn't say. In the dark he might get himself trapped. Maybe the best way was to simply kill the bandits and take the horses. But what if they weren't bandits? What if the rider had bought Macon's roan? It seemed unlikely that Macon would sell the horse, but what if he mistakenly killed an innocent man? Well, only time would tell. Until then, he would try to catch a nap.

The camp quieted early, just after full dark. Jesus saw no reflection of light on the brush. The men had kicked out their fire. The horses occasionally stomped or snorted, but otherwise the camp was silent.

Years on the dodge had made Jesus a cautious man. Now he was sure these men were on the run. They had a reason for putting out the fire. But something nagged at him. His wolf sense told him they knew he was there—and he was right. The unmistakable click of a pistol hammer told him he was caught.

"Mister," Harley said, "I saw that damn paint horse a mile away."

Jesus raised his hands slowly. "Macon? Is that

No Ordinary Thunder

you?"

"Sandoval?"

"*Sí*! *Sí, amigo*! It is me, Jesus! I thought you were dead. Please don't shoot me, *eh*?"

"I won't shoot you, but Dixon might. He's gettin' jumpy. The man tends to go off kinda sudden."

"*Amigo*, what happened to you? We were told the Apaches killed you on the trail. Where have you been?"

"Garralaga's prison in Monterrey. Damn poor place to spend your time. McNelly around?"

"He is a hard day's ride east of here. Who is with you?"

"Dixon and a fella we met in prison. Salyard's his name. He's handy in a fix, but hard to put up with. C'mon, let's start that fire. You got anything to eat?"

"*Sí*, I have some food. And I've been tasting your coffee all evening."

"Good. We've got plenty of it. Keep your mouth shut about me bein' a Ranger, though. Salyard don't know yet and I don't trust him. Somethin' about him sticks in my craw."

Salyard gasped and went for his pistol when Jesus walked into the camp. The man's frightening appearance so startled him that Salyard dropped his weapon and threw his hands in the air.

"Take it easy, Salyard," Harley said. "This man's a friend o' mine."

Dixon rose from behind his cover. Without a word he shook hands with Jesus. Harley supposed these were the two scariest looking men he'd ever seen—especially in one place.

"Salyard," he said, "meet Jesus Sandoval."

Jesus held out his hand, but Salyard seemed afraid to take it. The man's hesitation amused Harley, but didn't

No Ordinary Thunder

surprise him. Sandoval's piercing blue eyes were almost too scary to look at, even for someone who knew him. Maybe Salyard had never seen a blue-eyed Mexican before. He finally attempted to return the handshake, but Jesus grew tired of waiting. He retracted the offer and went to care for his horse.

"Well, how about this, Dixon?" Harley said. "Out here in the middle o' nowhere, and we run into our old pal, Jesus."

"Uh-huh."

"Now, that's a hell of an answer. Looks like you'd be happy to see a friendly face. Even if it is scarier than yours. You boys are gonna have to cheer up. You can't live forever, y'know."

"I ain't tryin' to live forever. I just got other things on my mind."

Harley knew what Dixon was thinking of—his wife, Rhoda, in Robeson County. The men had been together long enough that he could recognize the lonesome sound in his partner's voice. Dixon spoke of her often, in reverent tones, when no one but Harley could hear. He dearly wanted to go home to see his wife and children. But he was an outlaw with a price on his head. Robeson County might as well be ten thousand miles away.

"Well, let's get the fire goin'. Jesus says he's got some grub. A man can only eat so many apples."

There was little to speak of in the camp that night, for fear someone might say the wrong thing. The men loafed around, or stood their watch, and mostly tried to keep their mouths shut. The thoughts that wandered through their heads were the same as any man's. The things they must do. The things they wished they'd never done. The women that haunted their dreams.

In the morning they'd continue to ride east, directly into an inferno of violence. If what Dr. Warner said was true, they might be lucky to even reach McNelly's troop. At

No Ordinary Thunder

first opportunity, Harley would get the low-down from Sandoval. How many men McNelly had—what the next move was. But that would have to wait. For now, he'd try to forget what they were up against, relax, and get some sleep.

#

Harley and Sandoval loped toward the sunrise, keeping their distance well ahead of the others. Harley told the story of the prison break, and of the boy they'd left under Carlita's watchful eye. Jesus filled him in on Cortina's reaction to stealing the cattle from Chacal. He confessed that he enjoyed hanging the bandit, but gleaned no information for his trouble. When he learned of Chacal's involvement in the raid on his *rancho*—that the bastard had raped and killed his beautiful wife and daughter, the news sent him into a rage. He could not wait for information. He'd hung Chacal without a second thought. Since then, he told Harley, he'd learned to be more careful, to take his time, not kill so quickly. All men would talk, if given enough incentive.

"What about Eli?" Harley asked.

"He is with McNelly. I told him you said he wouldn't run."

"Eli's a good man. We've cut a long trail together. I was surprised to see Carlita in Rio Grande City."

"Without Chacal to lead them, the bandits of Laredo could do nothing right. Soon they had no money. Carlita will not be far from the money, *amigo*."

"Yeah, I expect you're right there. Can't blame her, I guess. Pretty tough world. I just hope she'll take care o' that boy."

Jesus stopped abruptly and held his hand up for the others to see. Someone, or something, was ahead of them in

No Ordinary Thunder

the brush. A slight trail of dust had given the position away. A half-mile maybe, no more.

The dust drifted east and covered ground at a good pace. No animal would move that fast in the heat unless someone pushed him. Traveling the same direction, the rider likely hadn't seen them.

"I would like to know who that rider is, *compadre*," Jesus said. "Shall we chase him down, or follow him?"

"We'll follow and keep pace. He'll stop somewhere along the trail. When he does, we'll take him."

"And if he runs?"

"If he does, we will."

Harley's prediction took less than an hour. The rider stopped to make coffee, eat a bite, and empty his complaining bowels. Having left his gunbelt hanging on the saddle horn, he found himself in a compromising position with Sandoval's knife at his throat.

"*Señor*," Jesus said, "that is a fine saddle you're riding. I think Dick Heye made that saddle, *no*?"

"I don't know who made it," the rider whispered. "I won it in a poker game. The horse, too. You can have 'em both if you want. I won't give you no trouble."

The horse in question was a sturdy gray gelding, with plenty of bone and plenty of wind, built to withstand the toughest, longest days under saddle. A horse like that would not come cheap. No cowboy in his right mind would risk losing him.

"*Amigo*, who would gamble with such a fine horse and saddle? I don't think I believe you."

"It's true, I tell you. I won 'em in San Antonio less than a week ago. I had three queens, he had three fours. If you'd take a step back and put that knife away, I'd get us outta this predicament. It's gettin' kinda rank, squattin' here."

Jesus laughed at the rider's humor, and let him compose himself. While pulling his pants up, the rider

No Ordinary Thunder

noticed the other members of the group helping themselves to his coffee. Any thought he had of making an escape, disappeared like the smoke from his fire.

"What you boys got in mind for me?"

"Oh, nothin' special," Harley said. "Been up around San Antone, huh?"

"Yes, sir. Been up there for a month or more."

"What you doin' down this way?"

"A man's got a right to travel, ain't he?"

"Yeah, I expect he does. But this is dangerous country, bandits and the like. Looks like a man'd stay clear o' such things. Unless maybe he had some business around here."

"No business. Just lookin' for the next card game. You the law or somethin'?"

"I'll ask the questions, mister. You just answer 'em. What's all this about the saddle, Jesus?"

"Eighteen Dick Heye saddles were stolen in the Nuecestown raid," Jesus said. "This is one of them. Maybe our friend was in that raid, *eh*?"

"Don't know nothin' about the raid," Harley said.

"What's your name, mister?"

"John Doe. You mind if I have some o' that coffee? I went to a lotta trouble to make it."

"Help yourself. We'll be leavin' soon. Think maybe we'll take you with us. You wanna come peaceably, or tied across that fancy saddle?"

John Doe looked them over, weighed his chances, and determined he had none.

"Peaceable sounds good to me. Where we headed?"

"You'll find out when we get there," Harley said. "Drink that coffee, and let's get goin'."

#

No Ordinary Thunder

McNelly's camp on the trail to Los Indios would have been hard to find if not for Sandoval. He seemed to know exactly where the Captain would be, though the two hadn't spoken in days. Harley never ceased to marvel at such men.

Nearing sundown, the Rangers had just put up for the night, the sentrys settling in at their posts. The young guard to the west recognized Sandoval, but not the four men with him. His eyes followed them closely as they rode into camp.

Eli dropped his coffee cup when he saw Harley Macon. The shock was almost too much for him, having believed for so long that his old partner was dead.

"Eli," Harley said, "it's good to see you up and doin'. You'd better close your mouth though, or you'll let the flies in."

The men dismounted and Harley shook Eli's hand. That was all there was to their reunion. Eli couldn't think of anything to say, and Harley was anxious to speak with McNelly.

"Where's the Captain?"

"I'm right here, Macon," McNelly said. "Where the hell have you been?"

"I've been down south aways. Colonel Garralaga enjoyed my company so much, he didn't wanna let me go."

McNelly laughed—an unusual sight—and offered his hand with pleasure.

"By God, it's good to see you. You look like hell. We'll have Dad work up something to eat. Got anything to tell me?"

"Not much. They're feedin' the Mexican Army on Texas beef. But they locked us up the day we got there. Other than that, I don't know any more than I did when I left Texas."

"Who are your friends?"

"Well, sir, this is Dixon. He's been with me since I

No Ordinary Thunder

left San Antone. I'd never have made it without him. Damned handy to have around. This fella with the gash in his head is First Sergeant Salyard. He served with Shelby's Iron Brigade. Found some trouble down in old Mex. And this stalwart gentleman here is none other than the mysterious John Doe. We caught him ridin' a fancy saddle. Jesus said you might wanna see him."

"John Doe?" McNelly asked.

"Yes, sir, Captain," Doe replied. "I know that sounds like a made up name, but it ain't. It's the only name I ever had. My ma had a real hard…"

"Save it!" McNelly snapped. "Where'd you get that saddle?"

"Like I told these fellas, I won it playin' cards. The horse, too."

McNelly shot Jesus a questioning glance. Jesus shook his head.

"Let's take a walk," McNelly said.

John Doe, surrounded by seven Rangers, was led forcibly to an ancient post oak and had his hands lashed behind his back. Jesus shook out his rope, pitched it over a limb, and settled the loop around the man's neck.

The saddle thief fought with all his strength, but was easily overpowered by the Rangers. He cursed them for cowards until the loop tightened, then chose to keep his mouth shut.

Jesus dallied his rope around the saddle horn, and backed his horse a few steps. John Doe's feet dangled inches from the ground, his long legs kicking madly.

"Where'd you get that saddle?" McNelly asked again.

Jesus let him down and gave him a chance to answer. But he didn't take it.

McNelly nodded and Jesus backed up, this time with a jerk. John Doe gasped and tucked his chin in an effort to keep his windpipe open. He fought and kicked, but

No Ordinary Thunder

made no attempt to speak. One of the Rangers lifted him by his legs, and dropped him several inches. After suffering such treatment three more times, John Doe decided to talk.

"I stole the saddle in Nuecestown, when we raided over there."

"Who were you riding with?" McNelly asked.

John Doe hesitated. Jesus backed his horse.

"Delgado," he said, before the rope drew tight.

"Delgado was in charge on that raid."

"Where were you headed when my men found you?"

"Headed east to meet him."

"Delgado?"

"Yeah. Cortina's waitin' on a cattle shipment. Delgado's supposed to bring 'em in."

"How many men?"

"Around fifty."

Jesus backed his horse again.

"No, no! I meant around twenty!"

"Which way?"

"South, along the coast, between Taylor Trail and Laguna Madre. East of Palo Alto Prairie."

"When?"

"Likely cross the river tonight, or maybe tomorrow mornin'."

"Sergeant Armstrong, have the troop saddle up. We're moving out in the quarter hour."

"Yes, sir, Captain. *Saddle up, Rangers! We're movin' out!*"

"Jesus," McNelly said. "He's all yours."

McNelly hit a long stride on the walk back to camp. Salyard stayed with him, anxious to tell him the news about Lowery. He could scarcely believe his good fortune. Macon

No Ordinary Thunder

was a Texas Ranger, and had led him directly to a band of lawmen with no qualms about dealing out justice. Never would he have believed it all to be so easy. He had only to report Lowery to Captain McNelly. The outlaw chief would be taken into custody, and he would get his fat reward. Maybe he was due a reversal of fortune. Maybe McNelly would hang Lowery beside the saddle thief, and that would be the end of it.

"Captain McNelly? Can I talk to you?"

"If you can do it walking. What's on your mind?"

"That Injun Macon calls Dixon is really Henry Berry Lowery, the guerilla fighter from Carolina. Bound to be a reward on him."

"And you want it, I suppose."

"Well, somebody's gonna collect. Thought it might as well be me."

"How'd you get that gash in your head?"

"He done it. Bashed me with a pistol."

"Uh-huh. Now you want pay-back?"

"No, sir. I just want that reward."

"I don't have time for this right now. We'll talk about the reward later. Mount up if you're going with us."

No Ordinary Thunder

Chapter 20

Harley smelled a fight in the air, as the Rangers made their way to Palo Alto Prairie. If the thief's story was true, they could expect upwards of twenty bandits. Sandoval's technique was generally known to bring out the truth.

Several of McNelly's men had been dispatched on a scouting mission before Harley arrived. The Rangers' number totaled about the same.

Few words were spoken on the trail, and then only at a whisper. Captain McNelly, a strict disciplinarian, made it plain that he liked to think while he traveled. He would not tolerate unnecessary distractions. The order for silence wasn't a problem, as most men riding into danger had little to say.

Many of the men, including Harley, were anxious for the fight to begin, that they might strike a hard blow for their families and Texas. Others were apprehensive, afraid that, with the Captain's blood boiling like it was, he might chase the bandits across the river into Mexico. They wanted no part of such an aggressive tactic.

The hardpan country of the Nueces Strip provided little else to think about. Scrub oak, salt cedar, a little marsh grass and Spanish dagger was about all there was to see.

The Rangers pressed east toward Laguna Madre, taking care to save their horses for the fight. The long trot in which the horses traveled produced a fine sheen of sweat on their necks. The ride would be a good warm-up for what was to come.

A forward rider cut the trail of the herd, about the time the sun climbed high enough to dissipate the ground fog. The rider stood in his stirrups, circled his hand above his head, and dropped it pointing south toward the river. The trail was no more than a few hours old.

The rider spurred his horse into a nice, easy lope.

No Ordinary Thunder

Captain McNelly bit into his second cigar of the day, and fell in behind leading a column of twos.

In no more than three miles, the forward rider reached a barren groundswell and pulled his horse to a stop. He again stood in his stirrups, circled his hand and dropped it twice. He had spotted the dust cloud of the bandits' herd, a few miles in the distance.

McNelly withdrew his binoculars to survey the scene, just in time to see that the bandits had sighted his column, as well. They crowded the herd into a hard run, firing their weapons, driving them toward Palo Alto. McNelly returned the glasses to his saddlebag, waved a hand to the column, and spurred his bay horse to the gallop.

"Well, Mr. Dixon," Harley said. "Looks like we're in it now."

Dixon grinned a not so easy grin. "Y'know, Harley, livin' with you is a hell of a lot more dangerous than the swamps in Carolina. If I ever get another chance, I'm leavin' you on your own."

"Aw, hell, this way you'll have somethin' to tell your grandkids about. If you live through it, that is."

"Very funny. My grandkids'll already have somethin' to talk about, remember? I swear, I might just shoot you myself. Just a wound, mind you. Maybe a leg. Nothin' serious. I'd hate to have to take care of you."

"I commend your gallantry, sir. Not the right leg, if it don't make any difference to you. I've been shot there before."

The Rangers steadily gained ground on the bandits for the next three miles or so. The bandits' horses were jaded from driving the stolen cattle all night. They could never hope to out-run the Rangers if they wanted to keep the herd.

Allowing they could not reach the river in time to escape, the bandits drove the cattle onto an island in the middle of the salt marsh. There they took what cover there

No Ordinary Thunder

was and prepared to make their stand.

McNelly slowed his column, let the horses blow, and let the bandits wait. Waiting set the nerves on edge, forced men to make mistakes. The longer they waited, the more rattled they would be.

Sergeant Armstrong rode up and down the line, encouraging the men to check their weapons. There might not be time later. Harley had been offered one of the Sharps .50's, but chose a Winchester '73 instead. It felt good in his hands and would replace the one he'd left in Mexico. Captain McNelly turned in his saddle and called Harley and Dixon to the front.

"Macon," he said, "Mr. Salyard tells me your friend here isn't named Dixon, at all, but Lowery—Henry Berry Lowery, the guerilla raider. Is that true?"

Harley swallowed hard and bit his tongue. So that was it. Salyard knew Dixon's identity. That's why he'd changed his mind and gone along with the prison break. To turn him in and claim the reward.

"It's true," Lowery said. "No need to put Harley on the hard seat."

"He's a good man, Captain," Harley said. "I never rode with any better."

"I believe you. I've heard the stories. But he's a wanted fugitive, Macon. How am I supposed to square that with the law?"

Harley didn't know the answer to the question, but wasn't ready to give up. "Nobody knows about this but the three of us. Can't we keep it that way?"

"Only if you think Salyard will keep his mouth shut. Somehow he doesn't strike me as the type."

Harley couldn't argue with that. Salyard would run to the law the first chance he got. Of course, they *were* riding into what might be a fierce battle. Maybe Salyard would catch a bullet, and the problem would solve itself.

"I'd've never made it outta that prison without his

No Ordinary Thunder

help, Captain. I ain't gonna turn my back on him, now."

"I'm not asking you to. Fighting men are hard enough to come by in this world. Lowery, you're not on the payroll. I can't order you to come with us, but I can't let you go. I'm sure you understand my position."

"I understand, Captain. Besides, if I learned anything in Mexico, it's that I don't care much for bein' in irons. Guess I'll just ride along, if it's all the same to you. You might find me pretty handy when things start poppin'."

"Good enough. By the time this is over, we may all be dead, anyway."

Delgado observed the Ranger column from one of the scarce, well-fortified positions on the island. His men were scattered throughout the marsh, taking advantage of every bit of cover available. Had he known the Rangers would slow their pursuit, he would've kept pushing hard for the river. As it was, the majority of his men had already dismounted, with only a few holding the herd to the south. He'd given thought to having them drive the cattle on, but concluded that he might need the firepower.

Two of his men ran when the Rangers were sighted, leaving him with just seventeen. The Rangers had that many, and more. But they would be forced to cross the marsh with little benefit of cover. His bandits would shoot them down like dogs.

If he could wipe out McNelly's Ranger troop, it would send a bold message to the Texans. The Strip belonged to Mexico—now and forevermore. Cortina's station would be elevated to that of a king, and a king would need his first knight. He, Delgado, would be that knight, riding through all of Mexico on a fine white horse,

No Ordinary Thunder

taking what he wanted, the hero of every young boy, the dream of every young woman.

Maybe he would someday sail on a great ship to Spain, or to the islands of the southern sea—a far cry from the tiny island he now occupied. He could envision the dark-skinned women, their bare breasts, their long legs. How he wanted to see those women.

McNelly's troops were closing in. With his spyglass, Delgado could see the rumor that he'd heard was true. The Rangers carried Sharps .50 caliber carbines. A Sharps would blow a big hole in a man. A hole as big as the man's fist. The bandits' advantage was superior cover, but staring down the bore of a Sharps .50 caliber could easily cause a man to lose heart. They had to hold their ground, or be overrun. Either way, Delgado was sure it would all be over soon.

#

"*Sergeant Armstrong! Form the line!*" McNelly shouted.

The effort brought on a coughing spell that left the Captain spitting up great curds of blood. He pulled out a handkerchief to cover his mouth that was also stained red with blood. Such times served to remind the men that even their brave leader, Captain McNelly, was human.

The Rangers formed their line in five pace intervals, double checked their weapons, and waited uncomfortably for the bloody coughing to stop. When it did, McNelly reviewed the line and said what he had to say.

"Men! Across that marsh, just waiting for you, are bandits that think they're bigger than the law—bigger than the laws of the United States—bigger than the laws of Texas. Today, we'll find out if they're right. They've robbed, and raped, and stolen our women into slavery.

No Ordinary Thunder

They've rustled, and burned, and murdered at will. Today, we will win, or we will lose. But it *will not* be a draw. Is that understood?"

"Yes, sir, Captain!" came the shouts.

"Good. That's the kind of talk I like to hear. Ride straight at them. Veer neither left nor right. Fire only at the man directly in front of you. Fire until that man is dead. Show them no mercy, Rangers. Expect none."

McNelly turned the handsome bay to face the marsh, and drew his brace of pistols.

"Don't fire until I do," he said. "I'll meet you in the middle, Rangers. *Forward at the walk!*"

Harley and Dixon flanked McNelly's left, while Eli and Sergeant Armstrong secured the right. The bandits laid down a sporadic field of fire, as the Rangers splashed through the hock-deep marsh. Their shots were wild, most of them dropping low, making a hollow sound as the bullets plowed through the water. McNelly held a painfully slow pace, in hopes that the bandits would burn up most of their ammunition. The sight of the Rangers' cool approach panicked many of the bandits. Some of them jumped their horses and ran, but plenty of them chose to stay and fight.

The bandits raised their guns and shot higher. At a hundred paces, Ranger mounts were dropping. The horses screamed, reared, twisted, and fell, as the bullets tore into their flesh. Rangers jumped clear of their falling mounts, and continued the slogging approach on foot. Captain McNelly had not yet given the order to fire.

Rangers looked up and down the line, afraid, but taking heart from their brave comrades. Eli still had a horse under him, but Ira Newton and Lewis Gould, as well as Salyard, had lost theirs to rifle fire. Sandoval swung wide,

No Ordinary Thunder

toward the thick brush, guiding his paint with his knees. He held a pistol in each hand, a long knife in his teeth—and wore a murderous expression, hard to describe.

Not a man faltered. Not one Ranger ran. With the fire coming hot and heavy, some of the Rangers began falling to wounds. Finally, at a distance of no more than thirty paces, Captain McNelly opened up with his pistols.

"Take them, Rangers!" he shouted.

The Rangers charged like a well-trained unit, firing their carbines at the nearest target, falling back to reload. Others maintained the charge, laying down fire with their pistols. The mounted Rangers rode the bandits down, many of them holding their reins in their teeth, firing two Colt revolvers.

"Don't let any escape!" McNelly ordered. "Circle them. Cut them down!"

Bullets whistled through the air, knocking bark off the trees, whining as they ricocheted into the distance. Bandits slopped through the salty marsh, attempting to run, trying to reach their horses. Most were killed before they made it.

Many of them ran into the surrounding brush, in an effort to escape the riders. But the Rangers dismounted and followed them in, mopping them up as they trudged through the mud. Blood mixed and mingled with the filthy water, splashing in small waves over their shattered dead bodies.

Near the edge of the timber, McNelly saw young Ranger Smith shoot an aged bandit as he tried frantically to mount his horse. The old man thrashed and floundered in the water, unable to regain his footing. McNelly tried to call to the boy, to warn him to be careful, but broke into a coughing spell before he got the words out.

The Ranger approached to finish the wounded bandit, but the man was not through fighting. The Ranger was careless. He came too close. McNelly whipped his

No Ordinary Thunder

horse to the gallop, a stream of blood choking him, running from his mouth.

The bandit raised his pistol, fired a single shot into the boy's chest, and killed him where he stood. The pleasure he received from killing young Smith only lasted a moment. McNelly fired as the bandit gained his feet. The old man didn't feel the bullet that tore half his head away.

McNelly dismounted and made his way into the brush. A wounded bandit with an empty gun, but a long shining knife, came at him—an evil grin of satisfaction showing on his ugly face. McNelly calmly raised his pistol and shot him in the mouth. The back of the bandit's head exploded, leaving a spider-like pattern of blood, brains and teeth on the post oak tree behind him.

"Catch horses, boys! Get after them," McNelly called.

The Rangers, Harley and Dixon among them, did as McNelly ordered, grabbing any horse they could get their hands on to pursue the fleeing bandits. They charged the bandits as best they could, but made poor time until they cleared the marsh. When they did, the pace picked up, and they began to close in fast.

Dixon reined in his horse, took careful aim with a bandit's rifle, and brought down the rider in the lead. Two horses fell to rifle fire. One of their riders died in the fall, the other was dispatched by a passing Ranger.

The running fight lasted five or six miles, and wore out a lot of good horses. But when the Rangers returned, the tired animals carried men tied across the saddles. Every bandit had been killed. The Rangers caught them all before they made it to the river.

McNelly found and mounted his horse. He rode across the bloody marsh, taking a toll of the dead. Occasionally there was a single shot by a Ranger finishing a bandit, but all in all, the marsh was eerily quiet. No birds sang, not even a breeze. Dead horses lay in the stinking

No Ordinary Thunder

water, while wounded ones drifted, confused and frightened. Some splashed around on three good legs, until one of the Rangers put them out of their misery. Others, untouched, stood on the battlefield, munching salt grass, sniffing the dead.

"*Sergeant Armstrong! Report!*" McNelly shouted.

Sergeant Armstrong loped his mount across the field, and pulled rein at McNelly's side. "Looks like we lost one man, Captain. Ranger Smith was killed. He was just a boy."

"I'm aware of that, Sergeant. Bandits?"

"Seventeen, sir. That's all the bodies we could find."

"Wounded?"

"Several Rangers wounded, sir, but all of them minor. Pretty lucky."

"A good morning's work. Wouldn't you say?"

"Yes, sir...except for the boy."

"He died a Texas Ranger, Sergeant. I told him before we struck for Palo Alto to stay in the rear. Do you know what he said? 'Me getting killed is no worse than some other Ranger getting killed.' That's what he said. We'll bury him in Brownsville. Full military honors. Anything else?"

"No, sir."

"We'll need a wagon to pick up the dead and haul them back to town. Dispatch a man to handle that."

"Take 'em back to town, sir?"

"That's what I said. We'll haul these killers and thieves to town and pile them in the plaza as a warning to every bandit on the river. Things are going to be different from now on. We'll find them and kill them, no matter where they go. Are my orders understood, Sergeant?"

"Yes, sir, Captain, but..."

"No buts. Commandeer another wagon to retrieve all the plunder. We'll turn it in to the sheriff, and have him

No Ordinary Thunder

dispose of it according to law, along with all the cattle."

"Yes, sir. We found a few of them Dick Heye saddles, Captain, and a lotta runnin' W brands. Looks like Mr. King's gonna get some of his horses back."

"That's fine, Sergeant. Go assemble the men. I'll be along."

"Yes, sir."

McNelly sat alone, his horse pawing the water, and contemplated the day. Seventeen bandits killed. One Ranger lost. A few minor wounds. More than just luck. Some might say miraculous.

Cortina would know that the game had changed. The Rangers' victory would encourage the Texans to fight on, and fight harder than ever before. Bandits from the south would wonder if it was worth it anymore. Such a victory had never been won against them. Within days, all of Mexico would hear of it. They would begin to wonder if they could continue to count on Texas beef for supper. The Texas Rangers had just answered that question.

McNelly rode to rejoin his men and get the troop organized for travel. When he reached them, it was plain their spirits were high, but Jesus appeared dejected. He led a fine steeldust gelding carrying a Dick Heye saddle, with an ugly crease in his shoulder. The saddle seat was covered with blood, two bullet holes in the pommel.

"Why so glum, Jesus?" McNelly asked. "I guess you wanted that horse?"

"No, *Capitán*. I don't want him. I want the man who rides him. He is Delgado's horse. Delgado is not among the dead."

No Ordinary Thunder

Chapter 21

Delgado hid in the heavy brush, and watched the Rangers gather up the bodies. He recognized Macon and the other Ranger, Plummer, from the raid on the stronghold of Zendejaz. At one point, Plummer walked within twenty feet of where he lay and killed his friend, Rojas, in a stand-up gunfight.

The bandit carried two pistols, the Ranger only one. Rojas fired until his guns clicked empty, but he panicked and let his shots go wild. Plummer was more conservative with his ammunition. He brought Rojas down with a single shot, hitting him in the hole that served as a nose.

The Ranger was close. He would be easy to kill, but Delgado had fired all his ammunition. If he tried to reload, he would betray his position, and Plummer would kill him for sure. He wasn't ready to die just yet, though he had to admit, death was probably the only thing that would release him from his pain.

He had a deep burn from a rifle bullet across the front of his left thigh, and a pistol round lodged in his right shoulder. But the wound that worried him most was the hole in his left side. He was thankful the bullet hadn't come from a Sharps .50 caliber. If it had, he'd be dead.

The bullet went clear through between the ribcage and the hipbone. He didn't think it hit anything important, but he'd lost a lot of blood and could feel himself weakening. He needed a doctor and he needed him fast, but had no choice but to wait until the Rangers cleared out. How he would get out of this mess and find help, he had no idea. If the Rangers decided to make another swing through the brush, he wouldn't have to worry about it.

At first opportunity, Delgado re-loaded his pistol with the four rounds he had left in his gunbelt, and tried to get comfortable in the brushy mud. He watched as the Rangers roped and dragged the bandits out of the marsh.

No Ordinary Thunder

They looked on the corpses with cold indifference, reacting only when they found the man with the scar on his cheek, that had quirted the Noakes woman in Nuecestown. Then the bull-dog sergeant with the big moustache had to settle them down.

They shouted all the things they wanted to do to the man, from cutting his ears off, among other things, to hanging him, even though he was dead. But the sergeant wouldn't allow it. Delgado could only imagine what they'd do if they found him.

The bullet in his shoulder hurt like hell, but the bleeding wasn't too bad. It felt like the pistol round had struck the bone and not gone in too deep. The hole in his side was another story. The wound bled profusely. He tried to staunch the bleeding by packing it with mud, but it didn't stop the flow.

He had to get away. He had to find help. If he waited much longer, he wouldn't have the strength to move. He felt himself nodding off, becoming complacent even in the face of such danger. He couldn't allow that to happen. He had to stay awake. Stay alert. If he fell asleep, they could walk up and shoot him, without him ever knowing.

The thought came to Delgado that he might not escape this time. Every man had his time to die. Maybe he'd gone as far as he was going. A man's luck only lasted so long, and up to now he'd been pretty lucky. But who could say? Maybe he still had things to do. Maybe he wasn't through killing Rangers yet.

He still had four rounds in his pistol. If it came to a fight, he'd do what he could with them. He needed only one round to finish himself, which he'd gladly do before letting the Rangers take him. If they found him alive, they'd probably hang him. They were plainly in a hanging mood. Or they might turn him over to Sandoval. He'd seen the killer riding among the Rangers. If his death was left to

No Ordinary Thunder

Sandoval, it might take a long time.

He felt so tired. Maybe, while he waited, he would take a short nap, and when he awoke, the Rangers would be gone. No, damn it. He had to stay awake!

"We lost one, boys!" he heard McNelly shout.

"Spread out. Find him. It's Delgado. Bring him in alive if you can. I want a word with him before we hang him."

Now he had no choice. It was fight or shoot himself. In a few minutes, the brush would be crawling with Rangers. He could already hear them moving slowly, cautiously, through the stinking mud.

One drew close. Close enough to shoot him. Delgado rolled to another position as fast as his wounds would allow. He cocked his pistol and made ready to fire. When he did, he saw the noise hadn't been made by a Ranger, but by a horse—a frightened, bloody, beautiful horse.

The animal had a burn on his hip, and the saddle hung under his belly. But he stood rock solid when he saw Delgado, as if waiting for the man to help him. Delgado made it to his feet and approached the horse, speaking softly, comforting him. He drew his knife and cut the cinch, letting the saddle fall into the salty mud. Mounting the horse wouldn't be easy without the saddle, but he didn't have time to fix it. He pulled the saddle out of the mud, and turned it over to use as a step. With a strength he didn't know he had, he pulled himself onto the animal's back, and walked him quietly toward the river.

The horse limped a little because of the burn, but, all in all, he was in good shape. Delgado slipped through the brush and made his escape, without firing another shot. He heard the Rangers cursing and shouting far behind him, when they found the saddle and the horse's tracks. He kicked the animal into the best lope he could muster, and held on tight to the horse's mane.

No Ordinary Thunder

#

Tensions ran high along the Rio Grande after the Palo Alto affair. Stacking the dead bandits in the plaza at Brownsville didn't bode well for Captain McNelly and the Texas Rangers. Harley argued against it, but McNelly had his mind made up. He was going to send a message.

By most, it was seen as a despicable act, meant only to incite another engagement with the bandits. They feared the engagement would be fought in the streets of their city, and their city had seen enough bloodshed. Others thought McNelly did it to bolster his status, but Harley knew better. McNelly wasn't building his own reputation, but the reputation of the Rangers. Finding themselves outnumbered was a detriment they'd lived with since their inception. They would fight to the death for Texas, no matter the odds. Either way, McNelly's message was clear. Steal cattle in Texas, and you'll pay with your life.

Rumors were rampant throughout the town. Harley heard the people talking every time he walked the streets. Some believed McNelly had bushwhacked a group of honest stockmen, merely driving their cattle to be sold at the stockyard in Brownsville. That was quickly disproved when the brands on the cattle were inspected. Some said McNelly and his Rangers were on the take—that they had cut the herd before turning them over to the law. Others said that many of the bandits tried to surrender, even waved a white flag, and were shot down like a pack of stray dogs. The Captain could have revealed his records and dispelled all the rumors. Harley encouraged him to do so. But it wasn't the rumors that bothered him. It was the merciless, hacking cough of tuberculosis.

The Rangers set up camp by the river, while McNelly checked into a hotel in Brownsville and tried to

No Ordinary Thunder

get some rest. But rest didn't come easy. The Rangers quickly grew bored waiting for McNelly to recover. He'd had their pay sent down from Austin, and they were ready to spend it. McNelly kept a tight leash on them, allowing just three men at a time to go into town, and then under strict orders of a two drink limit. No matter what was said or done, they were to defend themselves only if absolutely necessary.

Many of the citizens looked on the Rangers with scorn, even as they marched their fallen comrade to the graveyard. Though the locals might not be bandits and thieves, they had plenty of friends and relatives who were. The battle had hurt the economy. Everyone would have to do with a little less than before, and they were already getting by on less than they needed. Money from the rustling supported people on both sides of the border. One dead boy meant nothing to them.

The Rangers' blood still boiled from the fight, and they were itching for another one. Harley knew they might turn on each other soon, if they didn't find something to do. After all, a man could only wash his clothes so many times, or take so many baths, or play so many hands of poker. Within a few days, the whole troop was clean, half the men were broke, and the other half had money they couldn't go spend. Keeping a lid on the mounting pressure proved a difficult thing to do.

Salyard's presence made things no easier. In light of his performance at Palo Alto, the Captain had allowed him to stay on, determining to resolve the matter of Henry Berry Lowery when he got back on his feet. He'd given orders that Harley's Indian friend was not to leave the camp, but saw no reason to expose his identity.

Salyard kept his mouth shut about Lowery. He plainly didn't want to share the reward, but all the Rangers knew something was brewing. The friction between the two was obvious. Neither man took his eyes off the other.

No Ordinary Thunder

Salyard went to great pains to make sure neither Lowery nor Macon ever caught him alone, away from the safety of the camp.

Eli had come through the battle unscathed, and breathing the breath of new life. He worked around the camp with a vigor Harley couldn't remember ever seeing.

"I swear, Eli," he said. "A little blood-curdlin' combat seems to have done wonders for you. I expect you're anxious for another charge."

"I don't know if I'd say that. But, damn, it's good to be alive. I can't recall when I felt so fine."

"That's good to hear. I hope you feel the same when I say what I've got to say. I'm gonna ask McNelly to let me ride on over to Rio Grande City and take a look around. I want you to go with me, if he'll allow it. You game?"

"Hell, yes! I'd be proud to ride with you anywhere, Harley. And I won't let you down again, neither."

"You didn't let me down. Sometimes a man falls into things he can't find his way out of alone. I was just as drunk as you, and for a lot longer. It's over. Forget it."

Harley was aware that forgetting wasn't easy. He only wanted to reassure his old partner. He didn't know what Eli drank to forget, or if he drank to forget anything. But he certainly knew why *he* did—Abigail. The problem was that the drinking didn't make him forget. It only clouded his thinking for a while. He would never forget Abigail Mendenhall—her flashing blue eyes, her golden hair. Her miserable existence in that damned asylum.

"I didn't know you boys were so attached to each other," Dixon said. "You want me to leave you alone?"

"No," Harley said. "I want you to get on your horse, and get the hell outta here while the gettin's good. Salyard's already told McNelly your secret. Sooner or later, he'll tell someone else. When he does, there won't be any stoppin' 'em."

"What are you talkin' about, Harley?" Eli asked.

No Ordinary Thunder

"What secret?"

"Don't let it worry you, Pard. Dixon knows what I'm talkin' about."

"Glad you've got my best interest at heart," Dixon said. "It's a real comfort to know somebody cares. But if you think you're goin' back to see about that boy without me, then you'd better think again. Besides, you're bound to get into somethin' you can't handle on your own. I swear, you're a damn lightning rod."

"I ain't gonna be on my own, remember? I'm takin' Eli with me."

"If McNelly lets you. Hell, he may not let you go at all."

"He'll let me. You've been ordered under guard. If you try to escape, you might get shot, but that's a helluva lot better than swingin'. I wanna find out what's goin' on in Las Cuevas. Salinas is sure to be plannin' somethin'. I wanna know what it is, and so will McNelly."

"When you gonna see the Captain?" Eli asked.

"Well, there's no time like the present. I'll head up there, right now. Eli, you stick close to Dixon and keep an eye on things. If Mr. Salyard does anything suspicious, let me know about it."

"Y'know, Harley," Dixon said. "I'm surprised I've lived this long without you to take care o' me. Your concern is really touching."

Harley saddled his horse and rode to the hotel, though it was easily within walking distance. He lived by the old cavalry principle that a trooper never walked a single step, if there was a good horse standing ready. The roan liked the exercise, no matter how little, and entertained himself by watching the activity in the street. Harley kicked the dust from his boots, and stepped inside the lobby.

"I'd like to see Captain McNelly," he said.

"I'd like to see him leave," said the old man behind

No Ordinary Thunder

the desk, "only he don't never come out. I have to take his meals to him, then go pick up the dishes. Clean sheets every day. The man sweats like a leaky bucket. When am I supposed to get anything else done, can you tell me that? My employees won't even go in there."

The hotel proprietor plainly didn't care to have a consumptive boarding in his establishment. But McNelly, in his own convincing way, would not take no for an answer. The grumpy little owner directed Harley to the Captain's room, then made the long trip to the kitchen, mumbling something about losing rental business, and all the leftover pot roast he had.

"Captain!" Harley said, as he knocked on the door.
"It's me, Captain. Harley Macon."

A ragged, whispered voice invited him in. Harley hesitated, but couldn't let the Captain wait. He screwed a smile on his face and opened the door.

"Howdy, Captain. How you feelin' today?"
"How do I look?"
"A little better," Harley lied. "I expect we'll be movin' out soon."
"What do you want?"
"Well, I was thinkin' about driftin' over to Rio Grande City, with your permission, and checkin' on that boy we brought back from Mexico. While I'm there, maybe I can find out what's cookin' down south. The Mexican Army can't go long without beef. There's bound to be somethin' playin' at Las Cuevas. We can...."

McNelly fell into a coughing fit that lasted far too long for Harley's liking. He wondered if the whole damn thing was finished. How could the Captain go on in this condition? The man probably didn't weigh a hundred and twenty pounds. His skin was white, and his eyes were black. The waste basket beside the bed held a half-dozen bloody handkerchiefs. Harley poured McNelly a glass of water and waited for the coughing to stop.

No Ordinary Thunder

"We?" the Captain asked.

"Yes, sir. I thought I'd take Eli with me, if it's all right with you."

McNelly wiped the blood from his beard, and added the handkerchief to the basket. He drank the water and lay still as death, staring at the ceiling, his breathing hoarse and raw.

"Where's Sandoval?"

"We ain't seen him in a while. I expect he's out there among 'em."

"Let's wait until morning. If Sandoval doesn't show up, you can go. Take your friend Lowery with you, too. I've never set a wanted man free. You'll be responsible for him. But if he's not around, I might forget about him."

"Thank you, Captain. He's frothin' to go. What about Salyard?"

"Salyard's not a Ranger, and he's not wanted. He can come and go as he pleases. I can't hold him. I can order him out of camp, but if I do, he might follow you. He just might anyway, once you leave. He wants that reward mighty bad."

Harley thought it over a minute, and decided the Captain was right. There was nothing he could do to control Salyard. The man was as free as the breeze.

"Yes, sir, he just might. Well, if he does, he'll have to take his chances. Mr. Lowery ain't an easy man to shade."

"I'm sure that's true. But I don't condone murder. You be sure your friend knows that."

"Yes, sir, Captain. I'll be sure and tell him."

#

Salyard didn't like it when Sergeant Armstrong announced Dixon's reprieve. The thought of his lucrative

No Ordinary Thunder

future riding away didn't set well with him. Macon hadn't announced where he and the others were headed. He just spoke privately with Sergeant Armstrong, who said they were off on Ranger business. But Salyard had a pretty good idea. Maybe back to Rio Grande City to see about the boy, and that fine Mexican woman. There was little question of her feelings for Macon.

She was plainly a woman worth riding a long way to see. Her buxom figure gave a man plenty to think about in the late, lonely hours of the night. Salyard thought of her often when he tried to sleep, or when he was alone in the bushes doing his business. She was the kind of woman he'd dreamed of for years, in that stinking Mexican prison. Dreamed of until he was raw from dreaming.

But that wasn't the only thing women were good for. If she was willing to hide the boy for a Texas Ranger, she might be useful in other ways—like information. Maybe she knew of some gold making its way across the river. He watched as the three men saddled their horses, wolfed down a little salt pork, and braced Dad Smith's scalding coffee.

The weather was cool for a late June morning. Salyard listened closely as the Rangers huddled around the fire, murmuring their complaints of taking root by the river. But he heard nothing concerning Macon's destination. The men wanted action, but knew they weren't going to get it. Why didn't the Captain send some orders, some word? Why were they just sitting here? The bandits weren't going to cross stolen cattle right in front of them. Hell, Cortina might be gathering forces to cross the river and wipe them out. Every man among them wished they could go with Harley, but instead, they settled for a card game.

"How long you gonna be?" Sergeant Armstrong asked.

"Don't know," Harley said. "But I'll get word to you soon as I learn somethin'. Could take a while. Salinas

No Ordinary Thunder

might be layin' low."

"Well, you boys be careful. I don't know what's goin' on with this fella, Dixon, but I've got a feelin' Salyard's gonna be stickin' close to you."

"His bad luck if he does. We've put up with him about as long as we're goin' to."

"What's this all about, Harley? Why'd the Captain place Dixon under camp arrest?"

"I can't tell you, Sarge. Salyard's trouble. I can tell you that much. We need to shake him. If we don't, it's gonna go bad for him. If he tries to follow us, you think you can stall him a while?"

"Oh, I can maybe think o' somethin'."

"Good. Take care, now."

Harley offered his hand and mounted the roan. Salyard watched as the three of them rode north out of camp. He saw it as a feeble attempt to throw him off the trail. If Macon thought such a trick would work, he needed to consider his adversary. Salyard gathered his saddle and headed for the remuda, just in time to hear the men shouting that the horses were loose.

No Ordinary Thunder

Chapter 22

Salyard struggled to recall the lay of the terrain, on his ride back to Rio Grande City. He had only to cut south until he came to the river, then follow it west to get where he was going. But he wanted a route that would keep him hidden from anyone he might see on the trail. Riding the river was too dangerous. Rustlers, gypsies, and river pirates were never far from its banks. The trip east to join McNelly and the Rangers had been pretty blurry, his head swimming from the blow of Lowery's pistol. Try as he might, he could not locate a familiar landmark, adequate cover, or even a little shade. Only the arc of the sun kept him on course.

He hadn't had time to learn much about the country, on his way to Mexico with General Shelby. They passed through the state as fast as they could, traveling mostly at night in an effort to avoid the army and the blazing Texas sun—the same miserable sun that beat down on him now. How he wished he *could* travel at night, but on his own, without the river to guide him, he was sure he'd get lost.

So far he hadn't seen anyone. He saw plenty of tracks, but didn't think they belonged to Macon and the others. Most of the tracks pointed south, not west—a few horses, some of them driving small bunches of cattle. Salyard was no tracker, but he couldn't think of any reason to drive cattle through such a barren wasteland, unless the cattle were stolen. Only a thief, or a Texas Ranger, would frequent this terrible place.

The scattered horses back at the Ranger camp only slowed him down a few minutes. Macon and the others went north when they left, but Salyard was sure that was a ruse. Why would they go north? Everything they'd done up to now revolved around the Rio Grande. He'd followed their tracks a short distance, only to find that they'd split up and disappeared. No need to try and follow them further.

No Ordinary Thunder

He couldn't track them anyway. Rio Grande City, that's where they were going. Salyard was sure of it. He would ride until sundown, get a little sleep, and strike out again in the cool of the morning.

The following day brought more of the same. Mile after mile of empty prairie and merciless sun, with only the occasional rattlesnake or tarantula crossing his path to break the monotony. Salyard did his best to ration his water, but the sun was so hot, the air so dry, he knew it wouldn't last long. He'd already gone through a third of his canteen, with not a drop of moisture in sight. If he didn't find something soon, he'd have to give the remainder of the water to his horse. The little bit of dried meat he chewed on, only made him thirstier. Well, he could always make for the Rio if he had to.

Then shortly before sundown, he smelled the smoke. He figured the fire must be hidden in an arroyo. He could see no sign of life on the prairie. He judged the camp to be no more than a half-mile away.

Salyard dismounted and tied his bandana over his horse's nose, to keep him from nickering at the horses in the camp. He wanted a place to leave the animal and approach on foot, but fear of being left without a mount persuaded him otherwise. The horses had traveled together a while, were accustomed to the smells of their companions. Maybe they'd just let him walk in without any fuss at all. He knew it was a lot to hope for.

Salyard didn't think Macon would kill him without a call. But Lowery would. There could be no doubt about that. Now that he'd caught up to them, he wasn't sure what to do. He didn't see any point in negotiating a surrender. In the first place, Lowery wouldn't do it. The longer he tried to talk him into it, the better the chance one of the others would seize the opportunity to kill him. No, it would have to be an ambush. He'd have to kill Lowery first, then Macon. But killing two such deadly gunmen was a tall

No Ordinary Thunder

order, indeed. He'd need every element on his side. Everything would have to play out perfectly. Hopefully, after that, if it all went as planned, Plummer would give up, let him take Lowery's body, and he'd leave Texas a mighty rich man. Hell, he might even give Plummer a share of the reward, if he didn't cause him any trouble. If he did, well then, he'd just kill Plummer, too.

The walk to the arroyo seemed to take an hour. As Salyard drew nearer, he began to hear the voices of the men. They were jovial, passing a bottle around. But they weren't voices he knew. *Mexicans*! Two of them and one white man. Rustlers or bounty hunters? No matter. He had to get the hell out of there, now!

Just as he settled into the saddle, Salyard's mount picked the most inopportune moment to call to the concealed horses. In seconds, three rifles peeked over the edge of the arroyo, all of them pointed at Salyard, who immediately threw his hands in the air and proceeded to ask for mercy.

"I didn't hear anything. I didn't see anything. Just let me go, and I'll be on my way. I don't even know you fellas."

The mumbling among the men did not sound promising. They cursed, then laughed, then cursed some more, never once taking their eyes off him. Salyard was trapped, but not one to quickly surrender. He wondered if he should risk an escape. He was still a good distance from the bank of the arroyo. They'd been drinking. Maybe they couldn't shoot straight. Hell, not every man that carried a gun was a good shot. He, himself, was only fair, unless he had a stationary target. But he thought too long and the men in the arroyo made the decision for him.

"Step off that horse, mister," the white man said.

"Don't try anything. We'll kill you if you do. But you already knew that, didn't you."

"Yes, sir, I sure did. Don't mean no harm," Salyard

No Ordinary Thunder

said, as he carefully slipped down off his mount. "Ain't lookin' for trouble. Just makin' my way west. How far is it to Rio Grande City?"

"It's a long ride for a man alone. You're takin' quite a chance out here by yourself. Dangerous country, hereabouts."

"So I see. I'm friendly, mister. Got some business in Rio Grande City. Just tryin' to get to town, that's all."

"What kinda business?"

"The best kind—a woman."

"Well now, that's the best kind, all right. Come closer. Let's have a look at you."

Salyard walked forward. In the rapidly diminishing light, he could see their eyes carefully studying, trying to place him. Then, in an instant, he knew he'd been recognized.

"Ay, *amigo!*" one of the Mexicans said. "This man comes from the prison in Monterrey. I have seen him there working, many times."

"Aiee! Two hundred dollars reward," the other one shouted. "*Coronel* Garralaga wants this man very bad. We will take him back in the morning, *eh?*"

"Wait a minute," the white man said. "What about your friends, mister? Where are they?"

Salyard didn't know what to say. Should he try to make a deal? Would they trade the two hundred dollars on his head, for the six hundred waiting in Rio Grande City? Or would they want it all? The latter seemed the most likely. He certainly wasn't going to tell them about Lowery. At least, not yet. If it came to saving his life, he would, but not until then. The sad truth was that he was in a hell of a mess, with little or nothing he could do about it.

"Can't remember, huh? Well, put your hands up and come join us. We'll talk about your future."

The future seemed a thing far away. Salyard hadn't heard if the reward on him and the others was payable dead

No Ordinary Thunder

or alive. Garralaga might want them brought in alive, so he could have the pleasure of hanging them like he did Father Molino and the girl. If not, well, dead men were a lot less trouble to transport. Either way, he was caught. His fate lay in the hands of these men. By the look of them, killers all.

He led his horse into the arroyo and tied him alongside the other mounts, where he was roughly disarmed by a fierce looking Mexican with a rope scar around his neck. The Mexican took him by the shirt and threw him to the ground.

"Where did you say they were, *amigo*?"

Salyard fought back the urge to lunge at his assailant. What chance did he have of survival? He composed himself and asked for a cup of coffee instead.

"That's a good idea," the white man said. "Let's have some coffee and talk this over."

Upon closer inspection, something about the white man seemed familiar to Salyard. The way he moved maybe? The way he spoke? Then, in a moment, he had his answer. It all became clear to him. Certain of his position, he took a chance and confronted the man.

"Corporal Bell?"

Bell was stunned. "Corporal? Nobody's called me corporal since Shelby left Mexico years ago." He searched his memory for a hint of the old man's identity, but nothing came to mind. "Who the hell are you, mister?"

"First Sergeant Salyard. We came south together with General Shelby. Remember?"

"Sarge? You were in that prison? By God, I didn't know. Hell, I thought all you boys were dead. We all thought that."

"Most of 'em are. There might be a few left in there, but I didn't have time to look for 'em." Salyard rose and offered his hand to a friend he hadn't seen in years.

"Ay, I don't like this, *amigo*," the Mexican with the scar protested. "This man is your friend? Maybe you care

No Ordinary Thunder

more for him than the reward, *eh*? And where are the others? Lying out on the prairie waiting to kill us, maybe?"

"You ain't gonna turn me in for a lousy two hundred dollars, are you, Corporal?"

"No, I ain't." Bell suddenly pushed Salyard out of the way, drew his pistol and fired two rounds, murdering his unsuspecting companions. "But they would have."

Salyard marveled at the man's speed and deliberation. The Mexicans lay one beside the other, smoke exuding from the holes in their chests.

"I'll be damned. You're pretty handy with that gun," he said.

"Yeah. I've been gettin' plenty o' practice these last few years. Care to ride on? Gonna be a fine moon tonight."

"You just gonna leave 'em?"

"Yeah. They'd do the same for me."

"Good enough. Best offer I've had since I got here."

The men stripped the bandits of their meager belongings, tied their horses together, and led them out of the arroyo. Conversation turned to stories of the war, of life in prison and the Texas Rangers. But Salyard could only think of the advantage Bell's gun would give him when he faced Macon and the others. Who better to share the reward with than an old army buddy. And besides, maybe Bell would catch a bullet himself. It could happen.

"What's so important in Rio Grande City?" Bell asked.

"You ever heard of Henry Berry Lowery?"

#

Carlita had come to dote on Bobby, and he in turn had developed a patient's crush on her. She was more than willing to sleep on the davenport in her now off-limits room, and allow Bobby to keep the bed. But even her most

No Ordinary Thunder

select clientele were beginning to wonder if she'd retired from the world's oldest profession. Hiding the boy was becoming a bigger chore than she'd imagined. But he wasn't getting much better.

He still coughed, and hacked, and ran his fevers, though she hadn't seen him spit up any blood in a while. He tried to be gallant, even flirt with her, but his strength being so depleted, his attentiveness was usually short-lived. Soon he'd be unconscious again, struggling with the monsters in his dreams. Other times, she'd awake in the small hours of the night and find him staring wantonly at her, as she had a few minutes ago. He'd stayed awake just long enough to look into her eyes and kiss her hand. Men! They couldn't get women off their minds, even when they were sick.

But caring for Bobby had changed her, made her see the harsh realities of the life she'd led—the unabashed cruelty of the men she associated with. More and more, she thought of a settled life. A life with a man who would always be there. She'd had enough of men who could so readily rape and murder.

Anyone who could torture a young boy so, had no right to live in her estimation. When he slept peacefully, which wasn't often, he was like a small child, cooing at the pleasant visions in his mind. Then abruptly things would change and it would be all she could do to keep him quiet, his murmurings given over to snarls of murder and revenge.

Carlita could not bear the thought of Bobby being returned to the authorities. She kept a shotgun handy beside the boy's bed, and remained ever vigilant to his protection and care. Which is why she nearly jumped out of her skin when a tap came at the window.

"Carlita, honey. It's me, Harley."

Carlita rushed to the window and peeked out the shade. There stood Harley with his old, familiar smile. And next to him, Eli Plummer, who she never thought she'd see

No Ordinary Thunder

again. Looking back on recent events, the horrible things that had happened since he left, she could now hardly blame him for going.

"Come around to the door," she said. "I'll let you in."

Carlita hustled the men through the hallway into her room, barely noticed by the two house girls in the parlor, who were far more interested in each other. After all, Carlita owned the establishment. She could have two men if she wanted.

"Harley!" she said, throwing herself in his arms. "I heard about the Palo Alto fight. Thank God you're alive." Hesitating but a moment, Carlita embraced Eli as well, and unexpectedly asked his forgiveness.

"You were right to go when you did," she said. "I was wrong not to listen. I know you were trying to protect me. I wish now I'd gone with you. I'm sorry."

Eli hardly knew what to say. Such a welcome was the last thing he expected.

"It's all right," he said. "I'm glad you're safe, now."

"How's the boy?" Harley asked. "He still don't look so good."

"He comes and goes," Carlita said. "Where is your spooky friend?"

"Outside watchin' the horses. Lewd women make him nervous. Hear anything from across the river?"

"Am I to be your informant, now?"

"The job's open if you want it, honey. Didn't see many tracks on the way over here. Just small bunches. Salinas backin' off?"

"I haven't heard, but business has been a little slow. Not many cowboys in town."

"Well, maybe we did some good. At least, bought ourselves some time."

"Harley?" Bobby said. "Is that you? Are we ready to ride?"

No Ordinary Thunder

"He's delirious," Carlita said. "He often talks like you're here. It must be your voice."

"No, Bobby, we ain't ridin' out yet. You've got plenty o' time to rest up. Besides, where else you gonna find such a pretty nurse?"

"I think somebody's outside," Bobby said. He tried to sit up, but couldn't make it. He took Carlita by the hand, then drifted back into the dream world.

"His fevers still run high," she said. "He sometimes thinks someone is trying to come in through the window."

"Damn!" Harley said. "I'd hoped he'd be in better shape, by now."

"He is, then he's not. When he has the fever, he talks a lot, but makes little sense."

"Well, he's makin' sense this time," Eli said. "There *is* somebody outside. I can hear 'em talkin'."

Harley peeked carefully around the shade, and cursed under his breath.

"It's that damned Salyard! And he's got our man cold. Bell's with him. Where the hell did he come from?"

"See any others?" Eli asked. "There might be more outta sight."

"Nobody else I can see. Just the two of 'em."

Harley checked the load in his pistol. "By God, I think it's high time we put an end to this."

"Let's get 'em," Eli said, on his way to the door.

"Wait! We bust out there now, they'll kill him for sure. We'll go out the front door and circle the house. Don't fire 'til I do. Sorry to upset your customers, honey, but we've got it to do."

Carlita led them through the empty parlor and out the front door, giving each of them a kiss on the cheek for luck.

"Be careful," she said.

"That's the plan," Harley replied. "Stay away from

No Ordinary Thunder

the windows."

#

Henry Berry Lowery, exhausted from the trip, had only closed his eyes for a moment when he heard the sound of cocking hammers. Salyard and Bell sat their horses grinning. They'd captured their fortune without firing a shot. Salyard covered Lowery with his rifle, determined not to miss when the time came to kill the man that was soon to make him rich. Bell kept his rifle trained on the back door, casually waiting to shoot whoever came outside.

"Get on your horse, Mr. Lowery," Salyard said. "Nice and quiet."

"No. I don't think I will."

"No?"

"You heard me. If you want me, you can have at it right here. You too, Bell. Make your move."

Lowery's calm in the grip of such a tense situation shocked Salyard. He had fully expected the man to mount up and ride, as any thinking man would. But it didn't happen. Lowery stood his ground without so much as a flinch.

"I said, get your ass on that horse, mister!" Salyard walked his mount one step closer. Lowery didn't move a muscle. He just offered Salyard a contemptuous glare.

"You scared, Salyard? You scared to make your play?"

"You want it here, you son of a bitch? You'll get it here!"

His venomous words still hung in the air, when a deafening shotgun blast blew out the window, filling Salyard's face and chest with buckshot and splintered glass. His horse reared in terror, unseating his rider, who caught a foot in the stirrup as he fell. The horse galloped wildly into

No Ordinary Thunder

the night, dragging First Sergeant Salyard to whatever hell awaited him.

Bell whirled in his saddle and went into action, but not nearly fast enough to go against Lowery. The outlaw chief quickly filled each hand, and shot him to pieces before Bell even knew that it happened. He weaved in the saddle a moment or two, memorizing the face of his killer.

"If I'd… only known who I was… travelin' with… when we went to Monterrey, I might've… been a rich man, now." Bell gasped and drew his last ragged breath, slumped over, and dropped from his horse.

Bobby Fallon, pale and sick, leaned on the empty window frame, barely able to hold the heavy shotgun. With an effort that took all the strength he could summon, he had repaid the man who saved his life. Harley and Eli rounded the corner, just as he fell out the window.

"Catch him," Harley shouted.

Lowery turned and caught the boy, and rushed him back into the house. "Maybe we oughta get him outta here," he said. "The law's bound to show up soon."

"Don't worry about the law," Carlita said. "The sheriff is a friend of mine. He comes by to see the girls."

Harley laughed. "I might've known."

"Put him on the bed and go. I will tell the sheriff something."

"We'll get back to you," Harley said. "Take care, now. Let's go, boys."

As they filed out of the room, Eli, overcome by the feelings he'd long suppressed, pulled Carlita close to him, and kissed her long and deep. She drew away angry, but just for a moment. Taking Eli by the shirt, so hard she pulled tufts of hair from his chest, she returned the kiss with equal passion, and pushed him out the door.

No Ordinary Thunder

Chapter 23

The Texas Rangers found themselves with little to do, as the long, hot summer of '75 passed quietly into the fall. Harley spent much of his time telling stories of the war, and teaching younger hands the benefits and pitfalls of draw poker. His theory was simple. The less money a greenhorn had in his pocket, the less chance he'd have of falling into temptation.

The fight at Palo Alto had succeeded in slowing the rustling down, if not completely stopping it. Smaller bunches of cattle were now the target, with fewer thieves involved. The price of beef in Mexico soared to twelve dollars per head. Cortina had big contracts to fill, and had a hard time getting it done. The ranchers continued to fight back, though their stand had only a marginal effect. Violence and degradation along the Strip, at least were no longer the norm.

The Rangers, however, were taken to task for their behavior after the battle. McNelly took a lot of grief over his approach to law enforcement. Citizens all over the state were outraged at the reports of the bandits being stacked in the plaza like so much wood. Changes in the way the Rangers did business would have to be implemented.

No more would McNelly's aggressive tactics be tolerated. When a bandit was captured, he was to be delivered to the nearest law enforcement official, jailed and tried by a group of his peers—which just as often as not, consisted of men who somehow profited from his crimes.

Bandits made a mockery of the system, throwing their hands up and surrendering without a word of complaint, then riding out of town as free as a bird before the Rangers unsaddled their horses. Harley had seen it all before. The citizens crying the loudest for law and order, were the first to protest when the game got too rough.

Captain McNelly suffered terrible bouts with his

No Ordinary Thunder

illness, sometimes retreating to his home in Burton to recoup under the care of his wife. The Rangers would often go weeks without seeing him. As soon as possible, he was back in the fight, but the forays didn't last long. He was getting worse and the Rangers knew it.

Nervousness and boredom had them grouchy, anxious, needing something to do. They worried about their jobs. How long would Texas pay them to make mostly unsuccessful scouts throughout the Nueces Strip? How would Texas look on them, if they didn't finish what they set out to do?

Many of them spoke of leaving, of finding other jobs. But what other jobs were there? Cowboying paid less money—and even less than *that* for a green hand, which most of them were. The thought of looking at a cow's ass all the way to the Kansas Stockyards, didn't hold much appeal for them.

A few of the men had different ideas, Ira Newton and Lewis Gould among them. These were the men Harley worried about most. The wild daredevils who thought the reaper would never come for them. Young men who saw it all as a grand adventure. They spent their time restlessly cleaning and twirling their pistols. The tool of their trade. The one thing they were really good at.

There were other ways a man could make a living with a gun. Crossing the line was an easy thing to do. After riding with the Texas Rangers, chasing bandits, killers, and Comanche horse thieves, what would a man do, clerk in a store? Become a drunken sheriff like Eli had?

Things were changing all over the country. The Red River War in Northern Texas had finally ended. Quanah and the last band of free Comanches had surrendered and gone in to Fort Sill, to begin their new lives as peaceful reservation Indians.

Colonel George Armstrong Custer regularly guided columns of greed-crazed gold miners into the Black Hills

No Ordinary Thunder

of Dakota territory, land expressly ceded to the native people, "for as long as the grass shall grow."

People in the East wanted ice in their drinking water, cleaner streets and a softer life, with more leisure time to spend reading about courageous escapades in the Wild West. And in their camp near Edinburg, the Texas Rangers waited for some communication from their Captain. It came along the middle of November.

The telegram arrived by military courier, instructing the Rangers to mount up and strike for Ringgold Barracks at Rio Grande City on the double. The army had missed the river crossing of approximately two hundred and fifty head of stolen cattle, assumed to be bound for Las Cuevas. Captain McNelly, determined to stop the rustling once and for all, intended to ride into Mexico if he had to, and bring the cattle back.

The Rangers made the fifty-five mile trip from their camp near Edinburg to Ringgold Barracks in five hours—a ride Harley was sure would go down in the history books, if there was anyone left alive to tell the tale. They unsaddled their horses and left them to graze without a guard. The animals were exhausted. They weren't going anywhere.

Captain McNelly looked about the same as he did the last time Harley saw him, but he moved with a renewed vigor. He had a job to do and he was going to do it. The devil take the hindmost.

Jesus Sandoval showed up for the fight. Like McNelly, the Rangers hadn't seen him in a while, but there was little chance of him missing such an event. Riding beside him was Henry Berry Lowery, who had mysteriously disappeared after the Salyard/Bell killing, just to be on the safe side.

No Ordinary Thunder

Harley hoped he'd never see the man again—that he would go back home to his family. But he had to admit, Lowery was hell on wheels when the chips were down. A man like him could sure make a difference, with the scales tipped like they were.

The conversation McNelly carried on with Captain Randlett of Ringgold Barracks, about waiting for word from the consul at Matamoros, and waiting for approval of military support, ended the same way it began—with McNelly chewing his cigar like a piece of beefsteak and Randlett shaking his head in disbelief. Captain McNelly lined his Rangers up about midnight, and gave it to them straight.

"Boys, I've been informed that we will receive no support from the army if we cross into Mexico. Invasion, they call it. Seems that's against the rules. But Salinas and his bunch don't play by the rules. They come over here and take what they want, then high-tail it across the river where we can't get a hand on them. That all stops tonight.

"I can't order you to go with me. You signed on to fight in Texas, not Mexico. But I need you, boys. I can't promise you'll make it back, but I *can* promise you a damn good fight. Any man that wants to volunteer, step across the road."

Every man crossed, twenty-nine in all. Just thirty men, counting McNelly, against a bandit who could muster probably three hundred in an hour or less. There was no way of knowing how many already occupied the *rancho*. Harley remembered quite a crowd when he and Lowery were there. *Vaqueros*, slaves, women, kids. You didn't have to be a man to pull a trigger.

The Captain decided that most of the men would go over on foot, to increase the odds of surprise. A small rowboat, moored on the other side of the river, was the means he would use to get them there.

While the Rangers worked their way back and forth

No Ordinary Thunder

on the boat, Harley made his concerns known to Eli and Lowery. He also made another futile attempt to get Lowery to pack up and get out.

"Y'know, Harley, I'm startin' to think you don't want me around," Lowery said. "Kinda hurts my feelin's the way you're always tryin' to run me off."

"I just want you to go back to your family while you can. Hell, maybe you can go get 'em and bring 'em back to Texas. Ain't we been through all this?"

"Yeah. And you're the one who keeps bringin' it up! I went to see my family, if you'd like to know. Met 'em in Alabama. Where the hell you think I've been? The kids'r growin' like weeds, and Rhoda's prettier'n ever. But nothin's changed back there. The authorities still want me. They've killed off nearly all the rest. Only one was freed by the court. Rhoda don't wanna live in Texas. She wants to stay close to her kinfolks. So, Mr. Macon, when I get ready to go, I'll go. There won't be anything you can do to stop me. Unless you wanna arrest me."

"Very funny. Get in the boat."

#

Delgado woke early, considering his long night of indulgence. A pretty young girl lay beside him. She could be no more than fifteen. He couldn't remember her name, but her presence, the smells from the night they'd shared, woke him even further.

The delivery of the beef put General Salinas in an exceptionally good mood, it being the first large raid in some time. He provided lavishly for his guests, with plenty of food, wine, and willing women. Delgado graciously accepted the hospitality.

But with prices so high, and fewer men to handle the stock, low-level bandits were now trying to steal the

No Ordinary Thunder

smaller herds driven into Mexico. It was unlikely they would try to take such a large bunch, but to be sure the cattle made it to Monterrey, Salinas requested a troop of soldiers to escort the herd back to the garrison. The soldiers arrived late in the evening, a hundred and fifty or more.

Delgado's wounds had healed nicely. He'd spent nearly a month under the care of various women, who not only nursed him back to health, but also saw to his other needs. The slow summer gave him time to make the trip to Tampico with Cortina. At the General's side, he was treated like royalty, handed anything he wished for. While there he met many women from Cuba, which only made him want to go all the more. Maybe one day, when everything was settled, he would take a ship to the island like he'd often dreamed.

He was in good shape now. The hard ride into Texas had done him no harm, and he was ready for action. The soldiers would probably rest a day, maybe two, then return to the garrison. He would be more than happy to ride along. There was always plenty to do in Monterrey.

Las Cuevas stood silent in the gray morning light. No doubt the entire crew was sleeping off the night before. He had nearly fallen back to sleep himself, when the girl touched his manhood and brought him to life. She giggled at his rapid response.

Delgado took her by the hair and guided her gently under the covers. He lay back and tried to remember the girl's name, but he didn't try very hard. The girl had talent. Her technique made it difficult to concentrate. Besides, names mattered little in the throes of passion. All that mattered was the pleasure, the ecstasy. Delgado had almost reached that point, when he heard the echo of the first gunshots.

#

No Ordinary Thunder

Captain McNelly gave the order to fire, at the first sign of activity in the camp. But heavy ground fog had somehow thrown the Rangers off course. They had mistakenly attacked the line camp at Cachuttas about a mile south of the river, eliminating any possibility of surprise at the main camp of Las Cuevas. The inhabitants of Cachuttas, however, were taken completely by surprise.

They, too, had been celebrating the night before, and were in no better shape than those at the main camp. A few horses standing tied at the fence broke away and ran off when the bandits stumbled from their cover. Half asleep, fumbling with pants, boots, and control of their weapons, the bandits tried to make a fight of it. They got off no more than a shot or two before the Rangers cut them down. The Rangers suffered no casualties in the skirmish, but left several dead men in the brush. Some said twelve, some said more. To McNelly's astonishment, a few of them were Mexican soldiers.

"Oh, Lord," he said. "What the hell are these troops doing here?"

"They were not here yesterday," Jesus said. "They must have come in last night."

McNelly wasn't sure what to do, now that he'd lost the element of surprise. No doubt they'd heard the shooting down the road at Las Cuevas. Surely Salinas and his killers would be ready and waiting for them. And how many soldiers would the Rangers have to face?

The sun had burned off some of the fog, but it was still pretty heavy in the brush. The Rangers waited while McNelly talked it over with Jesus. But if they waited much longer, things would only get worse. Then, without a signal, McNelly and Jesus started jogging down the trail toward the main camp. The Texas Rangers, without hesitation, fell in close behind them.

A slow mile that seemed like ten, brought them to a ground swell near the edge of the camp at Las Cuevas.

No Ordinary Thunder

Below them lay the *rancho* Harley had described in detail to Captain McNelly. But it was the Rangers' turn to be surprised.

The drunken, sleepy, hung-over mob was still trying to catch their horses. When they finally got mounted, they sent out four scouts, all of which were shot from the saddle and hit the ground almost as one. The bandits had no idea the Rangers were so close. It was unlikely they even recognized what was happening. The shots from Cachuttas could have been fired in celebration, for all they knew. They were simply going to check.

At McNelly's command, the Rangers opened fire on the remaining bandits, nearly every shot dropping a horse or rider. The bandits fired, but could not find a target. Loose horses charged wildly through the brush. Rangers scrambled to get out of their way. Panic-stricken bandits darted for cover. Those who could catch a horse, mounted and galloped from the camp in every direction. The Texas Rangers, with the best cover around, settled in for some stylish shooting. The bandits continued looking for mounted riders. They hadn't yet even seen the Rangers in the brush.

Rancho Las Cuevas came alive, the entire camp in confusion. A good sized band raced out to locate the attackers, and blindly rode straight to their line. McNelly got off the first shot. After that, the bandits didn't have a chance. The Rangers shot them down like sitting ducks.

The bandits had no plan, no leader. It was all going too easy until a large, mounted force rode in from the direction of Camargo. Leading the men was General Juan Salinas, who in no time had assembled a large contingent of men around him. He ordered the men to split up and flank the Rangers. McNelly immediately saw his plan.

"Fall back to the river, boys!" he shouted. "Fall back! If they get behind us, we'll be trapped."

Bullets tore through the brush, as the Rangers began

No Ordinary Thunder

their retreat to the Rio Grande. The bandits approached the brush slowly at first, having already tried two frontal attacks, only to have their men shot to pieces. Their confusion made it plain they didn't know who, or what, they were fighting. They just knew there were a lot of guns in the brush. McNelly put it down as just pure luck. Had the bandits known the small number of their adversary, the Rangers would have easily been wiped out.

The boom of the Rangers' big Sharps carbines frightened the bandits' horses, helping to keep them at bay. But the bandits kept pushing through the heavy brush, firing, spurring their mounts forward.

The Rangers had the advantage of distance with the Sharps carbine, a weapon far more effective at long range than the bandits' Winchesters. They laid down a wall of gunfire—retreating, reloading, retreating again. But the Rangers were heavily outnumbered. More men had fallen in behind Salinas, stacking the odds three or four to one. Captain McNelly and the Rangers were still a long way from the river.

#

Bobby held Carlita in his arms, and tried to comfort her as they listened to the echoes of gunfire from across the river. She flinched at the sound of every report. Her tears soaked the front of the shirt she bought him. Never had she heard such fighting. Hundreds of shots interrupted the still morning. Rio Grande City lay quiet as a tomb.

Word of the Rangers' arrival the previous evening had spread through the town within minutes. Soldiers being entertained at Carlita's whorehouse were summoned to Ringgold Barracks at once. Other men, enjoying themselves in the house, hurried home to their wives and families. The streets, in minutes, resembled a ghost town.

No Ordinary Thunder

Captain McNelly made no bones about his plan to ford the Rio if need be. Apparently he'd deemed it necessary.

The worst of it for Carlita was knowing that Harley and Eli were probably in the middle of the battle. Harley's secret of rejoining the Rangers had been exposed the first time a newspaper reporter learned of his involvement. His name was plastered on every front page in Texas, reminding the citizens of his heroics in the war, of his excellent service to Texas in the past.

But the secret no longer mattered. The news made the people feel vindicated, reassured them the matter was in good hands. McNelly needed every brave man to ride with him. Harley Macon was back in the saddle.

Carlita knew what was at stake. If the Rangers lost the battle, any hope of peace on the Strip would be lost. Cortina and Salinas would rob Texas blind. How could she have ever fallen in with such men? With men who could do such terrible things? Bobby had made a complete recovery from the tortures he had endured, but only because of men like Harley. So many others, like that miserable Salyard, would have just left him in that prison.

Eli, upon hearing of Harley's alleged death, had become a different man. He couldn't bear the life he'd chosen, so he changed course and reclaimed his self-respect. Carlita vowed she would do the same.

Maybe Eli was the man to help her with the chore. Old ways die hard. She knew so few good men, if she didn't find one soon, she might never find one. The fear of loneliness began to overtake her. What if he didn't make it back?

"I'm goin' down there," Bobby said. "I can't sit here anymore."

"No!" Carlita screamed. "Stay here. You may be killed if you go."

"I don't care! If Harley's down there, maybe I can help. Sorry, ma'am, but I'm goin'."

No Ordinary Thunder

Bobby slipped away and out the door before Carlita could say another word. She'd done all she could to help the boy. What he did, he did for friendship, for honor. It was something she wasn't accustomed to, but now knew it was the most important reason of all.

#

Delgado rode beside General Salinas in the charge through the brush to the Rio. The General led the assault in gallant fashion, his men dashing and daring, driving the retreating Rangers at a furious pace.

But the bandits' gunfire had reached the Texas side of the river, their bullets kicking up dust all around the anxious soldiers. Captain Randlett, at last seeing his opportunity to join in the fray, announced that United States soil was under attack. He ordered his men to commence firing with their Gatling gun.

The first volley brought down a great number of riders—one of them General Salinas. He took the heavy round full in the chest. Delgado caught the General and tried to hold him in the saddle, though he felt sure the man was dead.

While valiantly trying to usher him to the rear, Delgado took a rifle bullet high in his back and lost his grip on Salinas. Just then, their horses were shot from under them and both men hit the ground hard. Delgado lay as flat as he could behind his dying horse, and checked the load in his pistol. General Juan Flores Salinas lay motionless, staring into the sun.

Bandits scrambled everywhere in search of sufficient cover. Men and horses littered the ground, within mere yards of the river. The Gatling gun belched fire and flame, taking a terrible toll on the bandits.

The Rangers had incredibly made it to safety,

No Ordinary Thunder

without a single loss. They dug into the bank and continued to fight, rather than cross over to Texas. Those bandits still mounted cut and ran for Las Cuevas, but many crept from dead horse to brush cover, in an attempt to escape the Rangers' guns. One of them, Eli recognized.

"That's Delgado, Harley. That one there. In the green shirt, behind the horse. I've seen him in Laredo before. I was just too drunk and scared to do anything about it."

Delgado! That son of a bitch! The five butchered Rangers on the Llano Estacado—the 1200 mile journey to catch Lean Wolf and his killers—Stone Horse, the Rangers' Tonkawa scout, who lost his life in the Zendejaz raid. The memories flooded Harley's soul like a polluted, poison river.

Delgado had made a bold escape, riding out of the canyon among the stampeding horse herd. And he'd escaped again at Palo Alto. But no one escapes justice forever. The man's time had come. He would not escape again. Harley would make damn sure of that.

"Good enough. As soon as he moves, cut him down."

Harley and Eli checked their rifles and waited. Delgado had nearly run out of cover. There were only a few more dead or wounded horses to hide him. But if he made it to the heavy brush, it might conceal him enough to let him slip away. The outlaw had only to move, and the Texas Rangers would balance the scales for Stone Horse's woman and little girl.

The morning sun grew hotter, the air still and stifling. Nothing moved on the battlefield, except the occasional wounded horse trying to thrash himself back to his feet. It was at just such a moment that Delgado made his play.

He fired two pistol shots from behind the horse. The second one burned a crease into Eli's scalp and knocked

No Ordinary Thunder

him backward into the river. Harley crouched lower, seeking better cover. Delgado rose from behind the writhing horse and ran as hard as his wound would let him.

Harley fired as fast as he could lever his rifle. Delgado went down, though Harley didn't think he'd hit him clean. He was right. Scrambling for all he was worth, Delgado made it to the brush, and cover.

"Eli! Dammit, are you hurt bad?"

Harley rushed to pull his friend out of the water. Eli lay still as death. The furrow in his scalp was not as bad as Harley had seen, but it was plenty bad enough. Harley slapped his face repeatedly, trying to bring him around. The technique finally worked.

"Damn, Harley. What happened?"

"Lay still, Pard. You've got a gash in your noggin."

"Is it bad?"

"It ain't good. Be still, now. We'll get you across the river.

"Bring that boat over here!" Harley shouted.

"We've got a Ranger down. Some o' you boys haul this man back across."

Harley took Eli's pistol, checked the load and shoved it into his belt. He checked the load in his own weapon again, and helped put Eli in the boat.

"Where's Dixon?" Eli mumbled.

"I expect he'll be around. When you see him, tell him I'll be back."

"Ain't you comin' with me, Harley?"

"No, I ain't, Pard. I'm goin' after Delgado."

"You gonna tell the Captain?"

"You tell him. I'm goin'."

Harley made his way upriver using every bit of cover the bank afforded. When he felt he'd traveled farther than Delgado could have, he slipped over the bank and into the brush.

It was slow, careful going. The bullet-riddled bodies

No Ordinary Thunder

of soldiers and rustlers lay strewn about the battlefield. Harley had to approach each one as if the victim was still alive. Fortunately, he found none that were, though he saw several trails in the dust where the wounded had crawled away.

Maybe twenty yards into the brush, Harley sensed movement on his left flank. He stopped and waited, but heard nothing. It was more a sense of knowing—a conditioning acquired through years of combat. Harley carried his pistol, leaving one hand free to negotiate the brush, but drew Eli's weapon from his belt, just to be sure. And he did it in the nick of time.

Delgado leaped from behind a dead comrade and blazed away with his pistol. Harley dove for cover, firing back with both weapons as he rolled across the ground. Delgado's green shirt made a perfect target for a man who had killed so many. Harley's bullet struck him in the chest. The concussion spun him around just as Harley fired again, his shot taking Delgado in the small of the back.

Delgado dropped to his knees, curiously examining the great hole above his belt. Harley rose to his feet and calmly placed his next shot through Delgado's silver hatband. The outlaw's head blew apart like a melon, and the battlefield grew quiet once more.

Nine dead men could be counted from the spot where Harley now stood. There was no telling how many more had given their lives—fallen dead throughout the stinking brush, for no more cause than a few stolen cattle. He had little time to think about it.

Harley whirled at the sound of someone running through the brush. He leveled his guns at Lowery.

"Dammit, don't you know better than to run up on a man like that? I might've blown your damned head off!"

Lowery raced to Harley's side, struggling to catch his breath.

"You get him?"

No Ordinary Thunder

"Hell yes, I got him. It was that murderin' bastard, Delgado. By God, that's been a long time comin'."
"You see them Mexican soldiers?"
"Yeah, I saw 'em. What about it?"
"The one on the black horse is Garralaga!"

No Ordinary Thunder

Chapter 24

The Las Cuevas affair had become an agonizing stalemate, and Harley didn't like it one bit. News of Garralaga's presence put him in a dark, dangerous mood. He wanted to do something, to make some kind of move, not just sit on his pockets and wait.

The Ranger troop held their ground at the river, demanding the return of the stolen cattle. The bandits continued to stall for time. They hurled harsh, threatening words when the body of General Salinas was found, shot to rags, crushed beneath his horse. Captain McNelly relayed a message through Sandoval that those doing the threatening could join their beloved general, if that's the way they wanted it.

Harley didn't believe in cease-fires. But one had been requested by the bandits' spokesman, until the dead and wounded could be recovered, and arrangements made to drive the cattle back to Texas in the morning. Captain McNelly agreed to the cease-fire, only as long as the bandits kept out of pistol range. The Captain made it plain he was in no mood to negotiate the terms.

A brisk wind picked up from the west, the sun and the temperature both slowly sinking. The Rangers hadn't had a thing to eat since they'd started their march twenty-four hours earlier, and they were hungry.

They'd ridden fifty-five miles at a steady gallop, a ride that came close to killing their horses. They'd completely wiped out the Cachuttas camp, and engaged in several hours of fierce combat with the bandits of Las Cuevas. They were hungry all right. Really hungry.

The army supplied bread, along with great pots of stew, and ferried them across the river on the boat. The starving Rangers quickly lined up to get it. While the troop devoured the coveted stew, sopping it up with huge chunks of fresh bread, Harley approached McNelly with the plan

No Ordinary Thunder

he and Lowery were hatching.

"Captain. Colonel Garralaga's leadin' these soldiers. Lowery saw him in the fight. Salinas is dead. I think these jaspers are stallin' so they can move the cattle to Monterrey after dark. If Garralaga's in charge, you can bet on it."

"You sure about that, Mr. Lowery?" McNelly asked. "You sure it's Garralaga?"

"I'm sure, Captain. I ain't likely to forget that face…ever!"

"You boys wouldn't be looking to settle a score, would you?"

"Well, sir, I can't say we wouldn't like to," Harley said, "and once we get in there, it might come to that. But if they can take that herd, after what we've done here today, there won't be any stoppin' 'em."

Captain McNelly wiped the stew from his whiskers on his shirt sleeve.

"We're already in a hell of a mess," he said.

"They're burning up the telegraph wires between here and Washington. I expect we'll all get fired when we get back to Texas. But I want those cattle."

"Garralaga needs 'em, Captain. His army's gettin' mighty hungry. Why else would they be stallin' like this? If they can drive the herd to Monterrey in the dark, they can drive 'em across this river in the daylight. But they want more time. That means only one thing to me."

"How are you planning to do it?"

"Just me and Lowery. We'll slip in there after dark, nice and quiet, and kill him, along with as many others as we can. They think we're stuck here. They think they've won. If we go in and finish this, they'll know they can't hide. We'll find 'em wherever they go."

"You might not be able to keep it quiet. What then?"

"I guess we'll just get by the best way we can."

No Ordinary Thunder

McNelly pondered the situation, but his analysis didn't take long.

"I heard you were a little crazy," he said. "Any truth to the rumor that you swam the Cumberland River in February, to burn a barge of Federal hay?"

Harley laughed. "Yeah. Damn, that water was cold."

"Of course, you know I can't authorize a plan like this. A man would have to take responsibility for his own actions."

"Yes, sir, Captain. We sure know that."

"We'll be crossing back to the Texas side after sundown. I expect you boys better eat up and get some rest."

#

Colonel Garralaga paced the floor, trying to get his thoughts together. Las Cuevas was quiet, almost silent, in the aftermath of the attack. Wounded men occupied every bed, and much of the floor space in the ragged *jacales*. With the exception of the room Garralaga used as a headquarters, the home of General Juan Salinas was also rife with wounded, dying men.

Women and children scurried from room to room, carrying water, applying bandages, administering to their needs as best they could. Wagons had been dispatched during the cease-fire to collect and haul the dead. With so many wounded or killed, Garralaga would count himself lucky to have enough men left to drive the herd.

The Rangers had made a bold move, crossing the river into Mexico. And though they hadn't succeeded in retrieving the cattle, Mexico paid a heavy price. General Salinas was a chief of operations along the border. Thousands of cattle made their way to Monterrey through

No Ordinary Thunder

his pens. Feeding the army without his leadership would be a difficult thing to do.

Delgado, one of Cortina's bravest men, would ride the rustlers' trail no more. His expertise at handling horses, cattle, and the worst of men, would be a serious detriment and sorely missed.

At last report, nearly eighty men had been lost in the fight, most of them seasoned *vaqueros*. Garralaga's men were soldiers, with little experience driving cattle. The sooner they got started, the better.

"*Sargento!*" Garralaga shouted. "Have the men ready to ride in one hour."

"*Sí, Coronel.* Will we leave any behind to secure the *rancho?*"

"No. We leave no one. We have only enough men to move the herd. Las Cuevas will have to see to itself. *Vayate.*"

Garralaga didn't like leaving the *rancho* unguarded, but he knew of no other way. He'd need every man to handle the cattle—and those he had may not be enough.

It was unlikely the Rangers would be back. Spies from across the river had already delivered the news. McNelly was in big trouble with the U.S. Government for invading Mexico. One report said the army received orders to stop him by any means necessary, if he tried another attack.

Still, there was no need to wait. If McNelly was in deep with the authorities, he might feel he'd have nothing to lose and throw caution to the wind. If he took the cattle back across the river, he would be lauded as a hero to the ranchers. The ranchers had plenty to say about the government in Texas.

Well, if the Rangers were to attempt another charge, they had better do it soon. Garralaga, exhausted, dropped into a comfortable chair. He would try to get some rest while his battered army prepared to move out.

No Ordinary Thunder

#

Harley found sneaking up to the main house at Las Cuevas almost effortless. Garralaga's worn-out troops were too busy preparing the column to move, grumbling at the prospect of driving cattle all night.

They'd ridden in from Monterrey only the night before, and spent the whole evening drinking. They'd been locked in combat with the Texas Rangers for most of the day, leaving them depleted, hungry, and needing sleep. They showed little interest in the two men leading horses around the camp.

The house bustled with the activity of caring for the wounded, but Garralaga was alone in the candle-lit room, from what Harley could see through the window. He looked to be asleep in a big stuffed chair, with his boots up on a table. Lowery tied the horses at the hitch rail, and checked the edge on his knife.

"What're you waitin' for?" he asked Harley.

"Nothin'. Let's go."

Harley eased his way through the door, but the ancient floor gave a warning groan. Garralaga woke with a start that tore him from his slumber. He reached for his pistol, but couldn't find it. He had removed it from his sash and laid it on a table beside the chair.

Lowery pushed Harley out of the way. He attacked the Colonel in full fury, striking him a vicious left-hook to the jaw. Garralaga fell backward into the chair. He reached again for the pistol on the table, but Lowery tackled him and turned the chair over. Lowery buried his knee into the Colonel's belly, driving the air from his lungs. Struggling for breath, Garralaga looked into his frightening eyes, and felt the cold, razor edge of a knife at his throat.

"Well, now. Looks like we got us a priest killer,"

No Ordinary Thunder

Harley said. "And a girl killer, too. Tell me, Colonel. What were that girl's last words before you hung her?"

Lowery pressed the knife a little harder. "Did she beg for her life, you son of a bitch? Did the good Father beg for his life? Or did you gag 'em so they couldn't talk?"

A trickle of blood dripped on the cowhide rug, as Lowery gently slid the knife across Garralaga's neck.

"Go ahead. Kill me, *Bastardo*! My men will be here any minute. You will never get out alive."

"Our objective is killin' you, mister. And that's what we're gonna do," Harley said. "Gettin' out'll just be gravy. Cut his throat and let's go."

"No," Lowery snapped. "We're gonna hang him."

"We ain't got time for that. No tellin' who's behind that door. Besides, there ain't anything in here to hang him from. Cut his throat. Let's get outta here."

Garralaga had a crazy look in his eye, like he might take the chance and yell for help. The fear on his face surprised even Harley, who had seen plenty of soldiers die. Lowery punched the man hard in the mouth, breaking some of his teeth out.

"You son of a bitch. You're gonna pay for what happened to that boy. Remember Bobby Fallon? Or don't you concern yourself with what your guards do to prisoners? Bring me a rope, Harley."

"No. Dammit! I said we ain't got time."

"Well then," Lowery said, "I guess we'll just have to take him with us."

#

Garralaga's milling troops shouted their confusion, as the galloping horses rode in from the south. The sergeant in charge could not tell how many there were. A great dust cloud followed behind them. A rider from Monterrey,

No Ordinary Thunder

maybe? Whatever their purpose, it must be important. The riders did not spare the horses.

"Go! Get the *Coronel*," the sergeant ordered a sleepy soldier.

The soldier ran for the main house to deliver the news, but before he got there, one of the riders shot him down. They raced through the camp, spurring for speed, the one in front holding the reins in his teeth, expertly firing two pistols. The other fired only one. He dragged something behind his horse, though the soldiers couldn't make out what it was.

"It's the Rangers!" the sergeant bellowed. "Get your weapons!"

It was too late for that. The Rangers were half-way through the camp, riding like mad-men, taking down a soldier with every shot. When he'd emptied one pistol, the first rider drew another weapon from his belt, firing again with deadly accuracy.

The unprepared soldiers didn't have a chance. The Rangers shot them down like paper targets, as many of them stood frozen in their tracks, unable to get into action. By the time the soldiers were ready to fight, the second rider loosed the load he was dragging, and the two men whipped for the river.

Their ragged delivery, a man with hands tied behind him and a rope around his neck, rolled to a stop at the feet of a horrified private. Upon leery inspection of the bloody corpse, he gasped and fell over backwards.

"It is the *Coronel!*" he cried. "The *Coronel* is dead."

The soldiers gathered around Garralaga's body, dismayed that such a thing could happen—that the Rangers could just ride in and kill an officer in the Mexican Army, and ride out again, unmolested.

Searching about for the sergeant in charge, they found him lying behind a barrel, a perfect .44 caliber hole in his forehead. Someone else would have to take

No Ordinary Thunder

command.

#

Harley and Lowery safely reached the river, where they stopped to let their horses blow. They had no fear of being pursued. The soldiers would never follow them into the darkness. Too much chance of an ambush.

The men had nothing in particular to say. They just sat in silence, retracing the last year and a half, each man sensing what the other was thinking. The thoughts men had when they'd suffered together, fought together, and saved each others' lives. Harley, as usual, instigated the conversation, as Lowery had little to say on any occasion.

"Well…where you goin' from here?"

"I ain't decided. Kansas, maybe. I heard they need lawmen up there."

"Lawman? You? Hell, if you're gonna do that, you might as well stay here. Maybe Laredo still needs a sheriff."

"Naw. Someone there'd recognize me. Sooner or later, McNelly'd come after me. That man's got a lotta bulldog in him. He'd have to do his job. Who's to say he won't clap me in irons, as soon as this thing's over?"

"McNelly's a fair man. He'll consider the work you've done here."

"Y'know, Harley, I don't think I'll take that chance. Besides, it looks like you've about got the Mexicans whipped."

"Listen, Lowery. I know you think you need to leave, but Texas needs every good man she can get. I expect you'd do 'til we find one."

"Arizona," Lowery said. "Reckon I could meet ol' Geronimo? I hear he's a wild ol' devil."

"Then you and him oughta get along just fine."

No Ordinary Thunder

Harley could see there was no point in talking. He offered his hand. The two shook long and hard. A simple nod concluded their parting.

In the light of a cool November moon, Henry Berry Lowery, the outlaw guerilla from North Carolina, turned his horse and rode upriver. Harley Macon, the Confederate legend, stepped his mount into the Rio Grande, and waded across to Texas.

#

Sunrise found Harley poking up the Rangers' fire, setting the coffee to boil. A stir came from a blanket lying close for the warmth. Bobby was the first to roll out and join him.

"Harley. Boy, am I glad to see you."

"Bobby? What're you doin' here?"

"I come down when I heard the Rangers were here, but the army wouldn't let me do anything. You all right?"

"Sure, I'm fine. How you doin'? You look a damn sight better than the last time I saw you."

"I am. We took Eli to Carlita's. He had a pretty bad gash in his scalp."

"Yeah, I know. How's he gettin' along?"

"Carlita says he'll be okay. Where's Dixon?"

"He's gone, son. Went to meet Geronimo."

"Huh?"

"It's a long story. How's Carlita?"

"She's been pretty glum for a while. She ain't hardly done any customers since I've been here. Says she don't want to anymore."

Captain McNelly, hearing the whispers at the fire, slid out of his wagon and joined the conversation.

"I don't see your partner, Macon. You didn't leave him over there, did you?"

No Ordinary Thunder

"No, sir. Seems he escaped in all the confusion. We left quite a few others, though."

"Dern. I hate to lose such a valuable prisoner. But then, he wasn't really under arrest, was he?"

"No, sir. He wasn't."

"Prisoner? What's he mean, Harley?"

"I told you, son. It's a long story."

"What about Garralaga?" McNelly asked, a little put out at being interrupted.

"He's dead, sir."

"You killed Garralaga?" Bobby gasped. "You killed him, Harley?"

"Mr. Dixon had the pleasure. You'd better get on back to Carlita's, son. This thing ain't over."

"No. I wanna stay and fight with you."

"Go on, boy," McNelly said. "We can't have any civilians getting killed."

The Captain's tone made it plain he didn't want any argument. Bobby gathered his blanket and walked away. He turned and looked back more than once.

"You tell Carlita we're all right," Harley said.

"Yes, sir. I will."

McNelly poured his first cup, though the coffee wasn't quite done. He sipped it cautiously, so as not to burn his mouth.

"Let's go, boys," he shouted. "It's time to make them prove it."

Captain McNelly and ten very anxious men ferried across the river into Mexico. A contingent of bandit spokesmen made their way down to join them. The deliberations began about the way McNelly expected they would, with the bandits stalling for more time. They were obviously confused. The deaths of Salinas, Garralaga and many others no doubt left them wondering what to do next.

No Ordinary Thunder

McNelly knew they didn't want to lose the cattle. The army needed the beef. They had to try something.

With nothing to lose, they appealed to the Rangers' religious persuasions. It was Sunday. The men didn't want to drive cattle on the holy day. They would happily drive the herd back first thing in the morning. Surely Captain McNelly, as a good Christian, would understand their reasoning.

But McNelly didn't understand. He was out of patience. He'd listened to all the excuses he was going to. At the close of negotiations, he gave the spokesman a wry smile. They drew their pistols in the same instant.

McNelly flew into action, bashing the man in the head with his gun, driving him to the ground. Harley shot the first bandit to go for a weapon, killing him on the spot. The Texas Rangers followed suit, drew their pistols as one, and disarmed the rest of the crowd. McNelly pulled the bloody man to his feet and held the gun to his head.

"Sergeant Armstrong!" he said. "Take this thief across the river. If he gives you any trouble, shoot him."

"Yes, sir, Captain."

"I'll kill this man in one hour," McNelly shouted, "if the cattle aren't started across by then. If they aren't started after I kill him, my Rangers and I will ford the river again. We'll wipe Las Cuevas off the face of the earth. We'll kill every damn one of you, if we have to chase you to Monterrey to do it. You'll never outrun us and keep the herd. One hour!"

The spokesmen drifted back into the brush. McNelly reached into his vest pocket and checked the time on his watch.

"Get back in the boat," he told his Rangers. "We'll cross over and get our horses ready to ride. Check your ammunition. If they try to move the herd, we cross the river."

McNelly waited on the Texas side, keeping a sharp

No Ordinary Thunder

eye open. The Rangers tightened their cinches and double-checked their guns.

The bandits had already lost nearly a hundred men, two of them, their leaders. McNelly doubted anyone felt compelled to take command, for fear he would be the next man killed. What they would do, he could only wait and see.

The Rangers rolled cigarettes and smoked them. They drank a little coffee, then rolled others and smoked them, too. None among them had time to roll a third.

"Look there, Captain," Harley yelled. "They're bringin' 'em back across!"

What was left of Garralaga's troops drove the cattle toward the river to the shouts and whoops of the Rangers. They were beat. The bandits had surrendered.

In less time than McNelly allowed, the stolen cattle were back on Texas soil, shaking the Rio Grande from their bellies. Not only the cattle McNelly came to retrieve, but every cow in the pens. The battle of Las Cuevas was over.

"Well, Captain," Harley said, "I guess we whipped 'em good, this time."

"Yeah, I guess we did. *Sergeant Armstrong*! Have the men start cutting the herd. When we get them split, we'll break up in groups and drive them back toward their home range. I'll telegraph the owners to meet them on the trail."

"Yes, sir, Captain."

"Anybody seen Sandoval?"

"He mounted up and headed east when they started 'em across."

"Well, I expect he'll be around."

"Captain," Harley said. "I'd like to go see a friend before we leave, if that's all right with you."

"The woman?"

"Yes, sir. One hell of a woman. While I'm there, I'll see if Eli's fit for travel."

No Ordinary Thunder

"All right. Go ahead, but get back here quick. This won't take very long."

#

Carlita left Eli resting on a sofa, and threw herself into Harley's arms when he walked through the parlor door. She kissed him and cried, so thankful for his safety, she buried her face in his chest, and held on with all her strength.

"I'm so glad you're alive. Both of you," she said. "The whole town's been walking on eggs, waiting to see what would happen at the river. Is it over?"

"Yeah, it's over," Harley said. "How's Eli?"

"I'm all right, Harley," Eli said. "I'm gonna be all right."

"That's good to know, Pard."

"You get Delgado?"

"Yeah, I got him. We got Garralaga, too."

"Dixon?"

"Gone to Arizona."

"Good. That's damn good."

"Carlita, it looks like your business may fall off a little," Harley said.

"I don't care about this business. I hate the men who come in here, even the rich ones. They are all the same."

"Goin' back to the cantina?"

"Maybe, I don't know. I don't want this anymore. I want what my mother had. A man to love me all the time, not just when he needs me to please him, or if he has a few dollars to spend. If I knew such a man, I would make him a good wife."

Carlita turned and looked into Eli's eyes, her gaze plainly asking the question.

No Ordinary Thunder

Eli, dumbfounded, couldn't bring himself to speak. He just couldn't say the words. Carlita sashayed to the sofa, and kissed him long and deep. Harley failed his attempt to curtail his laughter.

"Yes or no, Sheriff?"

"You'd better answer her, Eli. She ain't gonna wait forever," Harley said.

"Well, yes... I reckon. I expect I'll have to quit the Rangers, though."

"Good," Carlita said. "What woman would want a Texas Ranger for a husband?"

The house girls all gave a cheer as Carlita repeated the kiss. The piano player began a bright, happy tune, and they danced in celebration.

"I swear, Harley," Bobby said. "He's slower'n wet gunpowder."

"Yeah. Carlita'll help him. She's got a way about her. Well, I guess that settles that. What about you, son? What're you gonna do?"

"I'm goin' home to my ma. I didn't want her to see me the way I was. Now that I'm in better shape, I'll go home and let her know her boy's still alive."

"A boy could never survive what you did, son. I'd say you're as much a man as anybody. Maybe you can ride along with us aways."

"I'd like that, Harley. I'd really like that."

"Good. Now let's have a toast to the bride and groom."

A knock on the door disrupted the festivities. No one knocked on the door at Carlita's. The place was open to all. Harley swung the door wide with an invitation to join the fun. Standing at the threshold was Captain McNelly. He didn't look like he was in the mood.

"Macon. I've got a telegram here from the governor. He wants you to report to Austin right away." McNelly surveyed the room full of women, pouring

No Ordinary Thunder

whiskey, scantily clad. "If I were you, I'd leave now. Plummer, we're ready to move out, if you can ride."

"Sorry, Captain. This lady's just asked me to marry her. I expect I will. Been an honor ridin' with you, though."

"Uh-huh."

Harley read the telegram, but it gave no indication of what the governor wanted. He hated to leave the party, but such things could go on for a while. Besides, Eli and Carlita didn't need him hanging around. They had each other to think about—a life to plan together. He shook hands with McNelly, Eli, and Bobby, and kissed Carlita's salty, wet cheek.

"You will come back and see us, won't you?" she asked.

"Maybe so, honey. Who knows what the governor wants? I wish you all the best. Good luck to you both."

The crowd followed Harley onto the porch, waved good-bye and watched him ride away to the north. Maybe, he thought, he could find time to visit Cole and his family before reporting to Austin. He had to go through San Antonio, anyway. After all, he still owed Pap Teeters ten dollars damage on his saloon.

No Ordinary Thunder

Author's Note

Captain Leander McNelly continued his career as a Texas Ranger, but never again achieved the successes he'd had at Palo Alto and Las Cuevas. Stricter law enforcement guidelines made it harder to do his job, so he retired to his farm to raise cotton. McNelly succumbed to tuberculosis on September 4, 1877. He died at his home in Burton, Texas at the age of thirty-three.

Juan Nepomuceno Cortina was arrested and taken to Mexico City, for his support of General Porfirio Diaz, and his plot to overthrow the Mexican Government. After appointing himself President of Mexico on November 29, 1876, Diaz allowed Cortina to return to Tamaulipas. But he was soon under arrest again and taken back to Mexico City, where he lived the remainder of his life in exile. He died October 30, 1894.

General Juan Flores Salinas was killed in the battle of Las Cuevas, November 20, 1875. A stone monument commending his courage was erected at the spot where he fell.

Henry Berry Lowery, the outlaw chief, disappeared from the pages of history. Though there are many legends about this daring, enigmatic figure, including the theft of the $20,000 reward money, his part in this story is purely fiction.

Like Lowery, Jesus Sandoval, McNelly's "jailer", was lost to history after the Las Cuevas battle. His name, however, will likely never be forgotten along the Nueces Strip.

Made in the USA
San Bernardino, CA
16 June 2014

It is important to state that there is this belief that the power of darkness and witchcrafts gather to destroy people's destiny at midnight. Realizing this belief, I made up my mind that I will operate in the spirit realm, in prayers, during that same hour to pray for my children (biological, spiritual, adopted). I started this practice years ago and I am thankful to God for His grace and strength. It is important for parents to model the habit of praying to their children. Don't just tell them to pray, let them see you pray. They will follow your example faster than your advice!

Reading God's Word helps me to pray. I am a lover of God's word, and that has helped me in my prayer life. I encourage everyone to fall in love with the word of God and to also make sure that the children fall in love with the Word of God early in life. I introduced all my children to the Word of God early and often. Reading, studying,memorizing and obeying the Word of God is very important as we develop the lifestyle of prayer. Years ago, shortly after my husband passed, I perceived a spiritual attack looming, and my children and I started praying in our living room at night, declaring the judgment of the Lord upon the works of satan. We called the sword of the Lord to cut into pieces all the agents of darkness. In the morning, we physically saw dead, dismembered cats outside of our house. I have seen the Lord answer prayers in mysterious way. Sometimes the answer to your prayers will come immediately, other times the answers will come suddenly. Yet, other times, it might take time to receive your answers. But one thing I know is that the Lord answers prayers. Don't stop praying!

I understood by experience that you can pray for someone in another part of the world and that person will feel your prayer and the Lord will

do what you requested. There is power in the sent Word. Pray for others, whether they are far or near – send the word. This can be achieved if you get a prayer partner. I have a prayer partner that I pray with every week. Praying partners help you become accountable to one another. Being accountable and having an accountability partner is a good way of life. If you want to go fast, they say, go alone, but if you want to go far, go with others. This is a good word to live by in your prayer life. I encourage everyone to have a prayer partner.

One of my beloved prayer scriptures is one of the shortest verses in the bible, "Pray without ceasing." I took that literally. Instead of engaging in idle talk, I just developed the habit of talking to God. I really love talking to God because it makes me happy and gives me joy. This prayer book will help you accomplish that. For me, you don't have to encourage me to pray because I have seen prayer turn things around for me and for the people that I've prayed for. I remember when I was back in Nigeria, I declared it by faith that I will live the latter part of my life in the United States of America, I had no idea how it would happen. The Lord honored that prayer. I also prayed that all my children must know and serve God. The Lord honored that prayer also. Don't tell me that prayer doesn't work!

In fact, there is an event in my life that I remember very clearly. When I was raising my children in Nigeria, after dinner, I will tell them good night. But at midnight, I will wake up and start praying. But, my son, Bishop Israel will be peeping through the doors to see what I was doing. And, not too long, I saw him pick up this same habit of mine. And, he has never stopped since then.

One thing you must know is this: praying for others, even when you have your own needs, is powerful. I grew up praying for other people. Asking God to provide for them even when I didn't have enough to provide for my children. Every time, without fail, God, will suddenly open His windows and pour out His blessings by meeting our needs. Praying to God is what I do. It is what Bishop Israel does. Moreover, the Bible is the best and only place you can go to if you don't know how to pray and what to pray for. You can draw near to God when you pray. You can hear Him when you pray. I am a living testimony of this. I prayed and prayed and prayed and still praying and the Lord answered and is still answering me.

- Grandma Comfort Ajala.
[Mother of the Author of 'Let Us Pray']

Contents

Foreword 1

Thanksgiving 3

Dedication 10

Deliverance 14

Spiritual Warfare 17

The Church 54

Family 78

Protection 88

Divine Healing 99

Victory 102

Blessing 111

Pastors 121

Success 133

Foreword

The secret of my victories is prayer. The unrestricted access to God is my most cherished privilege. I was fortunate to know earlier in my life that prayer changes things, that prayer gives us strength, and that prayer helps us to have fellowship with God.

I am a product of a praying mother. It was not the spankings of my mother that changed me, it was her prayers. Keep praying, it makes all the difference.

Jesus gave us the pattern of prayer in the book of Matthew chapter 6, in verses 6 - 9, Jesus taught us that praying is a relationship-based communication:

*"But you, when you pray, go into your room, and when you have shut your door, pray to **your Father** who is in the secret place; and **your Father** who sees in secret will reward you openly. And when you pray, do not use vain repetitions as the heathen do. For they think that they will be heard for their many words. "Therefore, do not be like them. For **your Father** knows the things you have need of before you ask Him. In this manner, therefore, pray: **Our Father** in heaven, Hallowed be Your name."* (Matthew 6:6-9 NKJV)

When you pray, pray to your Father in the name of the Son, Jesus. The Father will honor every prayer prayed in this manner.

*"And in that day you will ask Me nothing. Most assuredly, I say to you, whatever you **ask the Father in My name He will give you.**"* (John 16:23 NKJV)

Let Us Pray

As you pray to the Father in the name of His Son, Jesus, pray in faith believing that you have what you asked for. Do not doubt that you've received your petition.

"...ask in faith, with no doubting, for he who doubts is like a wave of the sea driven and tossed by the wind. For let not that man suppose that he will receive anything from the Lord; he is a double-minded man, unstable in all his ways." (James 1:6-8 NKJV)

Every prayer in this prayer book is scripture based. Pray for yourself, your children, your spouse, your parents, your friends, your pastors and more.

Receive answers to all your prayers. Let Us Pray!

Bishop Israel Ade-Ajala

Thanksgiving

THANKSGIVING GIVES YOU ACCESS TO THE PRESENCE OF GOD. IF YOU CAN THINK, YOU WILL SEE THAT THERE ARE A MULTITUDE OF REASONS TO BE THANKFUL TO GOD FOR ALL HE HAS DONE FOR YOU. IN EVERYTHING AND FOR EVERYTHING GIVE THANKS (1 THESSALONIANS 5:18). WHEN YOU ARE THANKFUL, YOU ARE IN THE WILL OF GOD.

EVERY TIME THAT GOD IS FAITHFUL, YOU MUST BE THANKFUL. OH, GIVE THANKS TO THE LORD, FOR HE IS GOOD! FOR HIS MERCY ENDURES FOREVER. (PSALMS 136:1) LET US PRAY!

1. Psalms 31:21 *"Praise the Lord, for he has shown me the wonders of his unfailing love. He kept me safe when my city was under attack." (NLT).*

   Father, I praise you for keeping me, my family, my church, and all that surrounds me safe from January to December. Thank you for keeping us safe from the attacks of the enemies.

2. Psalms 75:1 *"Our God, we thank you for being so near to us! Everyone celebrates your wonderful deeds." (CEV).*

   Father, we thank you for your blessings in our lives, homes, jobs, businesses, and church. Thank you for providing our needs for our new church building!

Let Us Pray

3. *Romans 5:7-8 "For scarcely for a righteous man will one die; yet perhaps for a good man someone would even dare to die. But God demonstrates His own love toward us, in that while we were still sinners, Christ died for us." (NKJV).*

    My Lord and My King, I thank You for paying the price for me on the cross. Thank you, for paying my debt on Calvary.

4. *Luke 10:19 "See what I've given you? Safe passage as you walk on snakes and scorpions, and protection from every assault of the Enemy. No one can put a hand on you!" (Message).*

    Father, I praise you for keeping me, my family, my pastors, my church and all that surround me safe since January. Thank you for keeping us safe from the attacks of the enemies and for granting us victory on every side, in the name of Jesus!

5. *Psalms 106:1 "Praise the Lord! Give thanks to The Lord because He is good, because His faithful love endures forever." (CEB).*

    Let us thank God for all that He has been doing for us at our church and give Him praise.

6. *Proverbs 24:16 "No matter how many times you trip them up, God–loyal people don't stay down long; Soon they're up on their feet, while the wicked end up flat on their faces." (Message).*

    Father, thank you for keeping us on our feet, despite all the plans of the wicked. Thank you for keeping us standing with proof of your love and faithfulness.

7. *Psalms 75:4-5 "You tell every bragger, 'Stop bragging!' And to the wicked you say, 'Don't boast of your power! Stop bragging! Quit telling me how great you are.'" (CEV).*

Father, thank you for silencing every bragger against our destiny and the destiny of our church. Father, thank you for lifting us up amid opposition and hate. Thank you for allowing us to keep enjoying your love and mercy in the name of JESUS!

8. *Matthew 10:1 "And when He had called His twelve disciples to Him, He gave them power over unclean spirits, to cast them out, and to heal all kinds of sickness and all kinds of disease." (NKJV).*

Lord, we thank you for all that you are doing at our church. Father, reposition our church as a ministry, and use this church to destroy the satanic kingdom in this nation and all over the world in the name of Jesus!

9. *Psalms 75:1 "Our God, we thank you for being so near to us! Everyone celebrates your wonderful deeds." (CEV).*

Father, we thank you for your blessings in our lives, children, homes, jobs, businesses and church. Thank you for providing for our needs and for our church for these past years!

10. *Psalms 26:7 "Singing God-songs at the top of my lungs, telling God stories." (Message).*

Father, I declare that I will sing songs of thanksgiving, and I will tell of all your wonders in my life. My time to share testimonies has finally come in the name of Jesus!

Let Us Pray

11. *Revelation 13:8 And all the people who belong to this world worshiped the beast. They are the ones whose names were not written (Blotted Out) in the Book of Life that belongs to the Lamb who was slaughtered before the world was made. (NLT). Revelation 13:8 All who dwell on the earth will worship him. Those, whose names have not been written in the Book of Life of the Lamb, slain from the foundation of the world. (NKJV).*

Father, I thank you for the Lamb of God that was slain from the foundation of the world.

12. *Psalms 45:11 " So the King will greatly desire your beauty; Because He is your Lord, worship Him. (NKJV).*

Father, we thank you because of your beauty in our lives, in our homes, in our children, in our finances, and over our works. We are the envy of your blessing and favor and the World sees it! We celebrate your goodness.

13. *Psalms 144:1 1 "Praise the LORD, who is my rock. He trains my hands for war and gives my fingers skill for battle." (NLT).*

Father, we thank you for giving us victory in every battle we have fought this year. Thank you for making us winners and not losers in the name of Jesus.

14. *Judges 5:20 "The stars fought from heaven. The stars in their orbits fought against Sisera." (NLT).*

Father, thank you for fighting our battles and giving us victory. We praise you for defeating the Sisera of COVID-19 and other ravaging diseases. Lord, we praise you for protecting us from

what is killing others. We confidently say, "We lost no one to COVID-19!"

15. *1 Chronicles 29:11 "Yours, O Lord, is the greatness, The power and the glory, The victory and the majesty; For all that is in heaven and in earth is Yours; Yours is the kingdom, O Lord, And You are exalted as head over all." (NKJV).*

Father, we sincerely acknowledge, you are God that rules supreme in our affairs, thank you for the testimonies of your faithfulness, in our corporate and individual lives.

16. *Philippians 2:13 "For it is God who works in you both to will and to do for His good pleasure." (NKJV).*

Thank you Father for Your Grace and mercy; which enrolled me among the redeemed, the blessed, and the sanctified.

17. *Psalms 127: 2 "It is vain for you to rise up early, to sit up late, to eat the bread of sorrows; For so He gives His beloved sleep."*

Heavenly Father, here at this church, we thank you for granting us rest from toiling and laboring and replacing labor with your favor. Father, thank you for granting us the wisdom to achieve divine balance in all our endeavors and for releasing your peace that surpasses all understanding in Jesus' name.

18. *Psalms 102:2-5 "Praise the Lord, my soul, and forget not all his benefits; who forgives all your sins and heals all your diseases, who redeems your life from the pit, and crowns you with love and compassion; who satisfies your desires with good things so that your youth is renewed like the eagle's. (KJV).*

Let Us Pray

Father, we cannot forget the way you forgive us all for our sins and redeem us from the jaw of death. Take your glory Lord, over our senior pastor. Receive your praise Lord, over every member of this church family. Take your glory Lord.

19. *1 Corinthians 15:57 "But thanks be to God! He gives us the victory through our Lord Jesus Christ." (NIV).*

Father, in the name of Jesus, thank you for giving us victory constantly at our church over all the plans & works of the enemy. Thank you, Jesus!

20. *Numbers 6: 24-26 "May the Lord bless you and protect you. May the Lord smile on you and be gracious to you. May the Lord show you his favor and give you his peace." (NLT).*

Father, we thank you that you are the God of peace. We thank you that even when the earth is trembling, we can be still and know you are God. Nothing can separate us from You. We praise you for your protection and favor. As we sit in your presence and focus our hearts and minds on you, give us your perfect peace. We trust that no matter what, you will guide us, protect us, and be gracious toward us.

21. *Romans 15:13 "Now may the God of hope fill you with all joy and peace in believing, that you may abound in hope by the power of the Holy spirit." (NKJV).*

Father, we rejoice today because you never change. You are the same yesterday, today, and tomorrow. We thank you that your Holy Spirit is filling our family right now with unspeakable joy and peace that passes all understanding.

22. *2 Corinthians 9:15 "Thanks be to God for His indescribable gifts." (NKJV).*

Father, thank You for this church. Thank you for increasing your church. Thank you for the wonder working Word of life in this church.

Dedication

Daily dedicating oneself to the Lord is a great practice. Prayer of dedication is to present oneself to the Lord daily, monthly or yearly. It is a good thing to present your family, children, business and yourself to the lord. Romans 12: 1 says, "I beseech you therefore, brethren, by the mercies of God, that you present your bodies a living sacrifice, holy, acceptable to God which is your reasonable service. Let us pray!

23. *Job 34: 32 "So why don't you simply confess to God? Say, 'I sinned, but I'll sin no more. Teach me to see what I still don't see. Whatever evil I've done, I'll do it no more.'" (Message).*

Father, I confess and repent in totality, every sin that gave Satan and his demons entrance into my life, my business, and my finances in the name of Jesus; and I cast them out of my life in the name of Jesus.

24. *1 Samuel 28:15 "Why have you disturbed me by bringing me back?" Samuel asked Saul. "Because I am in deep trouble," he replied. "The Philistines are at war with us, and God has left me and won't reply by prophets or dreams; so, I have called for you to ask you what to do." (NLT).*

Father, cleanse me and purge me of anything and everything that can make me lose Your glorious presence. Lord, make Your presence more real to me day by day.

Israel Ade-Ajala

25. *Daniel 10:19 "And he said, "O man greatly beloved, fear not! Peace be to you; be strong, yes, be strong!" So when he spoke to me, I was strengthened, and I said, "Let My Lord speak, for you have strengthened me." (NKJV).*

Father, speak to me. Speak to my health, my finances, my marriage, my ministry, my career, my business, my children, my home, and my life. Strengthen me in the name of Jesus. Don't let me fall apart in the name of Jesus.

26. *Psalms 138:8 "You keep every promise you've ever made to me! Since your love for me is constant and endless, I ask you, Lord, to finish every good thing that you've begun in me!" (Passion).*

Father, finish every good thing you've begun in my life, home, career, finances, children, and business in the name of Jesus. Let the people see that your hand is upon my life and confess it in the name of Jesus.

27. *Matthew 6:31-33 "Therefore do not worry, saying, 'What shall we eat?' or 'What shall we drink?' or 'What shall we wear?' 32 For after all these things the Gentiles seek. For your heavenly Father knows that you need all these things. 33 But seek first the kingdom of God and His righteousness, and all these things shall be added to you." (NKJV).*

Father, I give you the first place and the full place in my business and in my career. I declare that I will serve you Oh Lord with the proceeds from my business faithfully, withholding nothing from you Oh Lord!

11

Let Us Pray

28. <u>Acts 6:7</u> *"And the word of God increased; and the number of the disciples multiplied in Jerusalem greatly; and a great company of the priests were obedient to the faith." (KJV).*

Father, let the knowledge of your word grow in us as individuals. Let it grow in our families and in our church family so that we will continue to affect our neighborhoods, our city, state and our nation for God, in the mighty name of Jesus Christ.

29. *2 Chronicles 7:14 "If My people who are called by My name will humble themselves, and pray and seek My face, and turn from their wicked ways, then I will hear from heaven, and will forgive their sin and heal their land." (NKJV).*

Father, as we pray and seek your face today, help us to turn from our wicked ways. Help us to be kind to one another the way we should. Forgive us for all sins and heal our land in the mighty name of Jesus Christ.

30. *1 Thessalonians 5:18 "In everything, give thanks; for this is the will of God in Christ Jesus for you." (NKJV).*

Thank you, Lord, for the blessings you have bestowed on our lives, children, home, jobs, businesses, and church. Father, thank you for providing us with more than we could ever have imagined in our homes and for our church.

31. *Psalms 86:12 "I will praise You, O Lord my God, with all my heart, And I will glorify your name forevermore." (NKJV).*

Father, we thank you for the gift of life, for the breath that sustains life, and for giving us life to continually praise You.

12

Israel Ade-Ajala

Thank you, Lord, for the help you have given us in the past and the help you will give us again in the future, in Jesus' name.

Deliverance

THE LORD IS A MIGHTY DELIVERER. TIME AND TIME AGAIN, HE HAS SHOWN UP FOR HIS CHILDREN. HE DELIVERED THE ISRAELITES FROM BONDAGE, DELIVERED DANIEL FROM THE LION'S DEN, AND DELIVERED THE THREE HEBREW BOYS FROM THE FIERY FURNACE. HE IS THE SAME YESTERDAY, TODAY AND FOREVER MORE. HE WILL DELIVER YOU AS YOU PRAY.

MANY ARE THE AFFLICTIONS OF THE RIGHTEOUS. BUT THE LORD DELIVERS HIM OUT OF THEM ALL (PSALMS 34:19) AS YOU SEEK THE LORD IN PRAYER, HE WILL HEAR YOU AND DELIVER YOU FROM ALL YOUR FEARS. LET US PRAY!

32. *Psalms 68:19-20 " What a glorious Lord! He who daily bears our burdens also gives us our salvation. He frees us! He rescues us from death." (TLB).*

Father, I cast my burdens on you. Set me free from the spirit of fear and worry in the name of Jesus. Rescue me from the traps of death laid for me by the evil ones, in the name of Jesus.

33. *Psalms 68:30 "Rebuke our enemies, O Lord. Bring them— submissive, tax in hand. Scatter all who delight in war." (TLB).*

Father, rebuke our enemies, bring them under our submission and let them pay back seven times what they have stolen from us, in the name of Jesus!

34. *1 Corinthians 14:33 "For God is not the author of confusion, but of peace, as in the churches of all saints." (KJV).*

Lord, we break every cycle of confusion operating in our lives, in our homes, and in our business or workplace, in the name of Jesus!

35. *Isaiah 45:3 "I will give you the treasures of darkness, riches stored in secret places, so that you may know that I am the LORD, the God of Israel, who summons you by name." (NKJV).*

Father, I pray for anyone whose business has been doing well before, but the enemy blew evil wind on it, and the business is in coma. I pray they receive your deliverance in the name of Jesus!

36. *Isaiah 61:7 "Instead of shame and dishonor, you will enjoy a double share of honor. You will possess a double portion of prosperity in your land, and everlasting joy will be yours." (NLT).*

God, arise and fill my mouth with laughter. Let my tears and shame expire, in the name of Jesus!

37. *Joshua 5:9 "Then the Lord said to Joshua, "This day I have rolled away the reproach of Egypt from you." Therefore, the name of the place is called Gilgal to this day." (NKJV).*

Father, today roll away every reproach of my life in the name of Jesus. Turn my tears to cheers in the name of Jesus.

38. *Exodus 12:42 "It is a night to be much observed unto the LORD for bringing them out from the land of Egypt: this is that night of the LORD to be observed of all the children of Israel in their generations". (KJV).*

Father, make tonight "that night of the Lord." Let it be my last day of struggling in life. Humiliate every Pharaoh trying to keep me in bondage in the name of Jesus!

39. *Psalms 105: 1-2 Oh, give thanks to the Lord! Call upon His name; Make known His deeds among the peoples! Sing to Him, sing psalms to Him; Talk of his wondrous works! (NKJV).*

Father, in the name of Jesus, we thank you for your wondrous works among us here at this house of God; For the healings, deliverances, blessings, gifts of life, and so many good things to mention, we Thank You, Lord.

40. *2 Samuel 22: 49-50 "He delivers me from my enemies. You also lift me up above those who rise against me; You have delivered me from the violent man; Therefore, I will give thanks to You, O Lord, among the Gentiles; And sing praises to Your name." (NKJV).*

Father, we thank and give you praise because you delivered our senior pastor and his family, the leadership, and individuals from those who revolted against us, and from violent men. You show mercy to Your anointed and our generations forever. Thank You Lord.

Spiritual Warfare

Spiritual warfare is not a strange thing to believers. Our enemy is satan and his demons. We rejoice because we fight in victory and not for victory. Jesus won the victory for us in Calvary.

"For The weapons of our warfare are not carnal but mighty in God for pulling down strongholds" 2 Corinthians 10:4. It is time to exercise your authority over Satan. Receive your victory. Let us pray!

41. *Psalms 108:13 "Through God we will do valiantly, For it is He who shall tread down our enemies". (NKJV).*

Father, I destroy every power preventing me from enjoying the goodness of The Lord in this land in the name of Jesus! Father, I declare that I will do great exploits in this land!

42. *1 Corinthians 3:11 "For no one is empowered to lay an alternative foundation other than the good foundation that exists, which is Jesus Christ!" (TPT).*

I decree and declare that every alternative foundation against my life is disempowered today, in the mighty name of Jesus! Jesus Christ is the foundation before all other foundations; Therefore, I am rooted in Christ the solid rock in the name of Jesus Christ!

43. *Psalms 144:5, 7-8 "Step down out of heaven, God; ignite volcanoes in the hearts of the mountains...Reach all the way from sky to sea: pull me out of the ocean of hate, out of the grip*

Let Us Pray

of those barbarians. Who lie through their teeth, who shake your hand then knife you in the back." (Message).

Father, disgrace all who are incensed against our pastors, all who work in this church, our church and every member of our church. In their presence, make us your voice and establish your presence in our midst, in the name of Jesus!

44. *Psalms 120:6-7 "My soul has dwelt too long with one who hates peace. I am for peace; But when I speak, they are for war." (NKJV).*

Father, we destroy every instrument of war – physical, verbal, or spiritual – raised against our church and church family, and against your servant and his family, in the name of Jesus!

45. *Micah 2:13 "Then I, GOD, will burst all confinements and lead them out into the open. They'll follow their King. I will be out in front leading them." (Message). Micah 2:13 "The One who breaks open the way will go up before them, they will break through the gate and go out. Their King will pass through before them, the LORD at their head." (NIV).*

By the reason of this season, I break out. – My King is JESUS! He passes before me. My Lord is JESUS! He is at my head. I am breaking forth; I am breaking through. I recognize no limit. – The BREAKER is going ahead of me. The Breaker's Anointing is going ahead of me, destroying every obstacle in my path. Mountains before me, obstacles in my way, by the reason of what Christ did, be moved in Jesus' name.

46. Romans 8:32 *"He who did not spare His own Son, but delivered Him up for us all, how shall He not with Him also freely give us all things?" (NKJV).*

Romans 8:31-32 *"So, what do you think? With God on our side like this, how can we lose? If God didn't hesitate to put everything on the line for us, embracing our condition and exposing himself to the worst by sending his own Son, is there anything else he wouldn't gladly and freely do for us?" (Message).*

Lord, I declare that every spiritual castration in my life is reversed.

47. Romans 8:11 *"But if the Spirit of Him who raised Jesus from the dead dwells in you, He who raised Christ from the dead will also give life to your mortal bodies through His Spirit, who dwells in you." (NKJV).*

Every deadness in my life, I command you to be quickened by the Spirit of God.

48. Ezekiel 18: 20 *"The soul who sins shall die. The son shall not bear the guilt of the father, nor the father bear the guilt of the son. The righteousness of the righteous shall be upon himself, and the wickedness of the wicked shall be upon himself." (NKJV).*

Father in your compassion and mercy, we come against any, and all generational curses that the enemy tries to unleash on any member of this church. We claim the blessings in the work of God that the teeth of your children at this church will never be

Let Us Pray

set on edge because of the errors or mistakes of their forebears in Jesus' name.

49. *Colossians 2:14-15 "having wiped out the handwriting of requirements that was against us, which was contrary to us. And He has taken it out of the way, having nailed it to the cross. 15. Having disarmed principalities and powers, He made a public spectacle of them, triumphing over them in it." (NKJV).*

Whatever cannot hold Christ, will not hold me down.

50. *Acts 2: 46-47 "So continuing daily with one accord in the temple, and breaking bread from house to house, they ate their food with gladness and simplicity of heart, praising God and having favor with all the people. And the Lord added to the church daily those who were being saved. (NKJV).*

Father in the name of Jesus, we declare that as we worship and praise you in this house and break bread, the spirit of revival will rest upon us that will breakout into the community, and Nation at large. We will go from house to house preaching the gospel and having favor with the people. Souls will be added to Your kingdom in Jesus Name.

51. *Isaiah 33:20 "Look upon Zion, the city of our appointed feasts; Your eyes will see Jerusalem, a quiet home, a tabernacle that will not be taken down; not one of its stakes will ever be removed, nor will any of its cords be broken." (NKJV).*

Father, frustrate and cast down every power planning to wage war against the divine vision of our church, every member of our church and his family, in the name of Jesus!

52. Exodus 4:19 "*Now the Lord said to Moses in Midian, "Go, return to Egypt, for all the men who sought your life are dead." (NKJV).*

Father, paralyze anyone or group of people planning to destroy my destiny in the name of Jesus.

53. Psalms 2:8 "*Ask of Me, and I will surely give the [a]nations as Your inheritance, And the very ends of the earth as Your possession." (NASB).*

Father, we ask that in this year, the Gospel of our Lord Jesus Christ will flourish and reign mightily across the nations of the earth. That many more nations will open their borders to Missionaries and to the Gospel of Christ. In such nations, violence shall cease, and peace shall reign!

54. Isaiah 50:7 "*For the Lord God will help Me; Therefore, I will not be disgraced; Therefore I have set My face like a flint, And I know that I will not be ashamed. (NKJV).*

Father, I bind every spirit of frustration, defeat, delayed blessing, and fear in my environment, in the name of Jesus!

55. Ecclesiastes 10:7; "*I have seen servants on horses, while princes walk on the ground like servants." (NKJV).*

Father, I destroy every vulture released by the enemy to eat or hinder my destiny and that of my family, in the name of Jesus!

56. Psalms 68:30 "*Rebuke our enemies, O Lord. Bring them— submissive, tax in hand. Scatter all who delight in war." (TLB).*

Let Us Pray

Father, rebuke my enemies, let them submit themselves to me and make me rulers over those who hate me in the name of Jesus.

57. *Matthew 14:24 "But the ship was now in the midst of the sea, tossed with waves: for the wind was contrary." (KJV).*

We stop every contrary wind against our church, every member of our church, and your servant and his family, in the name of Jesus!

58. *Matthew 9:37-38 "Then He said to His disciples "The harvest is truly plentiful, but the laborers are few. Therefore, pray the Lord of the harvest to send out laborers into His harvest." (NKJV).*

Father, open our eyes to the harvest before us. Lead us as a church to go out in the fields and get to work. We thank you that you will raise up men, women, and children to make disciples here and around the world.

59. *Job 5:12 "He frustrates the devices of the crafty, so that their hands cannot carry out their plans." (NKJV).*

Lord, build a wall of protection around our pastor, his wife, and their children, in the name of Jesus. Let every plan against them be frustrated, in the name of Jesus.

60. *Psalms 37:23-24; "The Lord directs the steps of the godly. He delights in every detail of their lives. Though they stumble, they will never fall, for the Lord holds them by the hand." (NLT).*

Father, I pray against every false open door (pseudo-blessing) that could lead to physical or spiritual destruction of our church members and its leadership, in the name of Jesus!

61. *Psalms 68:1-2 "God is already beginning to arise, and His enemies to scatter; let them also who hate Him flee before Him! As smoke is driven away, so drive them away; as wax melts before the fire, so let the wicked perish before the presence of God." (Amplified).*

Arise O God and scatter all the enemies of our church and let those who plan evil against our church and its members be put to shame.

62. *2 Corinthians 10:5 "Casting down imaginations, and every high thing that exalteth itself against the knowledge of God..." (KJV).*

I pray that every attack and evil imagination against our church, its leadership and membership are stopped, cast down and destroyed, in the name of Jesus!

63. *2 Chronicles 14:3 "For he removed that altar of foreign gods and the high places and broke down the sacred pillars and cut down the wooden images." (NKJV).*

I pray we destroy every strange and foreign altar raised against our church, every member of our church and your servant and his family, in the name of Jesus!

64. *Isaiah 37:14 "Then Hezekiah took the letter from the hand of the messengers and read it, and he went up to the house of the LORD and spread it out before the LORD. (NIV).*

Let Us Pray

Father, I declare that every letter, email, or text written against me and concerning my destiny, becomes my instrument of testimony, in the name of Jesus!

65. *Psalms 23:5 "You prepare a table before me in the presence of my enemies;You anoint my head with oil; My cup runs over." (NKJV).*

Father, those who say I will not reach my goal, vision, or destiny, paralyze them so that when I reach my goal, vision, or destiny, they will be able to see Your glory over me, in the name of Jesus!

66. *Psalms 7:6 "Arise, O Lord, in Your anger; Lift Yourself up because of the rage of my enemies; Rise up for me to the judgment You have commanded! (NKJV).*

Every rage of the enemy against my destiny, scatter in the name of Jesus!

67. *Psalms 37:14-15 "The wicked draw the sword and bend the bow to bring down the poor and needy, to slay those whose ways are upright. 15 But their swords will pierce their own hearts, and their bows will be broken." (NIV).*

Owner of evil load, I command you to carry your load in the name of Jesus!

68. *Jeremiah 31:29 "In those days they shall say no more: "The Fathers have eaten sour grapes, and the children's teeth are set on edge."(NKJV).*

Father, I declare that from today, the failure that happened in the lives of my parents will not happen in my life and in the lives of my children, in the name of Jesus!

69. *Psalms 3:7 "Up, God! My God, help me! Slap their faces, first this cheek, then the other, Your fist hard in their teeth!" (Message).*

Father, I command my guardian angels to slap all unprofitable and evil broadcasters of my goodness, and of our church and of our pastors; and silence them in the name of Jesus!

70. *Ezekiel 34:5 "And now they're scattered every which way because there was no shepherd—scattered and easy pickings for wolves and coyotes." (Message).*

Father, I destroy every organized network of demonic wickedness against our Shepherds and Pastors, and their family; and frustrate every negative utterance declared against them in the name of Jesus!

71. *Isaiah 49:26 "And your enemies, crazed and desperate, will turn on themselves, killing each other in a frenzy of self–destruction. Then everyone will know that I, God, have saved you—I, the Mighty One of Jacob." (Message).*

Father, I declare, any power planning untimely death for me this year, die in my place, in the name of Jesus!

72. *Hebrews 6:3 "And so, God willing, we will move forward to further understanding." (NLT).*

Let Us Pray

Father, I break myself loose from the bondage of life stagnation. I shall move forward and reverse every evil arrangement setup for my life, in the name of Jesus!

73. *Numbers 23:23 "For there is no sorcery against Jacob, nor any divination against Israel. It must be said of Jacob and of Israel, "Oh, what God has done!" (NKJV).*

Father, let every spell, jinx, and demonic incantation rendered against every member of our church be canceled, in the name of Jesus.

74. *Numbers 23:5 "Nevertheless the Lord your God would not listen to Balaam, but the Lord your God turned the curse into a blessing for you, because the Lord your God loves you. (NKJV).*

Father, I declare that every curse pronounced against our church, our pastors and every member of our church, turns into a blessing for us, in the name of Jesus! Disgrace every Balaam raised against us in the name of Jesus!

75. *Psalms 3:7 "Up, God! My God, help me! Slap their faces, first this cheek, then the other, Your fist hard in their teeth!" (Message).*

Father, I command my guardian angels to slap all unprofitable and evil broadcasters of my goodness, our church and our pastors, and silence them in the name of Jesus!

76. *Isaiah 49:26 "And your enemies, crazed and desperate, will turn on themselves, killing each other in a frenzy of self-destruction.*

Then everyone will know that I, God, have save
Mighty One of Jacob." (Message).

Father, I declare, any power planning untimely death for me
this year, die in my place, in the name of Jesus!

77. *Hebrews 6:3 "And so, God willing, we will move forward to*
further understanding." (NLT).

Father, I break myself loose from the bondage of life stagnation.
I shall move forward and reverse every evil arrangement setup
for my life, in the name of Jesus!

78. *Isaiah 49:26 "And your enemies, crazed and desperate, will turn*
on themselves, killing each other in a frenzy of self-destruction.
Then everyone will know that I, God, have saved you—I, the
Mighty One of Jacob." (Message).

Father, we send confusion into the camp of any group ganging
up against our pastors, and against our church. Let them turn on
each other in a frenzy of self-destruction, in the name of Jesus!

79. *Jeremiah 1:19 "They will fight against you, but they shall not*
prevail against you. For I am with you, says the LORD, to deliver
you." (NKJV).

Father, we declare that every attack against our pastors and their
children shall not prevail in the name of Jesus! We receive
victory for our pastors; grant them peace on every side in the
name of Jesus!

Let Us Pray

80. Jeremiah 31:29 *"In those days they shall say no more: "The Fathers have eaten sour grapes, and the children's teeth are set on edge." (NKJV).*

Father, I declare that from today, the failure that happened in the lives of my parents, will not happen in my life or in the lives of my children, in the name of Jesus!

81. Psalms 16:1-2 Preserve me, O God, for in You I put my trust. O my soul, you have said to the Lord, "You are my Lord, my goodness is nothing apart from You." (NKJV).

Father, frustrate every territorial spirit working against our church, pastors, and members of our church, in the name of Jesus!

82. Zephaniah 3:15 "The LORD has taken away your judgements, He has cast out your enemy. The King of Israel, The LORD, is in your midst; you shall see disaster no more." (NKJV).

Father, take away from our church any judgment against us, cast away all our enemies as you have promised. Rule in our midst throughout this year and let us see no disaster in the name of Jesus!

83. Isaiah 17:14 "Then behold, at eventide, trouble! And before the morning, he is no more. This is the portion of those who plunder us, and the lot of those who rob us." (NKJV).

Father, frustrate and disgrace anyone that threatens to plunder or rob our pastors of relevance and impact; home and abroad, in the name of Jesus!

84. Luke 8:17 *"For nothing is secret that will not be revealed, nor anything hidden that will not be known and come to light."* *(NKJV).*

Lord, bring to light and expose everything planned in darkness, against our church, its members, and our pastor's family, in the name of Jesus!

85. Judges 8:28 *"That is the story of how the people of Israel defeated Midian, which never recovered. Throughout the rest of Gideon's lifetime–about forty years–there was peace in the land." (NLT).*

Father, defeat and scatter all those who plot to see me fail and do not let them recover again, in the name of Jesus. Surround me all around with your peace.

86. Psalms 44:4-5 *"You're my King, O God—command victories for Jacob! With your help we'll wipe out our enemies, in your name we'll stomp them to dust." (Message).*

Father, we destroy and wipe out every attack and gang-up against our church, its members, and our pastors. We receive our victory in the name of Jesus!

87. Isaiah 50:11 *"But if all you're after is making trouble, playing with fire, go ahead and see where it gets you. Set your fires, stir people up, blow on the flames, but don't expect me to just stand there and watch. I'll hold your feet to those flames." (Message).*

Father, frustrate and destroy anything or anyone planning against our pastors, and their family. Hold the feet of the wicked

Let Us Pray

to the flames of fire that they set up for our pastors, in the name of Jesus!

88. *1 Corinthians 2:12 – Now we have received, not the spirit of the world, but the Spirit who is from God, that we might know the things that have been freely given to us by God. (NKJV).*

Father, everything that belongs to me that the enemy is trying to hide from me, restore them to me, in the name of Jesus. Lord let me begin to enjoy everything that you have freely given to me, (health, wealth, prosperity) in the name of Jesus!

89. *Isaiah 33:20 "Look upon Zion, the city of our appointed feasts; Your eyes will see Jerusalem, a quiet home, a Tabernacle that will not be taken down; not one of its stakes will ever be removed, nor will any of its cords be broken." (NKJV).*

Father, frustrate and cast down every power planning to wage war against the divine vision of our church, our pastors, and every member of our church, in the name of Jesus!

90. *Job 5:12 "He frustrates the devices of the crafty, so that their hands cannot carry out their plans." (NKJV).*

Lord, build a wall of protection around our pastors and their children, in the name of Jesus. Let every plan against them be frustrated, in the name of Jesus!

91. *Judges 8:28 "That is the story of how the people of Israel defeated Midian, which never recovered. Throughout the rest of Gideon's lifetime–about forty years–there was peace in the land." (NLT).*

Israel Ade-Ajala

Father, defeat and scatter all those who are plotting to see me fail, and do not let them recover again, in the name of Jesus. Surround me all around with your peace.

92. *Psalms 44:4-5 "You're my King, O God—command victories for Jacob! With your help we'll wipe out our enemies, in your name we'll stomp them to dust." (Message).*

Father, we destroy and wipe out every attack and gang-up against our church, its members and our pastors. We receive our victory in the name of Jesus!

93. *Psalms 18:24 "God rewrote the text of my life when I opened the book of my heart to his eyes." (Message).*

Father, rewrite the text of my life, fill in the details of your blessings and cancel every agenda of the wicked against me, my family, and our church, in the name of Jesus!

94. *Joshua 5:9 "Then the Lord said to Joshua, "This day I have rolled away the reproach of Egypt from you." Therefore, the name of the place is called Gilgal to this day." (NKJV).*

Father, I declare that every pain and struggle of the past year will not follow me into this new year. Roll away every reproach of my life, in the name of Jesus. In this new year, turn my tears to cheers, in the name of Jesus.

95. *Psalms 16: 9-10 "I'm happy from the inside out, and from the outside in, I'm firmly formed. You canceled my ticket to hell— that's not my destination!" (Message).*

Let Us Pray

Father, I cancel today every grave dug for any member of our church in this new year. I declare that no one will die in our midst, in the name of Jesus!

96. *Judges 8:28 "That is the story of how the people of Israel defeated Midian, which never recovered. Throughout the rest of Gideon's lifetime–about forty years–there was peace in the land." (NLT).*

Father, defeat and scatter all those who are plotting to see me fail and do not let them recover again, in the name of Jesus. Surround me all around with your peace.

97. *Psalms 44:4-5 "You're my King, O God—command victories for Jacob! With your help we'll wipe out our enemies, in your name we'll stomp them to dust." (Message).*

Father, we destroy and wipe out every attack and gang-up against our church, our members, and our pastors. We receive our victory, in the name of Jesus!

98. *Psalms 3:7 "Up, God! My God, help me! Slap their faces, first this cheek, then the other, Your fist hard in their teeth!" (Message).*

Father, I command my guardian angels to slap all unprofitable and evil broadcasters of my goodness and of our church and pastors, and silence them, in the name of Jesus!

99. *Ezekiel 34:5 "And now they're scattered every which way because there was no shepherd—scattered and easy pickings for wolves and coyotes."(Message).*

Father, I destroy every organized network of demonic wickedness against our Shepherds and Pastors, and their family; and frustrate every negative utterance declared against them, in the name of Jesus!

100. *Isaiah 49:26 "And your enemies, crazed and desperate, will turn on themselves, killing each other in a frenzy of self-destruction. Then everyone will know that I, God, have saved you—I, the Mighty One of Jacob." (Message).*

Father, I declare, any power planning untimely death for me this year, die in my place, in the name of Jesus!

101. *Hebrews 6:3"And so, God willing, we will move forward to further understanding."(NLT).*

Father, I break myself loose from the bondage of life stagnation. I shall move forward and reverse every evil arrangement setup for my life, in the name of Jesus!

102. *Matthew 14:24 "But the ship was now in the midst of the sea, tossed with waves: for the wind was contrary." (KJV).*

We stop every contrary wind against our church, our pastor's family and every member of our church in the name of Jesus!

103. *Psalms 68:28 "Your God has commanded your strength, strengthen, O God, what You have done for us." (NKJV).*

O Lord, let no man prevail against our church, its leadership, and membership, in the name of Jesus!

Let Us Pray

104. *Psalms 44:4-5 "You're my King, O God—command victories for Jacob! With your help we'll wipe out our enemies, in your name we'll stomp them to dust." (Message).*

Father, we destroy and wipe out every attack and gang-up against our church, its members, and our pastors. We receive our victory, in the name of Jesus!

105. *Matthew 10:1 "And when He had called His twelve disciples to Him, He gave them power over unclean spirits, to cast them out, and to heal all kinds of sickness and all kinds of disease." (NKJV).*

Lord, release fresh unction unto our church as a ministry, and use this church to destroy the satanic kingdom in this nation and all over the world, in the name of Jesus.

106. *Esther 7:10 "So they hanged Haman on the gallows that he had prepared for Mordecai. Then the king's wrath subsided. (NKJV).*

Father, let my enemies be hanged on the pole they had set up for me. Let them be hanged on the gallows which they had prepared for me.

107. *Psalms 18:36 "You cleared the ground under me, so my footing was firm. (Message).*

Father, hold me firmly and let nothing pull me down. Set my footing firmly on your word and make me an example of the power of your word in the name of Jesus.

34

Israel Ade-Ajala

108. Jeremiah 30:19 *"Then out of them shall proceed thanksgiving and the voice of those who make merry; I will multiply them, and they shall not diminish; I will also glorify them, and they shall not be small. (NKJV).*

Father, we destroy and pull down every form of limitation structured against our church in the name of Jesus Christ.

109. Matthew 9:38 *"Therefore pray The Lord of the harvest to send out laborers into His harvest." (NKJV).*

Lord, bring the workers of Your choice to our church and keep all other evil agents away, in the name of Jesus!

110. Numbers 23:23 *"No curse can touch Jacob; no magic has any power against Israel. For now, it will be said of Jacob, 'What wonders God has done for Israel!" (NLT).*

Father, we destroy every instrument of war (physical, verbal, or spiritual) raised against our pastors and their family, in the name of Jesus. Disgrace and humiliate those who want them to fail in the name of Jesus.

111. Isaiah 55:13 *"No more thistles, but giant sequoias, no more thornbushes, but stately pines— Monuments to me, to God, living and lasting evidence of God." (Message).*

Father, every root curse of poverty and inability to multiply resources, I command it to leave my life alone, in the mighty name of Jesus Christ!

Let Us Pray

112.   *Galatians 5:10 "...The one who is throwing you into confusion will pay the penalty, whoever he may be. (NIV).*

Father, in the mighty name of Jesus Christ, I break all satanic and wicked powers that keep me moving in a circle without any tangible result or achievement.

113.   *Isaiah 17:14 "At bedtime, terror fills the air. By morning it's gone—not a sign of it anywhere! This is what happens to those who would ruin us, this is the fate of those out to get us." (Message).*

Father, frustrate and disgrace anyone that threatens to plunder or rob our pastors of relevance and impact, home and abroad, in the name of Jesus!

114.   *Deuteronomy 1:6-7 "Back at Horeb, God, our God, spoke to us: "You've stayed long enough at this mountain. On your way now. Get moving." (Message).*

Father, in the precious name of Jesus Christ, I command every embargo of stagnation and limitation on my life to break and shatter to pieces now!

115.   *2 Timothy 1:7 "For God has not given us a spirit of fear, but of power and of love and of a sound mind." (NKJV).*

Father, because you have not given me the spirit of fear but of love, power, and of a sound mind, I hereby arrest the spirit of fear, anxiety, depression and cast them out of my life, in Jesus mighty name I pray!

36

Israel Ade-Ajala

116. *Exodus 4:17 "And you shall take this rod in your hand, with which you shall do the signs." (NKJV).*

Father, I hold the rod of God in my hands. I smash the head of every oppressor in the name of Jesus!

117. *1 Samuel 17:54 "And David took the head of the Philistine and brought it to Jerusalem, but he put his armor in his tent." (NKJV).*

O God, arise and place the head of my Goliath in my hands, in the name of Jesus!

118. *1 Samuel 30: 4 & 17 "Then David and the people who were with him lifted their voices and wept, until they had no more power to weep... Then David attacked them from twilight until the evening of the next day. Not a man of them escaped, except four hundred young men who rode on camels and fled." (NKJV).*

Father, crush and destroy the power that has made me cry in the name of Jesus!

119. *1 Samuel 17:49 "Then David put his hand in his bag and took out a stone; and he slung it and struck the Philistine in his forehead, so that the stone sank into his forehead, and he fell on his face to the earth." (NKJV).*

Father, let my stone locate the forehead of my Goliath and smash it, in the name of Jesus!

Let Us Pray

120. *Isaiah 54:15 "Behold they shall surely gather together, but not by me: whosoever shall gather together against thee shall fall for thy sake." (KJV).*

Father, scatter all those who gathered to celebrate my fall and clothe them with shame in the name of Jesus!

121. *Acts 23:21 "More than forty men are hiding and waiting to kill Paul. They have all taken an oath not to eat or drink until they have killed him. Now they are waiting for you to agree." (NCV).*

Father, we annul, revoke, and renounce every evil vow, every evil association, evil network, and evil alliance against the advancement of our church and of our pastors, in the name of Jesus.

122. *Proverbs 4:18 "The ways of right-living people glow with light; the longer they live, the brighter they shine." (Message).*

Father, in this year, no area of our lives will experience darkness, we shall live brighter, and we shall shine brighter in all areas of our lives, in the name of Jesus.

123. *Isaiah 54:17 "Weapons made to attack you won't be successful; words spoken against you won't hurt at all. My servant, Jerusalem is yours! I, the Lord, promise to bless you with victory." (CEV).*

Every weapon (physical, verbal, or spiritual) that is made to attack our pastors and their children, won't be successful. Every

wicked gossiper and evil broadcaster of our pastors and his family will suffer shame and devastations in the name of Jesus!

124.   *Psalms 68:30 "Rebuke our enemies, O Lord. Bring them–submissive, tax in hand. Scatter all who delight in war." (TLB).*

Father, rebuke all the enemies of our pastors, and their family. Let their enemies submit themselves to them and make our pastors rulers over those who hate him, in the name of Jesus.

125.   *Psalms 121:7-8 "The Lord keeps you from all harm and watches over your life. The Lord keeps watch over you as you come and go, both now and forever. (NLT).*

Father, we declare that no one in our church family will die this year. No one shall be missing nor suffer loss, in the name of Jesus.

126.   *2 Chronicles 29:36 "And Hezekiah and all the people rejoiced because of what God had done for the people, for everything had been accomplished so quickly." (NLT).*

Father, we declare no more delay and no more slowdown, in the name of Jesus. Everything will work out quickly for us this year in the name of Jesus.

127.   *Esther 7:10 "So Haman was hanged on the very gallows that he had built for Mordecai. And the king's hot anger cooled." (Message).*

Let Us Pray

Father, let my enemies be hanged on the pole they had set up for me. Let them be hanged on the gallows which they had prepared for me.

128.   *Numbers 16:48 "And he took his place between the dead and the living: and the disease was stopped." (BBE).*

Father, we declare that we take our place as the royal priesthood that God has made us, and we stop the plague of any pandemic in the name of Jesus!

129.   *Job 38:11 "I said, 'This far and no farther will you come. Here your proud waves must stop!'" (NLT).*

Father, we decree and declare that any pandemic and any disease thus far, you will come. Your proud waves stop now. You will go no farther, in the name of Jesus!

130.   *Numbers 16:48 "And he took his place between the dead and the living: and the disease was stopped." (BBE).*

We take our place as the royal priesthood that God has made us, and we stop the plague of any pandemic, in the name of Jesus!

131.   *Jeremiah 16:16-17 "But now I am sending for many fishermen who will catch them," says the LORD. "I am sending for hunters who will hunt them down in the mountains, hills, and caves. I am watching them closely, and I see every sin. They cannot hope to hide from me." (NLT).*

Father, arise and hunt down all those who are playing politics with the lives of the people of all over the world. Fish and flush

them out, in the name of Jesus. Expose their wickedness and let them have no place to hide again, in the name of Jesus.

132.   Psalms 24:9 *"So wake up, you living gateways, and rejoice! Fling wide, you ageless doors of destiny! Here he comes; the King of Glory is ready to come in." (Passion).*

Father, we declare every closed door of opportunities, of promotion, of success, of increase, of favor, and of honor begin to open for me now, in the name of Jesus. Lead the way and cause every closed door to open, in the name of Jesus.

133.   Psalms 69:29-30 *"But rescue me, O God, from my poverty and pain. Then I will praise God with my singing! My thanks will be his praise. (TLB).*

Father, rescue me from poverty and pain. Let favor locate me and terminate labor and toiling in my life, in the name of Jesus.

134.   Psalms 108:13 *"With God's help we will prevail with might and power. And with God's help we'll trample down our every foe!" (Passion).*

Father, I destroy every power preventing me from enjoying the goodness of The Lord in this land, in the name of Jesus!

135.   Isaiah 54:17 *"Weapons made to attack you won't be successful; words spoken against you won't hurt at all. My servant, Jerusalem is yours! I, the Lord, promise to bless you with victory." (CEV).*

Let Us Pray

Every weapon (physical, verbal, or spiritual) made to attack our pastors and their children, won't be successful. Every wicked gossiper and evil broadcasters of our pastors and their families will suffer shame and devastations, in the name of Jesus!

136.   Psalms 68:30 "Rebuke our enemies, O Lord. Bring them–submissive, tax in hand. Scatter all who delight in war." (TLB).

Father, rebuke all the enemies of our pastors and their families. Let their enemies submit themselves, and make our pastors ruler over those who hate them, in the name of Jesus.

137.   Job 5:12 "He aborts the schemes of conniving crooks, so that none of their plots come to term." (Message).

Father, we abort and nullify every scheme of conniving crooks against every member of our church family, in the name of Jesus. No one in our church will suffer defeat this year, in the name of Jesus.

138.   Isaiah 50:7 "But if all you're after is making trouble, playing with fire, Go ahead and see where it gets you. Set your fires, stir people up, blow on the flames, But don't expect me to just stand there and watch. I'll hold your feet to those flames. (Message).

Father, hold the feet of those who plan to hurt our church and members, to fire and let them burn in the flames that they set for us, in the name of Jesus.

139.   Psalms 121:7-8 "The Lord keeps you from all harm and watches over your life. 8 The Lord keeps watch over you as you come and go, both now and forever. (NLT).

Father, we declare that no one in our church family will die this year. No one shall be missing, no one will suffer loss, in the name of Jesus.

140.   2 Chronicles 29:36 "And Hezekiah and all the people rejoiced because of what God had done for the people, for everything had been accomplished so quickly." (NLT).

Father, we declare no more delay and no more slow-down in the name of Jesus. Everything will work out quickly for us this year, in the name of Jesus.

141.   Isaiah 26:6 "The time will come when Israel will take root and bud and blossom and fill the whole earth with her fruit!" (TLB).

Father, the time has come to establish your son, our pastor, as your voice to the nations. Let him take root in every continent of the world, and bud and blossom, in the name of Jesus. Justify your anointing upon his life through miracles, signs, and wonders in the name of Jesus.

142.   2 Chronicles 14:7 "...we have this peaceful land because we sought GOD; he has given us rest from all troubles." So they built and enjoyed prosperity." (Message).

Father, we declare peace and prosperity upon everyone that has given, and continues to give, to the ministries of our church. Let their hands always remain on top, and let none of them suffer loss, in the name of Jesus!

Let Us Pray

143.   Esther 2:21-22 *"Now Bigthana and Teresh were two of the king's eunuchs who guarded the doorway. While Mordecai was sitting at the king's gate, they became angry and began to make plans to kill King Xerxes. 22 But Mordecai found out about their plans and told Queen Esther. Then Esther told the king how Mordecai had discovered the evil plan." (NCV).*

Father, expose every evil plan and imagination against our pastors and their children. Let every Bigthana and Teresh hang themselves, in the name of Jesus.

144.   John 9:5 *"As long as I am with you my life is the light that pierces the world's darkness." (TPT).*

Father, let your light pierce every darkness in my life, home, finances, health, business, and family, in the name of Jesus. Shine your light on me and make me a success story in this nation, in the name of Jesus.

145.   Psalms 29:11 *"This is the one who gives his strength and might to his people. This is the Lord giving us his kiss of peace." (TPT).*

Father, give me Your kiss of peace in every area of my life, in the name of Jesus. As we come to the end of this year, let your peace surround me.

146.   Psalms 30:11 *"Then he broke through and transformed all my wailing into a whirling dance of ecstatic praise He has torn the veil and lifted from me the sad heaviness of mourning. He wrapped me in the glory garments of gladness." (TPT).*

Father, breakthrough for me and transform my tears and pain into a dance of ecstatic praise. Tear from me any garment capable of producing mourning or heaviness of the heart, and wrap me with glorious garments of joy and gladness, in the name of Jesus.

147. *Psalms 119:31 "Lord, don't allow me to make a mess of my life, for I cling to your commands and follow them as closely as I can." (TPT).*

Father, don't let me make a mess of my life, give me discernment to discover every trap the enemy has laid for me and to avoid them.

148. *Psalms 119:66 "Teach me how to make good decisions, and give me revelation-light, for I believe in your commands." (TPT).*

Father, teach me how to make good decisions and do not let me go astray, in the name of Jesus. Guide my steps and order my life to glorify You, in the name of Jesus.

149. *Psalms 31:16 "Smile on me, your servant. Let your undying love and glorious grace save me from all this gloom." (TPT).*

Father, continue to smile on our pastors and their children, in the name of Jesus. Let your undying love and glorious grace surround them continually and protect them from all haters, in the name of Jesus.

150. *Psalms 31:20 "So hide all your beloved ones in the sheltered, secret place before your face. Overshadow them by your glory-*

Let Us Pray

presence. Keep them from these accusations, the brutal insults of evil men. Tuck them safely away in the tabernacle where you dwell." (TPT).

Father, hide our pastors and their children in the secret place before your face. Let the glory of your presence overshadow them continually, in the name of Jesus. Keep them insulated and protected from accusations and insults of wicked and evil people, in the name of Jesus.

151. *Galatians 1:17 "And I chose not to run to Jerusalem to try to impress those who had become apostles before me. Instead, I went away into the Arabian Desert for a season until I returned to Damascus, where I had first encountered Jesus." (TPT).*

Father, deliver me from my sin of pleasing people. Lead me back to the place I had first encountered, Jesus. Lead me back to my first love and let the fire of the Holy Spirit burn brightly inside me and through me, in the name of Jesus.

152. *Galatians 1:24 "Because of the transformation that took place in my life, they praised God even more!" (TPT).*

Father, let the testimonies of your hand upon our church cause many to praise you even more, in the name of Jesus. Transform our lives continually so that we will always point people to your saving grace, in the name of Jesus. Let us bear fruit that will remain forever, in the name of Jesus.

153. *Psalms 28: 5 "Since they don't care anything about you, or about the great things you've done, take them down like an old building being demolished, never again to be rebuilt." (TPT).*

Father, take them down like old buildings being demolished. Take down all those who attacked, or plan to attack our church, our vision, our leadership, and membership. Never let our haters rise again in the name of Jesus.

154. *1 Kings 3:3 "Solomon loved GOD and continued to live in the God-honoring ways of David his father, except that he also worshiped at the local shrines, offering sacrifices and burning incense." (Message).*

Father, show me every local shrine in my life, and give me the courage to destroy them. Help me to live a life that pleases you, in the name of Jesus.

155. *Hebrews 10:24 "Discover creative ways to encourage others and to motivate them toward acts of compassion, doing beautiful works as expressions of love." (PASSION).*

Father, make me a blessing to nations. Make me a destiny helper and a lifter of the fallen. I declare that I will impact the lives of many, and nations will come to the brightness of my shining, in the name of Jesus.

156. *Exodus 1:7 "But the children of Israel were fruitful and increased abundantly, multiplied and grew exceedingly mighty; and the land was filled with them." (NKJV).*

Father, we declare that we shall continue to be fruitful and increase abundantly in this land. We shall become exceedingly mighty and powerful. We shall possess the gates of the cities, and make your glories known, in the name of Jesus.

Let Us Pray

157.   Psalms 119:39 "Defend me from the criticism I face for keeping your beautiful words." (TPT).

Father, defend and protect our pastors and their children from criticism and careless talk of haters. In the presence of their haters, make them your voice, in the name of Jesus.

158.   Isaiah 54:15 "Behold, they may gather together and stir up strife, but it is not from Me. Whoever stirs up strife against you shall fall and surrender to you." (AMPC).

Father, we declare that anyone gathering to stir up strife against our pastors and their children, shall fall and never rise again, in the name of Jesus. They shall go down in defeat and will never rise to prominence, in the name of Jesus.

159.   Zechariah 3:2 "And the LORD said to Satan, "The LORD rebuke you, Satan! The LORD who has chosen Jerusalem rebuke you! Is this not a brand plucked from the fire?" (NKJV).

Satan, the Lord of Host rebukes you over every city in the world, in the mighty name of Jesus! You will not prosper in this land again, in the mighty name of Jesus Christ. We declare peace over our cities, in the name of Jesus.

160.   Proverbs 3:5-6 "Trust in the LORD with all your heart and lean not on your own understanding; 6 In all your ways acknowledge Him, And He shall direct your paths. (NKJV).

Lord, we declare that all government leaders will fear the Lord and listen carefully to His voice, and that every decision they

make would be based on God's will and plan for our countries in this world.

161. Proverbs 29:2 *"When the righteous are in authority, the people rejoice; But when a wicked man rules, the people groan." (NKJV).*

Father, we pray that you will put righteous people in authority in every seat of government all over the world. Direct our heart to vote for those who will promote righteousness and not hate, bigotry or division, in the name of Jesus!

162. Psalms 2:10-11 *"Therefore, you kings, be wise; be warned, you rulers of the earth. Serve the LORD with fear and celebrate his rule with trembling. (NIV).*

Father, we pray for every president and their respective governments. That they will receive wisdom and lead their nations in the fear of God and in the beauty of holiness and love.

163. Psalms 33:12 *"Blessed and prosperous is that nation who has God as their Lord! They will be the people he has chosen for his own." (TPT).*

Father, we declare you as God and Lord over every nation of the world. Bless and prosper every nation again and again. Let your face shine continuously over every nation. No nation shall go down, in the mighty name of Jesus!

164. Job 14:4 *"Who can make a clean thing out of the unclean? No one!" (Amplified).*

Let Us Pray

Father, you are the only one that can cleanse the unclean. Do it again in every country and continent. Arise Oh Lord, hunt down all those playing politics with the lives of the people of this land, and expose their wickedness. Revive this world again and bless this land.

165.   *Psalms 69:23 "Let their eyes be darkened, so that they do not see; And make their loins shake continually. 24. Pour out Your Indignation upon them, And let Your wrathful anger take hold of them." (NKJV).*

Father, darken the eyes of my enemies of progress, make them shake continually and lift me up above their evil thoughts, in the mighty name of Jesus! Pour out your indignation upon them Lord, and let your wrathful anger take hold of them, in the mighty name of Jesus!

166.   *Proverbs 4:18 "But the path of the just is as the shining light, that shineth more and more unto the perfect day." (KJV).*

Father, we decree that the vision and mission of this church will go stronger and brighter with greater impact; from one generation to another, in the name of Jesus Christ.

167.   *Ephesians 6:19 "And pray for me, too. Ask God to give me the right words so I can boldly explain God's mysterious plan that the Good News is for Jews and Gentiles alike." (NLT).*

Father, by your Spirit, empower all our ministries in this church to deliver their functions with greater effectiveness for the glory of your holy name, and for the blessing of the people here at this

church. Grant greater insight unto all ministry leaders to obtain greater results, in the name of Jesus.

168.   Acts 26:16-18 *"But rise, and stand upon thy feet: for I have appeared unto thee for this purpose, to make thee a minister and a witness both of these things which thou hast seen, and of those things in the which I will appear unto thee; Delivering thee from the people, and from the Gentiles, unto whom now I send thee, To open their eyes, and to turn them from darkness to light, and from the power of Satan unto God, that they may receive forgiveness of sins, and inheritance among them which are sanctified by faith that is in me." (KJV).*

Father, I am the Light created to bring light to this dark world. Lord, Jesus, don't let my light become darkness. Don't let my light run out. Don't let my light burn out.

169.   Matthew 5:14-16 *"Ye are the light of the world. A city that is set on a hill cannot be hid. Neither do men light a candle, and put it under a bushel, but on a candlestick; and it giveth light unto all that are in the house. Let your light so shine before men, that they may see your good works, and glorify your Father which is in heaven." (KJV).*

Father, I am the solution to problems. Don't let me become the problem the world is solving. Increase my capacity to solve problems, in the name of Jesus Christ.

170.   Romans 15:18-19 *"For I will not dare to speak of any of those things which Christ hath not wrought by me, to make the Gentiles obedient, by word and deed, Through mighty signs and*

Let Us Pray

wonders, by the power of the Spirit of God; so that from Jerusalem, and round about unto Illyricum, I have fully preached the gospel of Christ." (KJV).

Father, in the name of Jesus, let the power of the Holy Ghost turn things around for my good, through mighty signs and wonders. Let the Person, Power and Principles of Christ be fully formed in me!

171.   *2 Thessalonians 1:3 "Dear brothers and sisters, we can't help but thank God for you, because your faith is flourishing and your love for one another is growing." (NLT).*

Father, let our children in this church continue to grow in the knowledge, the fear, and power of God continually.

172.   *Zechariah 2:3-5 "And there was the angel who talked with me, going out; and another angel was coming out to meet him, who said to him, "Run, speak to this young man, saying: 'Jerusalem shall be inhabited as towns without walls, because of the multitude of men and livestock in it. For I,' says the Lord, 'will be a wall of fire all around her, and I will be the glory in her midst." (NKJV).*

Father, increase this church numerically. Let multitudes of men and women flow into this Church and be established for life by the power of your Word.

173.   *Ezekiel 18:1-3 "God's Message to me: "What do you people mean by going around the country repeating the saying, The parents ate green apples, The children got the stomachache? "As*

sure as I'm the living God, you're not going to repeat this saying in Israel any longer." (Message).

I decree and declare that I will not fight my parents' battle. I set myself free from every generational evil pattern. I separate myself and my children from any generational problem, sickness, and poverty.

174. *Job 22:27-28 "You will make your prayer to Him, He will hear you, and you will pay your vows. 28 You will also declare a thing, and it will be established for you; so light will shine on your ways." (NKJV).*

Father, I declare light to shine on my ways. I declare light to shine on the path of my children. My children will see what they ought to see in Jesus' name.

175. *Isaiah 60:11 "Therefore your gates shall be open continually; they shall not be shut day or night, that men may bring to you the wealth of the gentiles, and their kings in procession." (NKJV).*

Lord, in this land, doors of advancement shall never be shut against our children. Their gates shall continually be open, wealth shall come to them.

176. *2 Chronicles 7:14 "If My people who are called by My name will humble themselves, and pray and seek My face, and turn from their wicked ways, then I will hear from heaven, and I will forgive their sin and heal their land." (NKJV).*

Lord, have mercy on us in this nation. Lord be gracious unto us and heal our land.

The Church

THE Gate of hell is fighting to render the church ineffective;
kingdomS of darkness lost that battle because the Lord himself
WAS building his church. The church is in many ways the
solution to the world problems. Let us stand together and pray for
the church of our lord Jesus Christ. (Matthew 16:18). Let us pray!

177. *Matthew 10:1 "And when He had called His twelve disciples
to Him, He gave them power over unclean spirits, to cast them
out, and to heal all kinds of sickness and all kinds of disease."
(NKJV).*

Lord, manifest your power in our church and use this church to
destroy the satanic kingdom in this nation and all over the world,
in the name of Jesus!

178. *Psalms 86:14-15 "O God, the proud have risen against me,
And a mob of violent men have sought my life, and have not set
You before them. But You, O Lord, are a God full of
compassion, and gracious, long-suffering and abundant in
mercy and truth." (NKJV).*

Father, I scatter every evil meeting summoned against the goal
and the vision of our church, our pastors, and every member, in
the name of Jesus.

179. *Isaiah 60: 22 "A little one shall become a thousand, and a
small one a strong nation: I the Lord will hasten it in his time."
(KJV).*

54

Father, pour upon us at this church Greater Grace, for unlimited Church Growth throughout this year. Supernaturally, increase us numerically, and let our impact spread into every soul in and around us!

180. *1 Corinthians 3:6 "My work was to plant the seed in your hearts, and Apollos' work was to water it, but it was God, not we, who made the garden grow in your hearts." (TLB).*

Father, throughout this year, let your WORD coming from this altar, prosper in my heart and profit my life.

181. *Jeremiah 1:19 "They will fight against you, but they shall not prevail against you. For I am with you, says the LORD, to deliver you." (NKJV).*

Father, I declare that every attack against our church, its members and our pastors, backfire, in the name of Jesus! We receive our victory in the name of Jesus!

182. *Ezra 6:3-4 "In the first year of King Cyrus, King Cyrus issued a decree concerning the house of God at Jerusalem: "Let the house be rebuilt, the place where they offered sacrifices; and let the foundations of it be firmly laid, its height sixty cubits and its width sixty cubits, with three rows of heavy stones and one row of new timber. Let the expenses be paid from the king's treasury." (NKJV).*

Father, complete our church building project, and let the expenses be paid from the King's treasury. Supply all the needed funds and send us financial Boaz in the name of Jesus!

Let Us Pray

183. 2 Chronicles 31:20 *"Thus Hezekiah did throughout all Judah, and he did what was good and right and true before the LORD his God." (NKJV).*

Father, help us to always do what is good, right. And true in your sight, as we serve you here at our church. Do not let us lose relevance, in the name of Jesus!

184. *Matthew 16:18-19 "And I also say to you that you are Peter, and on this rock I will build My church, and the gates of Hades shall not [g]prevail against it. And I will give you the keys of the kingdom of heaven, and whatever you bind on earth [h]will be bound in heaven, and whatever you loose on earth will be loosed in heaven." (NKJV).*

Father, we destroy every gang-up against the welfare and the growth of this church, in the name of Jesus! We crush every agenda of hell against the advancement of this church, in the name of Jesus!

185. *Zechariah 2:3-5 "And, behold, the angel that talked with me went forth, and another angel went out to meet him, And said unto him, Run, speak to this young man, saying, Jerusalem shall be inhabited as towns without walls for the multitude of men and cattle therein: For I, saith the Lord, will be unto her a wall of fire round about, and will be the glory in the midst of her." (KJV).*

Father, we declare that this church is a city without walls for the multitude of men and women trooping into worship & serve the

Israel Ade-Ajala

Lord in this place. This church, Your Growth and Your Glory, will know no bounds, in the name of Jesus Christ!

186. *Acts 5:12 "And through the hands of the apostles many signs and wonders were done among the people. And they were all with one accord in Solomon's porch." (NKJV).*

Father, in the name of Jesus, let there be a continuous eruption of miracles, signs, and wonders in all our services at this church, thereby drawing souls into the kingdom and into this church.

187. *Act 11:21- "And the hand of the Lord was with them, and a great number believed and turned to the Lord." (ESV).*

Father, in the name of Jesus, let your hand be upon us as we evangelize that people will believe and turn to you. With your fire burning through us, we will ignite the whole state and nation.

188. *Isaiah 56 :7 "Even them I will bring to My holy mountain and make them joyful in My house of prayer. Their burnt offerings and their sacrifices will be accepted on My altar; For My house shall be called a house of prayer for all nations." (NKJV).*

Father, make this church your house of prayer for all nations, in Jesus Name; Make everyone that comes here joyful, and accept our offerings and sacrifices, in Jesus Name.

189. *Acts 19: 11-12 "Now God worked unusual miracles by the hands of Paul, so that even handkerchiefs or aprons were*

Let Us Pray

brought from his body to the sick, and the disease left them and the evil spirits went out of them." (NKJV).

Father in the name of Jesus, saturate this church, the auditorium, grounds, and environment with your power, such that merely walking into it, will cause divine encounters. Healing, deliverance, and other miracles, signs, and wonders will continue to happen daily. These encounters will go round the world to draw men here to seek you in Jesus' name.

190. *Matthew 10:1 "And when He had called His twelve disciples to Him, He gave them power over unclean spirits, to cast them out, and to heal all kinds of sickness and all kinds of disease." (NKJV).*

Lord, reposition our church as a ministry, and use this church to destroy the satanic kingdom in this nation and all over the world, in the name of Jesus!

191. *2 Chronicles 31:20 "Thus Hezekiah did throughout all Judah, and he did what was good and right and true before the LORD his God." (NKJV).*

Father, help us to always do what is good, right, and true in your sight, as we serve you here at our church.

192. *Zephaniah 3:15 "The LORD has taken away your judgments, He has cast out your enemy. The King of Israel, The LORD, is in your midst; you shall see disaster no more." (NKJV).*

58

Father, take away from our church any negative propaganda against us. Cast away all our enemies as you have promised. Rule in our midst, and let us see disaster no more, in the name of Jesus!

193.   Exodus 36:5&7 "And they spoke to Moses, saying, "The people bring much more than enough for the service of the work which the Lord commanded us to do." .... for the material they had was sufficient for all the work to be done—indeed too much." (NKJV).

Father, supply all the finances, materials, and workers for the work of the new building. Let there be sufficiency and overflow, in the name of Jesus!

194.   Psalms 85:6 "Will You not revive us again, that Your people may rejoice in You?" (Amplified).

Father, send down the fire of revival upon our church and make us your voice in this land!

195.   Matthew 9:38 "Therefore pray The Lord of the harvest to send out laborers into His harvest." (NKJV).

Lord, bring the workers of Your choice to us and keep all other evil agents away, in the name of Jesus!

196.   Psalms 68:30 "Rebuke our enemies, O Lord. Bring them—submissive, tax in hand. Scatter all who delight in war." (TLB).

Let Us Pray

Father, scatter those who delight in spreading evil reports about our church, our pastors, and leadership, bring them to their knees with your righteous judgment in the name of Jesus!

197.   *Zechariah 8:3 "Thus says The Lord: "I will return to Zion, and dwell in the midst of Jerusalem. Jerusalem shall be called the City of Truth, The Mountain of The Lord of hosts, The Holy Mountain." (NKJV).*

Father return to our church in Your fullness, come and dwell in our midst and call our church the City of Truth in the name of Jesus.

198.   *2 Corinthians 7:1 "Therefore, having these promises, beloved, let us cleanse ourselves from all filthiness of the flesh and spirit, perfecting holiness in the fear of God." (NKJV).*

Lord, make our church a citadel of holiness, wonder, miracles, and glory upon the earth in the name of Jesus!

199.   *Exodus 14:21-22, "Then Moses stretched out his hand over the sea; and the Lord caused the sea to go back by a strong east wind all that night, and made the sea into dry land, and the waters were divided. So, the children of Israel went into the midst of the sea on the dry ground, and the waters were a wall to them on their right hand and on their left." (NKJV).*

Father, the glory that moved Moses forward in the Red Sea, let it move our church, its leadership, and membership forward, in the name of Jesus!

200. Psalms 115:14 *"The LORD shall increase you more and more, you and your children." (KJV).*

Father, increase our church more and more in the name of Jesus! Increase us and our children more and more, and let the whole world see it.

201. Psalms 68:28 *"Your God has commanded your strength; Strengthen, O God, what You have done for us." (NKJV).*

Lord, let no man prevail against our church, its leadership, and membership, in the name of Jesus!

202. 2 Thessalonians 3:1-2; *"Finally, brethren, pray for us, that the word of the Lord may run swiftly and be glorified, just as it is with you, and that we may be delivered from unreasonable and wicked men; for not all have faith." (NKJV).*

Father, let the Word of The Lord have free course and be glorified in our church and my life, in the name of Jesus!

203. Jeremiah 31:14 *"I will satiate the soul of the priests with abundance, and My people shall be satisfied with My goodness, says the LORD." (NKJV).*

Lord, satisfy our church, its members, and our pastors with abundance. Satisfy us with your goodness, in the name of Jesus!

204. Psalms 85:6 *"Will You not revive us again, that Your people may rejoice in You?"(Amplified).*

Let Us Pray

Father, send down the fire of revival upon our church, in the name of Jesus! From this year 2015 make us your voice in this land!

205.   *1 Kings 6:14 "So Solomon finished building the Temple." (NLT).*

Father, finish and complete the church building project through the hands of your servants, our pastors, in the name of Jesus!

206.   *Ezra 6:14 "So the elders of the Jews built, and they prospered through the prophesying of Haggai the prophet." (NKJV).*

Father, let every member of our church prosper greatly as they continue to build your church, in the name of Jesus.

207.   *Ezekiel 43:12 "And this is the basic law of the Temple: absolute holiness! The entire top of the mountain where the Temple is built is holy. Yes, this is the basic law of the Temple." (NLT).*

Father, sanctify this new building as Your most holy place. Let Your presence and glory always fill the house.

208.   *Psalms 68:19 "Blessed be The Lord, who daily loads us with benefits." (NKJV).*

Father, give us testimonies every day at our church for the glory of your name!

209.   *Matthew 9:38 "Therefore pray The Lord of the harvest to send out laborers into His harvest." (NKJV).*

Israel Ade-Ajala

Lord, bring the workers of Your choice to our church, and keep all other evil agents away, in the name of Jesus!

210.   *Exodus 36:5&7 "And they spoke to Moses, saying, "The people are bringing more than enough for doing this work that God has commanded us to do!" There was plenty of material for all the work to be done. Enough and more than enough."* (Message).

Father, supply all the finances, materials and workers for the work of the new building. Let there be sufficiency and overflow, in the name of Jesus!

211.   *Deuteronomy 1:11 "May the Lord, the God of your ancestors, increase you a thousand times and bless you as He has promised!" (NKJV).*

Lord, increase our church a thousand times more, and bless us, in the name of Jesus!

212.   *2 Corinthians 7:1 "Therefore, having these promises, beloved, let us cleanse ourselves from all filthiness of the flesh and spirit, perfecting holiness in the fear of God." (NKJV).*

Lord, make our church a citadel of holiness, wonder, miracles, and glory upon the earth, in the name of Jesus!

213.   *Psalms 68:1-2 "God is already beginning to arise, and His enemies to scatter; let them also who hate Him flee before Him! As smoke is driven away, so drive them away; as wax melts before the fire, so let the wicked perish before the presence of God."* (Amplified).

Let Us Pray

Arise O God and scatter all the enemies of our church. Let those who plan evil against our church, and its members, be put to shame, in the name of Jesus!

214.　*Exodus 33:18 "And he said, "Please show me Your glory." (NKJV).*

Father during this Convention, show us and manifest your glory in our midst and pour out your Spirit in greater measure into our lives, in the name of Jesus!

215.　*1 Samuel 3:21 "God continued to show up at Shiloh, revealed through his word to Samuel at Shiloh." (Message).*

Father, appear again to us during this convention. Reveal Yourself to us through Your Word from all the speakers. Manifest Your presence through signs and wonders, in the name of Jesus!

216.　*Mark 2:1-2 "After a few days, Jesus returned to Capernaum, and word got around that he was back home. 2 A crowd gathered, jamming the entrance so no one could get in or out. He was teaching the Word." (Message).*

Father, let the word go around that you are back home here at our church. Bring the crowd into our church and fill this house up. Release the WORD in season to us in the name of Jesus!

217.　*2 Chronicles 2:5 "The house I am building has to be the best, for our God is the best, far better than competing gods." (Message).*

Father, complete the building of this house, make it the best; send us all the financial and human resources needed. Rest your beauty upon this house and make our church your resting place in the name of Jesus!

218.   Isaiah 33:20 *"Look upon Zion, the city of our appointed feasts; Your eyes will see Jerusalem, a quiet home, a Tabernacle that will not be taken down; not one of its stakes will ever be removed, nor will any of its cords be broken." (NKJV).*

Father, frustrate and cast down every power planning to wage war against the divine vision of our church, our pastors, and every member of our church in the name of Jesus!

219.   Mark 2:1-2 *"After a few days, Jesus returned to Capernaum, and word got around that he was back home. 2 A crowd gathered, jamming the entrance so no one could get in or out. He was teaching the Word." (Message).*

Father, let the word go around that you are back home here at our church. Bring the crowd into our church and fill this house up. Release the WORD in season to us in the name of Jesus!

220.   2 Chronicles 2:5 *"The house I am building has to be the best, for our God is the best, far better than competing gods." (Message).*

Father, complete the building of this house; make it the best; send us all the financial and human resources needed. Rest your beauty upon this house and make our church your resting place in the name of Jesus!

Let Us Pray

221.   Psalms 85:6 "Will You not revive us again, that Your people may rejoice in You?" (Amplified).

Father, send down the fire of revival upon our church, in the name of Jesus! After these days of prayer and fasting, make us your voice in this land!

222.   Luke 8:17 "For nothing is secret that will not be revealed, nor anything hidden that will not be known and come to light." (NKJV).

Lord, bring to light and expose everything planned in darkness, against our church, its members, and our pastor's family, in the name of Jesus!

223.   2 Chronicles 31:10 "And Azariah the high priest, from the family of Zadok, replied, "Since the people began bringing their gifts to the Lord's Temple, we have had enough to eat and plenty to spare. The Lord has blessed His people, and all this is left over." (NLT).

Father, bless your people of our church as they continue to give to the completion of the building and prosper us greatly this year, in the name of Jesus!

224.   2 Chronicles 30:21 "And in every work that he began in the service of the house of God, in the law and in the commandment, to seek his God, he did it with all his heart, so he prospered." (NKJV).

Father, as we seek You and serve you with all our hearts at this church, prosper us and do not let our labor and service be in vain. Remember us for good, in the name of Jesus!

225. Isaiah 49:26 "And your enemies, crazed and desperate, will turn on themselves, killing each other in a frenzy of self-destruction. Then everyone will know that I, God, have saved you—I, the Mighty One of Jacob." (Message).

Father, I declare, any power planning untimely death for me this year, die in my place, in the name of Jesus!

226. Hebrews 6:3 "And so, God willing, we will move forward to further understanding." (NLT).

Father, I break myself loose from the bondage of life stagnation, I shall move forward; and I reverse every evil arrangement setup for my life, in the name of Jesus!

227. Zechariah 8:3 "Thus says The Lord: "I will return to Zion, and dwell amid Jerusalem. Jerusalem shall be called the City of Truth, The Mountain of The Lord of hosts, The Holy Mountain." (NKJV).

Father, send down the fire of revival upon our church in the name of Jesus! Let miracles, signs and wonders be daily occurrences and make us your voice in this land!

228. Exodus 36:5&7 "And they spoke to Moses, saying, "The people are bringing more than enough for doing this work that God has commanded us to do!" ... There was plenty of material

Let Us Pray

for all the work to be done. Enough and more than enough."(Message).

Father, supply all the finances, materials and workers for the completion of this new building. Let there be sufficiency and overflow in the name of Jesus!

229.   *2 Thessalonians 3:1-2; "Finally, brethren, pray for us, that the word of the Lord may run swiftly and be glorified, just as it is with you, and that we may be delivered from unreasonable and wicked men; for not all have faith." (NKJV).*

Father, let the Word of The Lord have free course and be glorified in our church and my life, in the name of Jesus!

230.   *Psalms 115:14 "The LORD shall increase you more and more, you and your children." (NKJV).*

Father, increase our church more and more, in the name of Jesus! Increase us and our children more and more, and let the whole world see it.

231.   *Jeremiah 31:14 "I will satiate the soul of the priests with abundance, and My people shall be satisfied with My goodness, says the LORD." (NKJV).*

Lord, satisfy our church, its members, and our pastors with abundance. Satisfy us with your goodness in the name of Jesus!

232.   *Psalms 28:4 "They talk a good line of "peace," then moonlight for the Devil. Pay them back for what they've done, for how bad they've been. Pay them back for their long hours in*

*the Devil's workshop; Then cap it with a huge bonus."
(Message).*

Father, visit those who are plotting against our church and its members with the same plot they are planning. Reward them with a huge bonus of their evil plots, in the name of Jesus!

233. *Isaiah 17:14 "Then behold, at eventide, trouble! And before the morning, he is no more. This is the portion of those who plunder us, and the lot of those who rob us."(NKJV).*

Father, frustrate and remove anything or anyone that wants to make our church lose relevance and impact home and abroad, in the name of Jesus!

234. *Exodus 33:18 "And he said, "Please show me Your glory." (NKJV).*

Father, manifest your glory in our midst and pour out your Spirit in greater measure in our lives. May we encounter the manifestation of your presence, heavenly encounters, signs, and wonders!

235. *1 Peter 2:4 "Welcome to the living Stone, the source of life. The workmen took one look and threw it out; God set it in the place of honor." (Message).*

Father, set our pastors up in the place of honor. Where they have been rejected, give them a place of honor. Let those who have worked against them begin to work for them. Let those that hated them begin to celebrate them, in the name of Jesus!

Let Us Pray

236. *Revelation 3:11 "I'm on my way; I'll be there soon. Keep a tight grip on what you have so no one distracts you and steals your crown." (Message).*

Father, disgrace and destroy anything or anyone trying to distract me to steal my crown, my peace, my joy, and my relevance, in the name of Jesus!

237. *Jeremiah 30:19 "Then out of them shall proceed thanksgiving and the voice of those who make merry; I will multiply them, and they shall not diminish; I will also glorify them, and they shall not be small. (NKJV).*

We demolish every artificial ceiling placed upon the growth of our church, in the name of Jesus. We nullify and cancel every curse pronounced on our church to limit growth in the name of Jesus.

238. *Zephaniah 3:15 "The LORD has taken away your judgements, He has cast out your enemy. The King of Israel, The LORD, is in your midst; you shall see disaster no more." (NKJV).*

Father, take away from our church any judgment against us. Cast away all our enemies as you have promised. Rule in our midst throughout this year and let us see no disaster, in the name of Jesus!

239. *Acts 2:5-6 "There were some religious Jews staying in Jerusalem who were from every country in the world. 6 When they heard this noise, a crowd came together. They were all*

surprised, because each one heard them speaking in his own language. (NCV).

Father, we declare that this church is a church for all nations and people. Let The Holy Spirit manifest in our midst, so that all will hear their language each time they come to service. Speak in this church, the language of healing, prosperity, deliverance, wisdom, financial strength, in the name of Jesus.

240. *Isaiah 33:20 "Look upon Zion, the city of our appointed feasts; Your eyes will see Jerusalem, a quiet home, a Tabernacle that will not be taken down; not one of its stakes will ever be removed, nor will any of its cords be broken." (NKJV).*

Father, frustrate and cast down every power planning to wage war against the divine vision of our church, our pastors, and members, in the name of Jesus!

241. *Mark 2:1-2 "After a few days, Jesus returned to Capernaum, and word got around that he was back home. 2 A crowd gathered, jamming the entrance so no one could get in or out. He was teaching the Word." (Message).*

Father, let the word go around that you are back home, here at our church. Bring the crowd into our church and fill this house up. Release the WORD in season to us in the name of Jesus!

242. *Deuteronomy 1:11 "May the Lord God of your fathers make you a thousand times more numerous than you are and bless you as He has promised you!" (NKJV).*

Let Us Pray

Father, increase our church a thousand times more in the name of Jesus! Increase us and our children more and more, and make us your voice in this land, in the name of Jesus!

243. *Isaiah 5:26 "He will send a signal to distant nations far away and whistle to those at the ends of the earth. They will come racing toward Jerusalem. (NLT).*

Father, blow your whistle far to the ends of the earth and in this city where you located us, and let the people come racing towards this church and give us a harvest of souls, in the name of Jesus.

244. *Acts 2:5-6 "At that time there were devout Jews from every nation living in Jerusalem. 6 When they heard the loud noise, everyone came running, and they were bewildered to hear their own languages being spoken by the believers." (NLT).*

Father, make your presence at this church known all over this city and nation, so that people of all races come to this church. Let everyone hear their language (healing, deliverance, financial prosperity or whatever they need to hear) each time they come to the service, in the name of Jesus.

245. *Nehemiah 6:15-16 "So on October 2 the wall was finished—When our enemies and the surrounding nations heard about it, they were frightened and humiliated. They realized this work had been done with the help of our God." (NLT).*

Father, complete the work of this church building, so that when people see and hear about it they will know that God was behind this work, in the name of Jesus. Give us strength, financially, to

Israel Ade-Ajala

complete the beautification of this building, in the name of Jesus.

246. *Exodus 4:31 "So the people believed; and when they heard that the LORD had visited the children of Israel and that He had looked on their affliction, then they bowed their heads and worshiped." (NKJV).*

Father, visit us again as a church and let the news spread all over the world that you are with us. Manifest your presence with miracles, signs and wonders, in the name of Jesus.

247. *Revelation 11:11 "Now after the three-and-a-half days the breath of life from God entered them, and they stood on their feet, and great fear fell on those who saw them." (NKJV).*

Father, breathe on us again. Let everyone that is sick be back on their feet. Lift us back on our feet spiritually, physically, emotionally, and financially, in the name of Jesus.

248. *Isaiah 28:5 "Then at last the Lord Almighty himself will be their crowning glory, the diadem of beauty to his people who are left." (TLB).*

Father, show yourself as the crowning glory of this church. Let the diadem of your beauty reflect on our family and let the world see it. This church will no longer be hidden, in the name of Jesus.

249. *Isaiah 52:1 "Wake up! Open your eyes! Beautiful Zion, put on your majestic strength! Jerusalem, the sacred city, put on*

Let Us Pray

your glory garments! Never again will the unclean enter your gates!" (TPT).

Father, we declare that after this Convention, our strength will be renewed, and nothing UNCLEAN will enter our lives again, in the name of Jesus. Your strength will become our strength and our glory garment will radiate all around the world, in the name of Jesus.

250. *Isaiah 49:12 "Look! They will come from faraway lands— some from the north, some from the west, and some from the land of Sinim." (TPT).*

Father, we declare an increase for this church during this Convention, in the name of Jesus. Let people come from faraway lands – from north, from the south, east and west of this land in the name of Jesus. Visit us in an unusual way during this Celebration and announce your presence in our mist through miracles, signs, and wonders, in the name of Jesus.

251. *Esther 8:17 "In each and every province and in each and every city, wherever the king's command and his decree arrived, the Jews celebrated with gladness and joy, a feast and a holiday. And many among the peoples of the land became Jews, for the fear of the Jews (and their God) had fallen on them." (Amplified).*

Father, let the fear of your doings at this church fall on this land and gain souls for yourself, in the mighty name of Jesus! Lord, make this church the tabernacle of celebration, gladness, and joy, in the mighty name of Jesus!

252. *Ezra 5: 4-5 "They also asked the Jews for the names of the men who were working on this building. 5. But the leaders of the Jews were under God's watchful eye. They couldn't be stopped until Dairus received a report and sent a reply to it." (God's Word Translation).*

Father, let the leaders of this church be under the perpetual God's watchful eye. Lord, watch over our pastors, and every family represented at this church, in the mighty name of Jesus! Let nothing stop us from achieving God's purpose and counsel for our lives. The enemy will not be able to stop or hinder our wives, children, husbands from prospering.

253. *Nehemiah 2:20 "So I answered them, and said to them, "The God of heaven Himself will prosper us; therefore, we His servants will arise and build, but you have no heritage or right or memorial in Jerusalem." (NKJV).*

Father, we declare that on this mountain, from this day forward, the God of heaven Himself will prosper every member of this church, in the mighty name of Jesus! We will not be weary, tired or discouraged in the race of life. God will prosper the work of our hands, our families, our church, and pastors, in the mighty name of Jesus!

254. *Proverbs 14:34 "Righteousness exalts a nation, But sin is a reproach to any people." (NKJV).*

We cry for help; deliver every nation from every reproach of sin. Set your face of mercy and compassion upon us all as a people; let righteousness reign!

Let Us Pray

255. *Matthew 16:18 "And I also say to you that you are Peter, and on this rock I will build My church, and the gates of Hades shall not prevail against it. 19 And I will give you the keys of the kingdom of heaven, and whatever you bind on earth I will be bound in heaven, and whatever you loose on earth will be loosed in heaven." (NKJV).*

Father, we pray that this church is built upon Jesus, the rock. Therefore the gates of hell will not prevail over us, enemies will not prevail over us, afflictions shall not prevail over us, evil shall not prevail over us, devil and all his cohort shall not prevail over us, in the mighty name of Jesus Christ.

256. *Acts 2:47 "Praising God continually and having favor with all the people. And the Lord kept adding to their number daily those who were being saved." (Amplified).*

Father, reposition our church to the status of Favor with all men! Help your Church to do what is right. Let your Church have once again, one voice!

257. *Psalms 80:19 "Restore us, O Lord God of hosts, cause Your face to shine, And we shall be saved." (NKJV).*

Father, restore our families, homes, ministries, and the church that we will always be the light and love of the world, in Jesus' name. Thank you for making your face shine on our families, homes, ministries, and everything that concerns us so that we will continue to make a positive impact.

258. *2 Timothy 4:2 "Preach the word! Be ready in season and out of season, convince, rebuke, exhort with all longsuffering and teaching." (NKJV).*

Father, help us as a church to proclaim Your truth and preach your message in season and out of season in Jesus' name. We thank you because your word is life to us, use your word to rebuke us, correct us, and encourage us, so that we will not fall by the wayside.

Family

The lord is particular about you and your family. The lord who increased you is able, more than able to preserve, protect, provide and promote your family as well. Stand in the gap and pray for yourself, your immediate, and extended family.

"here I AM and the children whom the lord has given me, we are for signs and wonders…" (Isaiah 8:18). Let us pray!

259. *Numbers 31:49 "They told Moses, "We, your servants, have counted our soldiers under our command, and not one of them is missing." (TLB).*

Father, as we approach the end of this year, let no one be missing in my home, my church, my family, in the name of Jesus. Increase us and don't let us diminish, in the name of Jesus.

260. *Psalms 45:11 "So the King will greatly desire your beauty; Because He is your Lord, worship Him. (NKJV).*

Father, let your beauty be revealed in my life, in my home, in my children, in my finances and over my work, and let the World see it, in the name of Jesus!

261. *Deuteronomy 1:11 "May the Lord God of your fathers make you a thousand times more numerous than you are and bless you as He has promised you!" (NKJV).*

Israel Ade-Ajala

Father, increase this church a thousand times more in the name of Jesus! Increase us and our children more and more and make us your voice in this land, in the name of Jesus!

262.   *1 Chronicles 29:2 "Using every resource at my command, I have gathered as much as could for building the Temple of my God. Now there is enough gold, silver, bronze, iron and wood, as well as great quantities of onyx, other precious stones, costly jewels, and all kinds of fine stone and marble." (NLT).*

Lord, we command an abundance of resources to come in for the finishing of the church building. Let there be enough and leftover money and resources to finish this project, in the name of Jesus!

263.   *Exodus 36:5 "And they spoke to Moses, saying, "The people bring much more than enough for the service of the work which the Lord commanded us to do." (NKJV).*

Lord, touch your people to give to this work, so that it is enough and let there be leftovers, in the name of Jesus!

264.   *Proverbs 11:29 "Exploit or abuse your family and end up with a fistful of air; common sense tells you it's a stupid way to live." (Message).*

Father, we declare healing for families all over the world. Lord, strengthen homes and families with peace and unity. We stand against every spirit that is breaking families apart, in the name of Jesus!

Let Us Pray

265. *Isaiah 54:13 "All your children shall be taught by the LORD, and great shall be the peace of your children." (NKJV).*

Father God, we ask for your protection over our children. Let no trouble fall on them, keeping them away from accidents. Allow no evil to influence their hearts. Cover them with the precious blood of Christ. Take charge over them so that they do not follow the crowd to do evil.

266. *Isaiah 54: 13-14 "All your children shall be taught by the Lord, And great shall be the peace of your children. In righteousness you shall be established, you shall be far from oppression for you shall not fear; And from terror, for it shall not come near you." (NKJV).*

Father, teach our children yourself and grant them great peace. Establish them in righteousness, let them be far from oppression, and let no terror come near them, in Jesus' Name.

267. *Psalms 143: 10-11 "You are my God. Show me what you want me to do, and let your gentle spirit lead me in the right path. Be true to your name Lord, and keep my life safe. Use your saving power to protect me from trouble." (CEV).*

Father, we present our children to you, please show them what you want them to do in this confusing world. Let your gentle spirit guide them in the right path and keep their lives safe, protect them from trouble by your saving power in Jesus Name.

268. *Isaiah 22: 21 "I will clothe him with your robe and strengthen him with your belt; I will commit your responsibility*

80

Israel Ade-Ajala

into his hand. He shall be a father to the inhabitants of Jerusalem and to the house of Judah." (NKJV).

Father, in the name of Jesus, clothe our bishop with your robe, strengthen him with your belt, and make him a father to this nation and beyond. Continue to use him mightily for your glory, in Jesus Name.

269.   *Philippians 2:13 "For it is God who works in you both to will and to do for His good pleasure." (NKJV).*

Father, I come against every work of the flesh, limiting the place of God inside me. I take grace to be God-inside-minded, Christ-minded, God pleaser, WORD-addict, Love-controlled, Soul-winner!

270.   *Romans 12:1-2 "I beseech you therefore, brethren, by the mercies of God, that you present your bodies a living sacrifice, holy, acceptable to God, which is your reasonable service. 2 And do not be conformed to this world, but be transformed by the renewing of your mind, that you may prove what is that good and acceptable and perfect will of God." (NKJV).*

Father, I receive new capacity to be committed to the Practice of the WORD of God! I break myself loose from the cycle of self-deception, into a lifestyle of Prompt Obedience to the Lord and his commands.

271.   *Revelation 3:12 "Then I'll write names on you, the pillars: the Name of my God, the Name of God's City—the new Jerusalem coming down out of Heaven—and my new Name." (Message).*

Let Us Pray

Father, write new names on me, my spouse, my children and my church. Where we have been called sick, let them call us healed; where we have been called poor, let them call us rich; where we have been called ordinary, let them call us great, in the name of Jesus!

272.   *Nehemiah 9:24 – Their children went in and took possession of the land. You subdued before them the Canaanites, who lived in the land; you gave the Canaanites into their hands, along with their kings and the peoples of the land, to deal with them as they pleased. (NIV).*

Father, let my children take possession of this land and deliver their enemies into their hands, in the name of Jesus. Make my children second to nobody, in the name of Jesus!

273.   *Jeremiah 31:29 "In those days they shall say no more: "The Fathers have eaten sour grapes, and the children's teeth are set on edge." (NKJV).*

Father, I declare that from today, the failure that happened in the lives of my parents will not happen in my life and in the lives of my children, in the name of Jesus!

274.   *Psalms 119:173 "Put your hand out and steady me since I've chosen to live by your counsel." (Message).*

Father, reach out your hand and steady me and let nothing shake or destabilize me, my home, or my work, in the name of Jesus.

82

275. Psalms 30:1 *"I give you credit, GOD – you got me out of that mess, you didn't let my foes gloat." (Message).*

Father, we thank you for your protection over my family, children, health, career, and my church since the beginning of this year. Thank you for not allowing our enemies to rejoice over us.

276. Psalms 31:21 *"Praise the Lord, for He has shown me the wonders of his unfailing love. He kept me safe when my city was under attack." (NLT).*

Father, I praise you for keeping me, my family, my church and all that surrounds me safe from January to December. Thank you for keeping me safe from the attacks of the enemies.

277. Psalms 115:14-15 *"God himself will fill you with more. Blessings upon blessings will be heaped upon you and upon your children from the maker of heaven and earth, the very God who made you!" (Passion).*

Father, I declare, this year, I and my children receive blessings upon blessings with unrivaled liftings. I declare that my children excel in all they do, in the name of Jesus.

278. Psalms 50:2 *"Out of Zion, the perfection of beauty, God will shine forth." (NKJV).*

Father, shine forth with new strength in my life, in the life of my spouse, my children, work, business, career, and church, in the mighty name of Jesus! I receive the beauty of God in me, and everyone that sees me will see this beauty and glorify God.

Let Us Pray

279.   Psalms 32:8 *"I hear the Lord saying, "I will stay close to you, instructing and guiding you along the pathway for your life. I will advise you along the way and lead you forth with my eyes as your guide." (TPT).*

Father, don't be far from our children, instruct our children and guide them along the pathway of their lives. Please God, teach and lead them the way they should go. Guide them with your eyes continually, in the mighty name of Jesus.

280.   Genesis 12: 2-3 *"I will make you a great nation; I will bless you And make your name great; And you shall be a blessing. I will bless those who bless you, And I will curse him who curses you; And in you all the families of the earth shall be blessed." (NKJV).*

Heavenly Father, we thank and we bless your name for your favor and blessings over our health, lives, families, ministries, businesses, and professions. Father, we ask that You bless us, that you will make us a channel of blessing to others, just as we have received freely from you, in Jesus' name.

281.   2 Timothy 1: 7 *"For God has not given us a spirit of fear, but of power and of love and of a sound mind." (NKJV).*

Father, you are the possessor of all knowledge and wisdom, in your mercy grant us divine wisdom as we make strategic and tactical decisions concerning all areas of our lives. Father, shut every false open door and unlock every door of blessings, which profit mightily with no sorrow whatsoever added, in Jesus' name.

282. Psalms 127:4 "Like arrows in the hand of a warrior, So are the children of one's youth." (NKJV).

Father, make our children arrows and no sorrows, in the name of Jesus!

283. John 10:5 "And a stranger will they not follow, but will flee from him: for they know not the voice of strangers." (KJV).

Father, there are many voices out there; we sanctify the hearing of our children. Keep our children from contrary and wicked voices.

284. 1 Chronicles 11:14 "But they stationed themselves in the middle of that field, defended it, and killed the Philistines. So the Lord brought about a great victory." (NKJV).

Father, make your word a tool of defense for our families against all devices of the wicked!

285. Joshua 24:15 "And if it seem evil unto you to serve the LORD, choose you this day whom ye will serve; whether the gods which your fathers served that were on the other side of the flood, or the gods of the Amorites, in whose land ye dwell: but as for me and my house, we will serve the LORD." (KJV).

Father, help me and my family to serve you with delight. Holy Spirit we surrender the affairs of our homes to you.

286. Psalms 90:14 "O satisfy us early with thy mercy; that we may rejoice and be glad all our days." (KJV).

Let Us Pray

Father, satisfy our children early. Oh Lord, bless their studies, for those who are working Lord, bless their career, for those who are married, bless their homes, for those who are getting married, bless their marriages, for those who are trusting God for a life partner, bless them with a godly life partner, that they may rejoice and be glad all their days, in Jesus mighty name.

287.   *2 Timothy 3:14-15 "But you must continue in the things which you have learned and been assured of, knowing from whom you have learned them, and that from childhood you have known the Holy Scriptures, which are able to make you wise for salvation through faith which is in Christ Jesus." (NKJV).*

Father, deliver our children from the lies of the world through social media and peer pressure, and make them hold on to what they have learned from the word of God through which they receive wisdom for a righteous living, in the mighty name of Jesus Christ.

288.   *Psalms 73:26 "My flesh and my heart fail; But God is the strength of my heart and my portion forever." (NKJV).*

Father, we pray for every family in this church. Be our strength in every area where we are weak (financially, emotionally, etc.). Rekindle the relationship between husbands and wives. Inject new love into our families. Be our portion now and forever, in the mighty name of Jesus.

289.   *Psalms 16: 8 "I have set the Lord always before me; because He is at my right hand I shall not be moved." (KJV).*

Father, we thank you for you are always at our right hand. You are the one that rules in our family affairs. Lord, we pray, let your praise be on our lips through thick and thin. Whatever comes our way, we will not be moved, in the mighty name of Jesus Christ.

290.   Psalms 127:3 *"Behold children are a heritage from the Lord. The fruit of the womb is a reward." (NKJV).*

Father, we pray for your protection over our children. You are their hiding place, and under your wings they shall continuously find refuge in Jesus' name. We thank you for not making them ashamed, protecting them from trouble wherever they go, and keeping evil far from them.

291.   Proverbs 4: 23 *"Keep your heart with all diligence, for out of it springs the issues of life." (NKJV).*

Lord, I pray my children's minds will be protected from evil and they will make wise choices in the face of peer pressure, in Jesus' name. We thank you that our children in this church will never perish, and no one will snatch them out of your hand.

Protection

GOD IS COMMITTED TO YOUR PROTECTION AND THE
PROTECTION OF YOUR POSSESSIONS AND EVERYONE
AROUND YOU. YOU ARE PROTECTED WHEN YOU GO
OUT, WHEN YOU COME IN, WHEN YOU LAY DOWN,
WHEN YOU WAKE UP. YOUR CHILDREN AT SCHOOL,
YOUR PARENTS AT WORK, WHEN YOU TRAVEL BY
ROAD, BY AIR, BY SEA OR BY RAIL, THE PROTECTION OF
THE LORD IS YOURS.

PRAY AND RECEIVE GOD'S PROTECTION BECAUSE YOU
DWELL IN THE SECRET PLACE OF THE MOST HIGH,
AND YOU ABIDE UNDER THE SHADOW OF THE
ALMIGHTY. (PSALMS 91:1). LET US PRAY!

292.   *Job 5:12 "He frustrates the devices of the crafty, so that their
hands cannot carry out their plans." (NKJV).*

Lord, build a wall of protection around our pastors and their
children, in the name of Jesus. Let every plan against them be
frustrated, in the name of Jesus.

293.   *Jeramiah 1: 19 "They will fight against you, But they shall
not prevail against you. For I am with you," says the LORD, "to
deliver you." (NKJV).*

Father, thank you for your protection and security over our
senior pastor and his family. The arm of flesh and its
machinations will never prevail against him and his family.

Father, thank you because You will cause your righteous right hand to protect, secure, and uphold our senior pastors in Jesus' name.

294. *Isaiah 33:24 "And the inhabitant will not say, "I am sick"; The people who dwell in it will be forgiven their iniquity" (NKJV).*

Father, protect me and every member of our church and the leadership from sickness, affliction and death. Let no one amongst us say, "I am sick." Let us enjoy divine health continually, in the name of Jesus!

295. *Psalms 16: 9-10 "I'm happy from the inside out, and from the outside in, I'm firmly formed. You canceled my ticket to hell—that's not my destination!" (Message).*

Father, I cancel today every grave dug for anyone in this church. I declare that no one will die in our midst, in the name of Jesus!

296. *Job 5:12 "He frustrates the devices of the crafty, so that their hands cannot carry out their plans." (NKJV).*

Lord, build a wall of protection around our pastors and their children, in the name of Jesus. Let every plan against them be frustrated, in the name of Jesus!

297. *2 Samuel 1:19 "Your pride and joy, O Israel, lies dead on the hills! Oh, how the mighty heroes have fallen!" (NLT).*

Father, my family is my pride and joy. Lord, protect us by your hand. Do not let any of my pride and joys die, however, destroy

Let Us Pray

all the devices and plans of the devil against my pride and joys, in the name of Jesus!

298.   *1 Kings 5:4 But now the Lord my God hath given me rest on every side, so that there is neither adversary nor evil occurrent. (KJV).*

Father, we thank you for the safety and peace you granted our city this week! We declare a greater atmosphere of peace, calmness and progress all over our cities, our states, and our country. Father we declare divine protection over all our officers: Law Enforcement, Fire Department, and First responders, in Jesus' name.

299.   *Numbers 31:49 "They told Moses, "We, your servants, have counted our soldiers under our command, and not one of them is missing." (TLB).*

Father, as we enter 2015, let no one be missing in my home, my church, my family, in the name of Jesus. Increase us and don't let us diminish in the name of Jesus.

300.   *Psalms 46:1 "God is our refuge and strength, A very present help in trouble." (NKJV).*

Father be my refuge this year, do not let me see evil. Protect me, my home, my children, any of my family members from an untimely death, in the name of Jesus.

301.   *Hebrews 13:12 "Jesus himself suffered outside the city gate, so that his blood would make people holy." (CEV).*

Blood of Jesus, laminate my life in the name of Jesus!

302. *Isaiah 33:24 "And the inhabitant will not say, "I am sick"; The people who dwell in it will be forgiven their iniquity" (NKJV).*

Father, protect me and every member of this church from sickness, affliction, and death. Let no one amongst us say, "I am sick." Let us enjoy divine health continually, in the name of Jesus!

303. *Numbers 31:49 "They told Moses, "We, your servants, have counted our soldiers under our command, and not one of them is missing." (TLB).*

Father, as we approach the end of this year, let no one be missing in my home, my church, my family, in the name of Jesus. Increase us and don't let us diminish in the name of Jesus.

304. *Psalms 68:28 "Summon your might; display your strength, O God, for you have done such mighty things for us." (TLB).*

Father, display your strength in my life, my home, my work, my ministry, my family, and my church and let me not be put to shame. Establish me for greatness, in the name of Jesus.

305. *1 Peter 1:5. "God is keeping careful watch over us and the future. The Day is coming when you'll have it all—life healed and whole." (Message).*

Father, let the great and prosperous future that you have for me begin today. Let my present show the preview of my future and

Let Us Pray

make the whole world concur that your hand is upon my life, in the name of Jesus!

306.   *Psalms 68:19-20 "What a glorious Lord! He who daily bears our burdens also gives us our salvation. He frees us! He rescues us from death." (TLB).*

Father, I cast my burdens on you. Set me free from the spirit of fear and worry, in the name of Jesus. Rescue me from the traps of death laid for me by the evil ones, in the name of Jesus.

307.   *Psalms 119:173 "Put your hand out and steady me since I've chosen to live by your counsel." (Message).*

Father, reach out your hand and steady me and let nothing shake or destabilize me in my home and work, in the name of Jesus.

308.   *Isaiah 49:23 "Kings will be your babysitters; princesses will be your nursemaids. They'll offer to do all your drudge work— scrub your floors, do your laundry. You'll know then that I am God. No one who hopes in me ever regrets it." (Message).*

Father, send us help in unlikely places in the name of Jesus! Bring help from governments, from corporations, from individuals and businesses, in the name of Jesus!

309.   *Nehemiah 9:21 – Yea, forty years didst thou sustain them in the wilderness, so that they lacked nothing; their clothes waxed not old, and their feet swelled not. (KJV).*

Father, sustain me for the rest of my life. Let my life bring glory to your name and remove shame far from me and my family, in the name of Jesus!

310.   Revelation 12:10 "Then I heard a loud voice saying in heaven, "Now salvation, and strength, and the kingdom of our God, and the power of His Christ have come, for the accuser of our brethren, who accused them before our God day and night, has been cast down." (NKJV).

Father, I declare that from today, I begin to enjoy in double portions, salvation, strength and the power of Christ in the name of Jesus! All my accusers are silenced, in the name of Jesus!

311.   1 Peter 2:4. "Welcome to the Living Stone, the source of life. The workmen took one look and threw it out; God set it in the place of honor." (Message).

Father, set my pastors up in the place of honor. Where they have been rejected, give them a place of honor there. Let those who have worked against them, begin to work for them. Let those that hated them, begin to celebrate them, in the name of Jesus!

312.   Luke 1:25 "Thus the Lord has dealt with me, in the days when He looked on me, to take away my reproach among people." (NKJV).

Father, from today, take away my reproach. Look down upon me and cause your favor to rest upon my household, in the name of Jesus!

Let Us Pray

313.   Psalms 119:16 "Take my side as you promised; I'll live then for sure. Don't disappoint all my grand hopes." (Message).

Father, bring to pass every promise you have given to me and cause me to give testimonies, in the name of Jesus!

314.   Revelation 12:7-8; "And war broke out in heaven: Michael and his angels fought with the dragon; and the dragon and his angels fought, but they did not prevail, nor was a place found for them in heaven any longer." (NKJV).

Father, I declare from today, no place will be found for Satan in my life, my home, my ministry, my family, my finances, or my church, in the name of Jesus!

315.   Revelation 3:11 "I'm on my way; I'll be there soon. Keep a tight grip on what you have so no one distracts you and steals your crown. (Message).

Father, disgrace and destroy anything or anyone trying to distract me to steal my crown, my peace, my joy, or my relevance, in the name of Jesus!

316.   Revelation 3:12 "Then I'll write names on you, the pillars: the Name of my God, the Name of God's City—the new Jerusalem coming down out of Heaven—and my new Name." (Message).

Father, write new names on me, my spouse, my children and my church! Where we have been called sick, let them call us healed; where we have been called poor, let them call us rich;

94

where we have been called ordinary, let them call us great, in the name of Jesus!

317. Isaiah 54:17 *"No weapon formed against you shall prosper, and every tongue which rises against you in judgment You shall condemn. This is the heritage of the servants of the LORD, and their righteousness is from Me." (NKJV).*

Father, destroy every satanic device employed or intended to be employed against any member Kingdom Connection Christian Center and their family, in the form of death, victimization, insanity, accident, and any other means, in the name of Jesus!

318. Numbers 31:49 *"They told Moses, "We, your servants, have counted our soldiers under our command, and not one of them is missing." (TLB).*

Father, as we approach the end of this year, let no one be missing in my home, my church, my family, in the name of Jesus. Increase us and don't let us diminish, in the name of Jesus.

319. Proverbs 23:18 *"You will be rewarded for this; your hope will not be disappointed." (NLT).*

Father, do not let my hope be disappointed in life, so reward me with abundance, in the name of Jesus.

320. Ezra 7:6 *"This Ezra was a scribe who was well versed in the Law of Moses, which the Lord, the God of Israel, had given to the people of Israel. He came up to Jerusalem from Babylon, and the king gave him everything he asked for, because the gracious hand of the Lord his God was on him." (NKJV).*

Let Us Pray

Father, let your hand of favor be upon my life and terminate my labor and toiling in the name of Jesus.

321. *1 Samuel 30:9-10 "David went, he and the six hundred men with him. They arrived at the Brook Besor, where some of them dropped out. David and four hundred men kept up the pursuit, but two hundred of them were too fatigued to cross the Brook Besor, and stayed there." (Message).*

Father, don't let me drop out in the battle of life, let your Holy Spirit build me up and give me strength in the name of Jesus. Give me strength to pray, to read the Word and walk in obedience to the WORD, strength to be faithful in all areas of my life.

322. *Psalms 18:20 "God made my life complete when I placed all the pieces before him. When I got my act together, he gave me a fresh start. (Message).*

Father, I place my life before you, every piece of it. Make my life complete this year, lacking nothing, in the name of Jesus.

323. *Psalms 18:28 "Suddenly, God, you floodlight my life; I'm blazing with glory, God's glory! (Message).*

Father, floodlight my life from today and let me be blazing with your glory in this year of shining glory. Let your glory shine through my life, finances, health, home, work, children, church, and city in the name of Jesus.

324. *John 10:5 "They won't follow stranger's voice but will scatter because they aren't used to the sound of it." (Message).*

Israel Ade-Ajala

Father, we declare your protection over our children. They will not follow a stranger's voice; they will prosper and serve you all their days in the name of Jesus.

325. *Psalms 118:16-17 "The right hand of the Lord is exalted; The right hand of the Lord does valiantly. I shall not die, but live, and declare the works of the Lord. (NKJV).*

Father, let the angels of deliverance that have been stationed around this place, now, let them be laying their hands on anyone here that has been having dreams of death, in the name of Jesus!

326. *Psalms 18:36 "You cleared the ground under me so my footing was firm." (Message).*

Father, hold me firmly and let nothing pull me down. Set my footing firmly on your word and make me an example of the power of your word, in the name of Jesus.

327. *Psalms 46:1 "God, you're such a safe and powerful place to find refuge! You're a proven help in time of trouble— more than enough and always available whenever I need you. (Passion).*

Father, be my refuge this year, do not let me see evil. Protect me, my home, my children, and all my family members from untimely death, in the name of Jesus.

328. *Numbers 31:49 "We have counted the soldiers under our command and not a man is missing." (Message).*

Let Us Pray

Father, as we approach the middle of this year, let no one be missing in this church, my home, my family, in the name of Jesus. Increase us and don't let us diminish, in the name of Jesus. Stretch Your hand and heal all who are sick amongst us in the name of Jesus.

329. *2 Chronicles 7:14 "If my people, which are called by my name, shall humble themselves, and pray and seek my face, and turn from their wicked ways; then I will hear from heaven, and will forgive their sins, and will heal their land." (NKJV).*

Father, as we pray individually and cooperatively today, hear and answer our prayers for revival in this nation and all over the world in Jesus' name. We thank You for healing the land and, we ask you to bring peace to the country of United States, Ukraine, and the entire world.

330. *Psalms 46:1 "God is our refuge and strength. A very present help in trouble." (NKJV).*

Father, we lift the hands of our senior pastor, his wife, and their children and always place them in your shelter in Jesus' name. We thank you because we know that you are their refuge and fortress, and you will preserve them all the time.

98

Divine Healing

Earthly ministry of Jesus Christ is often punctuated by miracles of healing, restoration and deliverance from sickness, diseases and death. Divine healing is still available today. Healing is children's bread. Ask for yourself and you will have, ask for others and they will receive.

"Beloved, I pray that you may prosper in all things and be in health, just as your soul prospers" (3 John 1:2) Let us pray for divine healing!

331. *Jeremiah 30:17 "For I will restore health unto thee, and I will heal thee of thy wounds, saith the LORD; because they called thee an Outcast, saying, this is Zion, whom no man seeketh after." (KJV).*

Father, we release your healing virtue on everyone sick in our midst. Restore health to them and heal them completely, in the name of Jesus!

332. *Psalms 68:19-20 " What a glorious Lord! He who daily bears our burdens also gives us our salvation. He frees us! He rescues us from death." (TLB).*

Father, I cast my burdens on you, set me free from the spirit of fear and worry in the name of Jesus. Rescue me from the traps of death laid for me by the evil ones in the name of Jesus.

Let Us Pray

333.   Psalms 16: 9-10 "I'm happy from the inside out, and from the outside in, I'm firmly formed. 10 You canceled my ticket to hell—that's not my destination!" (Message).

Father, I cancel today every grave dug for anyone in this church. I declare that no one will die in our midst in the name of Jesus!

334.   Isaiah 33:24 "No one in Zion will say, "I'm sick." Best of all, they'll all live guilt–free." (Message).

Father, I declare that no one in this church family will say again, "I'm sick." We shall continue to enjoy divine health in the name of Jesus. No one shall suffer loss in KCCC in the name of Jesus!

335.   Psalms 126:4 Now, Lord, do it again! Restore us to our former glory! May streams of your refreshing flow over us until our dry hearts are drenched again. (Passion).

Father, we declare restoration over all that has been stolen from us, in the name of Jesus. We declare that we recover all that has been taken from us; be it health, reputation, wealth, children, home, business, career, family, relationship, etc. We shout RESTORE, in the name of Jesus!

336.   Jeremiah 29: 11 1 "For I know the thoughts that I think toward you, says the LORD, thoughts of peace and not of evil, to give you a future and a hope."

Father, in the name of Jesus, we claim peace and a spirit of refreshing for every heart here at this church that may have been broken in one way or another due to a failed relationship. Father, we claim total restoration and wholeness for every such

situation. In the name of Jesus, we claim a future of divine expectation and eternal hope that comes only from your throne of grace, and we declare that all is well with our souls, in Jesus' name.

337.   *3 John 1:2 "Dear friend, I'm praying that all is well with you and that you enjoy good health in the same way that you prosper spiritually." (CEB).*

Father, in the name of Jesus, restore sound health and wholeness to any member that may be challenged in their health. Let them enjoy supernatural strength and wholeness.

Victory

SINCE YOU ARE BORN OF GOD, YOU HAVE OVERCOME THE WORLD. YOUR FAITH IS THE VICTORY THAT HAS OVERCOME THE WORLD. "...THANKS BE TO GOD WHO GIVES US THE VICTORY THROUGH OUR LORD JESUS CHRIST." (I CORINTHIANS 15:57). LET US PRAY AS WE RECEIVE OUR VICTORY THROUGH FAITH IN EVERY AREA OF OUR LIVES. LET US PRAY!

338. *Isaiah 61:7 "Instead of shame and dishonor, you will enjoy a double share of honor. You will possess a double portion of prosperity in your land, and everlasting joy will be yours." (NLT).*

God, arise and fill my mouth with laughter, let my tears and shame expire, and let me possess a double portion of prosperity in this land, in the name of Jesus!

339. *Psalms 20: 5-6 "When you win, we plan to raise the roof and lead the parade with our banners. (Message).*

Father, lead us on a victory parade in this land and let everyone watch to see it. Send us the help you promised. Work and fill up all the gaps (financial, social, spiritual) in our lives, in the name of Jesus!

340. *Joshua 5:9 "Then the Lord said to Joshua, "This day I have rolled away the reproach of Egypt from you." (NKJV).*

Israel Ade-Ajala

Therefore, the name of the place is called, "Gilgal" to this day." Father, today roll away every reproach of my life, in the name of Jesus. Turn my tears to cheers, in the name of Jesus.

341. *Genesis 45:4-5 And Joseph said to his brothers, "Please come near to me." So they came near. Then he said: "I am Joseph your brother, whom you sold into Egypt. But now, do not therefore be grieved or angry with yourselves because you sold me here; for God sent me before you to preserve life. In the presence of those who think I'm nobody." (NKJV).*

Oh God, arise and make me somebody, in the name of Jesus!

342. *Hebrews 12:24 "to Jesus the Mediator of the new covenant, and to the blood of sprinkling that speaks better things than that of Abel." (NKJV).*

Father, let the blood of Jesus speak and release my destiny and prosperity from the altars and warehouses of evil foundation, in the mighty name of Jesus Christ!

343. *Deuteronomy 28: 6 "Wherever you go and whatever you do, you will be blessed." (NLT).*

As a church and as individuals, we declare that wherever we go, whatever we do, we will be blessed, we will be victorious, we will see godly results, and we will see righteous increase.

344. *Ephesians 2:13 "But now in Christ Jesus you who once were far off have been brought near by the blood of Christ." (NKJV).*

Let Us Pray

I use the blood of Jesus Christ to release and bring my destiny and glory from anywhere they have been buried, in the name of Jesus.

345. *Hebrews 10:19 "Therefore, brethren, having boldness to enter the Holiest by the blood of Jesus." (NKJV).*

By the blood of Jesus Christ, I speak destruction into the camp of my enemies. I crush the powers of evil altars and evil priesthood of my household, in the mighty name of Jesus Christ!

346. *Hebrews 13:20-21 "Now may the God of peace who brought up our Lord Jesus from the dead, that great Shepherd of the sheep, through the blood of the everlasting covenant, 21 make you [a]complete in every good work to do His will, working in [b]you what is well pleasing in His sight, through Jesus Christ, to whom be glory forever and ever. Amen." (NKJV).*

I receive wholeness in every area of my life, (physically, spiritually, financially, emotionally) by the blood of Jesus Christ!

347. *Revelation 12:11 "And they overcame him by the blood of the Lamb and by the word of their testimony, and they did not love their lives to the death." (NKJV).*

From now henceforth, I will begin to enjoy the realities of new creation in testimonies, and victories with fresh wind by the blood of Jesus Christ, in Jesus' mighty name!

348. *Ephesians 1:4 "Just as He chose us in Him before the foundation of the world, that we should be holy and without blame before Him in love." (NKJV).*

Therefore, I confess that I am born again because I have been chosen by Christ Jesus before the foundation of the world. No condemnation, no downcast, no contradiction, in the mighty name of Jesus!

349. *Hebrews 4:3" For we who have believed do enter that rest, as He has said: "So I swore in My wrath, 'They shall not enter My rest,'" although the works were finished from the foundation of the world." (NKJV).*

Lord, I declare, in the name of Jesus Christ, that my deliverance from evil and idolatrous foundation has been finished from the foundation of the world. Father, I neutralize the claims and operations of evil and idolatrous foundation in my life, by the blood of Jesus Christ.

350. *1 Samuel 30:9-10 "David went, he and the six hundred men with him. They arrived at the Brook Besor, where some of them dropped out. David and four hundred men kept up the pursuit, but two hundred of them were too fatigued to cross the Brook Besor and stayed there." (Message).*

Father, don't let me drop out in the battle of life. Let your Holy Spirit build me up and give me strength, in the name of Jesus. Give me strength to pray, to read the Word and walk in obedience to the WORD. Give me strength to be faithful in all areas of my life.

351. *Nehemiah 12:43 "Many sacrifices were offered on that joyous day, for God had given us cause for great joy. The women*

Let Us Pray

and children rejoiced, too, and the joy of the people of Jerusalem was heard far away!" (TLB).

Father, in the year 2015, give us reasons to rejoice and to celebrate. Let people come and celebrate with us in the name of Jesus.

352. *Romans 8:2 "For the law of the Spirit of life in Christ Jesus has made me free from the law of sin and death." (NKJV).*

My Lord, My King, I praise You for my freedom from sin and death.

353. *Psalm 8:4-5 "What is man that You are mindful of him, And the son of man that You visit him? For You have made him a little lower than the angels, And You have crowned him with glory and honor". (NKJV).*

Father, crown me with glory and honor. Everywhere I go, let people see your glory and honor upon my life.

354. *Isaiah 60:3 "The Gentiles shall come to your light, And kings to the brightness of your rising." (NKJV).*

Father, let every imprisoned and buried potential in me begin to come forth now, for the whole world to see, in the name of Jesus.

355. *Psalms 73:24 "You guide me with Your counsel, leading me to a glorious destiny." (NLT).*

Father, I declare, no matter the situation I am facing, I shall become what God has made me to be, in the name of Jesus!

106

356. *Revelation 3:11 "I'm on my way; I'll be there soon. Keep a tight grip on what you have so no one distracts you and steals your crown. (Message).*

Father, disgrace and destroy anything or anyone trying to distract me to steal my crown, my peace, my joy, or my relevance, in the name of Jesus!

357. *Psalms 73:24 "You guide me with Your counsel, leading me to a glorious destiny." (NLT).*

Father, I declare, no matter the situation I am facing, I shall become what God has made me to be, in the name of Jesus!

358. *Psalms 20: 5-6 "When you win, we plan to raise the roof and lead the parade with our banners. May all your wishes come true! That clinches it—help's coming, an answer is on the way, everything's going to work out." (Message).*

Father, lead us on a victory parade in this land and let everyone watch to see it. Send us the help you promised. Work and fill up all the gaps (financial, social, spiritual) in our lives, in the name of Jesus!

359. *Psalms 30:11 "You did it: you changed wild lament into whirling dance; You ripped off my black mourning band and decked me with wildflowers. (Message).*

Father, thank you for changing my stories from failure to success, sickness to health, debt to prosperity, lack to abundance, nobody to significance, and hate to celebrity, in the name of Jesus!

Let Us Pray

360.   Psalms 26:4 *"I don't hang out with tricksters; I don't pal around with thugs (Message).*

Father, build walls of protection around me against tricksters and thugs, in the name of Jesus! Don't let me fall into their snares, in the name of Jesus!

361.   1 Samuel 17:54 *"And David took the head of the Philistine and brought it to Jerusalem, but he put his armor in his tent." (NKJV).*

O God, arise and place the head of my Goliath in my hands, in the name of Jesus!

362.   Psalms 26:2 *"Examine me, God, from head to foot, order your battery of tests. Make sure I'm fit inside and out." (Message).*

Father, I declare that Your hand will perfect my life, in the name of Jesus! I will not live my life as a mess financially, spiritually, or physically, in the name of Jesus!

363.   Psalms 26:7 *"Singing God-songs at the top of my lungs, telling God-stories." (Message).*

Father, I declare that I will sing songs of thanksgiving and I will tell of all your wonders in my life. My time to share testimonies has finally come, in the name of Jesus!

364.   Psalms 20: 5-6 *"When you win, we plan to raise the roof and lead the parade with our banners. May all your wishes come*

true! 6 That clinches it—help's coming, an answer is on the way, everything's going to work out." (Message).

Father, lead us on a victory parade in this land and let everyone watch to see it. Send us the help you promised. Work and fill up all the financial, social, and spiritual gaps in our lives, in the name of Jesus!

365. *Joshua 1:9 "This is my command—be strong and courageous! Do not be afraid or discouraged. For the Lord your God is with you wherever you go." (NLT).*

Father, manifest your presence in my life, home, children, work, finances, and in my health. Let my haters see you in my life and do not let the enemy rejoice over me, in the name of Jesus.

366. *Isaiah 30:19 "Oh yes, people of Zion, citizens of Jerusalem, your time of tears is over. Cry for help and you'll find it's grace and more grace. The moment He hears, He'll answer." (Message).*

Father, I declare that my tears are over, and my time of peace has arrived. Destiny helpers will locate me, and my family and we will enjoy favor every day, in the name of Jesus.

367. *Isaiah 54:14 "You'll be built solid, grounded in righteousness, far from any trouble—nothing to fear! far from terror—it won't even come close! (Message).*

Father, as we come to the end of this year, we declare that we are far from any trouble. Nothing will cause us to mourn, and

109

Let Us Pray

we shall end this year in peace and prosperity, in the name of Jesus.

368. *Psalms 144: 1"Praise the LORD, who is my rock. He trains my hands for war and gives my fingers skill for battle." (NLT).*

Father, we thank you for giving us victory in every battle we have fought this year. Thank you for making us winners and not losers, in the mighty name of Jesus.

369. *Psalms 33:12 "You have turned for me my mourning into dancing; You have put off my sackcloth and clothed me with gladness." (TPT).*

Father, we thank you for turning our mourning into dancing this year on this mountain. Thank you, for taking off our sack clothes and clothing us with gladness. Thank you for fighting our battles and giving us victory.

Blessing

"The lord will command the blessing on you in your storehouses and in all to which you set your hand, and He will bless you in the land which the lord your God is giving you." (DEUTERONOMY 28:8). You are not only blessed, you are also a blessing.

Let us pray the blessing!

370.   *Psalms 18:24 "God rewrote the text of my life when I opened the book of my heart to his eyes." (Message).*

Father, rewrite the text of my life, fill in the details of your blessings and cancel every agenda of the wicked against me, my family, and this church, in the name of Jesus!

371.   *Deuteronomy 15:6 "For the Lord your God will bless you just as He promised you; you shall lend to many nations, but you shall not borrow; you shall reign over many nations, but they shall not reign over you." (NKJV).*

Father, pour down your blessings on us. Establish the work of our hands. Make us lenders and not borrowers, rulers and not slaves over nations, in the name of Jesus!

372.   *Psalms 68:19 "Blessed be The Lord, who daily loads us with benefits." (NKJV).*

Father, give us testimonies every day, at this church, for the glory of your name!

Let Us Pray

373. Psalms 45:11 " So the King will greatly desire your beauty; Because He is your Lord, worship Him." (NKJV).

Father, let your beauty reflect in my life, in my home, in my finances, and over my work, and let the World see it.

374. Psalms 45:17 "I will make Your name to be remembered in all generations; Therefore, the people shall praise You forever and ever." (NKJV).

Father, use me to the glory of your name and cause your power to manifest in my life, my home, my ministry, my work, in the name of Jesus.

375. Psalms 68:28 "Summon your might; display your strength, O God, for you have done such mighty things for us." (TLB).

Father, display your strength in my life, my home, my work, my ministry, and my family. Let me not be put to shame, yet stablish me for greatness, in the name of Jesus.

376. Psalms 128: 5-6 "The Lord bless you out of Zion, and may you see the good of Jerusalem All the days of your life. Yes, may you see your children's children. Peace upon Israel!" (NKJV).

Father, bless us out of Zion and let us, our children, and our children's children, see the good of our land all the days of our lives, in Jesus' Name.

377. Psalms 115:14 "The LORD shall increase you more and more, you and your children." (NKJV).

Israel Ade-Ajala

Father, increase this church more and more, in the name of Jesus! Increase us and our children more and more, and let the whole world see it.

378. *2 Chronicles 30:21 "And in every work that he began in the service of the house of God, in the law and in the commandment, to seek his God, he did it with all his heart, so he prospered." (NKJV).*

Father, as we seek You and serve you with all our hearts at this church, prosper us and do not let our labor and service be in vain. Remember us for good, in the name of Jesus!

379. *Psalms 18:24 "God rewrote the text of my life when I opened the book of my heart to his eyes." (Message).*

Father, rewrite the text of my life, fill in the details of your blessings, and cancel every agenda of the wicked against me, my family, and this church, in the name of Jesus!

380. *Psalms 75:1 "Our God, we thank you for being so near to us! Everyone celebrates your wonderful deeds." (CEV).*

Father, we thank you for your blessings in our lives, children, homes, jobs, businesses, and church. Thank you for providing for our needs and for this new church building!

381. *Revelation 3:13 "Are your ears awake? Listen. Listen to the Wind Words, the Spirit blowing through the churches." (Message).*

Let Us Pray

Father, wake my ears up! Open my ears to listen and hear your voice. Don't let me go through life confused and defeated, in the name of Jesus!

382. *Deuteronomy 1:11 "May the Lord, the God of your ancestors, increase you a thousand times and bless you as He has promised!" (NKJV).*

Lord, increase this church a thousand times more and bless us, in the name of Jesus!

383. *Psalms 119:16 "Take my side as you promised; I'll live then for sure. Don't disappoint all my grand hopes." (Message).*

Father, bring to pass every promise you have given to me and cause me to give testimonies, in the name of Jesus!

384. *Psalm 119:170 "Give my request your personal attention, rescue me on the terms of your promise." (Message).*

Father, I declare that it is my turn to laugh and celebrate over my life, my home, my children, my business, my career, and my finances, in the name of Jesus!

385. *Micah 7:14 "O Lord, come and rule your people; lead your flock; make them live in peace and prosperity; let them enjoy the fertile pastures of Bashan and Gilead as they did long ago." (TLB).*

Father, lead us into prosperity, in the name of Jesus. Terminate financial struggle in our lives, in the name of Jesus! Open doors of advancement for us, in the name of Jesus!

386. Exodus 36:5,7 "And they spoke to Moses, saying, "The people are bringing more than enough for doing this work that God has commanded us to do!" 7 There was plenty of material for all the work to be done. Enough and more than enough." (Message).

Father, supply all the finances, materials and workers for the work of the new building. Let there be sufficiency and overflow, in the name of Jesus!

387. Numbers 11:31 - And there went forth a wind from the LORD, and brought quails from the sea, and let them fall by the camp, as it were a day's journey on this side, and as it were a day's journey on the other side, round about the camp, and as it were two cubits high upon the face of the earth." (KJV).

Father, let the wind from the Lord bring abundance to my life and terminate lack in my family, in the name of Jesus. Make me a blessing to my generation, in the name of Jesus!

388. 2 Chronicles 30:21 "And in every work that he began in the service of the house of God, in the law and in the commandment, to seek his God, he did it with all his heart, so he prospered." (NKJV).

Father, as we seek You and serve you with all our hearts at this church, prosper us and do not let our labor and service be in vain. Remember us for good, in the name of Jesus!

389. Psalm 27:3 "When besieged, I'm as calm as baby. When all hell broke loose, I'm collected and cool." (Message).

Let Us Pray

Father, stabilize me physically, spiritually, and financially, and let nothing rob me of your peace in the name of Jesus! Steady my hands as I navigate through the journey of life, in the name of Jesus!

390. *Psalm 31:6 "I hate all this silly religion, but you, GOD, I trust." (Message).*

Father, reveal yourself to me and bring me into your inner circle. Don't let me run around in a silly religion that leads to no profit. Make my life an example of your goodness, in the name of Jesus.

391. *2 Chronicles 14:7 "…We have this peaceful land because we sought GOD; he has given us rest from all troubles." So, they built and enjoyed prosperity." (Message).*

Father, we declare peace and prosperity upon everyone that has given, and continues to give, to the building of this church's sanctuary. Let their hands always remain on top and let none of them suffer loss, in the name of Jesus!

392. *Numbers 11:31 - And there went forth a wind from the LORD, and brought quails from the sea, and let them fall by the camp, as it were a day's journey on this side, and as it were a day's journey on the other side, round about the camp, and as it were two cubits high upon the face of the earth." (KJV).*

Father, let the wind from the Lord bring abundance to my life and terminate lack in my family in the name of Jesus. Make me a blessing to my generation, in the name of Jesus!

393. *Psalm 119:173 "Put your hand out and steady me since I've chosen to live by your counsel." (Message).*

Father, reach out your hand and steady me and let nothing shake or destabilize me in my home and work, in the name of Jesus.

394. *Revelation 3:12 "Then I'll write names on you, the pillars: the Name of my God, the Name of God's City—the new Jerusalem coming down out of Heaven—and my new Name." (Message).*

Father, write new names on me, my spouse, my children and my church. Where we have been called sick, let them call us healed; where we have been called poor, let them call us rich; where we have been called ordinary, let them call us great!

395. *Psalms 90:13-14 "Come back, God—how long do we have to wait? —and treat your servants with kindness for a change. Surprise us with love at daybreak; then we'll skip and dance all day long." (Message).*

O Lord, make me a candidate of supernatural surprises, in favor, finances, and promotion, and launch me into my next level, in the name of Jesus!

396. *Esther 7:2 "And on the second day, at the banquet of wine, the king again said to Esther, "What is your petition, Queen Esther? It shall be granted you. And what is your request, up to half the kingdom? It shall be done!" (NKJV).*

Let Us Pray

Father, I declare that all my petitions receive speedy attention in heaven today. Grant me all that I requested in the name of Jesus. Let me share the testimony of your faithfulness in my life again, in the name of Jesus.

397. Psalm 45:11 " So the King will greatly desire your beauty; Because He is your Lord, worship Him. (NKJV).

Father, let your beauty be revealed in my life, in my home, in my children, in my finances, and over my work and let the world see it, in the name of Jesus!

398. Isaiah 54:13 "All your children will be taught by the LORD, and they will have much peace. (NLT).

Father, we declare that our children will receive revelation of your word, they will enjoy peace and be above only, in the name of Jesus.

399. 1 Samuel 28:15 "Why have you disturbed me by bringing me back?" Samuel asked Saul. "Because I am in deep trouble," he replied. "The Philistines are at war with us, and God has left me and won't reply by prophets or dreams; so, I have called for you to ask you what to do." (NLT).

Father, cleanse me and purge me of anything and everything that can make me lose Your glorious presence. Lord, make Your presence more real to me day by day.

400. Psalms 5:12 "For You, O Lord, will bless the righteous; with favor You will surround him as with a shield." (NKJV).

Israel Ade-Ajala

Father, surprise me with favor this week, in the name of Jesus, and let your love surround me.

401.   1 Peter 1:5 *"God is keeping careful watch over us and the future. The Day is coming when you'll have it all—life healed and whole. (Message).*

Father, let the great and prosperous future that you have for me begin today. Let my present show the preview of my future and make the whole world concur that your hand is upon my life, in the name of Jesus!

402.   James 5:11 *"What a gift life is to those who stay the course! You've heard, of course, of Job's staying power, and you know how God brought it all together for him at the end. That's because God cares, cares right down to the last detail. (Message).*

Father, give me strength through your Holy Spirit to stay focused to the end. Make a gift out of my life and make my life a gift to my generation, and don't let my life end up in a mess. Take over my battle and work out the details of my life, in the name of Jesus!

403.   James 2:5 *"Listen, dear friends. Isn't it clear by now that God operates quite differently? He chose the world's down–and–out as the kingdom's first citizens, with full rights and privileges. This kingdom is promised to anyone who loves God. (Message).*

Father, I decree and declare that from this day forward I will enjoy all the full rights and privileges of your kingdom's first citizens. I reject eating from life's leftovers, in the name of Jesus!

119

Let Us Pray

404. *Exodus 1:7 "But the children of Israel were fruitful and increased abundantly, multiplied and grew exceedingly mighty; and the land was filled with them." (NKJV).*

Father, we declare that we shall continue to be fruitful, and increase abundantly, in this land. We shall become exceedingly mighty and powerful. We shall possess the gates of the cities and make your glories known, in the name of Jesus.

405. *Nehemiah 13:14 "Remember me for what I have done, my God, and don't wipe out the good things that I have done for your temple and for the worship that is held there." (GW).*

Father, remember everyone giving to this ministry through their time, talents, and treasure. Don't wipe out the good things they have done in this house. Answer all their prayers speedily, in the name of Jesus.

Pastors

"Brethren, pray for us!" (I Thessalonians 5:25). This was a request from a leader of the people. Your Pastor needS your prayers, love them openly, pray for them secretly.

Apostle Paul requested again in Hebrews 13:18, "Pray for us, for we are confident that we have a good conscience, in all things desiring to live honorably." It is to our advantage that we pray for our pastors. Let us pray for NOT ONLY our Pastor, BUT pastors everywhere.

406.   *Ecclesiastes 7:19 "Wisdom strengthens the wise more than ten rulers of the city." (NKJV).*

Father, strengthen our pastors and members of this church with wisdom and make us excel in all that we put our hands upon, in the name of Jesus!

407.   *Luke 8:17 "For nothing is secret that will not be revealed, nor anything hidden that will not be known and come to light." (NKJV).*

Lord, bring to light and frustrate everything planned in darkness against our pastors and their family, in the name of Jesus!

408.   *Ezekiel 34:5 "And they were scattered because there was no shepherd, and when they were scattered, they became food for all the wild beasts of the field." (Amplified).*

Let Us Pray

Father, destroy every organized network of demonic wickedness against our shepherds and pastors and their family; and render every negative utterance declared against them of no effect, in the name of Jesus!

409. *Joel 2:17 "Tell my servants, the priests, to cry inside the temple and to offer this prayer near the altar: "Save your people, LORD God! Don't let foreign nations make jokes about us. Don't let them laugh and ask, 'Where is your God?'" (CEV).*

Father, we declare that pastors and religious leaders will wake up to their duties of keeping the flock safe. Deliver our religious leaders from political pandering and turn their hearts towards the truth of your love. Open their eyes to understand their true calling, in the name of Jesus.

410. *Isaiah 61:6 6 You will be called priests of the LORD, ministers of our God. You will feed on the treasures of the nations and boast in their riches. (NLT).*

Father, we pronounce your blessings on pastors and religious leaders who have devoted themselves to the teaching of truth and love. Give them more insight to your Word, and provide for all their needs, in the name of Jesus.

411. *Zechariah 4:8-9, "Moreover the word of the Lord came to me, saying: "The hands of Zerubbabel Have laid the foundation of this temple; His hands shall also finish it. Then you will know That the Lord of hosts has sent Me to you. For who has despised the day of small things? For these seven rejoice to see." (NKJV).*

Father, we declare that the hands of your servants have started the building of the Temple, and their hands shall also finish it, in the name of Jesus.

412.   *Isaiah 44: 24 -25 Thus says the Lord your Redeemer, And He who formed you from the womb: "I am the Lord who makes all things, who stretches out the heavens all alone; Who spreads abroad the earth by Myself; Who frustrates the signs of the babblers, and drives diviners mad; Who turns wise men backwards, And makes their knowledge foolishness." (NKJV).*

Father, in the name of Jesus, frustrate all the signs of the babblers and the wicked ones against our senior pastor, his wife, and the children; drive the diviners mad, turn the wise men backwards and make their knowledge become foolish. Protect them from the wicked ones, in Jesus' name.

413.   *Psalms 128: 1-3 "Blessed is everyone who fears the Lord, Who walks in His ways. When you eat the labor of your hands, You shall be happy, and it shall be well with you. Your wife shall be like fruitful vine in the very heart of your house, Your children like olive plants all around your table." (NKJV).*

Father, teach us to walk in your fear and walk in your ways, so we can be happy when we eat the fruit of our labor in Jesus Name. Grant us peace and joy in our homes with our spouses and children, let us be fresh and flourishing to our old age, in Jesus' name.

414.   *Job 5:12 "He frustrates the devices of the crafty, so that their hands cannot carry out their plans." (NKJV).*

Let Us Pray

Lord, build a wall of protection around our pastors and their children, in the name of Jesus. Let every plan against them be frustrated, in the name of Jesus!

415. *Isaiah 49:3 "And said unto me, Thou art my servant, O Israel, in whom I will be glorified." You are my dear servant in whom I will shine." (KJV).*

Father, in this year, empower the pastors, elders, and deacons of this church with Divine Wisdom, for greater results, and for the expansion of the kingdom of God at this church.

416. *2 Thessalonians 3:1 "Finally, brothers, pray for us, that the word of the Lord may spread rapidly and be glorified, even as also with you;" (New Heart English Bible).*

Father, through the ministry of your servant, the senior pastor of this church, let testimonies abound to your word in his mouth. Father, surround your servant, the senior pastor of this church, his wife, and their children with peace like a river; round-about, in this year.

417. *Luke 8:17 "For nothing is secret that will not be revealed, nor anything hidden that will not be known and come to light." (NKJV).*

Lord, bring to light everything planned in darkness against this church, its members, and our pastor's family, in the name of Jesus!

Israel Ade-Ajala

418. *Acts 5:12 "And through the hands of the apostles many signs and wonders were done among the people. And they were all with one accord in Solomon's Porch. (NKJV).*

Father, through the hands of your servants and our pastors, let many more signs and wonders be done among us. Increase their spiritual authority and influence all over the world, in the name of Jesus.

419. *1 Peter 2:4. "Welcome to the Living Stone, the source of life. The workmen took one look and threw it out; God set it in the place of honor." (Message).*

Father, set our pastors up in the place of honor. Where they have been rejected, give them a place of honor there. Let those who have worked against them begin to work for them. Let those that hated them begin to celebrate them, in the name of Jesus!

420. *Psalms 144:5, 7-8 "Step down out of heaven, God; ignite volcanoes in the hearts of the mountains...Reach all the way from sky to sea: pull me out of the ocean of hate, out of the grip of those barbarians. Who lie through their teeth, who shake your hand then knife you in the back." (Message).*

Father, disgrace all who are incensed against our pastors, this church and every member of this church. In their presence make us your voice in this land and establish your presence in our midst in the name of Jesus!

421. *1 Chronicles 12:22 "Hardly a day went by without men showing up to help—it wasn't long before his band seemed as large as God's own army!" (Message).*

125

Let Us Pray

Lord, bring more workers of Your choice to this church, make me a worker of your choice at this church. and keep all other evil agents away, in the name of Jesus!

422. *Psalms 27:6 "God holds me head and shoulders above all who try to pull me down..." (Message).*

Father, hold our pastors above all who try to pull them down, in the name of Jesus! Make their haters become irrelevant and confused, in the name of Jesus!

423. *Psalms 27:12 "Don't throw me to the dogs, those liars who are out to get me, filling the air with their threats." (Message).*

Father, preserve and protect our pastors and their family from those wicked liars and evil broadcasters. Return their evil imaginations against our pastors upon their heads, in the name of Jesus!

424. *Luke 10:19 "See what I've given you? Safe passage as you walk on snakes and scorpions, and protection from every assault of the Enemy. No one can put a hand on you!" (Message).*

Father, I praise you for keeping me, my family, my pastors, my church and all those surround me, safe since January. Thank you for keeping us safe from the attacks of the enemies and for granting us victory on every side in the name of Jesus!

425. *2 Chronicles 31:20 "Thus Hezekiah did throughout all Judah, and he did what was good and right and true before the LORD his God." (NKJV).*

Father, help us to always do what is good and right and true in your sight as we serve you here at this church. Do not let us lose relevance, in the name of Jesus!

426. Isaiah 61:6 *"You will be called priests of the Lord, ministers of our God. You will feed on the treasures of the nations and boast in their riches. (NLT).*

Father, we declare that our pastors and all who work in this church will continue to enjoy favor in your sight. They will feed on the treasures of the nations and will never lack, in the name of Jesus.

427. Psalms 35:8 *"Surprise them with your ambush— catch them in the very trap they set, the disaster they planned for me." (Message).*

Father, ambush those who plan against our pastors and their family. Catch those who plan against our senior pastor the very trap they set for him. Let their disastrous plan return to their heads, in the name of Jesus.

428. Psalms 35:4 *"When those thugs try to knife me in the back, make them look foolish. Frustrate all those who are plotting my downfall." (Message).*

Father, frustrate all those who are plotting the downfall of our senior pastor and their children, in the name of Jesus. Let all their haters look foolish and drain them of their strength, in the name of Jesus.

Let Us Pray

429. *Psalms 68:1-2 "God! Arise with awesome power, and every one of your enemies will scatter in fear! 2 Chase them away— all these God-haters. Blow them away as a puff of smoke. Melt them away like wax in the fire. One good look at you and the wicked vanish..." (Passion).*

Arise O God and scatter all the enemies of this church and let those who plan evil against this church and its members, be put to shame.

430. *Exodus 33:18 "Then Moses said, "Now, please show me your glory." (NCV).*

Father, manifest your glory in our midst at this church and pour out your Spirit in greater measure in our lives. May we encounter the manifestation of your presence, heavenly encounters, signs and wonders!

431. *Psalms 132:17 "I will increase the anointing that was upon David, and my glistening glory will rest upon my chosen ones. (Passion).*

Father, increase the anointing upon our pastors and let your glory rest upon them in the name of Jesus. Lord, perform unusual miracles through the hands of your servants, in the name of Jesus.

432. *Revelation 11:5 "If anyone attempts to harm them, fire will flow out of their mouths and consume their foes. All who seek to harm them will die in this way." (Passion).*

Israel Ade-Ajala

Father, we declare fire to come out of the mouth of our senior pastor and consume all who hate him, his family and this church. Let all who seek to harm him, his family, or this church, die in this way, in the name of Jesus.

433. *Deuteronomy 33:11 "Bless the ministry of the Levites, O LORD, and accept all the work of their hands. Hit their enemies where it hurts the most; strike down their foes so they never rise again." (NLT).*

Father, increase your blessing on the ministry of our senior pastor. Hit their enemies where it hurts the most. Lord, strike down all those who hate them, so they never rise again, in the name of Jesus.

434. *Esther 9:3-4 "What's more, all the government officials, satraps, governors—everyone who worked for the king—actually helped the Jews because of Mordecai; they were afraid of him. 4 Mordecai by now was a power in the palace. As Mordecai became more and more powerful, his reputation had grown in all the provinces." (Message).*

Father, make our senior pastor a power in this land. Establish him as your voice and make government officials, governors, senators and business communities come to him for advice. Give him a name that no one can destroy, in the name of Jesus.

435. *1 Samuel 5: 11 "The people summoned the Philistine rulers again and begged them, "Please send the Ark of the God of Israel back to its own country, or it will kill us all." For the deadly*

129

Let Us Pray

plague from God had already begun, and great fear was sweeping across the town." (NLT).

Father, we command deadly plague from God over the enemies of our pastors, and their family. Frustrate all the haters of our senior pastor and their children, in the mighty name of Jesus Christ! Lord, let the fear of our senior pastor sweep across those who hate him and make him rulers over them, in the mighty name of Jesus!

436. *Psalm 71: 21 "You shall increase my greatness, And comfort me on every side." (NKJV).*

Father, increase the greatness of our senior pastor and make him comfortable on every side in the mighty name of Jesus! Strengthen Your servant, honor him, and bless him with every good blessing of Your love.

437. *2 Kings 19:34 "For I will defend this city, to save it, for mine own sake, and for my servant David's sake." (KJV).*

We declare by the Word of the Lord, Father, defend the family of our senior pastor by reason of your son' s obedience to your call. Defend his home!

438. *Proverbs 31:25 "Strength and honor are her clothing; And she shall rejoice in time to come." (KJV).*

Father, we declare concerning our senior pastor's wife, that the days of her rejoicing have come!

439. Isaiah 43:1-2 *"But now, says the Lord the one who created you, Jacob, the one who formed you, Israel: Don't fear, for I have redeemed you; I have called you by name; you are mine. When you pass through the waters, I will be with you; when through the rivers, they won't sweep over you. When you walk through the fire, you won't be scorched and the flame won't burn you."* (CEB).

Father, thank you for rescuing our senior pastor, his wife, and their children from the hand of the enemy. Now, let your presence be with them. When they pass through water, they will not get drowned. When they walk through fire, they will not be scorched, in the mighty name of Jesus Christ!

440. Isaiah 43:4 *"Because you are precious in my eyes, you are honored, and I love you. I give people in your place, and nations in exchange for your life."* (Amplified).

Father, according to your word, our senior pastor, his wife and their children are precious in your eyes. Honor them. Give people in their place and nations in exchange for their life, in the mighty name of Jesus Christ.

441. Matthew 4:16 *"The people which sat in darkness saw great light; and to them which sat in the region and shadow of death light is sprung up."* (KJV).

Father, by the power of your Word coming from this church's altar, command major transformations across the globe, kindle major revival fire in the life of men and women all around the world!

Let Us Pray

442. *2 Thessalonians 3:1 "Finally, dear brothers and sisters, we ask you to pray for us. Pray that the Lord's message will spread rapidly and be honored wherever it goes, just as when it came to you." (NLT).*

Father, in the name of Jesus, let the message you gave your servant, our senior pastor, spread rapidly and be honored in signs and wonders wherever it goes.

443. *Deuteronomy 34:7 "Moses was a hundred and twenty years old when he died, yet his eyes were not weak, and his vitality had not diminished." (Berean Study Bible).*

Father, in the name of Jesus, continue to increase the strength of your servant, our senior pastor, and his family on every side. As their days go, so let their strength increase.

Success

The Lord was with Joseph, and he was successful in the land of Egypt. God has built success into our DNA. You shall be like a tree planted by the rivers of water, that brings forth its fruit in its season, whose leaf also shall not wither, and whatever he does shall prosper. Success is your portion. Let us pray your success.

444. *Psalms 69:13 "But I keep right on praying to you, Lord. For now, is the time--you are bending down to hear! You are ready with a plentiful supply of love and kindness. Now answer my prayer and rescue me as you promised." (TLB).*

Father, bring to pass every promise you have given to me, and cause me to give testimonies, in the name of Jesus.

445. *Nehemiah 12:43 "Many sacrifices were offered on that joyous day, for God had given us cause for great joy. The women and children rejoiced, too, and the joy of the people of Jerusalem was heard far away!" (TLB).*

Father, in this year, give us reasons to rejoice and to celebrate. Let people come and celebrate with us, in the name of Jesus.

446. *Psalms 118:25 "Save now, I pray O Lord; O Lord, I pray, send now prosperity." (NKJV).*

Lord, send prosperity to this church and its members, in the name of Jesus! Let no one be missing!

Let Us Pray

447.   Daniel 1:17-20 "As for these four young men, God gave them knowledge and skill in all literature and wisdom; and Daniel had understanding in all visions and dreams. And in all matters of wisdom and understanding about which the king examined them, he found them ten times better than all the magicians and astrologers who were in all his realm." (NKJV).

Father, I receive access to supernatural knowledge and skill for my career and my business. Starting today, I am the best in what I do, in the name of Jesus. I know how to achieve excellent results with minimal resources, without sweat.

448.   Isaiah 48:16-17 "Come near to Me, hear this: I have not spoken in secret from the beginning; From the time that it was, I was there. And now the Lord God and His Spirit Have sent Me." Thus says the Lord, your Redeemer, The Holy One of Israel: "I am the Lord your God, Who teaches you to profit, Who leads you by the way you should go." (NKJV).

Father, I declare that all my business operations and career activities come under the FRESH ANOINTING of the Holy Spirit for supernatural profits and wealth creation!

449.   Deuteronomy 1:11 "May the Lord, the God of your ancestors, increase you a thousand times and bless you as He has promised!" (NIV).

Lord, increase this church a thousand times more and bless us in the name of Jesus!

450.   Deuteronomy 30:9 "Then the Lord your God will make you most prosperous in all the work of your hands and in the fruit of

your womb, the young of your livestock and the crops of your land…." (NIV).

Father, let my hands carry the anointing for prosperity, in the name of Jesus!

451. *Psalms 90:17 "May the favor of the Lord our God rest on us; establish the work of our hands for us—yes, establish the work of our hands." (NIV).*

Favor, envelope my life, in the name of Jesus! Divine favor, envelope my life, in the name of Jesus!

452. *Isaiah 40:29 "He gives power to the faint and weary, and to him who has no might He increases strength [causing it to multiply and making it to abound." (Amplified).*

Father, I declare that what has taken other people many years to achieve, I will achieve in a few months, in the name of Jesus!

453. *2 Chronicles 29:36 "Hezekiah and all the people rejoiced at what God had brought about for his people, because it was done so quickly". (NIV).*

Father, I receive divine acceleration in my life, in the name of Jesus!

454. *Psalms 90:13-14 "Come back, God—how long do we have to wait? —and treat your servants with kindness for a change. Surprise us with love at daybreak; then we'll skip and dance all day long." (Message).*

Let Us Pray

Lord, make me a candidate of supernatural surprises, in favor, finances, and promotion and launch me into my next level, in the name of Jesus!

455. *Psalms 73:24 "You guide me with Your counsel, leading me to a glorious destiny." (NLT).*

Father, I declare, no matter the situation I am facing, I shall become what God has made me to be, in the name of Jesus!

456. *Psalms 115: 14-15 "May the Lord richly bless both you and your children. 15. May you be blessed by the Lord, who made heaven and earth." (NLT).*

Father, I declare, this year, I shall be blessed with unrivaled lifting, and I shall be celebrated, in the name of Jesus!

457. *Psalms 69:13 "But I keep right on praying to you, Lord. For now, is the time--you are bending down to hear! You are ready with a plentiful supply of love and kindness. Now answer my prayer and rescue me as you promised." (TLB).*

Father, bring to pass every promise you have given to me and cause me to give testimonies, in the name of Jesus.

458. *Psalms 108:13 Through God we will do valiantly, for it is He who shall tread down our enemies. (NKJV).*

Father, this year we shall do valiantly in our finances, homes, business, ministry, education, and church. I destroy every power preventing me from moving forward, in the name of Jesus!

Israel Ade-Ajala

459. James 5:11 *"What a gift life is to those who stay the course! You've heard, of course, of Job's staying power, and you know how God brought it all together for him at the end. That's because God cares, cares right down to the last detail."* (Message).

Father, give me strength through your Holy Spirit to stay focused to the end. Make a gift out of my life and make my life a gift to my generation. Don't let my life end up in a mess. Take over my battle and work out the details of my life, in the name of Jesus!

460. James 2:5 *"Listen, dear friends. Isn't it clear by now that God operates quite differently? He chose the world's down–and–out as the kingdom's first citizens, with full rights and privileges. This kingdom is promised to anyone who loves God."* (Message).

Father, I decree and declare that from this day forward I will enjoy all the full rights and privileges of your kingdom's first citizens. I reject eating from life's leftovers, in the name of Jesus!

461. Psalms 45:11 *"So the King will greatly desire your beauty; Because He is your Lord, worship Him."* (NKJV).

Father, let your beauty reflect in my life, in my home, in my finances and over my work, and let the World see it.

462. Psalms 119:16 *"Take my side as you promised; I'll live then for sure. Don't disappoint all my grand hopes."* (Message).

Father, bring to pass every promise you have given to me and cause me to give testimonies, in the name of Jesus!

Let Us Pray

463.   Psalms 119:170 *"Give my request your personal attention, rescue me on the terms of your promise." (Message).*

Father, I declare that it is my turn to laugh and celebrate over my life, my home, my children, my business, my career, and my finances, in the name of Jesus!

464.   Psalms 119:170 *"Give my request your personal attention, rescue me on the terms of your promise." (Message).*

Father, bring to pass every promise you have given to me and cause me to give testimonies, in the name of Jesus!

465.   Micah 7:14 *"O Lord, come and rule your people; lead your flock; make them live in peace and prosperity; let them enjoy the fertile pastures of Bashan and Gilead as they did long ago." (TLB).*

Father, lead us into prosperity, in the name of Jesus. Terminate financial struggle in our lives in the name of Jesus! Open doors of advancement for us, in the name of Jesus!

466.   Psalms 90:13-14 *"Come back, God—how long do we have to wait? —and treat your servants with kindness for a change. 14 Surprise us with love at daybreak; then we'll skip and dance all day long."(Message).*

O Lord, I declare that I am a candidate of supernatural surprises, in favor, finances, and promotion and launch me into my next level, in the name of Jesus!

467.   Psalms 115: -15 "May the Lord richly bless both you and your children. 15 May you be blessed by the Lord, who made heaven and earth." (NLT).

Father, I declare, this year, I shall be blessed with unrivaled lifting, and I shall be celebrated, in the name of Jesus!

468.   Psalms 69:29-30 "But rescue me, O God, from my poverty and pain. Then I will praise God with my singing! My thanks will be his praise." (TLB).

Father, rescue me from poverty and pain. Let favor locate me and terminate labor and toiling in my life, in the name of Jesus.

469.   Psalms 1:3 "They are like trees growing beside a stream, trees that produce fruit in season and always have leaves. Those people succeed in everything they do." (CEV).

Father, I am planted in your house, let me produce fruit in season, and do not let my leaves dry. Keep me fresh by the power of your word, in the name of Jesus.

470.   Job 41:11 "I am in command of the world and in debt to no one." (CEV).

Father, I declare myself free from financial burden and debt, in the name of Jesus. God of abundance, I receive supernatural abundance of your provision to become a blessing to others around me, in the name of Jesus.

Let Us Pray

471. *Proverbs 4:18 says, "The path of the just is like a shining light, that shines brighter and brighter to the perfect day." (NKJV).*

Father, I declare that I will finish this year with joy and not with sadness, in the name of Jesus! I will finish this year on the positive financially, in the name of Jesus!

472. *Psalms 85:6 "Why not help us make a fresh start—a resurrection life? Then your people will laugh and sing!" (Message).*

Father, press the reset button and give us a fresh encounter with you this year. No more stale songs, but give us a new song this year, in the name of Jesus!

473. *Psalms 92: 12-13 "The righteous shall flourish like a palm tree, He shall grow like a cedar in Lebanon. Those who are planted in the house of the LORD Shall flourish in the courts of our God." (NKJV).*

Father, we pray that everyone connected to this church's family shall grow and flourish in health, finances, relationships, and businesses, in Jesus' name.

140

Made in United States
Troudale, OR
09/04/2023